"You're Awake," The Nurse Murmured.

A man turned and looked at her, too, his gaze piercing. He was strongly charismatic. Handsome as a pirate captain, exotically dark and obviously foreign. Masculine, strong. Anna blinked. There was a mark on his eye just like her baby's. A dark irregular smudge that enhanced both his resemblance to a pirate and his exotic maleness.

"Anna!" he exclaimed. A slight accent furred his words attractively. "Thank God you and the baby were not hurt! What on earth happened?"

"Are you the doctor?" she stammered.

His dark eyes snapped into an expression of even greater concern, and he made a sound that was half laughter, half worry. He bent down and clasped her hand. She felt his fingers tighten on hers in unmistakable silent warning.

"Darling!" he exclaimed. "The nurse says you don't remember the accident, but I hope you have not forgotten your own husband!"

Dear Reader,

Happy New Year from Silhouette Desire, where we offer you six passionate, powerful and provocative romances every month of the year! Here's what you can indulge yourself with this January....

Begin the new year with a seductive MAN OF THE MONTH, *Tall, Dark & Western* by Anne Marie Winston. A rancher seeking a marriage of convenience places a personals ad for a wife, only to fall—hard—for the single mom who responds!

Silhouette Desire proudly presents a sequel to the wildly successful in-line continuity series THE TEXAS CATTLEMAN'S CLUB. This exciting *new* series about alpha men on a mission is called TEXAS CATTLEMAN'S CLUB: LONE STAR JEWELS. Jennifer Greene's launch book, *Millionaire M.D.*, features a wealthy surgeon who helps out his childhood crush when she finds a baby on her doorstep—by marrying her!

Alexandra Sellers continues her exotic miniseries SONS OF THE DESERT with one more irresistible sheikh in *Sheikh's Woman*. THE BARONS OF TEXAS miniseries by Fayrene Preston returns with another feisty Baron heroine in *The Barons of Texas: Kit.* In Kathryn Jensen's *The Earl's Secret,* a British aristocrat romances a U.S. commoner while wrestling with a secret. And Shirley Rogers offers *A Cowboy, a Bride & a Wedding Vow,* in which a cowboy discovers his secret child.

So ring in the new year with lots of cheer and plenty of red-hot romance, by reading all six of these enticing love stories.

Enjoy!

Joan Marlow Golan

Joan Marlow Golan
Senior Editor, Silhouette Desire

Please address questions and book requests to:
Silhouette Reader Service
U.S.: 3010 Walden Ave., P.O. Box 1325, Buffalo, NY 14269
Canadian: P.O. Box 609, Fort Erie, Ont. L2A 5X3

Sheikh's Woman
ALEXANDRA SELLERS

Silhouette®

Desire

Published by Silhouette Books

America's Publisher of Contemporary Romance

SILHOUETTE BOOKS

ISBN 0-373-76341-7

SHEIKH'S WOMAN

Copyright © 2001 by Alexandra Sellers

All rights reserved. Except for use in any review, the reproduction
or utilization of this work in whole or in part in any form by any
electronic, mechanical or other means, now known or hereafter
invented, including xerography, photocopying and recording, or in
any information storage or retrieval system, is forbidden without
the written permission of the editorial office, Silhouette Books,
300 East 42nd Street, New York, NY 10017 U.S.A.

All characters in this book have no existence outside the imagination of
the author and have no relation whatsoever to anyone bearing the same
name or names. They are not even distantly inspired by any individual
known or unknown to the author, and all incidents are pure invention.

This edition published by arrangement with Harlequin Books S.A.

® and TM are trademarks of Harlequin Books S.A., used under license.
Trademarks indicated with ® are registered in the United States Patent
and Trademark Office, the Canadian Trade Marks Office and in other
countries.

Visit Silhouette at www.eHarlequin.com

Printed in U.S.A.

ALEXANDRA SELLERS

is the author of over twenty-five novels and a feline language text published in 1997 and still selling.

Born and raised in Canada, Alexandra first came to London as a drama student. Now she lives near Hampstead Heath with her husband, Nick. They share housekeeping with Monsieur, who jumped through the window one day and announced, as cats do, that he was moving in.

What she would miss most on a desert island is shared laughter.

Readers can write to Alexandra at P.O. Box 9449, London NW3 2WH, U.K., England.

For my sister Joy,
who held it all together in the bad times
and makes things even better in the good

Prologue

She crouched in the darkness, whimpering as the pain gripped her. He had made her wait too long. She had warned him, but he'd pretended not to believe her "lies." And now, in an empty, dirty alley, nowhere to go, no time to get there, her time was upon her.

Pain stabbed her again, and she cried out involuntarily. She pressed a hand over her mouth and looked behind her down the alley. Of course by now he had discovered her flight. He was already after her. If he had heard that cry...

She staggered to her feet again, picked up the bag, began a shuffling run. Her heart was beating so hard! The drumming in her head seemed to drown out thought. She ran a few paces and then doubled over again as the pain came. Oh, Lord, not here! Please, please, not in an alley, like an animal, to be found when she was most helpless, when the baby would be at his mercy.

He would have no mercy. The pain ebbed and she ran on, weeping, praying. *"Ya Allah!"* Forgive me, protect me.

Suddenly, as if in answer, she sensed a deeper darkness in the shadows. She turned towards it without questioning, and found herself in a narrower passage. The darkness was more intense here, and she stared blindly until her eyes grew accustomed.

There was a row of garages on either side of a short strip of paving. Then she saw what had drawn her, what her subconscious mind—or her guardian angel—had already seen: one door was ajar. She bit her lip. Was there someone inside, a fugitive like herself? But another clutch of pain almost knocked her to her knees. As she bent double, stifling her cry, she heard a shout. A long way distant, but she feared what was behind her more than what might be ahead.

Sobbing with mingled pain and terror, she stumbled towards the open door and pushed her way inside.

One

"Can you hear me? Anna, can you hear my voice?"

It was like being dragged through long, empty rooms. Anna groaned protestingly. What did they want from her? Why didn't they let her sleep?

"Move your hand if you can hear my voice, Anna. Can you move your hand?"

It took huge effort, as if she had to fight through thick syrup.

"That's excellent! Now, can you open your eyes?"

Abruptly something heavy seemed to smash down inside her skull, driving pain through every cell. She moaned.

"I'm afraid you're going to have a pretty bad headache," said the voice, remorselessly cheerful, determinedly invasive. "Come now, Anna! Open your eyes!"

She opened her eyes. The light was too bright. It hurt. A woman in a navy shirt with white piping was gazing at her. "Good, there you are!" she said, in a brisk Scots accent. "What's your name?"

"Anna," said Anna. "Anna Lamb."

The woman nodded. "Good, Anna."

"What happened? Where am I?" Anna whispered. She was lying in a grey cubicle on a narrow hospital trolley, fully dressed except for shoes. "Why am I in hospital?" The hammer slammed down again. "My head!"

"You've been in an accident, but you're going to be fine. Just a wee bit concussed. Your baby's fine."

Your baby. A different kind of pain smote her then, and she lay motionless as cold enveloped her heart.

"My baby died," she said, her voice flat as the old, familiar lifelessness seeped through her.

The nurse was taking Anna's blood pressure, but at this she looked up. "She's absolutely fine! The doctor's just checking her over now," she said firmly. "I don't know why you wanted to give birth in a taxicab, but it seems you made a very neat job of it."

She leaned forward and pulled back one of Anna's eyelids, shone light from a tiny flashlight into her eye.

"In a taxicab?" Anna repeated. "But—"

Confused memories seemed to pulsate in her head, just out of reach.

"You're a very lucky girl!" said the cheerful nurse, moving down to press her abdomen with searching fingers. She paused, frowning, and pressed again.

Anna was silent, her eyes squeezed tight, trying to think through the pain and confusion in her head. Meanwhile the nurse poked and prodded, frowned a little, made notes, poked again. "Lift up, please?" she murmured, and with competent hands carried on the examination.

When it was over, she stood looking down at Anna, sliding her pen into the pocket of her uniform trousers. A little frown had gathered between her eyebrows.

"Do you remember giving birth, Anna?"

Pain rushed in at her. The room suddenly filling with people, all huddled around her precious newborn baby, while she cried, "Let me see him, why can't I hold him?" and then...*Anna, I'm sorry, I'm so very sorry. We couldn't save your baby.*

"Yes," she said lifelessly, gazing at the nurse with dry, stretched eyes, her heart a lump of stone. "I remember."

A male head came around the cubicle's curtain. "Staff, can you come, please?"

The Staff Nurse gathered up her instruments. "Maternity Sister will be down as soon as she can get away, but it may be a while, Anna. They've got staff shortages there, too, tonight, and a Caes—"

A light tap against the partition wall preceded the entrance of a young nurse, looking desperately tired but smiling as she rolled a wheeled bassinet into the room.

"Oh, nurse, there you are! How's the bairn?" said the Staff Nurse, sounding not altogether pleased.

The bairn was crying with frustrated fury, and neither of the nurses heard the gasp that choked Anna. A storm of emotion seemed to seize her as she lifted herself on her elbows and, ignoring the punishment this provoked from the person in her head who was beating her nerve endings, struggled to sit up.

"Baby?" Anna cried. "Is that *my baby?*"

Meanwhile, the young nurse wheeled the baby up beside the trolley, assuring Anna, "Yes, she is. A lovely little girl." Anna looked into the bassinet, closed her eyes, looked again.

The baby stopped crying suddenly. She was well wrapped up in hospital linen, huge eyes open, silent now but frowning questioningly at the world.

"Oh, dear God!" Anna exclaimed, choking on the emotion that surged up inside. "Oh, my baby! Was it just a nightmare, then? Oh, my darling!"

"It's not unusual for things to get mixed up after a bang on the head like yours, but everything will sort itself out," said the Staff Nurse. "We'll keep you in for observation for a day or two, but there's nothing to worry about."

Anna hardly heard. "I want to hold her!" she whispered, convulsively reaching towards the bassinet. The young nurse obligingly picked the baby up and bent over Anna. Her hungry arms wrapping the infant, Anna sank back against the pillows.

Her heart trembled with a joy so fierce it hurt, obliterating for a few moments even the pain in her head. She drew the little bundle tight against her breast, and gazed hungrily into the flower face.

She was beautiful. Huge questioning eyes, dark hair that lay on her forehead in feathery curls, wide, full mouth which was suddenly, adorably, stretched by a yawn.

All around one eye there was a mocha-hued shadow that added an inexplicably piquant charm to her face. She gazed at Anna, serenely curious.

"She looks like a bud that's just opened," Anna marvelled. "She's so fresh, so new!"

"She's lovely," agreed the junior nurse, while the Staff Nurse hooked the clipboard of Anna's medical notes onto the foot of the bed.

"Good, then," she said, nodding. "Now you'll be all

right here till Maternity Sister comes. Nurse, I'll see you for a moment, please.''

The sense of unreality returned when she was left alone with the baby. Anna gazed down into the sweet face from behind a cloud of pain and confusion. She couldn't seem to think.

The baby fell asleep, just like that. Anna bent to examine her. The birthmark on her eye was very clear now that the baby's eyes were closed. Delicate, dark, a soft smudging all around the eye. Anna was moved by it. She supposed such a mark could be considered a blemish, but somehow it managed to be just the opposite.

''You'll set the fashion, my darling,'' Anna whispered with a smile, cuddling the baby closer. ''All the girls will be painting their eyes with makeup like that in the hopes of making themselves as beautiful as you.''

It made the little face even more vulnerable, drew her, touched her heart. She couldn't remember ever having seen such a mark before. Was this kind of thing inherited? No one in her family had anything like it.

Was it a dream, that memory of another child? Tiny, perfect, a beautiful, beautiful son...but so white. They had allowed her to hold him, just for a few moments, to say goodbye. Her heart had died then. She had felt it go cold, turn to ice and then stone. They had encouraged her to weep, but she did not weep. Grief required a heart.

Was that a dream?

She was terribly tired. She bent to lay the sleeping infant back in the bassinet. Then she leaned down over the tiny, fragile body, searching her face for clues.

''Who is your father?'' she whispered. ''Where am I? What's happening to me?''

Her head ached violently. She lay back against the pillows and wished the lights weren't so bright.

* * *

"My daughter, you must prepare yourself for some excellent news."

She smiled trustingly at her mother. "Is it the embassy from the prince?" she asked, for the exciting information had of course seeped into the harem.

"The prince's emissaries and I have discussed the matter of your marriage with the prince. Now I have spoken with your father, whose care is all for you. Such a union will please him very much, my daughter, for he desires peace with the prince and his people."

She bowed. "I am happy to be the means of pleasing my father.... And the prince? What manner of man do they say he is?"

"Ah, my daughter, he is a young man to please any woman. Handsome, strong, capable in all the manly arts. He has distinguished himself in battle, too, and stories are told of his bravery."

She sighed her happiness. "Oh, mother, I feel I love him already!" she said.

Anna awoke, not knowing what had disturbed her. A tall, dark man was standing at the foot of her trolley, reading her chart. There was something about him... She frowned, trying to concentrate. But sleep dragged her eyes shut.

"They're both fine," she heard when she opened them next, not sure whether it was seconds or minutes later. The man was talking to a young woman who looked familiar. After a second Anna's jumbled brain recognized the junior nurse.

The man drew her eyes. He was strongly charismatic. Handsome as a pirate captain, exotically dark and obviously foreign. Masculine, strong, handsome—and impossibly clean for London, as if he had come straight from a massage and shave at his club without moving through the dust and dirt of city traffic.

He was wearing a grey silk lounge suit which looked impeccably Savile Row. A round diamond glowed with dark fire from a heavy, square gold setting on his ring finger. Heavy cuff links on the French cuffs of his cream silk shirt matched it. On his other hand she saw the flash of an emerald.

He didn't look at all overdressed or showy. It sat on him naturally. He was like an aristocrat in a period film. Dreamily she imagined him in heavy brocade, with a fall of lace at wrist and throat.

She blinked, coming drowsily more awake. The junior nurse was glowing, as if the man's male energy had stirred and ignited something in her, in spite of her exhaustion. She was mesmerized.

"Because he's mesmerizing," Anna muttered.

Suddenly recalled to her duties, the nurse glanced at her patient. "You're awake!" she murmured.

The man turned and looked at her, too, his eyes dark and his gaze piercing. Anna blinked. There was a mark on his eye just like her baby's. A dark irregular smudge that enhanced both his resemblance to a pirate and his exotic maleness.

"Anna!" he exclaimed. A slight accent furred his words attractively. "Thank God you and the baby were not hurt! What on earth happened?"

She felt very, very stupid. "Are you the doctor?" she stammered.

His dark eyes snapped into an expression of even greater concern, and he made a sound that was half laughter, half worry. He bent down and clasped her hand. She felt his fingers tighten on her, in unmistakable silent warning.

"Darling!" he exclaimed. "The nurse says you don't remember the accident, but I hope you have not forgotten your own husband!"

Two

Husband? Anna stared. Her mouth opened. "I'm not—" she began. He pressed her hand again, and she broke off. Was he really her husband? How could she be married and not remember? Her heart kicked. Had a man like him fallen in love with her, chosen her?

"Are we married?" she asked.

He laughed again, with a thread of warning in his tone that she was at a loss to figure. "Look at our baby! Does she not tell you the truth?"

The birthmark was unmistakable. But how could such a thing be? "I can't remember things," she told him in a voice which trembled, trying to hold down the panic that suddenly swept her. "I can't remember anything."

A husband—how could she have forgotten? Why? She squeezed her eyes shut, and stared into the inner blackness. She knew who she was, but everything else eluded her.

She opened her eyes. He was smiling down at her in deep concern. He was so *attractive!* The air around him seemed to crackle with vitality. Suddenly she *wanted* it to be true. She wanted him to be her husband, wanted the right to lean on him. She felt so weak, and he looked so strong. He looked like a man used to handling things.

Someone was screaming somewhere. *"Nurse, nurse!"* It was a hoarse, harsh cry. She put her hand to her pounding head. "It's so noisy," she whispered.

"We'll soon have her somewhere quieter," said the junior nurse, hastily reassuring. "I'll just go and check with Maternity again." She slipped away, leaving Anna alone with the baby and the man who was her husband.

"Come, I want to get you out of here," he said.

There was something odd about his tone. She tried to focus, but her head ached desperately, and she seemed to be behind a thick curtain separating her from the world.

"But where?" she asked weakly. "This is a hospital."

"You are booked into a private hospital. They are waiting to admit you. It is far more pleasant there—they are not short-staffed and overworked. I want a specialist to see and reassure you."

He had already drawn Anna's shoes from under the bed. Anna, her head pounding, obediently sat up on the edge of the trolley bed and slipped her feet into them. Meanwhile, he neatly removed the pages from the clipboard at the foot of her bed, folded and slipped them into his jacket pocket.

"Why are you taking those?" she asked stupidly.

He flicked her an inscrutable look, then picked up the baby with atypical male confidence. "Where is your bag, Anna? Did you have a bag?"

"Oh—!" She put her hand to her forehead, remembering the case she had packed so carefully...and then had carried out of the hospital when it was all over. That long, slow walk with empty arms. Her death march.

"My bag," she muttered, but her brain would not engage with the problem, with the contradiction.

"Never mind, we can get it later." He pulled aside the curtain of the cubicle, glanced out, and then turned to her. "Come!"

Her head ached with ten times the ferocity as she obediently stood. He wrapped his free arm around her back and drew her out of the cubicle, and she instinctively obeyed his masculine authority.

The casualty ward was like an overcrowded bad dream. They passed a young man lying on a trolley, his face smashed and bloody. Another trolley held an old woman, white as her hair, her veins showing blue, eyes wild with fear. She was muttering something incomprehensible and stared at Anna with helpless fixity as they passed. Somewhere someone was half moaning, half screaming. That other voice still called for a nurse. A child's cry, high and broken, betrayed mingled pain and panic.

"My God, do you think it's like this all the time?" Anna murmured.

"It is Friday night."

They walked through the waiting room, where every seat was filled, and a moment later stepped out into the autumn night. Rain was falling, but softly, and she found the cold air a relief.

"Oh, that's better!" Anna exclaimed, shivering a little in her thin shirt.

A long black limousine parked a few yards away

purred into life and eased up beside them. Her husband opened the back door for her.

Anna drew back suddenly, without knowing why. "What about my coat? Don't I have a coat?"

"The car is warm. Come, get in. You are tired."

His voice soothed her fears, and the combination of obvious wealth and his commanding air calmed her. If he was her husband, she must be safe.

In addition to everything else, being upright was making her queasy. Anna gave in and slipped inside the luxurious passenger compartment, sinking gratefully down onto deep, superbly comfortable upholstery. He locked and shut the door.

She leaned back and her eyes closed. He spoke to the driver in a foreign language through the window, and a moment later the other passenger door opened, and her husband got inside with the baby. The limo began rolling forward immediately. Absently she clocked the driver picking up a mobile phone.

"Are we leaving, just like that? Don't I have to be signed out by a doctor or something?"

He shrugged. "Believe me, the medical staff are terminally overworked here. When they discover the empty cubicle, the Casualty staff will assume you have been moved to a ward."

Her head ached too much.

The darkness of the car was relieved at intervals by the filtered glow of passing lights. She watched him for a moment in light and shadow, light and shadow, as he settled the baby more comfortably.

"What's your name?" she asked abruptly.

"I am Ishaq Ahmadi."

"That doesn't even ring a faint bell!" Anna exclaimed. "Oh, my head! Do you—how long have we been married?"

There was a disturbing flick of his black gaze in darkness. It was as if he touched her, and a little electric shock was the result.

"There is no need to go on with this now, Anna," he said.

She jumped. "What? What do you mean?"

His gaze remained compellingly on her.

"I remember my—who I *am*," she babbled, oddly made to feel guilty by his silent judgement, "but I can't really remember my *life*. I *certainly* don't remember you. Or—or the baby, or anything. How long have we been married?"

He smiled and shrugged. "Shall we say, two years?"

"Two years!" She recoiled in horror.

"What of your life do you remember? Your mind is obviously not a complete blank. You must have something in there...you remember giving birth?"

"Yes, but...but what I remember is that my baby died."

"Ah," he breathed, so softly she wasn't even sure she had heard it.

"They told me just now that wasn't true, but..." She reached out to touch the baby in his arms. "Oh, she's so sweet! Isn't she perfect? But I remember..." Her eyes clenched against the spasm of pain. "I *remember* holding my baby after he died."

Her eyes searched his desperately in the darkness. "Maybe that was a long time ago?" she whispered.

"How long ago does it seem to you?"

The question seemed to trigger activity in her head. "Six weeks, I think...."

You're going to have six wonderful weeks, Anna.

"Oh!" she exclaimed, as a large piece of her life suddenly fell into place. "I just remembered— I was on my way to a job in France. And Lisbet and Cecile were going to take me out for a really lovely dinner. It seems to me I'm…" She squeezed her eyes shut. "Aren't I supposed to be leaving on the Paris train tomorrow…Saturday? Alan Mitching's house in France." She opened her eyes. "Are you saying that was more than two years in the past?"

"What sort of a job?"

"He has a seventeenth-century place in the Dordogne area…they want murals in the dining room. They want—wanted a Greek temple effect. I've designed—" She broke off and gazed at him in the darkness while the limousine purred through the wet, empty streets. Traffic was light; it must be two or three in the morning.

"I can remember making the designs, but I can't remember doing the actual work." Panic rose up in her. "Why can't I remember?"

"This state is not permanent. You will remember everything in time."

The baby stirred and murmured and she watched as he shifted her a little.

"Let me hold her," she said hungrily.

For a second he looked as if he was going to refuse, but she held out her arms, and he slipped the tiny bundle into her embrace. A smile seemed to start deep within her and flow outwards all through her body and spirit to reach her lips. Her arms tightened. Oh, how lovely to have a living baby to hold against her heart in place of that horrible, hurting memory!

"Oh, you're so beautiful!" she whispered. She shifted her gaze to Ishaq Ahmadi. He was watching her. "Isn't she beautiful?"

A muscle seemed to tense in his jaw. "Yes," he said.

The chauffeur spoke through an intercom, and as her husband replied, Anna silently watched fleeting expressions wander over the baby's face, felt the perfection of the little body against her breast. Time seemed to disappear in the now. She lost the urgency of wanting to know how she had got to this moment, and was happy just to be in it.

When he spoke to her again, she came to with a little start and realized she had been almost asleep. "Can you remember how you came to be in the taxi with the baby?"

Nothing. Not even vague shadows. She shook her head. "No."

Then there was no sound except for rain and the flick of tires on the wet road. Anna was lost in contemplation again. She stroked the tiny fist. "Have we chosen a name for her?"

A passing headlight highlighted one side of his face, the side with the pirate patch over his eye.

"Her name is Safiyah."

"Sophia?"

"Yes, it is a name that will not seem strange to English ears. Safi is not so far from Sophy."

"Did we know it was going to be a girl?" she whispered, coughing as feeling closed her throat.

He glanced at her, the sleeping baby nestled so trustingly against her. "You are almost asleep," he said. "Let me take her."

He leaned over to lift the child from her arms. He was gentle and tender with her, but at the same time firm and confident, making Anna feel how safe the baby was with him.

Jonathan. "Oh!" she whispered.

"What is it?" Ishaq Ahmadi said, in a voice of quiet command. "What have you remembered?"

"Oh, just when you took the baby from me...I..." She pressed her hands to her eyes. Not when he took the baby, but the sight of him holding the infant as if he loved her and was prepared to protect and defend the innocent.

"Tell me!"

She lifted her head to see him watching her with a look of such intensity she gasped. Suddenly she wondered how much of her past she had confided to her husband. Was he a tolerant man? Or had he wanted her to lie about her life before him?

She stammered, "Did—did—?" She swallowed, her mouth suddenly dry. "Did I tell you about...Jonathan? Jonathan Ryder?"

But even before the words were out she knew the answer was no.

Three

———

"**T**ell me now," Ishaq Ahmadi commanded softly.

She wanted to lean against him, wanted to feel his arm around her, protecting her, holding her. She must have that right, she told herself, but somehow she lacked the courage to ask him to hold her.

She had always wanted to pat the tigers at the zoo, too. Now it seemed as if she had finally found her very own personal tiger…but she had forgotten how she'd tamed him. And until she remembered that, something told her it would be wise to treat him with caution.

"Tell me about Jonathan Ryder."

Nervously she clasped her hands together, and suddenly a detail that had been nagging at her in the distance leapt into awareness.

"Why aren't I wearing a wedding ring?" she demanded, holding both hands spread out before her and staring at them. On her fingers were several silver rings of varied design. But none was a wedding band.

There was a long, pregnant pause. Through the glass panel separating them from the driver, she heard a phone ring. The driver answered and spoke into it, giving instructions, it seemed.

Still he only looked at her.

"Did I...have we split up?"

"No."

Just the bare syllable. His jaw seemed to tense, and she thought he threw her a look almost of contempt.

"About Jonathan," he prompted again.

If they were having trouble in the marriage, was it because he was jealous? Or because she had not told him things, shared her troubles?

She thought, *If I never told him about Jonathan, I should have.*

"Jonathan—Jonathan and I were going together for about a year. We were talking about moving in together, but it wasn't going to be simple, because we both owned a flat, and...well, it was taking us time to decide whether to sell his, or mine, or sell both and find somewhere new."

Her heart began to beat with anxiety. "It is really more than two years ago?"

"How long does it seem to you?"

"It feels as if we split up about six months ago. And then..."

"Why did you split up?"

"Because...did I not tell you any of this?"

"Tell me again," he repeated softly. "Perhaps the recital will help your memory recover."

She wanted to tell him. She wanted to share it with him, to make him her soul mate. Surely she must have told him, and he had understood? She couldn't have married a man who didn't understand, whom she couldn't share her deepest feelings with?

"I got pregnant unexpectedly." She looked at him and remembered that, sophisticated as he looked, he was from a different culture. "Does that shock you?"

"I am sure that birth control methods fail every day," he said.

That was not what she meant, but she lacked the courage to be more explicit.

"Having kids wasn't part of deciding to live together or anything, but once it happened I just—knew it was what I wanted. It was crazy, but it made me so happy! Jonathan didn't see it that way. He didn't want…"

Her head drooped, and the sound of suddenly increasing rain against the windows filled the gap.

"Didn't want the child?"

"He wanted me to have an abortion. He said we weren't ready yet. His career hadn't got off the ground, neither had mine. He—oh, he had a hundred reasons why it would be right one day but wasn't now. In a lot of ways he was right. But…" Anna shrugged. "I couldn't do it. We argued and argued. I understood him, but he never understood me. Never tried to. I kept saying, there's more to it than you want to believe. He wouldn't listen."

"And did he convince you?"

"He booked an appointment for me, drove me down to the women's clinic…. On the way, he stopped the car at a red light, and—I got out," she murmured, staring at nothing. "And just kept walking. I didn't look back, and Jonathan didn't come after me. He never called again. Well, once," she amended. "A couple of months later he phoned to ask if I planned to name him as the father on the birth certificate."

She paused, but Ishaq Ahmadi simply waited for her to continue. "He said...he said he had no intention of being saddled with child support for the next twenty years. He had a job offer from Australia, and he was trying to decide whether to accept or not. And that was one of the criteria. If I was going to put his name down, he'd go to Australia."

His hair glinted in the beam of a streetlight. They were on a highway. "And what did you say?"

She shook her head. "I hung up. We've never spoken since."

"Did he go to Australia?"

"I never found out. I didn't want to know." She amended that. "Didn't care." She glanced out the window.

"Where are we going?" she asked. "Where is the hospital?"

"North of London, in the country. Tell me what happened then."

Her eyes burned. "My friends were really, really great about it—do you know Cecile and Lisbet?"

"How could your husband not know your friends?"

"Are Cecile and Philip married?"

He gazed at her. "Tell me about the baby, Anna."

There was something in his attitude that made her uncomfortable. She murmured, "I'm sorry if you didn't know before this. But maybe if you didn't, you should have. "

"Undoubtedly."

"*Did* you know?"

He paused. "No."

Anna bit her lip. She wondered if it was perhaps because she hadn't told him that she had reverted to this memory tonight. Had it weighed on her throughout the new pregnancy? Had fears for her new baby surfaced and found no outlet?

"Everything was fine. I was pretty stressed in some ways, but I didn't really have doubts about what I was doing. At the very end something went wrong. I was in labour for hours and hours, and then it was too late for a Caesarean...they used the Ventouse cap."

She swallowed, and her voice was suddenly expressionless. "It caused a brain haemorrhage. My baby died. They let me hold him, and he was...but there was a terrible bruise on his head...as if he was wearing a purple cap."

No tears came to moisten the heat of her eyes or ease the pain in her heart. Her perfect baby, paper white and too still, but looking as if he was thinking very hard and would open his eyes any moment...

She wondered if that was how she had ended up giving birth in the back of a cab. Perhaps it was fear of a repetition that had made her leave it too late to get to the hospital.

"Why weren't you there?" she asked, surfacing from her thoughts to look at him. "Why didn't you take me to the hospital?"

"I flew in from abroad this evening. And this was six weeks ago?"

"That's how it feels to me. I feel as though it's the weekend I'm supposed to be going on that job to France, and that was about six weeks after the baby died. How long ago is that, really?"

"Did you ever feel, Anna, that you would like to—adopt a child? A baby to fill the void created by the death of your own baby?"

"It wouldn't have done me any good if I had. Why are you asking me these questions now? Didn't we—''

"Did you think of it—applying for adoption? Trying to find a baby?"

"No." She shook her head. "Sometimes in the street, you know, you pass a woman with a baby, or even a woman who's pregnant, and you just want to scream *It's not fair,* but—no, I just...I got pretty depressed, I wasn't doing much of anything till Lisbet conjured up this actor friend who wanted a mural in his place in France.''

She leaned over to caress the baby with a tender hand, then bent to kiss the perfectly formed little head. "Oh, you are so beautiful!" she whispered. She looked up, smiling. "I hope I remember soon. I can't bear not knowing everything about her!''

He started to speak, and just then the car drew to a stop. Heavy rain was now thundering down on the roof, and all she could see were streaks of light from tall spotlights in the distance, as if they had entered some compound.

"Are we here?''

"Yes," he said, as the door beside her opened. The dark-skinned chauffeur stood in the rain with a large black umbrella, and Anna quickly slipped out onto a pavement that was leaping with water. She heard the swooping crack of another umbrella behind her. Then she was being ushered up a curiously narrow flight of steps and through a doorway.

She glanced around her as Ishaq, with the baby, came in the door behind her.

It was very curious for a hospital reception. A low-ceilinged room, softly lighted, lushly decorated in natural wood and rich tapestries. A row of matching little curtains seemed to be covering several small windows at intervals along the wall. There was a bar at one end, by a small dining table with chairs. In front of her she saw a cluster of plush armchairs around a coffee table. Anna frowned, trying to piece together a coherent interpretation of the scene, but her mind was very slow to function. She could almost hear her own wheels grinding.

A woman in an Eastern outfit that didn't look at all like a medical uniform appeared in the doorway behind the bar and came towards them. She spoke something in a foreign language, smiling and gesturing towards the sofa cluster. She moved to the entrance door behind them, dragged it fully shut and turned a handle. Still the pieces refused to fall into place.

Anna obediently sank down into an armchair. A second woman appeared. Dressed in another softly flowing outfit, with warm brown eyes and a very demure smile, she nodded and then descended upon the baby in Ishaq Ahmadi's arms. She laughed and admired and then exchanged a few sentences of question and answer with Ishaq before taking the infant in her own arms and, with another smile all around, disappeared whence she had come.

"What's going on?" Anna demanded, as alarm began to shrill behind the drowsy numbness in her head.

"Your bed is ready," Ishaq murmured, bending over her and slipping his hands against her hips. At the touch of his strong hands she involuntarily smiled. "In a few minutes you can lie down and get some sleep."

His hands lifted and she blinked stupidly while he drew two straps up and snapped them together over her hips. Under her feet she felt the throb of engines, and at last the pieces fell together.

"This isn't a hospital, this is a plane!" Anna cried wildly.

Four

"Let me out," Anna said, her hands snapping to the seat belt.

Ishaq Ahmadi fastened his own seat belt and moved one casual hand to still hers as she struggled with the mechanism. "We have been cleared for immediate take-off," he said.

"Stop the plane and let me off. Tell them to turn back," she cried, pushing at his hand, which was no longer casual. "Where are you taking us? I want my baby!"

"The woman you saw is a children's nurse. She is taking care of the baby, and no harm will come to her. Try and relax. You are ill, you have been in an accident."

Her stomach churned sickly, her head pounded with pain, but she had to ignore that. She stared at him and showed her teeth. "Why are you doing this?" A sudden wrench released her seat belt, and Anna thrust herself to her feet.

Ishaq Ahmadi's eyes flashed with irritation. "You know very well you have no right to such a display. You know you are in the wrong, deeply in the wrong." He stabbed a forefinger at the chair she had just vacated. "Sit down before you fall down!"

With a little jerk, the plane started taxiing. "No!" Anna cried. She staggered and clutched the chair back, and with an oath Ishaq Ahmadi snapped a hand up and clasped her wrist in an unbreakable hold.

"Help me!" she screamed. "Help, help!"

A babble of concerned female voices arose from behind a bulkhead, and in another moment the hostess appeared in the doorway behind the bar.

"Sit down, Anna!"

The hostess cried a question in Arabic, and Ishaq Ahmadi answered in the same language. *"Laa, laa, madame,"* the woman said, gently urgent, and approached Anna with a soothing smile, then tried what her little English would do.

"Seat, madame, very dingerous. Pliz, seat."

"I want to get off!" Anna shouted at the uncomprehending woman. "Stop the plane! Tell the captain it's a mistake!"

The woman turned to Ishaq Ahmadi with a question, and he shook his head on a calm reply. Of course he had the upper hand if the cabin crew spoke only Arabic. Anna had a dim idea that all pilots had to speak English, but what were her chances of making it to the cockpit?

And if it was a private jet, the captain would be on Ishaq Ahmadi's payroll. No doubt they all knew he was kidnapping his own wife.

Ahmadi got to his feet, holding Anna's wrist in a grip

that felt like steel cables, and forced her to move towards him.

The plane slowed, and they all stiffened as the captain's voice came over the intercom—but it was only with the obvious Arabic equivalent of ''Cabin staff, prepare for takeoff.'' Ishaq Ahmadi barked something at the hostess and, with a consoling smile at Anna, she returned to her seat behind the bulkhead.

Ishaq Ahmadi sank into his seat again, dragging Anna inexorably down onto his lap. ''You are being a fool,'' he said. ''No one is going to hurt you if you do not hurt yourself.''

She was sitting on him now as if he were the chair, and his arms were firmly locked around her waist, a human seat belt. The heat of his body seeped into hers, all down her spine and the backs of her thighs, his arms resting across her upper thighs, hands clasped against her abdomen.

Wherever her body met his, there was nothing but muscle. There was no give, no ounce of fat. It was like sitting on hot poured metal fresh from the forge, hardened, but the surface still slightly malleable. The stage when a sculptor removes the last, tiny blemishes, puts on the finishing touches. She had taken a course in metal sculpture at art college, and she had always loved the metal at this stage, Anna remembered dreamily. The heat, the slight surface give in something so innately strong, had a powerful sensual pull.

She realized she was half tranced. She felt very slow and stupid, and as the adrenaline in her body ebbed, her headache caught up with her again. She twisted to try to look over her shoulder into his face.

''Why are you doing this?'' she pleaded.

His voice, close to her ear, said, "So that you and the baby will be safe."

She was deeply, desperately tired, she was sick and hurt, and she wanted to believe she was safe with him. The alternative was too confusing and too terrible.

The engines roared up and the jet leapt forward down the runway. In a very short time, compared to the lumbering commercial aircraft she was used to, they had left the ground.

As his hold slackened but still kept her on his lap, she turned to Ishaq Ahmadi. Her face was only inches from his, her mouth just above his own wide, well-shaped lips. She swallowed, feeling the pull.

"Where are you taking me?"

"Home." His gaze was steady. "You are tired. You will want to lie down," he murmured, and when the jet levelled out, he helped her to her feet and stood up. He took her arm and led her through a doorway.

They entered a large, beautifully appointed stateroom, with a king-size bed luxuriously made with snowy-white and deep blue linens that were turned down invitingly. There were huge, fluffy white pillows.

It was like a fantasy. Except for the little windows and the ever-present hum you would never know you were on a plane. A top hotel, maybe. Beautiful natural woods, luscious fabrics, mirrors, soft lighting, and, through an open door, a marble bathroom.

"I guess I married a millionaire," Anna murmured. "Or is this just some bauble a friend has loaned you?"

"Here are night things for you," he said, indicating pyjamas and a bathrobe, white with blue trim, that were lying across the foot of the sapphire-blue coverlet. "Do you need help to undress?"

Anna looked at the bed longingly and realized she was

dead on her feet. And that was no surprise, after what she had apparently been through in the past few hours.

"No," she said.

She began fumbling with a button, but her fingers didn't seem to work. Even the effort of holding her elbow bent seemed too much, so she dropped her arm and stood there a moment, gazing at nothing.

"I will call the hostess," Ishaq Ahmadi said. And that, perversely, made her frown.

"Why?" she demanded. "You're my husband, aren't you?"

His eyes probed her, and she shrugged uncomfortably. "Why are you looking at me like that? Why don't you want to touch me?"

She wanted him to touch her. Wanted his heat on her body again, because when he touched her, even in anger, she felt safe.

He made no reply, merely lifted his hands, brushed aside her own feeble fingers which were again fumbling with the top button, and began to undo her shirt.

"Have you stopped wanting me?" she wondered aloud.

His head bent over his task, only his eyes shifted to connect with hers. "You are overplaying your hand," he advised softly, and she felt another little thrill of danger whisper down her spine. Her brain evaded the discomfort.

"Did you commission work from me or something? Is that how we met?" she asked. She specialized in Mediterranean and Middle Eastern designs, painting entire rooms to give the impression that you were standing on a balcony overlooking the Gulf of Corinth, or in the Alhambra palace. But what were the chances that a wealthy Arab would want a Western woman to paint trompe l'oeil fifteenth-century mosaic arches on his palace walls when he probably had the real thing?

"We met by accident."

"Oh." She wanted him to clarify, but couldn't concentrate. Not when his hands were grazing the skin of her breasts, revealed as he unbuttoned her shirt. She looked into his face, bent close over hers, but his eyes remained on his task. His aftershave was spicy and exotic.

"It seems strange that you have the right to do this when you feel like a total stranger," she observed.

"You insisted on it," he reminded her dryly. He seemed cynically amused by her. He still didn't believe that she had forgotten, and she had no idea why. What reason could she have for pretending amnesia? It seemed very crazy, unless...unless she had been running away from him.

Perhaps it was fear that had caused her to lose her memory. Psychologists did say you sometimes forgot when remembering was too painful.

"Was I running away from you, Ishaq?"

"You tell me the answer."

She shook her head. "They say the unconscious remembers everything, but..."

"I am very sure that yours does," Ishaq Ahmadi replied, pulling the front of her shirt open to reveal her small breasts in a lacy black bra.

She knew by the involuntary intake of his breath that he was not unaffected. His jaw clenched and he stripped the shirt from her, his breathing irregular.

She wasn't one for casual sex, and she had never been undressed by a stranger, which was what this felt like. The sudden blush of desire that suffused her was disconcerting. So her body remembered, even if her conscious mind did not. Anna bit her lip. What would it be like, love with a man who seemed like a total stranger? Would her body instinctively recognize his touch?

She realized that she wanted him to make the demand on her. The thought was sending spirals of heat all through her. But instead of drawing her into his arms, he turned his back to toss her shirt onto a chair.

"What will I remember about loving you, Ishaq?" she whispered.

He didn't answer, and she turned away, dejected, overcome with fatigue and reluctant to think, and lifted her arms behind her to the clasp of her bra. She winced as a bruised elbow prevented her.

Her breath hissed with the pain. "You'll have to undo this."

She felt his hands at work on the hook of her bra, that strange, half electrifying, half comforting heat that made her yearn for something she could not remember. She wondered if they *had* been sexually estranged. She said, "Is there a problem between us, Ishaq?"

"You well know what the problem between us is. But it is not worth discussing now," he said, his voice tight.

She thought, *It's serious.* Her heart pinched painfully with regret. To think that she had had the luck to marry a man like this and then had not been able to make it work made her desperately sad. He was like a dream come to life, but…she had obviously got her dream and then not been able to live in it.

If they made up now, when she could not remember any of the grievances she might have, would that make it easier when she regained her full memory?

As the bra slipped away from her breasts, Anna let it fall onto the bed, then turned to face him, lifting her arms to his shoulders.

"Do you still love me?" she whispered.

His arms closed around her, his hands warm on her bare skin. Her breasts pressed against his silk shirt as her arms cupped his head. He looked down into her upturned face with a completely unreadable expression in his eyes.

"Do you want me, Ishaq?" she begged, wishing he would kiss her. Why was he so remote? She felt the warmth of his body curl into hers and it was so right.

A corner of that hard, full mouth went up and his eyes became sardonic. "Believe me, I want you, or you would not be here."

"What have I done?" she begged. "I don't remember anything. Tell me what I've done to make you so angry with me."

His mouth turned up with angry contempt. "What do you hope to gain with this?" he demanded with subdued ferocity, and then, as if it were completely against his will, his grip tightened painfully on her, and with a stifled curse he crushed his mouth against her own.

He was neither gentle nor tender. His kiss and his hands were punishing, and a part of her revelled in the knowing that, whatever his intentions, he could not resist her. She opened her mouth under his, accepting the violent thrust of his hungry, angry tongue, and felt the rasp of its stroking run through her with unutterable thrill, as if it were elsewhere on her body that he kissed her.

Just for a moment she was frightened, for if one kiss could do this to her, how would she sustain his full, passionate lovemaking? She would explode off the face of the earth. His hand dropped to force her against him, while his hardened body leapt against her. She tore her mouth away from his, gasping for the oxygen to feed the fire that wrapped her in its hot, licking fingers.

"Ishaq!" she cried, wild with a passion that seemed to her totally new, as the heat of his hands burned her back, her hips, clenched against the back of her neck with a firm possessiveness that thrilled her. "Oh, my love!"

Then suddenly he was standing away from her, his hands on her wrists pulling her arms down, his eyes burning into hers with a cold, hard, suspicious fury that froze the hot rivers of need coursing through her.

"What is it?" she pleaded. "Ishaq, what have I done?"

He smiled and shook his head, a curl of admiring contempt lifting his lip. "You are unbelievable," he said. "Where have you learned such arts, I wonder?"

Anna gasped. He suspected her of having a lover? Could it be true? She shook her head. It wasn't possible. Whatever he might suspect, whatever he might have done, whatever disagreement was between them, she knew that she was simply not capable of taking a lover while pregnant with her husband's child.

"From you, I suppose," she tried, but he brushed that aside with a snort of such contemptuous disbelief she could go no further.

"Tell me why you won't love me," she challenged softly, but nothing was going to crack his angry scorn now.

"But you have just given birth, Anna. We must resign ourselves to no lovemaking for several weeks, isn't it so?"

She drew back with a little shock. "Oh! Yes, I—" She shook her head. He could still kiss her, she thought. He could hold her. Maybe that was the problem, she thought. A man who would only touch his wife if he wanted sex. She would certainly hate that.

''I wish I could *remember!*''

He reached down and lifted up the silky white pyjama top, holding it while she obediently slipped her arms inside. He had himself well under control now, he was as impersonal as a nurse, and she tasted tears in her throat for the waste of such wild passion.

Funny how small her breasts were. Last time, they had been so swollen with the pregnancy...hadn't they? She remembered the ache of heavy breasts with a pang of misery, and then reminded herself, *But that's all in the past. I have a baby now.*

''Do you think I'll remember?'' she whispered, gazing into his face as he buttoned the large pyjama shirt. It seemed almost unbearable that she should feel such pain for a baby who had died two years ago and not remember the birth of the beautiful creature who was so alive, and whose cry she could suddenly hear over the subdued roar of the engines.

''I am convinced of it.''

''She has inherited your birthmark,'' she murmured with a smile, touching his eye with a feather caress and feeling her heart contract with tenderness. ''Is that usual?''

He finished the last button and lifted his eyes to hers. ''What is it you hope to discover?'' he asked, his hands pulling at her belt with cool impersonality. ''The... Ahmadi mark,'' he said. ''It proves beyond a doubt that Safiyah and I come of the same blood. Does that make you wary?''

''Did you think I had a lover?'' she asked. ''Did you think it was someone else's child?''

His eyes darkened with the deepest suspicion she had yet seen in them, and she knew she had struck a deep chord. ''You know that much, do you?''

Somewhere inside her an answering anger was born. "You're making it pretty obvious! Does the fact that you've now been proven wrong make you think twice about things, Ishaq?"

"Wrong?" he began, then broke off, stripped the suede pants down her legs and off, and knelt to hold the pyjama bottoms for her. His hair was cut over the top in a thick cluster of black curls whose vibrant health reflected the lampglow. Anna steadied herself with a hand on his shoulder and stifled the whispering desire that melted through her thighs at the nearness of him.

They were too big. In fact, they were men's pyjamas.

"Why don't I have a pair of pyjamas on the plane?" she asked.

"Perhaps you never wear them."

He spoke softly, but the words zinged to her heart. She shivered at the thought that she slept naked next to Ishaq Ahmadi. She wondered what past delights were lurking, waiting to be remembered.

"And you do?"

"I often fly alone," he said.

It suddenly occurred to her that he had told her absolutely nothing all night. Every single question had somehow been parried. But when she tried to formulate words to point this out, her brain refused.

Even at its tightest the drawstring was too big for her slim waist, and the bunched fabric rested precariously on the slight swell of her hips. Ishaq turned away and lifted the feathery covers of the bed to invite her to slip into the white, fluffy nest.

She moved obediently, groaning as her muscles protested at even this minimal effort. Once flat on her back, however, she sighed with relief. "Oh, that feels good!"

Ishaq bent to flick out the bedside lamp, but her hand stopped him. "Bring me the baby," she said.

"You are tired and the baby is asleep."

"But she was crying. She may be hungry."

"I am sure the nurse has seen to that."

"But I want to breast-feed her!" Anna said in alarm.

He blinked as if she had surprised him, but before she could be sure of what she saw in his face his eyelids hooded his expression.

"Tomorrow will not be too late for that, Anna. Sleep now. You need sleep more than anything."

On the last word he put out the light, and it was impossible to resist the drag of her eyelids in the semi-darkness. "Kiss her for me," she murmured, as Lethe beckoned.

"Yes," he said, straightening.

She frowned. "Don't we kiss good-night?"

A heartbeat, two, and then she felt the touch of his lips against her own. Her arms reached to embrace him, but he avoided them and was standing upright again. She felt deprived, her heart yearning towards him. She tried once more.

"I wish you'd stay with me."

"Good night, Anna." Then the last light went out, a door opened and closed, and she was alone with the dark and the deep drone of the engines.

Five

―――

"Hurry, hurry!"

The voices and laughter of the women mirrored the bubble of excitement in her heart, and she felt the corners of her mouth twitch up in anticipation.

"I'm coming!" she cried.

But they were impatient. Already they were spilling out onto the balcony, whose arching canopy shaded it from the harsh midday sun. Babble arose from the court-yard below: the slamming of doors, the dance of hooves, the shouts of men. Somewhere indoors, musicians tuned their instruments.

"He is here! He arrives!" the women cried, and she heard the telltale scraping of the locks and bars and the rumble of massive hinges in the distance as the gates opened wide. A cry went up and the faint sound of horses' hooves thudded on the hot, still air.

"They are here already! Hurry, hurry!" cried the women.

She rose to her feet at last, all in white except for the tinkling, delicate gold at her forehead, wrists, and ankles, a white rose in her hand. Out on the balcony the women were clustered against the carved wooden arabesques of the screen that hid them from the admiring, longing male eyes below.

She approached the screen. Through it the women had a view of the entire courtyard running down to the great gates. These were now open in welcome, with magnificently uniformed sentinels on each side, and the mounted escort approached and cantered between them, flags fluttering, armour sending blinding flashes of intense sunlight into unwary eyes.

They rode in pairs, rank upon rank, leading the long entourage, their horses' caparisons increasing in splendour with the riders' rank. Then at last came riders in the handsomest array, mounted on spirited, prancing horses.

"There he is!" a voice cried, and a cheer began in several throats and swelled.

Her eyes were irresistibly drawn to him. He was sternly handsome, his flowing hair a mass of black curls, his beard neat and pointed, his face grave but his eyes alight with humour. His jacket was rich blue, the sleeves ruched with silver thread; his silver breastplate glowed almost white. Across it, from shoulder to hip, a deep blue sash lay against the polished metal.

The sword at his hip was thickly encrusted with jewels. His fingers also sparkled, but no stone was brighter than his dark eyes as he glanced up towards the balcony as if he knew she was there. His eyes met hers, challenged and conquered in one piercingly sweet moment.

Her heart sprang in one leap from her breast and into his keeping.

As he rode past below, the white rose fell from her helpless hand. A strong dark hand plucked it from the air and drew it to his lips, and she cried softly, as though the rose were her own white throat.

He did not glance up again, but thrust the rose carefully inside the sash, knowing she watched. She clung to the carved wooden arabesques, her strength deserting her.

"So fierce, so handsome!" she murmured. "As strong and powerful as his own black destrier, I dare swear!"

The laughter of the women chimed around her ears. "Ah, truly, and love is blind and sees white as black!" they cried in teasing voices. "Black? But the prince's horse is white! Look again, mistress!"

She looked in the direction of their gesturing, as the entourage still came on. In the centre of the men on black horses rode one more richly garbed than all. His armour glowed with beaten gold, his richly jewelled turban was cloth of gold, ropes of pearls draped his chest, rubies and emeralds adorned his fingers and ears. His eyebrows were strong and black, his jaw square, his beard thick and curling. He lifted a hand in acknowledgement as those riders nearest him tossed gold and silver coins to the cheering crowd.

Her women were right. Her bridegroom was mounted on a prancing stallion as white as the snows of Shir.

"Saba'ul khair, madame."

Anna rolled over drowsily and blinked while intense sunlight poured into the cabin from the little portholes as, *whick whick whick whick,* the air hostess pulled aside the curtains.

Her eyes frowned a protest. "Is it morning already?"

The woman turned from her completed task and smiled. "We here, madame."

Anna leapt out of the bed, wincing with the protest from her bruised muscles, and craned to peer out the porthole. They were flying over water, deep sparkling blue water dotted with one or two little boats, and were headed towards land. She saw a long line of creamy beach, lush green forest, a stretch of mixed golden and grey desert behind, and, in the distance, snow-topped mountains casting a spell at once dangerous and thrilling.

"Where on earth are we?"

"Shower, madame?"

"Oh, yes!"

The hostess smiled with the pleasure of someone who had recently memorized the word but had produced it without any real conviction and was now delighted to see that the sounds did carry meaning, and led her into the adjoining bathroom.

Anna waved away her offer of help, stripped and got into the shower stall, then stood gratefully under the firm spray of water, first hot, then cool. This morning her body was sore all over, but her headache was much less severe.

Her memory wasn't in much better shape, though. It still stopped dead on the night before she had been due to leave for France. Now, however, she could remember a shopping expedition with Lisbet during the afternoon, going home to dress, meeting Cecile and Lisbet at the Riverfront Restaurant. Now she could remember leaving the restaurant, and almost immediately seeing a cab pull up across the street. "You take that one, Anna, it's facing your direction,'' Lisbet had commanded, and she had dashed across the street...

She could remember *that* as if it were yesterday.

Of the two years that had followed that night there was still absolutely nothing in her memory. Not one image had surfaced overnight to flesh out the bare outline Ishaq Ahmadi had given of her life since.

When she tried to make sense of it all, her head pounded unmercifully. The whole thing made her feel eerie, creepy.

Last night's dream surfaced cloudily in her mind. She had the feeling that the man on the black horse was Ishaq Ahmadi.

She wondered if that held some clue about her first meeting with him. Had she seen him from a distance and fallen in love with him?

That she could believe. If ever there was a man you could take one look at and know you'd met your destiny, Ishaq Ahmadi was it. But he was definitely keeping something from her. If once they had loved each other, and she certainly accepted that, there was a problem now. It was in his eyes every time he looked at her. His look said she was a criminal—attractive and desirable, perhaps, but not in the least to be trusted.

Anna winced as she absently scrubbed a sore spot. The accident must have been real enough. Her body seemed to be one massive bruise now, and she ached as if she had been beaten with a bat.

That thought stilled her for a moment. Panic whispered along her nerves. Suppose a man had beaten his pregnant, runaway wife and wanted to avoid the consequences...

Anna reminded herself suddenly that they would be landing soon and turned off the water. In the bedroom mirror she stared at herself. She was still too thin, just as she had been after losing her baby two years ago. There were dark circles under her eyes to match the bruising on her body.

She had a tendency to lose weight with unhappiness. Anna sighed. By the look of her, she had been deeply unhappy recently, as unhappy as when she had lost Jonathan's baby. But the question was—had she lost the weight *before* she left Ishaq, or *after?*

Her clothes were lying on the neatly made bed. The shirt had been mended, the suede pants neatly brushed. Anna's breath hissed between her teeth. *It's terrific, Anna. Stop dithering and buy it!*

She had bought this shirt on that Friday afternoon and worn it that night to dinner in the Riverfront. These were the clothes that she could remember putting on that night. Her jacket was missing, that was all.

Anna stood staring, her heart in her throat. With careful precision she reached down and picked up the shirt. The tag was completely fresh. Either she was confusing two separate memories in her mind…or she and Lisbet had bought this shirt yesterday.

"Ah, I was just coming for you," Ishaq Ahmadi said, as she opened the door. "We are about to land. Come and sit down."

He sank into an armchair as Anna obeyed. Beside him the nurse sat with the baby in her arms. The air hostess was behind the bar. Anna could smell coffee.

"I'll take the baby," she said, holding out her arms.

To her fury, the nurse glanced up at Ishaq Ahmadi.

"Give me the baby," she ordered firmly.

Ishaq Ahmadi nodded all but invisibly, and the nurse passed the baby over. Safiyah was sleeping. Anna

stroked her, the hungry memory of the son who had not
lived assuaged by the touch of the tiny, helpless body,
the feather-soft skin, the curling perfect hand. Her
mouth, full, soft and tender, was twitching with her
dream, as were her dark, beautifully arched eyebrows.

Anna glanced up at Ishaq Ahmadi and thought that he
had probably once had the same mouth. But now its
fullness was disciplined, its softness was lost in firmness
of purpose, its tenderness had disappeared.

She wanted to believe that he was telling the truth.
That he was her husband and that this was the child of
their mutual love. She wanted to believe the evidence of
the shirt was somehow false. Her heart was deeply
touched by the baby, the man. It was possible, after all.
She might have packed the shirt away, left everything
with friends, perhaps, and then, fleeing to those friends
from her husband, had recourse to her old clothes.

Or confusing the memory of two different shopping
trips might be a sign that her more recent memory was
returning.

"Where are we?" she asked, watching out the window as the wheels touched down in the familiar chirping
screech of arrival.

Palm trees, sunlight, low white buildings, the name on
the terminal building in scrolling green Arabic script, the
red Roman letters underneath moving past too fast for
her to read...

"We are in Barakat al Barakat, the capital of the Barakat Emirates," he said.

"Oh!" She had heard of the Emirates, of course. But
she knew almost nothing about the country except that
it was ruled by three young princes who had inherited
jointly from their father. "Is it—is it your...our...
home?"

"Of course."

"Are you Barakati?"

"Of course," he said again.

She had some faint idea that amnesia victims didn't forget general knowledge, only personal. So how was it that she couldn't remember anything about the country that was her home? Her skin began to shiver with nervous fear.

A few minutes later the door opened. Bright sunshine and fresh air streamed into the aircraft, bringing with it the smell of hot tarmac and fuel and the sea and…in spite of those mundane odours, some other, secret scent that seemed full of mystery and magic and the East.

An official came deferentially aboard in an immigration check that was clearly token, and her lack of a passport wasn't even remarked on. Anna flicked a glance at Ishaq as the men spoke. Well, it wasn't surprising that he was as important as that. She could have guessed it just by looking at him.

Down below a sparkling white limousine waited, and the chauffeur and a cluster of other people were standing on the tarmac.

"Give the baby to the nurse," Ishaq Ahmadi said when the official departed with a nod and smile. Anna immediately clutched Safiyah tight.

"She's sleeping," she protested, with the sudden, nameless conviction that if she obeyed him she would never see the baby again.

"Give the baby to the nurse," he repeated, approaching her.

Anna evaded him, and stepped to the open doorway of the aircraft. "If you try to take her away from me, I'll scream. How far does your influence go with the people out there?"

Out on the tarmac her appearance in the doorway caused a little stir. People were gazing her way now.

Ishaq's jaw tightened and his eyes flashed at her with deep, suspicious anger. "How cunning you think you are. So be it."

He came up beside her and, with an arm around her waist, stepped with her through the door onto the top step. He stopped there, and to Anna's utter amazement, two of the men below produced cameras and began snapping photos of them.

"What on earth—?" she exclaimed.

She heard him murmur what sounded like a curse. "Smile," he ordered, with a grimness that electrified her. "Smile or I will throttle you in front of them all."

"What is it?" she whispered desperately. "Who are you?" and then, crazily, after a beat, "Who am I?"

"You will not say anything, anything at all, to the journalists."

"Journalists?"

She stared at the photographers in stunned, stupid dismay. What was going on? What could explain what was happening to her?

Ishaq went down the narrow stairs one step ahead of her, turning to guide her down. His hand was commanding, and almost cruel, against her wrist. In crazy contradiction to her feelings, the sun was heaven, the breeze delicious. Light bounced from the tarmac, the car, the plane with stupefying brilliance.

A man with a camera jumped right in front of them, and Anna recoiled with a jolt. "Excuse me!" she murmured, outraged, but he only bent closer. "Please, you'll disturb the baby!"

"Ingilisiya!" someone cried. *"Man hiya?"*

"Louk these way, pliz!"

The chauffeur had leapt to open the door of the limousine, and Ishaq shepherded her quickly to it. Before Anna's eyes could adjust to the blinding sunlight she was in the dimness of the car, the door shutting her and the baby behind tinted glass.

The voices were still calling questions. She heard Ishaq's deeper voice answer. A moment later he was slipping into the seat beside her. The nurse got into the front seat. The chauffeur slammed the last door and the limousine moved off as a cameraman bent to the window nearest Anna and snapped more pictures.

She turned to Ishaq.

"What's going on?" she said. "Why are there journalists here?"

"They are here because they permanently stake out the airport. The tabloids of the world like to print photographs of the Cup Companions of the princes of Barakat as they come and go in the royal jets. Usually it does not matter. But now—" he turned and looked at her with a cold accusation in his eyes that terrified her "—now they have a photograph of the baby."

Too late, she realized how foolish she had been to defy him when she knew nothing at all.

Six

The limousine turned between big gates into a tree-lined courtyard and swept to a stop in front of a two-storey villa in terra-cotta brick and stone with a tiled roof. The facade was lined with a row of peach-coloured marble pillars surmounted with the kind of curving scalloped arches Anna was more used to painting on clients' walls than seeing in real life.

Anna's heart began beating with hard, nervous jolts.

"Are we here?" she murmured, licking her lips.

It was a stupid question, and he agreed blandly, "We are here."

The door beside her opened. Anna got awkwardly out of the car, the baby in one arm. She stood looking around as Ishaq Ahmadi joined her. The courtyard was shaded with tall trees, shrubs and bushes, and cooled with a running fountain, and she had a sudden feeling of peace and safety.

"Is this your house?"

He bowed.

The baby woke up and started making grumpy noises, and the nurse appeared smilingly at Anna's side. She clucked sympathetically and made an adoring face at the complaining baby, then glanced up at Anna.

Anna resolutely shook her head and, with a defiant glance at Ishaq Ahmadi, shifted the baby up onto her shoulder. The baby wasn't going out of her sight till she understood a lot more than she did right now.

But he merely shrugged. A servant in white appeared through one of the arches, and they all moved into the shade of the portico.

Her eyes not quite accustomed to the cool gloom, she followed Ishaq Ahmadi into the house, through a spacious entrance hall and into the room beyond. There the little party stopped, while Ishaq Ahmadi conversed in low tones with the servant.

Anna opened her mouth with silent, amazed pleasure as she gazed around her. She had never seen a room so beautiful outside of a glossy architectural magazine. An expanse of floor patterned in tiles of different shades and designs, covered here and there with the most beautiful Persian carpets she had ever seen, stretched the length of a room at least forty feet long.

There were low tables, sofas covered in richly coloured, beautifully woven fabric like the most luscious of kilims, a black antique desk, and ornately carved and painted cabinets. Beautiful objets d'art sat in various niches, hung on the walls, stood on the floor.

A wall that was mostly window showed a roofed balcony overlooking a courtyard, in which she could see the leafy tops of trees moving gently in the breeze. The balcony was faced with a long series of marble pillars supporting sculpted and engraved stone arches and walled with intricately carved wooden screens. Beyond the treetops, she saw a delicious expanse of blue sky and sea.

Anna closed her eyes, looked again. Heaved a breath. She felt the deepest inner sense of coming home, as if after interminable exile. She belonged here. She sighed deeply.

She turned to Ishaq Ahmadi. "Why was I in London?" she asked.

He raised his eyebrows in enquiry.

"I've been doubting you and everything you told me," she explained. She closed her eyes and inhaled, letting out her breath on another deep sigh of relief. "But I *know* this is home. Why did I leave, Ishaq? Why did you have to bring me home by force?"

He looked at her with an unreadable expression.

"Do you tell me you remember the house?"

She shook her head. "No…not really *remember*. But I have the feeling of belonging."

"You are a mystery to me," he said flatly. "Give Safiyah to the nurse, and let us have something to drink."

The manservant was waiting silently, and Ishaq turned to him with a quiet order. With a slight bow the man moved away.

Meanwhile, with a caress, a kiss and a lingering glance, Anna let the nurse take Safiyah from her arms. The woman smiled reassuringly and disappeared through a doorway, leaving Anna alone with Ishaq Ahmadi.

Who was opening a door onto the magnificent balcony. "Come," he said, in a voice that instantly dispelled her more relaxed mood. "We have things to discuss."

He slipped off his suit jacket and tossed it onto a chair. She hesitated.

"My dear Anna, I assure you there is nothing to fear on the terrace," he said. "No one will throw you over the edge, though it is undoubtedly what you deserve."

What she deserved? Well, there was no answer she could make to that until she remembered more.

"Do I—have I left any clothes here?" Anna asked, rather than challenge him, feeling she could hardly bear any more wrangling. She couldn't remember ever having felt so tired. "Because if so, I'd like to change into something cooler."

"I am sure there is something to accommodate you. Shall I show you, or do you remember the way?" Then, correcting himself, "No, of course, you remember nothing."

She followed without challenging that mockery as he closed the door again and led her along half the length of the room and down a flight of stairs. There they walked along a hall and he opened a door.

If she had been hoping that the sight of her bedroom would trigger memories, that hope died as she entered the utterly impersonal room. For all the feeling that the room had been inhabited for centuries, there was not one photograph, one personal item on view. A few bottles of cosmetics on a dressing table were the only evidence that a woman slept here.

Well, she had known from the beginning that her marriage was troubled, so there was no reason to weep over this confirmation. Anna opened the door of a walk-in closet. Inside there were empty hangers, a few items in garment bags, a pair of sandals on the floor, a case neatly placed on a shelf.

So she had left him. She had preferred to run to London to have her baby in the back of a cab rather than stay with her handsome, passionate husband. Anna bit her lip. And he had come and kidnapped her and brought her back.

And she had no idea what that meant. Was she to be a prisoner now? Would he keep the baby and banish her? Or did he mean to try again to make a troubled marriage work?

She heaved a sigh, but there was nothing to be gained in trying to second-guess him. She was desperately disadvantaged by her memory loss, utterly dependent on him for any description of what had gone wrong between them.

Anna stripped, found some clean underwear in a drawer. Bathing her face and wrists in cool water, she paused and stared at her reflection. The face that looked back at her was not the face of a woman who was happy about having left her husband. Her eyes, normally a deep sapphire blue, looked black with fatigue.

Or perhaps it was the marriage itself that had done that to her.

The bra was too large for her. So she had been away some time? She abandoned the bra, slipping into briefs and a pale blue shirt and pant outfit in fine, cool cotton. The shirt was long, Middle Eastern fashion. It was size medium, and she had always bought petite. Anna shook her head. Nothing fit, in any sense of the word. One of the thong sandals was broken and she decided to go barefoot.

Ishaq, having changed his suit for a similar outfit to her own in unbleached white cotton, and wearing thong sandals, was waiting for her outside the door.

He led her up to the main room again.

"What time is it?" she asked as he opened the balcony door. He obediently consulted the expensive watch on his wrist.

"Eleven."

"It feels more like six in the morning to me," she remarked, yawning and stepping outside. "I feel as if I've hardly slept."

From here she could see that the house was built in a squared C shape, and the broad balcony she was on ran around the three sides. One storey below, the courtyard was deliciously planted with trees and shrubs around a fountain. Beyond that there were other levels of the terrace, connected with arches and stone staircases, but mostly hidden from view by the greenery.

"It is seven in the morning in London. We have travelled east four hours," he replied.

She laughed at her own stupidity. "Oh, of course! Well, it just goes to show how confused I am!"

"No doubt."

The balcony was partitioned with beautiful wooden arches in the most amazing scrollwork. As they walked through one of these archways, Anna paused to touch the warm, glowing wood. "I paint arches like this on the walls of rooms," she observed. "But I've never before seen the real thing at first hand." Then she turned with a self-conscious laugh. "Well, but except—"

"Except for the fact that you live here," he said blandly.

They strolled through another arched partition, past windows leading to magical rooms. The house seemed very old, the brick and tiles well-worn by time and the tread of generations. Flowering plants tumbled in the profusion of centuries over the balcony and down to the terrace below, others climbed upwards past the opening towards the roof.

"Is this your family's house?"

"I inherited it from my father early this year."

"Oh, I'm sorry," she murmured, and then shook her head for how stupid that must sound to him—his wife, who must have attended the funeral with him, formally commiserating with him months after the fact.

"Sorry," she muttered. "It's hard to…"

Past the next archway a group of padded wicker chairs and loungers sat in comfortable array by a low table near a tiny fountain. Anna sighed. Her weary soul seemed to drink in peace so greedily she almost choked. There were flowers and flowering bushes everywhere. The breeze was delicious, full of wonderful scents. The sound of running water was such balm. The whole scene was luxuriously, radiantly, the Golden Age of Islam.

"This is beautiful!"

As he paused, Anna stepped to the scrollwork railing and glanced down. She could hardly believe that any normal process of life had brought her to such a magnificent home.

The villa was not small. That was an illusion at the entrance level. Below her on various levels now she had a clearer view of the stepped terraces full of flowers and greenery, and discovered that the courtyard led to a terrace with an inviting swimming pool unlike any she had ever seen. It was square, set with beautiful tiles both around the edge and under water.

The house was built on a thickly forested escarpment above a white sand beach that went for miles in both directions. Straight ahead of her, across the bay, she saw the smoky blue of distant hills. To the left, several miles away around a curving shoreline, she could just catch sight of the city. Beyond the bay the sea stretched forever, a rich varied turquoise that melted her anxiety and fatigue with each succeeding rush of a wave onto the sand.

The murmur of voices told her that the servant had reappeared, and she turned to see him pushing a trolley laden with a large cut-glass pitcher of juice and a huge bowl of lusciously ripe fruit. All the glass was frosted, as if everything had been chilled in a freezer. In a few deft movements, the man transferred the contents of the trolley to the table, and at a sign from his master, retired.

As she sank onto a lounger Ishaq poured a drink and handed it to her without speaking. She put the ice-cold glass to her lips and drank thirstily of the delicious nectar, then lifted her feet onto the lounger and leaned back into a ray of sun that slanted in. The breeze caressed her bare toes. Behind her head a flowering shrub climbed up a pillar and around an arch, a carpet of pink blossoms. Anna smiled involuntarily as the heavy tension in her lifted. For a moment she could forget her fears, could forget how he had brought her back home, and simply be.

He sank into the neighbouring chair, facing her at an angle, leaned back and watched her over the rim of his glass. His gaze set up another kind of tension in her, that warred with the peace she was just starting to feel.

"So, Anna," he said. She closed her eyes against the intensity she felt coming from him.

"Ishaq, I'm tired. Can't we leave this for another day?"

"Delay would suit you, would it? Why?"

"I really am at a loss to understand you," she sighed. "I'm here, the baby's here, what else do you want?"

He smiled. "You have no idea what it is I want?"

"If I don't even remember being married to you, how can I possibly be expected to guess what you want?"

she exploded. She could feel that she was very near breaking point.

"All right," he said. "Let us deal with what you do remember. As far as you remember, six weeks ago you gave birth and the child died."

She closed her eyes. There was no softness in his tone, and she wondered what kind of fool she had been to tell him, when she remembered nothing about what kind of man she had married. She must have had good reason for not telling him.

"That's how it feels."

"You were distraught over this loss."

"Yes, of course I was." She gave him a steady look, desperately hoping she would be able to hold her own against him. "And I remind you that you were not then part of my life, Ishaq."

"You wondered about the possibility of adopting a baby, but as a single woman you were not eligible through conventional channels."

"What?" She blinked at him. "I never said that! Why are you putting words in my mouth?"

"Anna, time is short. I intend to find the truth."

"The truth of *what?*" she exploded. "You keep telling me different things! How can you expect me to remember anything when you keep changing your story? What is it you want? Why is time short? Why are you playing these games? Why does the past matter now? It's over, isn't it?"

"You wanted a baby very much," he continued, as if she hadn't spoken.

"Ishaq—"

"You wanted a baby very much?"

"No, I did not want 'a baby' very much!" she said through her teeth. "I wanted *my* baby. My baby, Noah, who had every right to be born healthy and strong. I wanted him. I still do. You're going to have to face it, Ishaq. It's not something that gets wiped out by time. He's there in my heart, and he will never leave. Safiyah joins him there, but she won't replace him. Noah will always be in my heart.''

It was the first time she had spoken of the baby in such a way. Her urgency meant she spoke without defending herself against the pain, and her breath trembled in her throat and chest. She felt the lump of stone in her chest shift, and thought, *Six weeks of hiding from the hurt is one thing. But what kind of marriage can it be if I've been keeping this inside for two years?*

He was leaning forward, close to her, but staring down into the glass he held loosely between his spread knees.

''What drew us together?'' she asked.

He lifted his eyes without moving his head.

''Have I never been able to be open about my feelings before? Is our relationship entirely based on sex or something?''

His eyes took on a look of admiration laced with contempt. ''In spite of having no memory of me, you feel sexual attraction between us?''

''Don't you?'' she countered.

His look back at her was darkly compelling, and her skin shivered. There *was* a strong sexual pull. And if that was the centre of their bond, it would be foolish to pretend to exclude it from their negotiations.

He reached out and ran a lean finger along her cheek, and the little answering shiver of her skin made her heart race. ''Have you forgotten this?''

She gulped. Oh, how had she ever, ever managed to attract him? He was so masculine, so attractive, and yet with an air of risk, of danger. Like the powerful muscles under the tiger's deceptively furry coat, under Ishaq Ahmadi's virile masculinity there was a threat that he would make a bad enemy.

"It seems rather wasteful on my part," she agreed with a crazy grin, wanting him to smile without any edge. "But I'm afraid I have."

"Then I will have the pleasure of teaching you all over again," he said lazily. His hand cupped her cheek and he looked searchingly into her face. "Yes?"

She had no argument with that. She bit her lip, smiling into his eyes, nearer now. "It might even be the thing to bring back my memory."

"Yes, of course! That is the most ingenious excuse for making love that I have heard. But you always were imaginative, Anna."

His lips were almost touching hers, and her skin was cold and hot by turns. His hand cupped her neck and his fingers stroked the skin under the cap of hair.

She felt the rightness of it. She wanted to lean against him and feel the protection his strength offered, feel his arms clasp her firmly, feel herself pressed against his chest again. For in his arms, just as in this house, she knew she was home.

He moved his mouth away from hers without kissing her, moved to her eyelid. She closed her eyes in floating expectation, feeling the sun's heat and Ishaq's warmth as if both derived from one source.

He trailed light kisses across her eyelids, brushed her long curling lashes with his full lips, trailed a feathery touch down the bridge of her nose. His thumb urged her chin upwards, and her head fell back in helpless longing.

She felt starved for the touch, as if she had been longing for it for months. Years. Her arms wrapped him, her hand on his neck delighting in the touch of the thick hair.

At last he kissed her lips, and it was right, so right. As if some deep electrical connection had been made. She felt it sing against her mouth and melt her heart, and she felt his hand tighten painfully on her arm and knew that he felt it, too. Whatever had gone wrong between them, it was not this.

He was gnawing on her lower lip with little bites that sent shafts of loving and excitement through her. His other hand came up and encircled her throat, too, and he held her helpless in his two hands while his mouth hungered against hers, stealing and giving pleasure.

Anna pressed her hand against his chest, thrilling to the strength of heart and body she felt there. It was both new and old. She felt as if she had loved him in some long-distant past, some other life, and at the same time that it was all totally new. She seemed never to have been warmed with such delight by a kiss, never yearned so desperately for a man's love.

He wrapped her tight in his arms and drew her upper body off the lounger and across his knees with a passion that made her tremble. Now his mouth came down on hers with uncontrolled longing, and he kissed her deeply and thoroughly until her bones were water and her heart was alive with wild, wild need.

His mouth left hers, trailed kisses across her cheek to her ear, down her neck to the base of her throat, and slowly back up the long line of her throat.

"Ishaq!" She cried his name with passionate wonder before his kiss could smother the sound on her lips. "Ishaq!"

His lips teased the corner of her mouth and moved up towards her ear.

"Tell me the truth, Anna," he whispered. "Tell me, and then let me love you."

"Tell you?" She would tell him anything, if only he would carry on kissing her. But she had nothing to tell. "Tell you what?" He did not answer, only stared compellingly at her, and she slowly turned away her head. "I don't remember," she protested sadly, feeling the passion die within her. "Why won't you believe me? What have I done to forfeit the trust you must once have had in your wife?"

His eyes squeezed shut, and she felt how he struggled for control of himself and bit by bit gained it. Then he lifted her to rest in the lounger again, took his hands away, and sat looking at her. She saw burning suspicion in his eyes.

"What is it?" she pleaded. "What do you want me to tell you? What have I forgotten?"

He shook his head, reaching for his glass, and nervously she picked up her own. He drank a long draft of juice, and set the glass down carefully.

"What have you forgotten, you want to know?" He looked at her levelly. "You have forgotten nothing, Anna. Except perhaps the humanity that is the birthright of us all. Tell me where Nadia is."

Anna closed her eyes, opened them. Swallowed.

"Nadia?" She repeated the name carefully. "Who is Nadia?"

Ishaq smiled. "Nadia, as you very well know, is the mother of the baby you kidnapped and have been pretending is your own."

Seven

The storm of passion he had raised in her body was now a dry emptiness that left her feeling sick. "What?" An icicle trailed along her spine. She blinked at him, mouth open, feeling about as intelligent as a fish. "What are you talking about?"

He watched her in silence. When she moved, it was to set her glass down on the table very carefully.

"I don't know anyone nam…the mother of the baby? Of Safiyah?" Her voice cracked. "She's not my baby?"

He was silent. She stared into his face. Was this the truth, or some kind of mind game?

"You're trying to break me," she accused hoarsely. "Tell me the truth. If you have any humanity at all, if you have one ounce of human feeling in you, tell me the truth. Is Safiyah our baby?"

"You know very well that she is not," he said. "Will

you never come to the end of your play-acting? What can you stand to gain from this delay?''

Anna heard nothing except *she is not.*

"She's not?'' she repeated. "She's not?''

He sat in silence, watching her, his sensual mouth a firm, straight line.

"If she's not mine, then...I haven't forgotten two years of my life, either,'' Anna worked out slowly. She wrapped her arms around her middle and looked away from his gaze, rocking a little. "And we aren't married, and this is not my home. It was all lies.''

She looked into his face again, saw the confirmation of what she had said, and turned hopelessly to gaze around her. A quiver of sadness pierced her. It had seemed so right. Being here, the baby, the man—it had felt real to her. She shook her head. "But how...is one of us crazy?''

He looked like someone sitting through a badly acted play. "You, if you imagined you could get away with it,'' he offered.

Her mouth was bone-dry. One hand to her throat, she tried to swallow, and couldn't. "I don't know anyone named Nadia,'' she began, with forced calm. "I was in an accident and I woke up in hospital and they told me my baby was okay. You said you were my husband and I had amnesia. That's all I know. That is literally all I know.''

Ishaq Ahmadi—if that was his name—leaned back in his chair. "You knew enough to pretend the baby was your own,'' he pointed out dryly.

She shook her head in urgent denial. "My memory was a complete jumble. You can't know what it's like unless you've experienced it. First I thought I was back at the time I was in hospital for...when my baby died.

When they said, 'Your baby's fine,' I thought..." She stopped and swallowed. "I thought Noah's death had been a bad dream. I thought I'd dreamt the whole six weeks since. I thought I had another chance."

She forced down the taste of tears at the back of her throat.

"And then you came along," she said, in a flat voice. "You turned everything on its head."

It was all so crazy, so horrible, she could hardly take it in. She put a hand to her aching forehead. "Where did the baby come from? Why did you tell me we were married?" she demanded, fighting to keep sane. He'd be convincing her the world was flat next.

"For the same reason you pretended to believe me."

"No!" she cried. "No! You know perfectly well—" She broke off that argument, knowing it was futile. "What is this? Why are you doing this?"

"You can guess why."

She shook her head angrily. "I can't guess anything! How dare you do this to me! Messing with my mind when I was concussed, telling me I was suffering from amnesia! What do you want? What can you possibly want from me? Why, *why* did you say she was our baby?"

"Because husbands have rights in such cases that others do not have."

She blinked at the unexpectedness of it. It was perhaps the first time he had given her a straight answer to any question.

"Are you the baby's father?"

He paused, as if wondering how much to tell her. "No. Nadia is my sister. "

"How did I come to be in the hospital with her baby? Did you plant her on me somehow?"

One eyebrow lifted disbelievingly. "Not I. That's what I want you to tell me. I found you there together."

Anna shook her head confusedly. "I don't understand. Then how do you know this is your sister's baby?"

"By the al Hamzeh mark." He rubbed his eye unconsciously.

"By the—*what?*" She jerked back in her chair. "Are you telling me that you abducted a baby and a total stranger from a hospital and brought us across four time zones on the strength of the baby's *birthmark?*" she shrieked incredulously.

He gazed at her for a moment. Anna shifted nervously.

"Nadia was in labour and on her way to the hospital when she disappeared. A few hours later you turned up in another, nearby hospital, pretending to be the mother of a newborn baby with the al Hamzeh mark."

"How did you know I *wasn't* her mother? The nurses told me it was my baby. So how did you know better? Is there really nobody else in the world with that mark except you and Nadia?"

"The nurse who examined you knew very well it was not your baby. She had written notes on your chart to that effect. You may read the notes, if you doubt me. I have them. She made a note for the hospital to check with the police for any reported incidents of baby stealing from maternity wards and to keep you in for observation till the matter was investigated."

Anna blinked and opened her mouth in amazed indignation. "But then why—but they—I *told* them my baby died, and they said, No, here's your baby, she's alive!"

He shrugged.

Anna couldn't fit any one piece of the puzzle with another. She shook her head helplessly, feeling how slowly her mind was working. "Anyway, if you knew I wasn't Safiyah's mother, why bother to abduct me? Why didn't you just take the baby? I wouldn't be likely to complain, would I, if I was faking it?"

"I wanted information from you. And you were in no state to—"

"Information about what?" she interrupted.

"About how you got possession of Safiyah."

This was unbelievable.

"Like for example?" she demanded. "What are you suggesting? That I—jumped Nadia while she was in labour, dragged her off somewhere, and then stole her baby when it was born?"

"That is one possible scenario, of course. Is that what happened?"

"Well, thank you, I'm starting to get a picture here," Anna said furiously. "On no evidence whatsoever, you have decided that I am a baby snatcher. And that gives you the right to treat me like a criminal. You don't owe me an iota of respect, or the decency of truth. Nothing. Because of what you *suspect*. Have I got that now?"

Now she understood the reason for his questions earlier. The ugliest doubt of her own sanity brushed her. Was it possible? Had grief made her crazy enough to want a baby at any cost? Could she have done such a thing and forgotten all about it? Was that even the reason for her amnesia? No. *No*.

"And what do you imagine I did with Nadia?" she went on, when he didn't speak.

"That is one of the things I want you to tell me," he said.

Anna leapt to her feet. "How dare you talk to me like this? I did not do it! You have absolutely no grounds *whatsoever* for making such an appalling accusation!"

"I have not accused you. But you were in that cab with a newborn baby who is not your own. That needs some explaining."

She was not listening. She stormed on. "How dare you take such extreme action on no evidence at all...lying, abducting me, making me believe I'm half crazy! Telling me...my God, and we almost made love!" she raged, her cheeks blazing as she suddenly remembered the scene.

"Was that my doing?" he asked dryly. "Or was that your attempt to get my guard down?" He was speaking as if this were only another such attempt. As if he believed nothing she said.

The flame of rage enveloped her, licking and burning till she felt something almost like ecstasy.

"Don't *you* accuse *me!*" she stormed. "*I've* never said anything but the truth! All the manipulation has come from your corner! You even lied about your name, didn't you? Last night it was the Ahmadi mark. Just now you called it the al Hamzeh mark!"

Ishaq Ahmadi looked bored. "Never lied to me? You lied to me not half an hour ago."

"I have not lied to you!"

He got to his feet, facing her over the lounger, and Anna stepped back, but not fast enough to prevent his grasping her wrist.

"What do you call it? You told me you recognized this place, that you knew you had come home! You have not been within a thousand miles of this place."

Her eyes fell before the searching gaze. "Why did you say it?" he prodded.

She was silent. She had felt a sense of homecoming, probably only because she wanted to feel it. Wanted the baby to be hers, wanted him to be her husband. So desperately wanted all the sorrow and anguish of her terrible loss to be years in the past. There had certainly been enough clues that he was lying, if she had wanted to put them together.

"What did you hope to gain?" he pressed.

"Suppose you tell me!" she blazed, pain fuelling her anger in order to hide from him. She wrenched her wrist from his hold. "What advantage could there possibly be in saying something like that?"

"Perhaps you hoped to lower my guard and make your escape?"

"By sleeping with you, I suppose! Sexually amoral, too. That's quite a charming list you've made up there."

"You lied. You must have had a reason."

"Dear Kettle, yours sincerely, Pot!" she exclaimed mockingly. "I have only your word for what's going on, you know. And your word hasn't exactly proved unassailable. You..."

She stopped. "Why did you think I would believe you in the hospital, if things are as you say? You must have known I had amnesia. You must have been deliberately playing on the fact. Otherwise, why wouldn't I just tell the nurse you were an impostor?"

"I did not imagine that you would believe me. I thought you would prefer to pretend to do so, however, rather than run the risk of being revealed as a kidnapper and arrested by the police." Now she remembered that curious, warning pressure on her hand as she lay so dazed in the casualty ward. "And I was right. You could not afford to make a stand, because that would mean an immediate inquiry. And any inquiry would have shown that the baby could not be yours."

"If I hadn't been totally out of it I would have made a stand soon enough," she said. She suddenly felt too weak to support her own anger. All her energy had been used up; she was empty. She had no more strength for holding pain at bay.

Her baby seemed to reach for her heart, the touch of that tiny soul unlocking the deepest well of grief in her. She shook her head and forced herself to confront Ishaq, to cloak her weakness from this dangerous adversary.

"If you hadn't lied about absolutely *everything*... If a lie is big enough, they'll believe it! Are you proud to be taking your lead from a monster?

Anger flickered in his eyes.

"I do what is necessary to protect those I love," he said coldly. She believed him. She saw suddenly that he was a man who would make a firm friend as well as an implacable enemy and, in some part of her, she could grieve for the fact that she was destined to be his enemy.

"Well, bully for you!" she cried, her voice cracking with fatigue. "I want to get out of here and go home to my life. So suppose you tell me what you want from me?"

Ishaq Ahmadi inclined his head. "Of course. You have only to tell me where Nadia is and how you got her baby. Then you are free to go. I will of course pass the information and your name on to Scotland Yard."

With a grunt of exasperation that almost moved into tears, Anna whirled to stride away from him. Against the wall of the house a railing protected a worn brick staircase running down to the courtyard below, and again she felt that crazy sense of belonging. *I have gone up and down that staircase a hundred times.*

She shook her head to clear it, stopped and turned to face him.

"Why don't you believe me?" she demanded. He lifted an eyebrow, and she fixed her eyes on his. "No,

I really mean it. My explanation of events is as reasonable as anything else in this—'' she lifted her hands ''—in this unbelievable fantasy, so why won't you even give it a moment's consideration? You absolutely dismiss everything I tell you. Why?''

A sudden, delightful breeze whipped across the terrace, stirring her hair and the leaves, whipping the cloth on the table, snatching up a napkin and carrying it a few yards. Her nostrils were suddenly filled with the heady scent of a thousand flowers. The servant appeared as if from nowhere to chase down the napkin.

''Because what you tell me has no logic even of its own. How did you come to be in the hospital with this baby?''

''Funny, that's exactly why I *believed* you,'' she said on a desperate half laugh. ''How did I get there? That's the question, all right.''

''Your story has no foundation. It rests on sand.''

''What about the cab driver?'' she exclaimed. ''What did he say about it?''

''He was quite seriously hurt. He cannot yet be questioned.''

''Where did the accident happen?''

''The taxi pulled into the path of a bus on the King's Road at Oakley Street,'' he replied, as if she already knew. ''You were in the back with the baby. There can be no doubt of that.''

She damned well was not, but she didn't waste time on what he thought he knew. She wanted to sort this out.

''Oakley Street. That's only a couple of minutes from the Riverfront.'' The Riverfront Restaurant was moored near Battersea Bridge. ''What time was the accident?''

"Not long after midnight, according to the police report."

She wondered how he had got access to the police report, but didn't waste time asking. "We asked for our bill around midnight, I'm pretty sure."

She squeezed her eyes shut. That meant her memory loss covered a very short period. If only a few minutes had elapsed from the time she got into the cab till the accident...

"If you're right, the only possible explanation is that the baby was in the cab when I got into it," Anna said, and as she said it, the truth finally pierced her heart. That darling baby whom she already loved was not to be hers to love...any more than her son had been.

Ishaq Ahmadi snorted. "Excellent. If only you had thought of this explanation a few hours ago."

Anna shook her head, swallowing against the feeling that was welling up inside her, a flood of the deepest sadness. She had no right after all to hold and love that beautiful, perfect baby, no matter how empty her arms were, how much she yearned.

"Perhaps a little later you will remember this. At a convenient time you will perhaps remember getting into a cab and discovering a baby cooing and kicking there."

His words hurt her. *Noah,* she thought. *Oh, my baby! You never kicked and cooed....*

Suddenly all her defences were gone. She felt like a newborn herself. She dropped her arms to her sides.

"Maybe I didn't catch that cab. I don't actually remember getting into it. Drivers change shift around midnight, don't they? Maybe he wouldn't take me and we went up to the King's Road to try and get cabs there. Maybe..."

She was babbling. She didn't know if she was making

sense. She blinked hard against the unfamiliar tears that threatened, against the sudden pressure on the wall that had held down her feelings for so long. She wanted to put her head back and howl her loss to the whole mad world that had let it happen, let her perfect baby die.

"Yes?" he prompted.

"I don't know," she said, despair welling up. How could she sort anything out when she could not remember? It was boxing in the dark. Was it possible she had forgotten some horrible conspiracy? Had her grief driven her to the madness of taking someone else's baby to fill her empty heart? Women did such things.

Tears began to slip down her cheeks. She couldn't seem to control them. Her head was pounding; it must be the heat. She staggered a little.

"I'm tired," she realized suddenly. "Really tired." She put out her hand to an arch for support, but it was further away than it seemed. A sob came ripping up from her stomach, bringing with it bile and the juice she had just drunk, and feeling came surging on its heels.

"Oh!" she cried. "Oh, I can't..." Her fingers caught at something, a branch, perhaps, but she couldn't hold on, and at the next sob her knees gave way.

The branch was Ishaq's arm. He caught her around the waist when she buckled, supporting her as grief and bile spilled from her amid howls of anguish.

"My baby!" she cried desperately, as the image of Safiyah blended with that of her own darling son, and seemed to be torn anew from her arms and her heart. Her throat opened, and at last she howled out the uncomprehending, intolerable misery that had been her silent companion for so many days and weeks. "Oh, my baby! My baby! Why? *Why?*"

Eight

"*Princess, it is too dangerous!*" pleaded the maidservant. *She stood wringing her hands as her mistress, gazing into the mirror, tweaked the folds of the serving girl's trousers she wore.*

She glanced up, eyes sparkling in the lamplight. "*He is a brave man, the Lion. He will admire bravery. If I could, I would challenge him in the field of battle.*"

"*If anyone discovers you—*"

"*I will flee. And you will be waiting for me, with my own raiment,*" *she said firmly.*

She admired herself one last time in the mirror. The short jacket just covering her breasts, the pants caught tight below the knee, the delicate gold chain around her ankles fanning out over her feet to each toe, the circlets of medallions around her waist and forehead, the glittering diaphanous veil that did not hide the long dark

*curls…the costume of her father's winebearers suited a
woman well.*

*A smile pulled at her dimpled cheek as she turned
away and kissed her maid. "Fear not," she said. "I am
quick of mind and fleet of foot and I shall elude all save
him I would have capture me." A delicious thrill rushed
through her and she picked up the white rose that lay
waiting and tucked it into her waist.*

*A few minutes later the two women crept together
down the dark, secret passages of the palace towards
the sounds of revelry in the great banqueting hall.*

*Inside the hall, the narrow doorway was hidden by a
large carpet hung upright to provide a narrow passage
against the wall, but as they glided in behind it, light
from the banquet beyond revealed more than one spy
hole in the fabric. She pressed her eye to one and gazed
hungrily.*

*The men sat and lay around the laden cloth on cush-
ions and carpets, drinking and eating, laughing, toasting
the bridegroom, who sat beside her father. At the far
end of the room musicians played. Serving men moved
about the room, carrying huge platters massed with
food. A whole roast sheep was being set down before
the bridegroom.*

*But she had no thought for her intended. Her eyes
searched the faces of the men seated nearest the prince,
looking for the one they called al Hamzeh. The Lion.
The birthmark made her search easy, even at such a
distance, and her heart thudded in pain and delight as
her eyes found him.*

*She took the golden pitcher from her frightened maid-
servant's hands then and glided stealthily out into the
room, her movements measured by the bell-like tinkle of
her jewellery. She walked down the room towards the*

Lion, as if in answer to a summons, as she had watched
the cup bearers do.

He sat cross-legged on the carpet, leaning against a
mound of silken cushions at his elbow, listening as someone described some feat of the bridegroom's at the hunt.
His dark hair, glowing in lamplight, fell in tousled curls
over the glittering gold embroidery of his jacket. On his
fingers heavy carved gold held rich rubies and emeralds;
high on his arm she noted the seal of his office, a signet
in gold and amber. He seemed to glow independent of
the lamplight. She watched in a fever of desire as he bit
into a sweetmeat and his tongue caught an errant morsel
of powdered sugar from his full lower lip.

She approached, and bent over to fill the cup that he
held in one strong careless hand. The scent of him rose
up in her nostrils, spices and musk and camphor from
his clothes, and from his skin the clean perfumed smell
of a man just come from the hammam.

As if he sensed something in the winegirl, the Lion
lazily turned his head and let his eyes follow the smooth
arms up to her white breast, her half-hidden cheek. Instead of turning her face demurely away, she met his
gaze with a look of passionate challenge. He started, his
lips parting with questing amaze.

She let fall the white rose by the goblet, the little note
fluttering like a lost petal from its stem. His eyes flicked
to the rose, and she saw by his stillness that he understood. He turned and looked up at her, and now his gaze
devoured the sweet face so passionately that her own
eyes fell.

His hand moved possessively to gather up the rose
before it could be noticed by anyone else—enclosing it
jealously to keep it from other eyes, crushing it in a

*signal of all-consuming passion. She melted into an-
swering passion as she felt his gesture on her own skin.*

*A thorn pierced his flesh and he smiled, as if a little
pain was no more than to be expected from love.*

Anna awoke in a strange bed and gazed around her.

Her headache was gone, and she felt deeply refreshed,
as if she had made up for all the lost sleep of weeks past
in one go. But the sunlight filtering through the shutters
was still bright.

She had wept till she was completely drained and exhausted. She had wept it all out, for the first time, and
then had fallen into a deep sleep. And now a burden had
lifted from her. The heavy weight was gone.

Now healing could begin.

And of all people it was Ishaq Ahmadi who had sat
beside her and witnessed her grieving. He had not said
much, but his quiet presence had been exactly right.
Someone to listen without feeling driven to reassure.
Someone to hear and accept while understanding that
nothing could be done to change her world for her.

With more interest in life than she had experienced
for weeks past, Anna leaned up on one elbow and gazed
around her.

She was in a different bedroom entirely from the one
she had changed her clothes in. This was a very spacious
room, beautifully decorated in blues and dark wood,
with a door leading to the terrace. There were two other
doors, and in the hopes that one of them led to a bathroom, Anna sprang out of bed and crossed an expanse
of soft silk carpet woven in shades of blue and beige.

She got the bathroom first time, and when she returned
to the bedroom, there was a smiling maid waiting for
her. The bed was made as neatly as if Anna had never

slept in it, and on the bed were laid clothes, as if for her
choice.

"*Saba'ul khair, madame,*" the maid murmured, duck-
ing her head.

Anna smiled. "*Salaam aleikum,*" she offered. It was
the only phrase she knew in Arabic.

It was a mistake, because the woman immediately
burst into delighted chatter, indicating the terrace beyond
the windows and the clothes on the bed.

Laughing, Anna shook her head. "I don't speak Arabic!" she said, holding up her hands in surrender, but
when she saw that among the offered outfits were several
swimsuits, she turned towards the windows. The woman
was opening the slatted wooden shutters so she could
see more clearly what was out there.

The room was at one of the tips of the C. On the far
side of the broad terrace was the swimming pool she had
seen from above. Ishaq Ahmadi was sitting at a table in
a beach robe, reading a newspaper. A meal was being
served to him.

Anna's stomach growled. She turned to the bed and
picked up a swimsuit in shades of turquoise. It was beautifully cut and looked very expensive. Underneath that
was another one, identical except for the size. With a
frown of interest Anna picked up a few other items. Everything had been supplied in two sizes.

It might be conspicuous consumption, but as for refusing to accept his casual largesse, well, Anna was dying for a swim. So she stripped off her clothes and
inched into one of the blue suits. It had an excellent fit,
and she turned to examine herself briefly in a large mirror. She was thin, but the antique mirror was kind. Her
shape was still unmistakably feminine. The suit em-
phasised her slender curves. The gently rounded neck-

line produced a very female cleavage, and her back, naked to the waist, had an elegantly smooth line. Her legs were lean but shapely, even if the large purple bruise on one thigh showed cruelly against her too-pale skin.

It was a long time since she had examined her reflection for femininity and attractiveness. Now it was perhaps a sign of her return to feeling that she was anxious to look attractive.

The maid held a cotton kaftan for her, and she slipped her arms into the sleeves with a murmur of thanks. It was plain white with an oriental textured weave and wide sleeves, and she knew without looking at the label that it had cost a small fortune. She chose a purple cotton-covered visor and a pair of sunglasses from a small spread of accessories.

He had thought of everything. He must have phoned a very exclusive boutique—or had one of his servants do so. Well, she would be glad if the utter stupidity of her trip here was relieved by a few hours of sun before she flew back to a wintry Europe. And though the items would be beyond her budget, they wouldn't amount to much for a man who owned a house like this.

The maid drew open the door for her, and Anna stepped out under the arched overhang and into the luscious day and walked across the tiled paving, past shrubs and flowers, past palm trees and small reflective pools, towards the swimming pool.

The air was cooler, and the sun had moved in the opposite direction to what she would have expected. She had thought the courtyard faced south, but in that case the sun was setting in the east.

Before she could reorient herself she had arrived at Ishaq's table beside the pool in a corner where the house met the high perimeter wall, nestled attractively under an arching trellis thick with greenery and yellow blooms.

He closed his paper as the servant pulled out a chair for her. A second place had been set.

"Good afternoon," she said, sinking down into it.

"Afternoon?" Ishaq queried with a smile, and she simultaneously took in the fact that his meal was composed of fruit and rolls.

"*Café, madame?*" murmured the servant, and she smelled the strong, rich odour and demanded, "What time is it?"

"Just after nine," said Ishaq Ahmadi.

"In the morning!" A breathless little laugh of comprehension escaped her. "Have I slept an entire day?"

"I am sure you needed it. You must be hungry."

"Ravenous!" She flung down her sunglasses, then leaned back out of the shady bower so that the sun caught her face, and felt that she was happy in spite of everything. "Oh, this is heaven! What a wonderful place!"

He smiled. He had lost some of the hard edge of suspicion he had carried since they first met. And she—well, she had shown him things about herself that no one else in the world had seen. So it was only natural that she felt closer to him now.

He offered the basket of rolls. "Perhaps you would like what you call a full English breakfast?"

Taking a roll, Anna smiled up at the servant who was setting cream and sugar just so by her coffee cup. "I could devour a plate of bacon and eggs," she told Ishaq, then checked herself. "Oh, but—"

"I am sure the cook has some lamb sausage."

"That sounds delicious."

Ishaq translated her wishes to the servant. As the man

slipped away, he said, "I do not ask my staff to cook pork for non-Muslim guests. I hope you will not object to doing without it during your stay."

"My *stay?*" She looked at him. "I want to go home. Are you planning on forcing me to stay here beyond today?"

"Force you? No," he replied calmly. "But you might reconsider when you look at this."

His hand was resting on the arm of his chair, holding the newspaper he had been reading. He lifted it to present her with the paper, front page up.

Trahie Par Son Milliardaire De Cheikh! screamed the French headline, which she could vaguely translate as *Betrayed By Her Millionaire Sheikh,* and Anna only shook her head. But then her eye was drawn further down the page, to a large photograph.

"That's me! That's you and me!" she cried in astonishment, snatching the paper without apology and spreading it under her horrified nose.

It was a photo taken at the airport, of herself, holding Safiyah, and Ishaq Ahmadi with one arm around her, guiding her to the limousine. An inset photo showed a sultry, big-lipped blonde whose face Anna vaguely recognized.

Very clearly marked—and too dark, so someone had obviously retouched the photo—was the al Hamzeh mark on the eye of Ishaq and of Safiyah.

"Oh, good grief!" Anna cried weakly. "Is this…" She glanced at the stack of papers on the table beside him, knowing the answer even as she asked. "Is it in the English papers?"

"Very much so," he agreed lazily.

She jumped up and ran to the stack. Of course, today

was Sunday. The English Sunday tabloids were notorious for their love of scandal among the rich and famous.

Sheikh Gazi's Secret Baby!
Sheikh's Mistress In Baby Surprise!
Mystery Beauty Has Playboy Gazi's Baby!

All the tabloids save one had run it on the front page, with a variant of the photograph she had already seen. Every headline insinuated or said outright that the woman in the photo was the sheikh's mistress and the mother of his child. Worst of all, in virtually every photograph Anna's face was clear and unmistakable. She looked exactly like herself. And her arms were around the baby in a firm maternal hold that spoke louder than the headlines.

Still in a state of stunned disbelief, Anna chose one of the papers and returned to her seat, sinking slowly into it as she read the story.

Sheikh Gazi al Hamzeh, the wealthy, jet-setting Cup Companion and trusted confidant of Prince Karim of West Barakat, startled the world yesterday with the revelation that his long-time English mistress has given birth to his child.

The infant is thought to be over a month old. "The birth was kept secret till Gazi could gain the prince's approval to acknowledge the child," said a source close to the sheikh.

Prince Karim, whose own son was born in July, is understood to be urging the sheikh to marry his so far unidentified mistress, seen here with the sheikh on arrival at Barakat al Barakat.

"Sheikh Gazi has gone to extraordinary lengths to protect the privacy of his mystery girlfriend," says our own society columnist, Arnold Jones

Bremner. "Virtually no one outside his circle knows who she is."

Although the couple have been seen in some of London's most exclusive private clubs over the past year, they use a service entrance. This is the first photograph of them together.

Insiders say the couple are unlikely to marry.

Anna lifted her eyes to "Ishaq Ahmadi."

"*'Long-time mistress!'*—where did they get this?" she demanded. Her gaze hardened. "Is this what you told them?"

He laughed. "They did not trouble to ask me. The truth might have got in the way of invention. Suppose you had been the baby's English nanny! Where would their front page be then?"

"They asked you questions at the airport," Anna said stonily. "I heard them. And you answered."

His jaw tightened. "Recollect that it was you yourself who insisted on presenting them with the tantalizing sight of the baby. But for that our arrival would have been unremarkable."

"What does *Paris Dimanche* say?" she asked, to catch him out. If the stories matched, surely that meant there had been one source?

He looked as if he saw right through her suspicious mind, but made no comment, merely lifted the paper and negligently began to translate.

"Sheikh Gazi al Hamzeh, the Hollywood-handsome, polo-playing millionaire considered one of the world's most eligible bachelors, has dashed the hopes and broken the heart of beautiful model/actress Sacha Delavel, his close friend, with the revelation that he is on the point of marrying the mother of his child. 'It comes as a total shock,' Mademoiselle Delavel reportedly told friends from the privacy of a villa in Turkey, where she is said to have fled as the news broke. 'I never knew of her existence until today.''"

He tossed the paper aside as Anna's breakfast was placed before her. He deliberated over the fruit in the bowl and chose a ripe pomegranate as if he had nothing else on his mind. Then he neatly began to slice into the rind.

For some reason this story was much more infuriating than the other.

"I suppose when you're next seen with Sacha Delavel *I'll* be the one billed as having the broken heart," Anna snapped.

Ignoring her, he delicately, patiently prised open the pomegranate to reveal the luscious red rubies within. Anna shivered as if she were watching him make intimate love to another woman.

"Sacha Delavel and I danced together at a charity ball given for Parvan war relief a few months ago in Paris. They have searched their picture library and found some nice photos of the two of us, which are on page seven. The rest is invention."

She watched as he sank strong white teeth into the red fruit. Liquid spurted from the seeds over his hands and mouth, but he was concentrated on his pleasure. A thrill of pure sensation pierced her, and with a little gasp Anna dropped her eyes to her own breakfast.

"Did they get your name right? You're Sheikh Gazi al Hamzeh?"

"In the West I commonly use that name," he admitted wryly.

"Oh!" she remarked with wide-eyed sarcasm. "*It's* not your real name, either?"

"My name is Sayed Hajji Ghazi Ishaq Ahmad ibn Bassam al Hafez al Hamzeh," he said, reeling the name off with the fluency of poetry. "But this is difficult for English speakers, who do not like to take time over other people's names. Nor do they trouble to pronounce consonants that don't appear in English."

She couldn't think of any comeback to that. They ate in silence for a few minutes. With little flicked glances she watched him enjoy the pomegranate, and marvelled that anyone could believe that ordinary Anna Lamb was the mistress of such a powerful, virile, attractive man, or that he had dropped someone as beautiful as Sacha Delavel for her.

But she was pretty sure that people *would* believe it, now. It had been in the papers, after all. Probably even her own friends would wonder. Not Cecile or Lisbet, of course. But others less close to her.

"What do we do about this?" she finally asked, indicating the papers.

"Do?" Sheikh Gazi shrugged and wiped his hands and mouth with a snowy napkin. "Ignore it."

"*Ignore* it? But we have to make them retract. We could sue."

"And sell more papers for them."

"But it's all lies!"

Sheikh Gazi smiled at this indignation. "People will soon forget."

"But—aren't you going to do *anything?*"

"The editors hope that I will. Then they would have something to run with. A story denied is a story. Do you really want to see *Sheikh Gazi Denies Baby* as next Sunday's headline? Or do you prefer *Gazi Is Not The Father, Says Anna*?''

"But people will think—it says that you and I are..." She licked her lips and faded off, startlingly aware of the day, the heat, the luscious taste of fruit in her mouth, the smell of the sun on his skin. *They think we're lovers.* The thought hovered between them, shimmering like heat.

"And the more you say now, Anna, the more they will go on thinking it," he said.

"But I—I have to go back to London immediately. To France," she amended. "What if the papers find out my name?"

"They will certainly do so," he warned her softly. "As soon as the papers are read in London this morning—" he glanced at his watch "—it is nearly six o'clock there now—someone who knows you will call a journalist and name you."

They were reading the story before most people in England were awake. She realized he must have some mechanism for getting the Sunday papers as soon as they rolled off the presses at midnight and flying them out to Barakat.

"Your price per copy must be astronomical," she observed dispassionately. "Do you have a regular Sunday delivery of the European papers?"

"No," he said.

The servant came with a new pot of coffee. He whisked their half-drunk cups away and poured fresh coffee into clean cups. Even with her worries, Anna had attention to note the luxury of that.

"Today was special, huh?" She had always dreamed of being famous one day, but for her work, not for something like this. ''Well, so some friend or client will spill the beans. Then what? Will they phone me?''

''Phone you? They will phone you, they will phone your friends, they will come to your front door. At least one paper will offer you money for an exclusive, and if you accept, the editor will do everything to convince you to make the story of your sheikh lover more extreme and exciting.''

''What do you mean?''

''Before they are through you will be tricked or persuaded into confessing that we have made passionate, death-defying love in the back of a limousine as it drove through London and Paris, in moonlight on the deck of my yacht, high in the air in the royal jet, on the magical white sand beach down there, and even on the back of my favourite polo pony as it galloped through the forest. Naturally we have been insatiable lovers. And of course they will publish photos of you posed in my favourite piece of sexy underwear.''

His words sent electric twitches all across her scalp and down her spine, and Anna sat up abruptly and sugared her coffee. Was he being assailed by the same treacherous thought she was—that since everyone believed it anyway, they might as well make it the truth?

Nine

"**I**'m not going to be selling anyone any story," she said, setting the spoon in the saucer with a little snap. "Your polo pony's reputation is safe from me."

He lifted his hands in a shrug.

"But it really burns me that everyone I know is going to half believe I had your baby. What am I going to tell *them?*"

"That the story is false."

Her anger exploded on a little breath. "Oh, sure! You seem to forget that I actually have been pregnant. Only my close friends know my baby died. I haven't told anyone. I've hardly seen anyone since it happened. Everybody is going to wonder."

He looked at her. "I see."

"And what happens when I don't have the baby with me? People are going to think I walked away and let you keep her."

"Is it so bad? Fathers do get custody," he pointed out, so offhand she gritted her teeth. "And you have a career that takes you—"

She ground out, "I would no more give up my baby to its father for the sake of my career than—" She broke off with an exasperated sigh.

"Blame it on me," he suggested. "Everybody knows Arabs are an uncivilized bunch of barbarians who kidnap their own children."

"Will you stop laughing at me?" she demanded hotly.

"I will stop laughing when you stop being foolishly outraged by something so unimportant. It is not the end of the world, Anna. People will accept that the story was false when you tell them, or they will not. Either way they will cease to care within a week. These things—" he flicked the pile of newspapers with a gesture of such deep and biting contempt she flinched "—they feed the lowest tastes in humans, and like any junk food the purveyors of it make it addictive and completely without nutrition in order to create a constant demand for more. One story runs into another in people's minds. It is a taste for scandal and outrage this feeds, not a desire for factual information."

"I want to make them print a retraction," she said doggedly.

"Anna, by next Sunday, if we give them no more fuel for their fire, no one will remember whether you had a sheikh's baby or bribed a government minister, and no one will care! Do you know how many times my picture has appeared in these rags? Do you think anyone who gobbles such stories along with their Sunday toast remembers my name? I am 'that sheikh' if they think of me at all, and they confuse me with half a dozen other Cup Companions, or even with the princes themselves.

Even with something like the al Hamzeh mark to distinguish me, people say to me, *Oh, you were in the paper, weren't you? What was that about again?* when the story was about the ex-Sultan of Bagestan.''

"You just told me a minute ago that they're going to chase me down like dogs," she said irritably.

"*Yes,* if you put yourself in their way." He gazed compellingly at her, lifting his closed fist, the first knuckle extended towards her, for emphasis. "*Yes,* if you give them fodder by complaining. This is a story that has another one or two headlines in it at most—*if* we give it to them! If not, it will die now. This is not, as they say, a story with legs."

"What does that mean?" she asked doubtfully, half convinced. He seemed to know so much about it.

"To have legs? It is newspaper jargon. It means a story that is going to run under its own steam."

She sat in silence, her chin in her hands, absorbing it.

"There is nothing to be gained by issuing a denial, Anna. The best you can do, if you wish it to go no further, is stay out of sight for a while."

She tried again. "It's not as though I'm a celebrity, is it? It's you they're really interested in. If I can just get to France, I'll be fine. Alan's house is pretty remote."

"Let me offer you an alternative to France, Anna." His gaze was now utterly compelling. Although he was trying to disguise it, she realized that he wanted something from her, and the butterflies in her stomach leapt into a dance so wild she was almost sick.

She licked her lips. "And what would that be?"

"You could stay here with me until the heat dies down," he said.

* * *

A long moment of stillness was interrupted by the shrill cry of a bird in a nearby tree. Anna dropped her napkin by her plate with a matter-of-fact gesture.

"I—" she began, and then broke off. Her blood pounded in her stomach, making it feel hollow in spite of the meal she had just eaten.

"Do not turn me down without giving it some thought, Anna. There is advantage to you in staying away from the press for the moment. And I assure you I will do everything in my power to make your stay enjoyable."

Anna licked her lips. What was he really offering her here? A mere bolt-hole, or her very own Club Med holiday complete with dark lover? With any ordinary man, she would be in no doubt, but he was a man whose interest would flatter the most famous and beautiful women in the world. Why should he want her?

"For how long—a week?" she asked.

He shrugged and lifted a hand. His hands were graceful and strong, and she wondered if he played a musical instrument. Or perhaps a man got hands like that playing music on women's bodies…she stomped on the little flames that licked up around her at the thought.

"Perhaps a week, a few weeks. It depends."

On what? she wondered. Not on newspaper interest, obviously, when he had already assured her that would scarcely last till next Sunday.

Was he imagining that he would put her through her paces and see how long she kept him interested? She was unlikely to keep a millionaire playboy sheikh who hung out with the likes of Sacha Delavel interested for long. She had never studied sex as an art, and she would bet that he had.

"But people would find out I was here, wouldn't

they? It would just confirm the story. So whenever I
went back I'd have to face journalists wanting me to talk
about it. Wouldn't I?''

He shrugged and plucked a grape from the bowl. She
had the feeling again that he was hiding something.

''Where's the advantage in delaying the inevitable?
At least if I go back now I can deny it. If I stay here
even for a week no denial is ever going to sound cred-
ible.''

It suddenly occurred to her that she sounded like
someone wanting to be convinced, and she shut up.

''Can you think of no advantage from such a holiday?
Barakat is a very exclusive holiday destination. No package tours come here. We have only a few resorts. That
beach is as crowded now as it ever gets.''

She couldn't refrain from a glance in the direction he
indicated. The strip of white sand curving around the
bay in front of them was virtually deserted. So it actually
wouldn't be stretching credibility too far to suggest that
they had made love there, she found herself thinking
absently…

Some part of her urged her to simply capitulate, and
let nature take its course. But a little voice was warning
her to be wary. Sheikh Gazi was not disinterested. What
purpose would her staying serve for him? Was he really
attracted to her, or was he deliberately letting her think
so to disguise his real motives? And if he *didn't* want
her sexually, what did he want?

Had he in fact been offering *her* sex as a bribe? He
wanted her to stay and he knew she was attracted. Plenty
of women would jump at the chance for a holiday in
this paradise with a man like Gazi—and a sheikh, too!—
devoting himself to them. Was he assuming she was one
of them?

Anna, examining the grape between her fingers with minute fixity, blushed to the roots of her hair. After a moment she slipped it into her mouth.

"I would of course reimburse you for your time," he said, and that certainly proved the suspicion. He was simply trying whatever was handy by way of a bribe. If sex wasn't enough, he would throw in cash. God, what that said about his opinion of her!

"Really," she observed, her voice distant, almost absent.

"At your professional rate, of course."

She flicked him a look. "Which profession would that be?"

He chose to ignore the irony. "Which profession? I don't—you are an artist, you say. Artist, designer, interior decorator, whatever fees are your usual fees."

"Since you're doing me the big favour by allowing me to hide here, I don't really see why *you* should pay *me,*" Anna said sweetly. "Isn't the shoe on the other foot? Or perhaps you have some reason of your own for wanting me to stay?"

He sat for a moment tapping a thumb on his cup, considering.

"Yes," he said at last. "I also have reasons for wishing it."

"Well, well! And what would those reasons be?"

"I cannot discuss it with you," he said. The look in his eyes was an assessment, but a long way from sexual assessment. She realized abruptly that he did not trust her, or fully accept her version of events, even now. But he might be willing to make love with her if that was what it took to keep her here. Rage swept her, with a suddenness that astonished her.

"Suppose I take a stab at guessing?"

He watched her.

"Let's see, now," she began. She tilted her head and looked at him. "You're sure about that judgement, are you—that this story hasn't got legs, as you call it?"

"That a Cup Companion has a child with his mistress may offend the religious in Barakat, but for a Western audience it means nothing. You must be aware of the truth of this. As you pointed out, you are not a celebrity yourself. That gives the story only limited interest."

She nodded thoughtfully. "That's okay as far as our affair and our secret baby go, but that's all lies anyway. But there's something you're leaving out of the calculation, isn't there? I mean, that's not the only story here, not by a long way."

She saw a flicker of feeling in his eyes, instantly veiled. He fixed her with a dark, impenetrable gaze. "And what else is there?"

Anna did not stop to consider how unwise it might be to show such a man how thoroughly she understood his motives.

"You abducted a baby from an English hospital, Sheikh Gazi—and according to the papers, you're one of the trusted Cup Companions of Prince Karim. That's got legs, don't you think? You also abducted an Englishwoman. And you got us out of England and into Barakat without passports. That's got legs, too. In fact, it's got so many legs it's a centipede.

"And forgive me if I suggest that you wouldn't have done any of that just for sheer amusement. So the real reason you took such risks, Sheikh Gazi, whatever it is— that's a story that'll have legs, too."

He was silent when she finished, and her ears were suddenly filled with the thunder of her own agitated heartbeat. Too late, Anna reflected that perhaps her reasoning processes hadn't fully recovered from her accident. What on earth had made her challenge the man here on his own ground?

"How well you grasp the facts," Sheikh Gazi said softly, tossing his napkin down beside his plate. "But I advise you to consider a little longer before you try to blackmail me, Anna."

His eyes were absolutely black. His gaze stabbed her, and her heart pounded hard enough to make her sick.

"I am not trying to blackmail you!" she shouted, rejecting her own dimly realized understanding that her little summation might well have sounded like it. "Why are you constantly accusing me of the lowest possible crimes?"

"What, then?" he said, his lips a tight line in a face that suddenly seemed sculpted from stone. "Just a pleasant little gossip to pass the time of day with me?"

She gritted her teeth. "Tell me, is it your wealth and position that give you the right to trample over other people, or is it just that women in general are beneath contempt?"

"I do not hold women in contempt," he said in flat repudiation.

"I have a life," she interrupted rudely before he had finished. "Forgive me if I find it offensive to be offered a holiday on the casual assumption that my career can be put on hold in order to save you from the consequences of your own actions." She tilted her head.

"I also resent being taken for such a fool. It's not me who's going to suffer if I deny this ridiculous story, is it? It's you. I have nothing at all to fear from the truth. Now—" She held up her hands. "I have no intention of telling anyone anything, except that you are not my lover and I am not the mother of your baby. But I do intend to get out of here and back to my own life. So unless you're considering adding forcible confinement to the list of your crimes—"

"You are annoyed because I have underestimated your intelligence," he interrupted with a sudden return to reasonableness that secretly irritated her. "Fair enough, but if you can see so far, a little more thought will tell you—"

"Please don't spell out anything more for poor little me," Anna snapped, lifting a hand. "I really think I understand enough. The rest I don't want to know. You might decide at some future date that I am a danger to you if I learn any more now."

His face closed, and she saw that he could be deeply ruthless when he chose.

"You are determined to consider only your own convenience."

"Me?" She could hardly speak for outrage. With biting sarcasm, she began, "I quite understand that *you* feel your concerns should come first with everyone you meet, Sheikh Gazi—no doubt it follows from having more servants than is good for you. But forgive me if *I* consider it quite reasonable that I should put myself and my clients first."

He gazed at her for a moment. "My concern is for my sister," he said quietly. "Let me—"

She lifted her hands, pushing the palms towards him. "Well, that's admirable! But I have already told you I know nothing about your sister. She is a total stranger to me. And my life has been quite disrupted enough on her behalf, thank you! Now I'd like to get it back on the rails."

Sheikh Gazi acknowledged this with a hard, business-like little nod. "Let us hope that future generations consider such devotion to your art a worthwhile sacrifice."

"It's no sacrifice on my part, believe me!" Anna exclaimed explosively, if not quite truthfully. "Not that I would *begin* to suggest that you rate your claims too high!"

He went absolutely still with fury. For a moment they stared at each other. Anna's skin twitched wildly all over her back and breasts as emotion flared in him, and she wondered what her reaction would be if he reached for her. If he started to make love to her, it was entirely possible she'd end up agreeing to anything he asked her to do, short of murder.

As if in answer to her thoughts, Sheikh Gazi shoved back his chair and got to his feet. He shrugged out of his bathrobe, letting it fall onto the chair. Then he stood there, naked except for a neat black swimsuit in body-hugging Lycra. She could not avert her fascinated gaze.

Wind seemed to blow up out of nowhere, seducing all the flowers on the trellis overhead to give up their perfume, tousling her hair and robe, caressing her skin, so that all at once her whole body came alive.

He was gorgeous—there was just no other word. Beautifully proportioned legs, powerful thighs, neat-muscled waist curving up to a very male expanse of chest with just the right amount of curling black hair, broad shoulders that were held with the minimum of tension, strong arms.

Probably she would never get another chance at such death-defying sexual excitement as he had just offered. When she was an old woman probably she would look back on this day and call herself seventeen kinds of fool for turning him down.

Her gaze locked with his, her heart jumping, her stomach aquiver. She was acutely aware that the bed she had spent the night in was only yards away across the terrace.

He could convince her to stay. Even knowing his passion was totally calculated, a payment for services rendered, she would still burn up if he touched her. The thought of him using his sexual expertise to reduce her to willing cooperation in his plans, whatever they were, made her legs weak.

Sheikh Gazi al Hamzeh's lips parted. "Then you will not wish to avail yourself of my offer," he said, with bone-chilling politesse. "I will arrange for your return to London as soon as possible." Then he turned, stepped to the edge of that delightful pool, and dove in.

Ten

It wasn't as easy as that. Anna would of course not be allowed to re-enter Britain without a passport. Her passport was in London, however, in her flat. The keys to her flat were in her handbag, which was presumably still at the hospital. Before anything else, someone had to be nominated to go to the hospital and pick up her belongings, then go to her flat, find her passport, and send it to her.

Anna wanted to ask Lisbet to do it, but Sheikh Gazi frowned when she suggested it. "The hospital must be dealt with very diplomatically. And anyone going into your flat may be questioned by journalists," he warned.

"Lisbet's an actress. She'll know how to handle that."

"*Allah!*" he murmured in horrified tones. "You surely do not want someone to whom publicity is the breath of life being asked by the press about your private life?''

"Lisbet won't say anything. If anyone is going to be rooting around my flat in my absence, I'd rather it was Lisbet,'' she said doggedly.

"And your other friend—Cecile?''

"If Cecile was challenged by a reporter, she'd collapse and give them my entire life back to when I sucked my thumb, and be under the impression that she had handled them very well. I love her, but really, she just has no idea.''

"There must be another way,'' said Sheikh Gazi. "I will consider.''

Anna had to insist on being allowed to call her client to explain her delay. "What is the point? You will be there in a day or two,'' Sheikh Gazi argued.

"The point is I was due there yesterday,'' Anna said, thinking how different the perception of time was in the Barakat Emirates. It was true there was no one at the villa to worry, but what if Alan phoned from London and got no answer? A day or two was plenty of time to get worried.

Sheikh Gazi gave in very gracefully when she explained how Sunday meant Sunday to the English, and a delay till Tuesday or even Wednesday was significant.

"Of course, darling. Whenever,'' Alan Mitching said when she tried to explain. "You relax and enjoy yourself. The villa's not going to disappear. No one's using the place till Christmas. You can get the keys from Madame Duval anytime.'' She had the feeling that Alan was sitting there with a tabloid leaning against his breakfast teapot, avidly reading about her and Gazi.

"Will you tell Lisbet that I'll be in touch?''

"Of course.''

Having won this argument, Anna found it harder to press the other. So when Sheikh Gazi suggested that it would be best for someone from the Barakati Embassy in London to get her passport, since they could put it in the diplomatic pouch, she felt almost obliged to be as gracious as he had been in giving in.

He insisted on her being examined by a specialist, in spite of the fact that she would be back in London within a day or two and could see her own doctor. Although the man spoke German and French, he knew so little English Gazi had to translate for him.

"He says you are well, there is no lasting damage," Gazi told her, and she suddenly discovered, by the depths of her own relief, how frightened she had been, and was grateful to him for insisting.

Two days later, when she was expecting to hear that her passport had arrived in that day's diplomatic pouch, word came through that the hospital would not give up her handbag without a signed authorization.

It seemed things were going to move at a Middle Eastern speed. It was hard to find the energy to push for a faster conclusion, though, especially as the surroundings were so blissful. Her fatigue seemed to be taking this opportunity to catch up with her. Anna found she had no physical energy for anything but swimming, lying in the sun, or wandering around the beautiful house, and no mental energy at all.

She signed a permission and Sheikh Gazi sent it off by special messenger, and another day drifted past like the others.

The desert sky was black as a cat, with a thousand eyes. The wind blew, hot and maddening, around the turrets, driving her thin robe against her body, biting sand against her cheeks and into her eyes. She crept precariously along the parapet, feeling how the wind clutched at her, trying to fling her down.

He was there before her with a suddenness that made her gasp, his arms around her, dragging her against himself.

"You came," he whispered hoarsely.

The wind whipped at her, but not so harshly as his passion. Her back arched over his arm as her eyes glowed up into his. "How could I not?" she half laughed, half wept. "Am I not lost, and are not you the polestar? Am I not iron, and you the lodestone?"

Holding her with one powerful arm, he bent over her and tenderly drew the scarf from her mouth to gaze at her face in the moonlight. He drank in her beauty with a hunger that melted her, his eyes burning with desire.

"How beautiful thou art," he murmured, and his hand captured one of hers and drew it to his mouth. He pressed the fingers, then the palm, against his burning lips, water in the desert.

He kissed her throat, white in the moonlight, and she trembled with her first taste of such passion. His eyes pierced hers again. "Thou art no slave girl!" he said.

She smiled. "No. No slave girl."

"Tell me thy father's name, and I will send to him for thee. I will make thee my wife."

She shook her head. "Thou art the trusted companion of a prince," she whispered. "And truly, I am no better than a slave. Do not seek to know my father, but only know that I willingly give up all for one taste of thy love. The world holds nothing for me."

He bent his head and his mouth devoured hers with a violence of passion. The wind gusted with a sudden fury, dashing sand cruelly against them. He tore his mouth from hers.

"Your lips are nectar. Tell me thy father's name, for I will not take thee like a slave, but wed thee in all honour."

"Ah, do not ask, Beloved!" she pleaded, but when he insisted, she smiled sadly and said, "Mash'Allah! My father is King Nasr ad Daulah."

He stared at her. "But the king has only one daughter! The Princess Azade, and she—"

"True, oh Lion! Three days hence the Princess Azade is destined to become the wife of the prince to whom you are sworn in allegiance. But for one taste of your love she forsakes all."

The baby was a source of deep delight. Safiyah seemed to have cast off the trauma surrounding her birth completely. She was a happy, deep-thinking spirit who loved to lie with Anna on the terrace under a flowery, shady trellis and watch the blossoms just overhead dance in the constant, cooling breeze.

"There couldn't be a better crib toy," Anna told Sheikh Gazi. Because, whatever their differences, they were united in a deep fondness for the baby. "It's even got musical effects." The birdsong from the trees planted around the terrace and the forest beyond was nearly constant, and it was clear from Safiyah's expression that she loved to listen.

Anna was picking up a little Arabic from the nurse, in the usual women's exchange of delight and approval with a baby. *Walida jamila* was the first expression she learned. She was pretty sure it meant *pretty baby,* and she and the nurse could say it back and forth to each other, and to the baby herself, with endless delight.

And every day she felt a little more of her long-standing fatigue and unhappiness being leached out of her body and self by her surroundings.

The only fly in the ointment was Sheikh Gazi himself. His job had to be very fluid, because he worked from home, and he was almost constantly around. He sat beside the pool in his trunks, tapping away at his laptop or talking into a dictaphone or telephone, while Anna swam and sunned and played with the baby. She was constantly aware of him.

They ate together at nearly every meal. He had a powerful radio, on which he regularly listened to the news from several countries, and in different languages. They often discussed what was happening in the world, and although he was insightful and seemed very informed, he always listened to her opinions with respect.

He talked only a little about himself, though. When she asked, he told her that his job was to coordinate the publicity and public relations side of West Barakat's trade relations with the world, but spoke little more about it. Instead he talked about Barakat's history and culture.

He played music softly as he worked. Anna, who had rarely listened to Middle Eastern music, found it haunting, and in some mysterious way perfect for her surroundings. At intervals, too, could be heard from the city the wail of the muezzin, the Islamic call to prayer, and it all seemed to fit into one marvellous whole.

Sometimes it seemed as if the accident had been a doorway to another reality. A curious little space-time warp had appeared, and she had been shunted through—into some other life stream, where she joined up with a different Anna. An Anna who had made a different choice long ago, and now belonged here. Sometimes it seemed just as if Gazi had been telling the truth—as if they had been married for years.

Except for one thing.

However delicious the weather, however exotic the food his servants brought them, however sexy he looked emerging from the pool, his strong body rippling and his smoky amber skin beaded with water, however electrically she felt his presence—he never again suggested to Anna, by word or by deed, that her holiday out of time might include him as a lover.

He seemed totally immune to her physical presence. Whatever had made him kiss her with such passionate abandon on two occasions, he wasn't interested now.

She had never before met a man who had given up a pursuit of her after one little rejection, but that was what Gazi had apparently done. Or maybe it was simply that, in turning down his request to stay, she had lost her chance at the free lovemaking. In short, since she had refused his actual invitation to stay and was here only from necessity, he didn't feel obliged any longer to pretend he wanted to make love to her.

In every other way, they were practically the ideal family.

The fact that the constant delay getting her passport meant she had ended up staying after all never was mentioned between them. Anna sometimes wondered what his reaction would be if she made the suggestion that since she was, however inadvertently, acceding to his demands, he ought to live up to the original offer.

If you left out of the reckoning a teenage crush on a rock star, it was the first time in her life that she had felt such powerful romantic interest in a man who felt none in return, and it wasn't a sensation she enjoyed. Half the time she was determined not to accept even if he did change his mind, and the other half she had to restrain herself from making a clear pass.

He really was moving heaven and earth in the effort to understand her concept of time, and when she reminded him that another day was passing, he shook his head in frustration with his own stupidity and picked up the phone at once. But unfortunately, he was met with the same lack of focus at the other end. He ended up shouting in outraged impatience down the phone to a Barakati Embassy employee and hung up cursing.

"They understand nothing, these government employees!" he exploded. "To them nothing can be done without the correct documentation and by following established procedure! The person who collected your keys from the hospital put them in the safe last night, and today there is no one in the embassy to give permission for opening this safe." He glanced at her hesitantly. "I can phone Prince Karim, Anna. He is very absorbed with certain affairs of state, but...if I explain, he would call and order them to open the safe. Shall I do this?"

Anna blushed. "No, no, of course not! You can't bother the prince for that!" she exclaimed. And although he hid his relief, she could tell that it was not a request he had wanted to make.

And so another day slipped away.

Though she had told him she wouldn't be here long enough for it to be necessary, Gazi had been adamant about providing her with clothes suitable for the climate. So she had chosen a small but lovely wardrobe of mixed Middle Eastern and Western clothes from a selection sent in for her approval by a couple of city boutiques.

During the day she often wore nothing more than a bathing suit under a cotton kaftan. She never left the house, but for the moment she had no desire to do so, and it was great to be able just to slip off the kaftan any time and dive into the delicious pool.

The water was salt because the pool was, in accordance with Barakati law, Gazi told her, supplied by the ocean and not from the limited fresh-water resources of the country. So there was no smell of chlorine hovering over the garden or on her skin, and it felt like bathing in a natural pool.

She loved the sun, and although in this climate she was careful with exposure, she knew it was a source of deep healing. Her pale skin was a mark of her unhappiness and ill health, and she was delighted when it turned a soft brown.

The healthier she felt, the more physically she responded to Sheikh Gazi's constant presence, reading, tapping into the computer, talking on the phone. Sometimes she would lie on her lounger feeling the sun's hot caress and feel such a surge of desire for him she was convinced he was on the point of coming over to her, but when she glanced over he usually wasn't even looking at her. Or if he was, his face was tight with disapproval.

Every evening Anna dressed for dinner with the casual elegance her new clothes allowed. Made herself as beautiful as she could, without ever fooling herself she was competition for anyone like Sacha Delavel. She was being a fool, she knew, but she couldn't help wanting to see in his eyes, if only once, that she was attractive enough to disturb him.

Sometimes she would remember those moments when he had kissed her. She had felt such passion in his arms and his mouth, seen such burning desire in his eyes, that she had responded by going almost out of her skull with delight.

But now she had to wonder if that had been entirely
faked. If he had merely been offering her a sample of
the treats on offer. No doubt he could fake the whole
thing if necessary. But she never felt that intensity in
him now…and she found that was what she really
wanted. She wanted to know she could touch his mind,
his heart, his feelings. Not simply that he could perform
a sexual service like a gigolo, if she insisted. That was
how she stopped herself making a move.

They talked and laughed together over the delicious,
candlelit meals until she was weak with wanting him.
She was almost sure that the dark fire she sometimes
surprised in his eyes held admiration.

Sometimes she couldn't believe that things he said
could be anything other than a prelude to lovemaking.
But if so, his feeling never lasted more than a brief moment. Although she was somehow kept in a constant
fever of anticipation and wishing, he never touched her.
And if she touched him, even with a spontaneous pat on
the arm as she spoke, he would stiffen and look at her
with an unreadable look that made her lift her hand.

It didn't help her get a handle on her feelings to discover Gazi was the best listener she had ever met in her
life. He drew her out as if he was really interested in
her life and her opinions, her experiences and her
dreams. He showed particular interest in her art, wanting
to know what had drawn her to want to reproduce Middle Eastern art on the walls of England's houses.

The house itself was like the magician's cave, with
masterpieces of ancient scrollwork and sculpture in
every corner. The patterned tilework was unbelievably
artistic, the colours from a palette of magic. Anna spent
hours wandering and examining the treasures.

At her request Gazi would explain the significance of

certain symbols, read and translate the beautiful calligraphic designs, so thoroughly she felt she was in a personal tutorial with a professional expert.

"How do you know so much about it?" she asked him in amazement when he had described how certain tiles had been painted and fired, and he threw her a look.

"This is my people's culture and history and art," he said, in a voice like a cat's tongue on her skin. "It is some of the greatest artistic and architectural achievement in the history of the human race. How should I not be familiar with it? Every Barakati is familiar with such things, as familiar as an English person with Shakespeare. But in addition it is my job to know such things."

She was certainly learning more about her area of interest than she had ever learned at art college, and bit by bit she was packing in a wealth of inspiration that could probably carry her for years.

If only she didn't feel that she was also packing in future heartbreak.

"Something has to give," Anna muttered after several days of inaction.

Sheikh Gazi was on the phone trying to get through to the Barakati Embassy in London.

"Yes, today I will insist—why does no one answer?" Gazi said, exasperatedly listening to a recorded message. "It is noon in London, where is everyone? Ah, of course!" He lifted a hand. "Today is Friday, *juma,* they are all at the mosque." He put down the phone. "I will try again later."

"Friday?" she murmured, almost unable to believe that so much time had passed.

"The Friday prayer is the minimum required act of

worship in the week. It is my own fault, I should have remembered.''

He had certainly remembered earlier in the day, Anna thought absently. A bit before noon, he and the entire staff had left the house in a minivan, everyone dressed in their best. She and Safiyah had been left alone for an hour, and when the van returned only Gazi and the nurse were in it.

''Is that where you all went earlier? To the mosque?'' Anna asked.

''Yes, all of my household who wish it have the right to be driven to the mosque for *juma*. It is far to walk. Then they go home to their families. Tonight you and I will eat at the hotel.''

A little later Anna poured a subtle, spicy perfumed oil into her bath and afterwards dressed with care in a flowing, ivory silk *shalwar kamees* embroidered at breast and sleeve with deep blue thread and flat beads of lapis lazuli. Her tiny silver ear studs and silver rings were all the jewellery she had, but they at least suited the outfit. A gauzy navy stole and pair of navy leather thongs on her bare feet completed her outfit.

In the early evening she joined him at the front door, where a sports car was waiting. He drove them up the road to the Hotel Sheikh Daud for dinner in luxurious elegance on a balcony overlooking the sea. From here the view was much more open; she could see the whole stretch of the shoreline around the shallow bay, out into the water of the Gulf of Barakat.

Lights twinkled from the city, on the yachts out in the bay, and in the sprinkling of houses nestled in the forest along the shore. The sea and the sky were one deep, rich black, so that it seemed to her that the sky itself rushed onto the shore and retreated again, with that hypnotic roar and hiss.

A young woman sang haunting Barakati love songs, the food was deliciously cooked, and Gazi's eyes were on her almost constantly. Anna found herself floating away on a dream. A dream that was composed of Gazi's mouth, Gazi's eyes…

He watched her, knowing what she wanted. Her wide mouth stretching in a tremulous smile, her head tilting back to offer her slim throat, as if she knew how that posture in her excited him. His own mouth was tight with control.

"This song is so beautiful," she said dreamily, at the end of the meal, when their coffee cups were drained and the singer sang again. "Tell me what the words mean."

He unlocked his jaw. "They mean that a man is refusing to fall into a trap that a woman has set for him," he replied. "A woman he desires but does not trust. She dresses in beautiful jewels and robes, she perfumes her hair, she smiles, until he is driven mad with passion. But he cannot give in."

In a brief pause in the music, his voice rasped on her ears, and Anna pressed her lips together. "He can't?"

"He knows that she is forbidden to him."

The music resumed on a haunting, wailing note, like a woman in the act of love. She made a little face of disappointment, and he thought that she would not look so if he made love to her.

"Why?" Her eyes, inviting him, were dark as the night sky, her face beautiful as the moon.

"Because she is a cheat," Gazi said harshly.

The singer's voice joined the music again with a keening plaint. Fixed by his narrowed gaze, Anna could not turn away.

"So what happens?"

"He decides to make her admit her betrayal," Gazi said softly. "He will pretend to love her, so that she will confess."

"And he calls *her* a cheat?" she asked.

"The song is about how the man fools himself as to his own motives. He is lying to himself. It is not for the reason he gives himself that he is going to make love to her, but because she has succeeded—before he even began."

The music stopped, amid applause from the restaurant patrons.

"You are beautiful, Anna," he told her in a voice like gravel. "You tempt me, with your soft looks, your willing mouth. I lie awake at night, wishing I were fool enough to believe that I could make love to you without danger. But it is not to be, Anna. You will not succeed."

Eleven

At first, hearing the word *danger,* her heart thrilled, because she believed he meant that he was in danger of falling in love with her. But his voice and the expression in his eyes were so hard...and suddenly she understood.

She drew back into her chair, her brain sharp with suspicion. "My God, you still think—!" Suddenly it all fell into place. "I've been here a *week* now, waiting for someone to perform a simple errand that Lisbet could have done in an hour! You've been delaying deliberately! What is going on?"

"I thought this way would be easier," he said, but she knew it was a lie.

"Easier for you!" she stormed. "Easier for you to keep me here against my will. Did you call back the embassy today, when the staff returned from the mosque?"

Gazi slapped a hand to his head. "Ah! I forgot!" He

lifted his wrist and glanced at his watch. "Too late now. It is past seven o'clock in London."

"You forgot. And today's Friday, and I suppose the Barakati Embassy in London closes over the weekend?"

"All embassies in London, I believe, do so. I am sorry, Anna."

Anxiety choked her. Most of a week had gone by. He had manipulated her into doing exactly what he wanted, and fool that she was, she had spent the time dreaming.

"Is there a British Embassy in Barakat al Barakat?" she demanded.

"But of course!" he assured her blandly. "The British have always been on excellent diplomatic terms with Barakat, even though they never conquered us. The embassy is in Queen Halimah Square."

"If my passport isn't here by Monday, I want to go to the embassy and ask them to issue me a temporary travel document so I can go home," Anna told him sternly.

"Very wise," he said, nodding. "Yes, an excellent solution."

"I want to stay here in the hotel tonight," she said.

He shrugged. "As you wish. Will you go now and check in?"

Anna half got to her feet. "Yes, I—" She stopped, one hand on the back of her chair, and a nearby waiter came to her aid. She stood up because she had to, but stayed looking down at Gazi al Hamzeh. "I don't have a credit card or anything."

"Perhaps if you explain your situation, they will give you credit. Foreigners need passports to register in hotels here, but I am sure you can convince them to wait until you can apply to your embassy on Monday."

Before she could come to any decision he was on his

feet beside her, and the maître d' was hurrying over to
bow his distinguished guest out.

Anna had always believed she had her fair share of
courage. But she could not summon enough to make a
stand now. The thought of trying to make herself understood, in a foreign language, a foreign country, while
making a charge of abduction against a leading citizen—
a Cup Companion of the ruling prince! And Gazi, as if
knowing exactly what she was trying to get the courage
for, remained deep in friendly conversation with the
man, all the way to the door.

And only she knew, and he knew, that the dark expression in his eyes as he smiled at her was the look of
a watchdog guarding a criminal.

They did not speak on the drive back to his house.
Anna went straight to her own room, without a word.

She spent a restless night. Only the fact that, thanks
to the tabloids, half the world knew where she was kept
her from complete panic. She tossed and turned and
looked back over the week and realized how easy a mark
she had been. Time had slipped by, with sun and food
and good talk…. He had her exactly where he wanted
her. He had accused her of trying to tempt him. But it
was Gazi who had been using constant temptation to
keep her brain muddled.

How easily manipulated she had been by his interest
in her! He had let her talk and talk. *It's a known brain-
washing technique!* she reminded herself disgustedly.
*It's what cults do with their marks—give them massive
doses of attention. Love-bombing.* And even knowing
that, how easily she had fallen for it.

And his Arab incompetence, his lack of appreciation
of Western ideas of time—she began to blush for how
easily she had fallen for the stereotype. Of course he had

been faking all that. She had never met a man with a more incisive, better-informed mind. He spoke at least three languages! What could have possessed her to fall into the trap of believing that he could be so inefficient and ineffectual, could lack a basic understanding of Western culture?

She saw now that he had begun this act only after she refused his invitation. He had deliberately become a caricature Arab. Anna snorted. It must have taken an extremely efficient organization to effect the abduction of her and the baby. That was a plan he had certainly conceived on his feet, and it had been flawlessly executed. From the time he found her in the hospital to the time the plane took off scarcely two hours had elapsed.

Clearly he had a crack team. Yet somehow he had fooled her into believing he couldn't organize getting her *handbag* from the very hospital he had abducted her and the baby from!

And still she had no idea why. What did he want from her? Why did he continue to think she was engaged in some kind of dishonesty? And above all, what was his reason for wanting to keep her here?

"Fly with me!"

"Willingly would I fly with thee, Beloved. But where can we fly, that is not ruled by your father or my prince?"

"India," she breathed.

He smiled at her, knowing she knew nothing save the name. "India is far, very far."

"For you I would suffer any hardship!" she cried.

"Beloved, if they catch us before we reach India, they will not let us live."

She smiled. "Choose fleet steeds, then, my Lion!"

He stood gazing out over the far horizon. "And if I say, stay here and live thy life as thy destiny demands—"

"I will fling myself from this parapet tomorrow night rather than wed him."

He turned and caught her to his chest, and stared into her eyes, his love a torment, because he was destined never to enjoy her beauty. But he could not tell her so. He put his lips on hers and tasted their deaths.

"Why then, we will fly to India," he said.

The dreams were profoundly disturbing, though she never quite remembered them. She would awaken suffocating with love and anguish, her heartbeat pounding through her system, yearning for him so desperately she could almost feel her dream lover beside her, as if his arms had only now let her go.

Her dream lover was Gazi al Hamzeh. And the dream seemed another reality, one that she half watched, half lived…always yearned for.

"I have had a phone call," Gazi said at breakfast. "Your passport has been picked up from your apartment. Today, if you wish, you can fly back to London. I will arrange for someone to meet you at the Immigration desk at Stansted airport with your passport."

She looked at him, one eyebrow raised. "If I wish? Of course I wish."

"You are determined to return?" he said softly. They were at a table on the balcony, looking out over the sun-kissed courtyard in the cool of the morning.

"Has not my home seemed to you like a good place to recuperate from your accident and restore yourself after your sorrows?" he asked, gesturing out to the paradise below them.

"In case you haven't noticed, I've had a week of that," she said. All her hackles were rising as she scented danger. Did he mean to prevent her again?

Gazi took another sip of the perfectly brewed coffee, set the cup in the saucer, and with an almost invisible flicker of his eyes, dismissed the attentive serving man, who nodded and slipped away.

"Anna, I would like to tell you…to explain something to you."

"With a view to changing my mind about leaving?"

He hesitated. "Perhaps. No—not necessarily. But in hopes that what you learn may change your mind about other things that you might plan to say or do."

"Such as talk to the media."

"And other things."

Anna was curious, but she hesitated. "Suppose you tell me what you want to tell me and it turns out you don't change my mind about anything at all?"

Gazi shrugged. "Then of course you will do whatever suits you."

She wondered if that was the truth. He had already kept her here a week against her will. What new ploy might he come up with? But, she reflected, at least she would know more about why. That had to be an advantage.

"Fire away," she said, with a casualness she was far from feeling.

"Nadia, my sister, the mother of Safiyah, is missing. This you know. We are very worried about her."

"Who is 'we'?"

"I and my family. If you permit, I will tell you Nadia's story from the beginning," he said, and waited for her nod before beginning. "Three years ago, my father announced that he had chosen a husband for my sister.

None of us knew until that moment that he was even considering such a step. It was an even greater surprise when we learned that he had chosen a man named Yusuf Abd ad Darogh. This was not a man my sister had any admiration for. She begged my father to go no further in it.''

"Oh," she murmured.

"I tried to reason with my father." Anna picked up the echo of frustration and sorrow in his voice and tried to stop her heart softening towards him. "But my father was of the old school. In spite of all that we said, in spite of her deep unhappiness, Nadia was married to Yusuf.''

He gazed down at his coffee cup, which his hand absently clasped in a strong, loose embrace. Following the direction of his abstracted gaze, Anna had to close her own eyes. Something in the incipient power of the hold made her want to feel it close around her arm, her body....

"Yusuf's job then took him to the West," he was saying as she surfaced. "He works for a large Barakati company, and he and Nadia moved to London. I am in London frequently, and of course I visited or spoke to Nadia on each visit. One of my brothers also.

"For the first year or so, things were apparently not intolerable. Then time went by, and Nadia did not become pregnant. She was becoming more and more anxious about it. We suspected that Yusuf was blaming her for it.''

Anna was listening now with her mouth soft, her eyes fixed on him, her sympathies entirely with Nadia. She heard an anxiety in his tone that proved that he loved his sister, and she couldn't help wanting to help him.

"Then at last Nadia became pregnant. But it made

Yusuf no happier. It became difficult for us to get any reading on how Nadia was. More and more there was some excuse why visits were not convenient just at the moment, or she could not come to the phone. When we did visit we somehow were never allowed time with Nadia alone. And we gradually came to understand that she was only allowed to speak to any member of her family on the phone when Yusuf was in the room with her."

Anna shivered. "She must have felt totally helpless," she said.

"I am sure you are right, but if so, she was never able to express it."

He paused and cleared his throat. "My father died. When they returned to Barakat for the funeral, Nadia was wearing *hejab*. Here in Barakat even a simple headscarf is not worn outside of the mosque except by the religious old women. Nadia was wearing full black robe and scarf, no lock of hair showing, which is extreme by Barakati standards, and nothing she herself would have wished. It is certain that she was made to do it by Yusuf.

"Shortly after this, when they returned to England, Nadia became ill with the pregnancy. Too ill to speak to us when we phoned. Or there were other excuses."

Gazi paused, and an expression of self-reproach tightened his mouth for a moment. "There was a great deal to see to about my father's estate. I was here in West Barakat virtually full-time for weeks. One day my brother and I realized that neither of us had been allowed to speak to Nadia for almost two months."

Anna was listening too hard to be capable of making a sound.

"We knew it was fruitless to try to phone again. Yusuf would only put us off. My brother and I flew in together on Friday last week and arrived unannounced at their apartment. We found—we found Yusuf running around the streets like a wounded animal, screaming for Nadia and saying that she had disappeared.

"He said that she had gone into labour shortly before our arrival, and he had gone out to the garage—it is in a mews behind the house—for the car. When he drew up at the front door, it was open and Nadia was gone. That is what he said."

Anna bit her lip. "Was it—do you think he was lying?" she whispered.

"There is no way to be sure," Gazi replied. "It is possible he had warning that we were on our way and staged a show for our benefit. What reason could Nadia have for running away at such a time? She would want to go to the hospital to have her baby safely."

"You don't think she was desperate and it was maybe—her only chance to escape?" Anna offered quietly.

At this, Gazi bent forward, his hands clasped between his knees. "Perhaps it is so, Anna, perhaps it is so. But now do you see how important your involvement is? You are the only lead we have. The question we must ask is, how did you come to be in a taxi with Nadia's baby? The answer to this may tell us much."

She gazed at him, feeling how strong the pull was. He had half hypnotized her, made her want to declare she was on his side. It was like pulling a tooth to stand up and walk away, out of his potent orbit. But she needed to think clearly, and she couldn't sitting so close to him. She had to do it.

Moving a little distance from the table towards an archway covered with greenery, she turned and said, "Well, thank you for telling me that. But it's *still* not the whole story, is it?"

"Why do you think so?" asked Sheikh Gazi. His gaze was just slightly wary, but she noted the change, and it proved her right.

She lifted her hands. "Because it's got more holes than a sponge! Excuse me, but there you are out combing the streets for your pregnant sister, and you just happen to search the casualty ward of the Royal Embankment Hospital, is that what I hear?"

He was watching her with steady disapproval. "There was an item on the radio that made me think I would find Nadia and her baby there. Instead I found you."

"On the radio?" she demanded disbelievingly.

"Yes, Anna," he said, and she was glad to make him understand how it felt to have his word doubted. "A silly item, meant to be amusing—'mother, baby *and* cab driver all in hospital and doing well.'"

"Ah! Okay, you found me. And you found a baby you were instantly convinced was Nadia's. And what do you do? Do you call the police and tell them your suspicions? Do you claim the baby and take it home to Papa? No, strangely enough, you *kidnap* me and this infant you are convinced is your niece, and you immediately cart us off to Barakat! Now, that needs a little more explaining than the current version of your story offers. Because even a man with your influence and connections, it seems to me, and no doubt they reach to the very top, isn't going to risk breaking the laws of two countries without a very substantial reason.

"Unless, of course, your contempt for women runs so deep you forgot that Safiyah and I had any human rights at all. You're quick to condemn your brother-in-law for keeping your sister a prisoner, but have you noticed that you are at this moment doing exactly the same thing to me?"

She saw that he was angered by that. "I do not keep you prisoner!" he exploded.

"What do you call it?" Anna cried. She suddenly doubted whether the best course after all was challenging him. Her safest alternative probably had been to pretend to go along with whatever he suggested and then, when his guard was down, make good her escape. But she was too late.

"Why don't you tell me the truth, Sheikh Gazi?"

"I have told you the truth, so far as it goes." His eyes were hard. "Recollect that you have still offered no coherent account of how you came to be in possession of my sister's baby."

"Recollect that you have offered no convincing proof that the baby *is* your sister's!"

"There can be no question of it. My brother remains in London, pursuing enquiries. If any woman had reported her child missing, he would have discovered it."

"How do you know that some past girlfriend of your own hasn't given birth and abandoned the baby? Maybe I found her!"

"You are being ridiculous," he said, his face hard. "The baby was in a satchel that had obviously been prepared for a hospital maternity visit. In that satchel, which has now been picked up from the Royal Embankment Hospital, were items recognizably my sister's."

"All right, let's assume Safiyah is your sister's baby, then. What do you suspect *me* of? Your little team has had the keys to my apartment for the best part of a week by now," she told Gazi coldly. "Don't you feel that if there was anything at all to connect me with your sister they'd have found it?"

Gazi took a breath, trying for calm. "Nevertheless, it

is very difficult to imagine any scenario in which you are completely uninvolved. You must see that. What am I to guess? That the hospital mistakenly mixed up two casualties, leaving Nadia with no baby? That Safiyah was abandoned at the precise place where you had your accident?''

''As far as I'm concerned, either of those is more likely than that I went out of my tiny mind and kidnapped a baby, all during the one half hour of my life that I don't happen to have any memory of.''

''All right.'' Gazi's full, usually generous mouth was drawn tight. ''I will tell you more. Nadia's husband, Yusuf, may suspect that the baby is not his. In Yusuf's mind his suspicion would be enough. In such a case, it is not easy to guess what he intended to do, but it is almost certain that he would not allow Nadia to keep the child and raise it as his own.''

She felt a little chill in the warm breeze, and shuddered.

''It was in the hopes of preventing Yusuf discovering that we had found Safiyah that we rushed her out of the country in the way we did. This would have succeeded, but for your actions. The press has created huge potential risk by running photos of me arriving in Barakat al Barakat with a baby. Yusuf of course now suspects that the child is Nadia's.''

His voice was hard with suspicion. Anna frowned and took a step back towards the table where he sat. ''You thought I deliberately showed the baby to the cameras to let Yusuf know you had her?''

He was sitting in a casual but not a relaxed posture, one elbow on the chair arm, his hand supporting his cheek. ''There seemed very little other excuse for such wanton disregard of the baby's safety.''

Anna gasped indignantly. "I did it to protect the baby from *you*!" she informed him hotly, flinging herself back into her chair. "I didn't know the paparazzi were even there. You had convinced me the baby was ours, but you sure hadn't convinced me you had any affection for me! I thought you were going to try to snatch her! You told me nothing but lies! How was I supposed to guess what was going on?"

He raised an eyebrow, but did not comment, merely said, "Fortunately the press blunted the damage by printing that the baby is ours, and even hinted that Safiyah is several weeks old."

She laughed in irritation. How stupid did he think she was? "Fortunately? You told them that, didn't you? You've already admitted that your job is in press relations, so you've got all the necessary contacts."

He waited for her to finish and then went on. "It was of crucial importance in deflecting Yusuf's suspicions. Yusuf will believe what he sees in print if we reinforce it. Or at least, don't contradict it. That is why I hoped that you would agree to remain unavailable for a while. Not to deny the press stories."

"And when I refused, you forced my compliance through trickery."

"There are lives at stake," Sheikh Gazi said.

"Why the hell didn't you tell me there were lives at stake, then, instead of trying to bribe me with sun and fun and money and sex?"

"Sex?" he asked, his eyebrow up. "Do I try to bribe you with sex, or has that been the other way?"

Suddenly danger of a different sort whispered on the breeze. Anna snapped, "What reason could you possibly have for suspecting that I would want to bribe you with sex? What would I hope to achieve?"

"That is something only you know!" he bit out, his own anger flaring suddenly, making Anna jump. "I find you with my sister's baby, you can give no reasonable explanation, you deliberately show her to reporters after I have successfully smuggled her out of England—" He broke off. "Did you give me any reason to trust you? You threatened me with exposure for having abducted Safiyah! What—"

"I *never* threatened you! I told you I had no intention of exposing you! I said I would do nothing more than deny—"

They were by this time almost shouting.

"To go back to England and to deny that Safiyah is our child is to send Yusuf a notarized declaration that she is Nadia's daughter," Gazi said coldly. "Now, if you are involved with Yusuf in any way, I ask you to tell me what your involvement is. And if you are not involved, I ask you to go on with the charade that has been created until we find the truth.

"For the love of God, Anna!" he cried as she hesitated. "My sister may be at this moment her husband's prisoner. Or hiding in some alley, snatching food from rubbish tins. Have you a heart, Anna, to appreciate what she may be suffering, and to help her?"

Twelve

She met him at the stables, in her disguise as a page, while the sounds of revelry still rose on the air from the palace. He dared use no light, nor kiss her, but only turned silently to lead her through dark, tortuous passages to the great city wall.

She climbed the rope ladder ahead of him, bravely, without a murmur of fear, and he thought what a wife she would have made him, if things had been otherwise.

On the other side, still without speech, he led her to the outcrop within which he had tethered two horses. With one quick embrace only, one whispered word of courage, he tossed her into the saddle.

They rode out towards the dawn.

They arrived in London at midmorning, and it was only when she felt the wheels touch down and saw the familiar landmarks that Anna started breathing again.

She had agreed to return to London and make her arrangements as quietly as possible, to head straight to France and hide out at the villa of her clients without speaking to the media.

At Immigration, they were met as promised, by an escort of three bodyguards, one of whom handed over her passport. Sheikh Gazi, she noticed, was travelling on a Barakati diplomatic passport, and they were allowed to enter Great Britain with barely a nod. No one even questioned why or how she had left the country without a passport.

Then they came through the doors into the terminal and were faced with a crowd of excited paparazzi.

Anna stopped as if she had walked into a wall. She could hear the noise of clicking cameras, but the shouted questions might as well have come from the Tower of Babel for all she could understand. She swayed.

"How on *earth* did they find out we were arriving?" she cried, astonished at the sheer numbers.

"Anna, Anna!" "Can you look this way?" "Smile for the folks, Anna!" "Are you happy? How's the baby, Anna?" "Did the baby come with you?" "What's your baby's name, Anna?"

Then a strong arm was around her, and Sheikh Gazi's hand was gripping her arm above the elbow, urging her forward. He leaned into her ear and murmured, "Walk quickly but on no account run. Let me handle them."

This was a command she was only too relieved to obey.

His voice was low and for her ear alone, and in spite of everything it raised yearning in her heart, and heat in her blood. "Look at me."

She looked nervously over her shoulder into his face, and met a glance of such lazy, sexy approval her stomach rolled over. Anna stumbled, and his strong embrace steadied her. She smiled involuntarily, her whole self stretching and basking in his unexpected admiration like a cat in a sunbeam.

The photographers cried out their satisfaction. "Kiss her, Gazi!" someone cried, and Anna's heart thumped. But the sheikh only laughed lightly and shook his head.

They moved quickly after that, his bodyguards doing no more than create a little breathing space as the group of journalists ran beside them through the terminal to the exit, calling questions.

"How do you feel about the baby, Sheikh Gazi?"

"What do you think, Arthur?" he called, as if it should be obvious.

"Did you get Prince Karim's approval?"

"He has never disapproved, to my knowledge."

"When's the wedding? Have you set the date?"

"No," the sheikh's deep voice responded above her ear.

"Are you going to?"

Sheikh Gazi threw the last questioner a smile. "Julia, you'll be the first to know."

Questions and answers were following each other in such a rapid-fire way it was a moment before Anna took it all in. She blinked and turned to him. "What are you—?" she began, but he put a warning grip on her arm.

"Let me handle it, Anna!" he said again.

It terrified her. He was doing it again. Forcing her into compliance through circumstance. She had not agreed to look the press in the eye and pretend it was true, and now she was frightened. Had he ever told her the truth? Was she a pawn in something she didn't know about? Suddenly she doubted the truth of everything he had

said. He had a much deeper reason for this constant manipulation of her. He must.

Anna swallowed, coughed and forced herself to turn
to the nearest man with a notebook.

"I am not Sheikh Gazi's mistress," she said.

"Great!" he said, scribbling. "Can I say fiancée?"

"No! Don't say I'm his fiancée! And the baby is
not—"

"The baby is not with us!" Gazi cried over her,
drowning her out. "The doctor thought it better."

His arm went tight around her and he was swooping
her through the main exit to where a limousine waited
by the curb, the rear door already open.

Anna threw one wild look along the half-deserted
road. Wherever she ran now, she would be chased by
all these journalists, and they would certainly catch up
with her. What would she say then, what could she do?
She could not simply deny that she was his mistress and
that the baby was hers and then expect to disappear.
They would hound her unmercifully for the whole story.
And if she told it…Gazi had powerful friends.

Feeling like every kind of coward, Anna got into the
limousine. Gazi quickly followed. One of the bodyguards got into the back with them, the other two in front
with the driver, and a second later they were pulling
away from the happy mob of journalists.

She turned to Sheikh Gazi al Hamzeh. "How did they
know we were arriving?" she demanded furiously.

"In a moment," he said, then turned to the other man.
"Anything?" he asked.

The man shook his head. He looked younger than the
sheikh, and she thought she could detect a facial resemblance between them. "Still not a trace," he said. "She
has evaporated into air, Gazi. Yusuf insists he knows

nothing, and unless we're willing to show our hand with him, there's no saying if that's the truth or not.''

He had none of the air of a man talking to his employer. As if in confirmation of this judgement, he turned suddenly to Anna. ''Hi, Anna,'' he said, with an engaging smile. ''I'm Jafar. People here call me Jaf.''

''Hello,'' she said slowly. She glanced back and forth between the two men.

''Jafar is my brother,'' Sheikh Gazi said quietly.

''It's great of you to play along, Anna,'' said Jaf. ''We really appreciate it.''

Anna didn't return his smile. ''Thank your brother,'' she said. ''I had nothing to say about it.''

She seemed to herself not to start breathing again until the familiar sights of Chelsea met her eyes and she could believe that Gazi was going to do what he said and take her home.

There were a few journalists on the street in front of the ramshackle Victorian house where she had an apartment, and as the three went up the walk there were more shouted questions.

Anna left it to Gazi to talk to them, already rooting for her keys in the little shoulder bag Jaf had given back to her at the airport. But no key chain met her searching fingers. Anna clicked her tongue and lifted the bag to eye level, just as Gazi produced her keys and unlocked the door.

So Jaf had passed over her keys to Gazi instead of herself.

They all moved inside the small front hall and closed the outer door on the paparazzi. Then she held out her hand and said sharply, ''My keys, please.''

She waited, staring at him, until Gazi put her keys in her hand. A moment later she stepped through her own

door, followed by Jaf and Sheikh Gazi, and led the way
upstairs.

The phone was ringing. Anna moved into the main
room as the answering machine picked up. She stood
looking around her for a moment, trying to orient herself
in her own life.

The room was long, with windows at each end. The
south-facing half, overlooking the street, was her sitting
room, with a fireplace, sofa and chairs; the north, whose
windows overlooked an overgrown courtyard with a tree,
was her studio, with trestle tables, trolleys, rolls of paper,
a couple of painted screens that she was working on for
a client. Two broad expanses of wall down both sides
of the room were covered with sketches, paintings, photos, colour swatches and other bits and pieces of her
working life.

Underneath them, painted on the plaster, was a series
of arches not unlike those she had seen for real in Gazi's
house. Anna blinked and wondered if it was merely her
own mural that had given her the idea she was at home
there.

It just did not feel like only a week since she had
dressed for her meal with Cecile and Lisbet. She felt
strange, removed from her old life, as if she hadn't been
here for months.

"Hello, Anna. This is Gabriel DaSouza from the
Sun...."

She mentally shut out the voice coming from the an-
swerphone, and moved towards the sofa. On the table in
front of it was spread the week's mail, including a few
scribbled notes from the press.

Anna frowned, wondering who had placed them there,
and just then heard a step in the kitchen. She whirled,
her heart jumping into her throat.

"Hi!" said Lisbet. "I made the coffee while I was waiting. Jaf figured we'd all need it."

Lisbet kicked off her shoes and under Jaf's interested gaze slid her long, black-stockinged legs behind Anna on the sofa as she accepted the cup of coffee Anna had poured for her.

"Frankly, it's a mystery to me, too," she told Anna. "You ask what happened—absolutely nothing. Someone pulled up in a cab and got out, you got in. The cab drove off. It took Ceil and me a couple of minutes to flag another one. Ceil dropped me at home. That was all I knew until someone phoned me at sparrow's peep Sunday morning to say was that Anna Lamb in this morning's *Sun?* I said it couldn't possibly be you. And then Alan said you'd called him...."

Jaf leaned forward, taking his own cup from Anna's hand. "Someone got out of the cab, you say. Did you notice who?"

Lisbet pursed her lips and shook her head. "It was on the other side of the street and I wasn't really paying attention."

"Try to think back. You may have seen something. One person, a couple?"

Lisbet obligingly closed her eyes and tried to visualize the scene. "There was a tree just there—someone came past it, but whether that was whoever got out of the cab or not...one person, I think. Dressed in black, maybe, with street lighting it's—wait! There was someone in black a couple of minutes later, too. I wonder if it was the same person? By the bridge."

Lisbet opened her eyes. "I noticed her because she seemed to be wearing one of those black things that cover a woman from head to foot and I thought it was strange to see a Muslim woman by herself there at night.''

"Battersea Bridge?" Jaf prompted.

Lisbet nodded. "Yes, the Riverfront isn't far from there, and we were sort of strolling in that direction after Anna left, looking for a cab. This woman crossed the road ahead of us and went onto the bridge. But I don't know that she was the person who got out of the cab Anna caught. There was something about her that drew my eye, I can't really say what it was.''

Anna, meanwhile, put her hands up to her face. A woman in black. She smelled the scent of the river at night, autumn leaves…. She dropped her hands again and found Sheikh Gazi's eyes on her.

"What have you remembered?" he asked softly.

She shook her head sadly. "Nothing.''

They sat drinking coffee without speaking for several minutes. Lisbet was lost in thought. She surfaced and said, "Unless something completely weird and incredibly unlikely happened after you got into that cab, Anna, the accident must have happened within a couple of minutes. He turned the corner, drove straight along Oakley to the King's Road and smashed into the bus. Five minutes max.''

"That's what I think.''

"So either someone walked up to the accident scene and slipped the baby into the crashed cab knowing that an ambulance would be coming, which, let's face it, is pretty far-fetched, or…or you got into a cab with a baby already in it.''

"Yes.'' Anna nodded.

"Or else some completely off-the-wall thing happened in the hospital.''

As her friend put into words just what she herself had

been trying to say to Sheikh Gazi, Anna felt what a huge relief it was to have her integrity reaffirmed after his suspicions. She glanced at him to see how he was taking this, but his face gave nothing away.

Lisbet went on, "So putting myself in Nadia's place…I'm running away from an abusive husband, but I'm already in labour, right? So I—what? Give birth in the back of a cab? But then the driver would have radioed an emergency call to get an ambulance to the scene, wouldn't he? Was there such a call?"

"No," said Jaf, sitting forward. Lisbet was certainly convincing while she was getting into a part.

"Or he would get her straight to a hospital. What he *wouldn't* do is pull up on the Embankment and drop his passenger, with or without her baby. So, let's assume for the moment that Nadia was the person who got out of the cab that you got into, Anna, and that she left the baby in it. Doesn't it follow that she had already given birth, and *then* flagged the cab to take her somewhere?"

"Yes…" Anna said slowly, the excitement of discovery building in her. This was starting to feel right.

Jaf said, "The baby was absolutely newborn, wrapped in a woman's bathrobe and laid inside a satchel. She had not been washed. The hospital guessed that the driver had stopped to assist in the birth and then had hastily wrapped the baby and resumed the journey to the hospital, when the accident occurred. He is still not able to be questioned."

Anna glanced at Gazi. "She might have given birth in the apartment, and when he went for the car, she just ran out into the streets."

Lisbet pursed her lips.

"You and your brother were both out of town, right?

Who in London could Nadia go to, with her baby? Who could she trust not to call her husband?''

Jaf shook his head. ''She had no childhood friends in London, only those she had met since moving here three years ago. And we think her social life was very restricted.''

''So maybe something like a women's shelter would have been her only option. Was she on her way to one? Have you checked whether there are any shelters in the neighbourhood of Battersea Bridge?''

Jaf smiled. ''We have not before thought about concentrating on this area, of course. I will see what can be done, but women's shelters are very secretive.''

''The big question is, what changed Nadia's mind? Why did she leave the baby in the cab? If she *was* going to a shelter, surely...'' Lisbet faded off thoughtfully.

Sheikh Gazi intervened at last. ''That is the flaw in an otherwise excellent argument. If she went to a women's shelter, why not take the baby with her? And in addition, whether she went to such a place, or to friends we know nothing about, why has she not called us?''

Lisbet hesitated. ''I hate to—uh.'' She glanced at Anna for guidance. Anna, catching her meaning, shrugged.

Lisbet turned to Gazi. ''I have one advantage over you here. I *know* that Anna isn't involved in the way you suspect. I know that she doesn't know any guy named Yusuf, and that she wouldn't be involved in anything like baby-snatching if she did,'' she said firmly, and Anna suddenly felt like crying. ''I also know that if she says she was confused after the accident and has amnesia about a critical moment, that's the exact truth. So.''

She heaved a breath. No one else spoke. ''I don't want

to distress you, and please forgive me if this suggestion is way off beam, but is it possible that…I mean, unhappy people have been known to…do you think Nadia went to the bridge because jumping seemed the only way out?''

Thirteen

"**I**'ve got to go,'' Lisbet said, looking at her watch a few minutes later. "We've got a night shoot up on Hampstead Heath tonight and I'm due in Makeup in an hour.'' She turned to Anna. "Do you want to come and hang out for a while?''

The question was put casually, but Anna knew that it was her friend's way of extricating her from a difficult situation. If she went with Lisbet, Sheikh Gazi and his brother would have no option but to leave.

But she found herself shaking her head. "I've got to get to France, Lisbet. I'm only half packed and I have to organize my ticket.''

Lisbet lifted an eyebrow as if she understood more than Anna was confessing. "Well, phone me on my mobile later. I'll probably be hanging around doing nothing most of the night.''

"All right.''

Lisbet slipped into her shoes and a smart little jacket, put sunglasses on her nose.

"Would you allow me to take you where you have to go?" Jaf offered, and Lisbet's mouth was pulled in an involuntary, slow smile.

"Sure," she said easily.

"They will photograph us," Jaf warned, gesturing towards the windows and the photographers still waiting in the street below. "Do you mind?"

Lisbet laughed. "I'm an actress, Jaf. Publicity is everything."

A moment later Gazi and Anna watched from the windows as Lisbet and Jaf braved the journalists and slipped into the back of the limo. As the limo pulled away she turned to look at him, and all at once the silence weighed very heavily in the room.

"Well," Anna said. "Sorry we couldn't be more help."

Sheikh Gazi took her hand, but not in a handshake, and stared into her eyes. "You can be of more help," he said, in a rough, urgent voice. She felt a surge of energy from him travel up her arm to her throat and chest.

"I really—" Anna coughed to clear her throat. "I really can't, you know, unless I remember something. But I do think Lisbet's right. The baby had to be in the cab when I got into it."

"That is not what I mean, Anna."

Her heart began a wild dance in her breast. She stared at him, licked her lip unconsciously and, taking her hand from his, turned away to hide the heat she felt burning up in her cheeks.

He was mesmerizing, he really was. He had the most extraordinary ability to turn himself off and on. A few

minutes ago, listening to Lisbet, he had gone to low
voltage, Anna thought wildly, effacing himself in some
mysterious way to watch and listen. Now he was high-
powered again.

"I'm almost afraid to ask," she joked, nervous of her
own deep response.

He looked at her with a frown and turned her towards
him, his eyes searching her face till she felt exposed and
vulnerable, was trembling. She had never felt so emotionally fragile just at a man's look. Almost shaking with
nerves, she lifted her hands up and placed them against
his chest. She felt his body react to the jolt of the connection, and his eyes darkened suddenly, like a cat's.

And then his arms were around her, and he was staring down into her upturned face. "Anna," he murmured,
his lips inches from her own. She felt him tremble and
with fainting pleasure recognized in him a mixed desire
to cherish her and yet crush her against himself.

Then he closed his eyes, and she felt him tense with
a huge effort of will. In the next moment she was released. He dropped his arms and stepped back.

"We must talk," he said.

A little laugh of bitter disappointment escaped her. So
she was still the woman who was a cheat, whose temptation he must resist.

"Must we?"

"Anna, what your friend said has changed the picture.
You must see this."

"Yes, and how does it affect me?" she asked,
blowing air out hard and turning away as she tried to
get a grip on the passionate ache her arms felt to hold
him.

"It is no longer enough, Anna, that you agree simply
to disappear to France and say nothing to the press."

She turned to look over her shoulder at him with deep hostility. "Why not?" she demanded.

"They are out there, Anna. They know you now—they will chase you for the story."

"And whose fault is that? Are you suggesting it was *not* your brother who notified everyone and his dog of our arrival time?"

"No, you are right. It was Jaf who did this. I am sorry. We thought only to take one last advantage of your presence, to get one more story that might convince Yusuf. But now things are more desperate."

"But Lisbet didn't tell you anything you didn't already know—or guess."

"Yes," he contradicted. "May we sit down again?"

It was a command, and her reaction was to turn towards a chair. A sudden draft made her feel how the temperature was dropping outside—or perhaps it was inside her own heart—and Anna stooped and flicked on the gas fire in the fireplace before flinging herself into an armchair on one side of it.

The gas ignited with a whoosh. Sheikh Gazi took the chair opposite her, on the other side of the fireplace. Then for a moment he turned his gaze to blink thoughtfully at the flames leaping up around the fake coal.

She watched him. The bone structure of his face was emphasized by the firelight flickering over it in the gathering dusk, revealing sensitivity at temple and mouth. In this light he looked like an old portrait of a saint, sensuous and ascetic together. She suddenly saw, behind the playboy handsomeness, that he was a man used to the rigours of self-discipline. And he was exerting it now.

Sheikh Gazi stared into the fire. He began speaking slowly. "Ramiz Bahrami has been my close friend most of my life. His family is from one of the ancient tribes in the mountains of Noor, but his father moved to the capital to serve the old king. Ramiz and I went to school in the palace and later to university together. He is a close, personal friend of Prince Karim. Highly trusted.''

Anna blinked, her lips parting in surprise, and he flicked his eyes from the fire to her face. She saw open pain in them, and her heart hurt for him.

''My sister Nadia and Ramiz fell in love. She could not have chosen a better man. It was when Ramiz approached my father to ask for permission to marry Nadia that we were all rocked by the information that my father had already chosen Yusuf for her.

''I told you I argued with my father. I tell you now I never pleaded so strongly with him about anything before or since. But he would not give in. Ramiz was a university-educated, moderate Muslim with political ambitions, and Yusuf was mosque-educated, ignorant of the world, devout. It was one thing for my father to let his sons be educated at university. It was another thing entirely to give his daughter to such a man.''

He was silent for a moment, staring into the flames.

''How did Ramiz react to his refusal?'' she prompted softly.

''They both took it hard. Very hard. Ramiz appealed to the prince to intervene, but although Prince Karim did make a request, he knew very well that a father cannot be ordered even by a prince in such a matter.

''Ramiz wanted to run away with her. I would have assisted them, but Nadia was raised with a strong sense of religious duty. She felt it right to obey my father, even in this. And she knew that such a thing in any case would ruin Ramiz's political career.''

He breathed. ''She said no. I was sorry for it, and yet I knew she was right.''

If he was trying to get her onside with this recital, he was succeeding. Anna's heart was deeply touched.

"Ramiz left the country before the wedding—Prince Karim kindly sent him on some mission abroad. He did not return until Yusuf and Nadia had come here to London."

"Has Ramiz married?" Anna asked softly.

He looked at her, shaking his head once. "No. He devoted himself to work. Karim trusts him absolutely. For the past year he has been engaged on something that took him to various countries. For a while he was in Canada.

"It is only since Nadia's disappearance that I have learned from the prince that Ramiz spent part of the past year here in London."

She gasped. "Do you think they met?"

"Now that the pieces come together a little, I begin to believe that they met. I think that this was the root of Yusuf's jealousy, of his suspicion that Nadia's baby was not his own."

"Did Yusuf know that Ramiz and Nadia were in love?"

"It is possible that my father confided something to Yusuf. I cannot say it is not so. My father might have hoped in this way to prevent trouble by alerting Yusuf to the danger."

She could say nothing. What a wholesale betrayal of a daughter.

Gazi took a breath. "Anna, the story is not over. Ramiz disappeared several months ago, and Prince Karim cannot be certain where he was at the time of his disappearance. But it is very possible that he was in England."

"Are you...are you saying Yusuf killed him?"

Again pain was mirrored on his face. "We can't be certain. Ramiz may even be alive. But it seems more of a possibility now that Ramiz's disappearance, rather than being connected with his secret work for Prince Karim, was because of his personal life."

"Do you think that Yusuf is right? Is Safiyah Ramiz's baby and not his own?"

"How can I be certain unless we have tests done? It will be some time before this can be arranged. And time is something we do not have.

"Anna, if your friend is right, and it was Nadia she saw that night...if Nadia is dead and Ramiz also, then it is possible that Safiyah is the only heir either of them will ever have.

"As things stand, as the legal father under English law, Yusuf has the right to custody of Safiyah. I cannot give up custody of the only child my sister and my friend will ever have to such a man as this, and with such a motive to hate her.

"Anna, I ask you, as a woman who knows the value of one child's life, to go on with the pretence we have started. Let the world think we are lovers. Pretend Safiyah is our child. Stay with me until we have discovered the fate of Nadia and Ramiz."

He wasted no time acting on her capitulation. By the time she had hastily thrown a few things into a bag, completed her half-made arrangements for leaving the flat unoccupied for a few weeks, and written a note for the downstairs tenant, another limousine was waiting to sweep them off to London's most prestigious hotel.

There they went to a huge suite on the top floor, with wonderful views overlooking Hyde Park. "We must give the press as much fodder as we can," he told her.

"The more Yusuf reads about us in the papers, the more he will believe."

Before anything else, Gazi insisted that Anna should be examined by another medical expert on head injury. The surgeon, who seemed to be a personal friend, however, was as cheerful as his counterpart in Barakat had been.

"It's not uncommon for accident victims to experience amnesia such as yours," he reassured Anna. "The period of time immediately surrounding the trauma is lost. In fact, it's unlikely you'll ever regain those minutes. But there is absolutely nothing to worry about."

After that she went to the private Health Suite, where she had a steam bath and a massage, and emerged feeling totally pampered. Then she went downstairs to see a top hairdresser, and then a makeup artist.

She returned to the suite to find that several outfits had been sent up from a boutique downstairs for her choice.

"Choose something for tonight," Gazi ordered her. "We will have dinner in a club. Tomorrow we will go shopping in the stores."

She chose a simply cut, utterly luxurious full-length coat and spaghetti-strap dress in black velvet. She had never worn anything so expensive in her life. The outfit clung to her, emphasizing her fashionable thinness.

She emerged from her bedroom, feeling she had never looked so stylish in her life, to find Gazi at a desk in the sitting room of the suite. He looked up, and for an instant his eyes burned her. Then he dropped his eyes and snapped open one of several cases on the desk.

"Diamonds, perhaps," he said with forced casualness, offering it to her.

Anna gasped when she looked inside. "Oh, goodness, where did these come from?"

He raised an eyebrow. "From the jeweller downstairs." He lifted from its silky bed a fabulous necklace that seemed to burn with cold fire, and when he slipped it around her neck she was almost surprised that it didn't scorch her skin. "Do you like diamonds, Anna?"

She laughed, delighted at the utter madness of her life, and turned to the mirror above the fireplace. "I've never really been on speaking terms with diamonds," she said. "But I'm quite happy to wear a necklace like this tonight, I promise you!"

Later, sitting at the table beside her on an intimately small, semicircular bench seat in a place so famous Anna had to pinch herself to believe it, Gazi observed, "Diamonds are too cold for you. You should wear coloured stones. Sapphires, to match your eyes."

Anna only laughed, shaking her head, and fingered one of the earrings.

"You must wear a variety of jewels over the next day or so," he said. "Then, it will please me if you will choose the set you like best to keep. As a gift of gratitude."

Anna almost choked on the tiny garlic mushroom she was eating as a starter. "Choose a *set* of jewels?" she exclaimed, putting a hand to her throat, and feeling the diamonds glowing there. "You're joking! These must be worth a fortune!"

"What you are doing for Nadia is worth much more to me," Gazi said.

Anna gazed down at the beautiful diamonds encircling her wrist, shaking her head. "Thank you. Not that I have anything against jewellery, Sheikh Gazi, but there's something else that I'd much rather have.'' She looked up. ''It would be a real favour, if you—''

His face darkened with an unreadable expression. His gaze raked her with an intensity that held more fire than the diamonds, leaving her gasping for air. Anna breathed and thought, *God, he thinks I'm going to ask him to make love to me—* But before the thought was completed, the sheikh was in control of himself again.

''Whatever you ask for, if I can,'' he said levelly.

She could hardly speak, for the thought of what that unguarded moment had told her was choking her. Desire pulled at her, drew her lips into a trembling smile. She could not control that, for what else could his look mean, but that he wanted her, and for some reason known to himself, was exercising rigid control?

In the moment when that control had slipped, she had felt a powerful passion emanating from him. Her whole body seemed to be made of butterflies now, all fluttering, so that nothing but thought held her being together. She was so fragile she would dissolve in the smallest gust of wind.

She knew that he could not remain in control if she challenged him. The thought was like champagne to her system, making her drunk.

She swallowed and tried to speak.

''Tell me,'' he commanded, and Anna struggled to bring her own thoughts back in line.

''I just—it just occurred to me that you could maybe mention to people that I'm a mural artist, specializing in Middle Eastern themes. It would be such fabulous publicity for me. And if as a result I got even one commission from—'' she lifted a hand and gestured around the room, where more than one table had recognizable faces

"—from someone like this, well, I'd be muralist to the stars, wouldn't I?"

He stared at her, his eyes narrowed. "And you would rather have this than precious stones?"

Anna smiled, biting her lip. "It would be a lot more useful over the long term."

"You are a very unusual woman."

Jealousy clawed her, and she didn't think before she spoke. "But then I suppose the favours I'm providing are a little different than what you're used to, too."

His eyes went black as he got it, and his hand found hers on the table between them and crushed it as he stared into her eyes. All the breath left her body in one grunting moan at the suddenness of the change in him. She thought, *I've done it, he's lost control,* and the thought made her blood wild.

"It will not be a favour, Anna, from me or from you, when it happens," he growled between his teeth, and kissed her hand with a mouth drawn tight with passionate control. "It is a necessity between us. You know it."

She felt passion like burning heat in his touch, saw it in his eyes, felt it rush through her body so powerfully she was dimly grateful she was not standing. Gazi was trembling as his hand released hers and came up to stroke her temple, her cheek. She shivered.

"Is it not so? Do you not feel it so?"

She couldn't have said a word to save her life, she was so swamped with feeling. She tried to swallow, but her throat was choked.

"I have seen it in your eyes, Anna! In every move you make!" he insisted. "Do you deny it?"

She opened her mouth and dropped her head back, trying to catch her breath. Electric sensuality roared through her, setting every part of her alight.

"I have wanted you until I was mad," he whispered hoarsely. "Your perfume, your mouth, your body stretched out in the sun...what it cost me, hour after hour, day after day, to see you there, to feel how you wanted to tempt me—*ya Allah!* how I wanted you!"

"Gazi!" she whispered helplessly.

"And do you challenge me now with talk of favours? Favour?" His voice grated over her charged nerves, blinding her with sensation, making her faint. "Shall I ask you for this as a favour, and offer you jewels in return? How much will you ask, I wonder? A diamond for each kiss, Anna? Another for every thrust of my tongue into your sweet mouth, to make us both mad with wanting more? And what, to touch your breasts? A bracelet of sapphires?"

His voice dropped to a tiger's hungry growl. She could feel his breath against her neck. "To open your legs for me, Anna, what for this favour? A necklace, a tiara? I give it to you, yes! If it were necessary I would bury you in jewels, make love to you on a bed of diamonds and rubies and then give them all to you."

His eyes burned her, heat licking through her body, melting everything into wild need.

"But it will not be necessary, Anna—will it? Do you think I do not know that to make you open your legs I need only ask with my tongue for entry? If I press my kiss on you there, Anna, who does whom the favour? Tell me that you too do not want this, if you can. Tell me the thought of my tongue on your body is not part of your dreams as it is of mine."

"Stop," she moaned helplessly. "My God, Gazi, stop, I'm—"

"Think of opening your legs to my kiss, Anna," he commanded, watching how desire burned her and made her tremble, devouring her need. "Think of my tongue, my mouth, think how the heat will stir you, make you need what only I can give you. How you will cry out, and beg for more."

"Gazi," she pleaded. "Gazi, I can't take it."

"Yes," he said, deliberately misunderstanding her. "Yes, you can take more than this. You must. Do you think I can stop there? No, once we start, Anna—"

He lifted her hand to his mouth again, and bit the fleshy part of her palm between strong white teeth. A thousand nerves leapt into wildest reaction, and she could scarcely stifle the moan that rose to her throat.

"What comes next, Anna? Who will beg whom for the favour of my body inside you, hmm? Will we not beg each other for it? Say it!" he commanded.

She wondered dimly how she would survive. She opened her eyes and mouth at him, struggling for control.

"Tell me!" he commanded again.

She licked her dry lips, opened her mouth for air. "Tell you what?"

"Tell me whether you will ask me for the favour, Anna. Tell me that you will want it, too. Or will it be a favour you grant me when I ask?"

Feeling coursed up and down her body, through every cell.

She dropped her head. "You know I want you," she said, scarcely getting the words out.

It was as if she struck him with all her strength. She saw his back straighten with a jolt, his head turn to one side. His eyes never left hers, and she saw blackness like the centre of a storm, and realized that he had, at last, been driven beyond his strength.

Fourteen

It was at that moment that their lobsters arrived. She saw Gazi flick an unbelieving glance at the waiter, and at the plate, saw his hand clench. Then his eyes moved from the deliciously steaming lobster slowly up to her face, and he smiled a smile that sent little rivulets of sensation all over her.

They were silent as the pepper grinder made its ritual pass over both plates and then Gazi picked up a claw of the lobster between his strong fingers. His hands clenched till the knuckles showed white, and she quivered where she sat, knowing it was a sign not of exertion, but control. The shell broke open to reveal the tender white meat.

His hand not quite steady, he dipped the triangular wedge of flesh in butter, lifted it and held it out invitingly to her mouth. Anna tried to speak, failed, licked her lips and then submitted, leaning forward a little to take the meat between her teeth and pull it delicately from the shell.

He watched her chew and lick the butter from her mouth, with a smile that took her breath away. She dropped her eyes to her own plate, picked up the cracker and broke a piece of shell, then did as he had done, dipping the tender juicy flesh into butter, and holding it for him to eat.

When his teeth closed firmly on the meat, biting it, drawing it out, and then eating it with sudden, uncontrolled hunger, a shaft of purely sexual sensation went through her. Anna grunted, and his eyelids flickered.

The meal that followed was torment, the torment of overcharged senses. Anna had never experienced a sensuality to equal it in all her life. They fed themselves and each other without plan, with their bare hands, with forks, biting, chewing, licking, and fainting with delight at each touch of lips and tongue on buttery flesh.

And all the time he talked to her, in a low, intimate voice that was another charge on her drunken senses. "You lay in the sun, Anna, the sweat breaking out on your skin, on your thighs, till I could think of nothing but my tongue licking it off, till I could taste the salt of you actually in my mouth…and you knew it and I knew you knew it."

"No," she whispered.

"How I wanted to punish you for tempting me. I dreamed of how I would do this, how I would make you weep with desire and wanting. How my hands and mouth would touch you, caress you, stroke you…my hands on your damp skin, stroking your feet, your thighs, your stomach, your breasts. Sometimes, when you lay on your back, it was like death, the wanting to walk over to you, to put my hand on the fabric of your suit and draw it aside and kiss you there.

"I told myself my tongue would torment you till you wept for the thrust of my body, and then I would refuse, so that you should know what torment was mine.

"But I knew I was a fool. If once I had touched you, I would have lost all. If I made you beg, at the first pleading I would have to thrust into you. I could not have resisted then."

"Gazi," was all she could whisper.

"Yes, I dreamed of you saying my name in this way," he said roughly, as if the sound of her voice was too much, and held another delicate morsel up to her lips. "And you will say it again for me, in every way that I dreamed."

He looked down at her body, at the bare, soft brown shoulders, the slender curved arms, the soft folds of the fine velvet that covered her breasts. Her nipples pressed against the delicate velvet cloth, announcing her sexual arousal.

She was constantly half fainting. Her blood ran between head and body with a wild rushing that drowned her. She saw him looking down at her body, saw his eyes darken.

He offered her another buttery bite. Looking into his stormy, hungry eyes, she thought of how she would kiss his flesh, too, and gently took what he offered onto her tongue, half smiling at him in sensuous promise.

The breath hissed between his teeth. "You drive me to the edge," he said in a voice like gravel.

When the meal was over, Anna could scarcely stand. She staggered, her knees turned to butter, and was sure she must look drunk, if anyone were watching them, but she didn't want to find out. Gazi took the coat from the attendant and held it for her, and she could feel his arms like iron with the effort it took not to pull her into his embrace as she slipped her arms inside the sleeves.

Neither of them even noticed the photographers' cameras as they went, hand in hand, his grip so possessive it hurt her, out to the waiting car.

His control lasted until the limousine door shut them in. With a steady hand he pressed a switch, and a blind hummed up to cover the glass between the passenger compartment and the driver's. Another switch plunged them into darkness. Music was already softly playing. Outside the black-tinted windows, the city lights began to slide past.

He reached for her, passion tearing at them both, and with a cry she was in his arms. He drew her across his lap, her head in one possessive hand, his other arm wrapping her waist under the velvet coat, and lifted her up to his mouth for the wildest, hungriest kiss either of them had ever experienced. They were pierced with passionate sweetness, and moaned their pent-up need against each other's lips.

Never had a kiss sent so much pleasure through her body, so that she trembled and clung, shivering with desire. Never had his mouth been so hungry for a woman, so that no matter how he drank, he could not get enough of her. Her arms wrapped his head, her fingers threaded the dark curls, while her mouth opened to his wild demands.

The car stopped, a door slammed, and at last, heaving with breath, they broke apart. She lay looking up at him, seeing nothing but the glint of light on his curling hair; he stared blindly down at her. Like two animals, scenting each other in the darkness.

"We are at the hotel," he murmured.

Her hand was clenched in his hair and Anna had to command her fingers to let him go. She felt the hard, uncomfortable pressure from his groin against her side and smiled as he helped her to sit up.

"All right?" he asked, and she heard the click as he unlocked the door. The chauffeur opened it, and a moment later they were inside the hotel and stepping into the luxurious, golden-lighted elevator that carried them upwards.

In the darkened sitting room, two lamps cast soft pools of light, and a fire had been lit in the grate. They moved towards it without speaking. Beside the fireplace a small table held a decanter and glasses.

"Will you have a brandy?" Gazi asked as he helped her out of her velvet coat. The silky lining brushing her skin was almost more than she could bear. She nodded mutely as he tossed the coat onto a sofa, and he turned to the table.

He lifted the stopper out of the decanter and set it down with a small sound that seemed to resonate around them. The slight gurgling of the liquid, even, was another branch laid on the erotic fire.

He handed her the goblet, the brandy a glowing, rich, warm amber in the bottom. Picking up his own, he swirled, drank, and set the glass down again. Then he bent and hungrily kissed her.

The taste of brandy hit all her senses as he kissed it into her mouth, onto her tongue. Anna felt shivers of sensation from her brain to her toes, and with her free hand clutched at his jacket front, her head going back to allow him the fullest access to her mouth.

His hands enclosed her, one arm around her waist, one hard on her naked shoulder. He lifted his mouth from her mouth, and moved hungrily down the line of her throat. The taste of brandy on her tongue smoked through her system, and hot on its trail little flames of sensation licked their way.

His hand found the little velvet buttons at her back, and one by one began to undo them. Her eyes closed dreamily, the better to follow the progress of his determined fingers down her spine, from between her shoulder blades, down and down along her spine to her waist, while her skin became ever more sensitive.

The buttons stopped below her waist, leaving the whole long stretch of her back naked and accessible to his teasing, tasting hands, and he stroked and caressed the bare skin while his mouth sought hers again.

The room was warm. All her shivers arose in his touch, a curious heated chill running crazily all over and through her. She buried her hand in the thick curls on his head and obediently bent backwards as he pressed her body tight against him.

Her glass was slipping from her grasp, and as he straightened he took it from her and set it down. Then he stood close, looking down at her. The straps of her dress had loosened and were slipping off her shoulders, and she instinctively bent her elbows up, placing her hands against her throat.

"Let it fall," Gazi commanded softly, and his voice, too, was all erotic sensation, compelling her obedience. She dropped her arms to her sides, and the velvet whispered slowly, slowly down over her breasts, leaving them naked to the touch of the fireglow.

He closed his eyes, opened them again, and that, too, created sensation in her. The dress rested precariously on her hips for a moment, clung there, and then, as if reluctantly, slithered down the gentle curve and fell with a little swoop to her feet.

She stood revealed in tiny black briefs, smoky lace-top stockings, delicate high-heel mules, and the diamond circlets at throat and wrist.

His hands reached out to slide with possessive heat down her back and encircle her rump, and he drew her against him, gazing into her eyes with a hotter, brighter flame than the fire provided.

"You will drive me out of my mind," he growled, and as her head fell helplessly back he pressed his lips against the pulse at the base of her throat. Her hands wrapped his neck, slid down his back onto the silky fabric of his jacket.

"Take this off," she murmured, as her hands moved to his chest and slipped inside and against his shirt, pushing the jacket down his arms. He shrugged out of it and let it fall, and now she flirtatiously pulled at his neat black bow tie, untied it, and with a hungry, teasing smile, slowly pulled it away.

He smiled, his eyes dark, and let her work on the tiny buttons, one by one, of his shirt. His chest was darkly warm in the firelight, and as she pulled the shirt down his arms, she laid a line of kisses in the neat curling mat of hair, up and across his shoulder to his throat.

"You have not taken off my cuff links," Gazi murmured protestingly, as his mouth smothered hers in a kiss so hungry she moaned.

Anna smiled. "You're at my mercy, then," she whispered, drawing the shirt further down his arms to pinion him.

He smiled a smile, and lifted his arms, the muscles bulging for a moment of exertion, and then she heard the sound of tearing fabric and the distant clink of but-

tons hitting somewhere, and his arms were free, each
wrist carrying a tattered half shirt. He stopped a moment
to tear himself free, tossing the remnants of the shirt
wildly away. Then his arms wrapped her tight, dragging
her against him with a ruthlessness that told her she had
released a demon in him, and swung her up to carry her
to his bedroom.

"A little further, Beloved, before we rest."

*"Ah, how weary I am with riding! How far to India
now, my Lion?"*

*He looked over his shoulder at the cloud in the dis-
tance. "Not far, my princess. Courage."*

*But her eyes followed his, and now she, too, saw the
signs of pursuit. "Riders!" she cried. "Oh, Lion, is it
my father?"*

*"A caravan," he lied. "On its way, like us, to India.
We shall join them."*

*She spurred her mount to a gallop again, and bit her
cheek not to cry out against the pain and weariness.
They rode in silence, as those behind grew steadily
closer.*

"Will they catch us, Lion?" she asked.

He did not answer.

Anna awoke from the dream just before dawn, still in
his arms. Rain drove against the windows and she lay
listening to the music of it.

Never in her life had she been held with such passion
as she had felt in Gazi's hands, never had she experienced such a wild storm of pleasure and need as had
swept her in his embrace.

When he entered her, it was all fresh, all new, for the
joy she experienced had touched a part of her that no

one had ever touched in her. Everything that had gone before was like a sepia photograph in comparison. She had clung to him, accepting the thrust of his body from the depths of her self, weeping as pleasure suffused her.

She loved him. She looked into his face now, the faint glow of dawn showing her the mark on his eye, and a passion of tenderness overwhelmed her. Her heart melted in its own burning, and was reborn stronger, surer, understanding things that until yesterday she had only dimly glimpsed.

Of course he did not love her. He was attracted, but for a man like him sexual passion was more a part of his being than her effect on him. She had no illusions about ordinary Anna Lamb's ability to touch his heart.

It would break her heart when her time with him was over. Maybe it would have been better for her if she had resisted the temptation of his lovemaking…but Anna had the feeling that, however much this affair cost her in the end, when she was an old woman she would look back on her moments with Sheikh Gazi as something she was glad to have experienced.

She felt chilly suddenly, and instinctively slipped closer to him. Still asleep, he reached for her, and drew her in against his warm, naked body as if that was where she belonged.

The Sunday papers were delivered to the suite, and as they sat over their breakfast at a table set cozily in front of a bright fire, Gazi and Anna glanced through them.

The story of their arrival in London was not extensively reported, though it had got a few mentions in gossip columns. Only one paper ran a picture on the front page. It was a shot of her looking up at him, and she thought the look between them should set the paper on fire.

Gazi glanced from the paper to her with a look that made her heart jump with sadness, though she couldn't have said why. Perhaps because her pictured face was that of a woman deep in love, and that troubled him.

He shook his head over the favourite story, a rehashed royal scandal. "We must do better than this," he said matter-of-factly, tossing the last tabloid aside and picking up his coffee. "Yusuf cannot be counted on to read gossip columns."

Anna gazed at him. "Do better, how?"

"First things first," Gazi said, with a smile that stopped her heart. "I must take you shopping."

Anna had only ever dreamed of the kind of shopping trip that followed. He seemed to want to buy her everything he saw. She protested several times that he was buying too much, but he simply ignored her.

"Never has so much been purchased by so few in so short a time," she joked, as he signalled his approval to yet another outfit, one only suitable for a yacht cruise. At last he said, in a bored voice, "Anna, you must have clothes if we are going to carry this off."

"But where will I ever wear these?"

"On my yacht," he said with surprise.

"But, Gazi—" she began again, and he made an impatient sound.

"Anna," he told her in a low voice. "I ask you to remember that you are the pampered darling of a rich Arab, and the mother of his only child. Please, Anna! Cannot you find it in you to be capricious, difficult to please, even a little greedy? You should be saying, 'Can't I have both, darling?' not 'Gazi, you are spending too much on me!' You are doing me a great favour, much more than you know, and it is only right that I should reward you according to my means. Do you think a few thousands spent on clothes means anything to me?''

Then she gave herself up to it—total, guilt-free shopping.

''Can I buy one for Lisbet?'' she asked, when he encouraged her to buy several fashionable pashminas in a variety of colours. Gazi shrugged his approval. ''Buy her a dozen, Anna,'' he said.

His cellphone rang several times as they shopped, and he had brief discussions with the callers. When they had finished their shopping at one famous store, Anna was surprised to hear Gazi say that they would take everything with them.

The store produced several uniformed footmen to carry their packages. Gazi chose a medium-sized shopping bag and handed it to Anna. ''Carry this, Anna,'' he said, and took two small boxes under his own arm.

Followed by the footmen, whose arms were full, he led the way to the exit. Outside they were met by two or three photographers, who snapped their cameras as the little procession, the image of conspicuous consumerism or remnant of a vanished era, depending on your point of view, walked along the pavement to the limousine waiting a few yards away.

When they got into the car, she grinned at Gazi. ''You're really good at this!'' she said.

''It is a part of my job to be good at it. In any case, it is not difficult to manipulate something like the media,'' he said. ''Greed is the biggest weakness anyone has, whether an institution or an individual.''

She eyed him. ''Do you think it's right to manipulate people?''

"Anna, if I said to the editors of those papers, 'In the hope of saving my sister's life I need you to run a certain story,' do you think they would agree?"

She thought. "I don't know. Wouldn't they?"

"It is possible. But it is also possible that one of them at least would consider the fact that I am afraid for my sister's life at her own husband's hands a much better story. I do not wish to see a headline tomorrow reading *Save My Sister, Pleads Arab Playboy.*"

She was silenced.

They returned to the hotel, where they had a few hours to prepare for a black-tie function in the evening. Anna had the full treatment again, massage, manicure and pedicure, and professional makeup job.

By the time she was ready for the party she was feeling utterly pampered, and she knew she had never looked better in her life. Her hairstyle wasn't violently different from her old one, but it was a thousand times better cut. Little locks of hair tumbled this way and that over her scalp and down the back of her neck in charming confusion, with half a dozen sapphire-and-diamond trinkets nestling artistically among them, which seemed to reveal a dark sensitivity in her sapphire eyes. Her individual looks and fine bone structure had been dramatized with subtle shading and black eyeliner, and her wide, expressive mouth was coloured dark maroon.

She wore an ankle-length coat dress with a stand-up shirt collar, bodice snugly fitted to the waist, and slightly flaring skirt that was open at the front to well above the knee. It was made of soft-flowing midnight-blue and creamy tan silk brocade that matched both her skin and the deep blue of her eyes. It gave the impression that she was naked under a covering of lace. For warmth she carried one of her new cashmere pashminas, in matching midnight-blue.

She was all blue, black and tan. With clear nail varnish on her short artist's nails, and stockings that matched the navy of the dress, the only flash of real colour was her wine-dark lips. Anna looked dramatic and sensational and, staring at herself in the mirror, she thought that, although she would never be a beauty, perhaps tonight it was just a little less unbelievable that she might be the consort of a man like Sheikh Gazi al Hamzeh.

He was looking extremely rich and handsome himself, in a black dinner jacket with diamond cuff links and diamond button studs nestling among the intricate pleats of an impeccable white silk shirt.

He lifted his head from the contemplation of the fire as she entered the room, and his eyes found her in the huge slanted mirror just above the mantel. His glance darkened in a way that sent blood rushing to her brain, and for a moment neither moved.

Formal wear seemed to emphasize the patch around his eye. He really was a swashbuckler tonight. Anna shivered with a frisson of pure sexual excitement.

"Hi," she said, lifting a hand to shoulder height and waggling her fingers at him, a crazy grin splitting her face.

He turned. "Hi," he returned, smiling with one corner of his mouth, his eyes still intent. "You are very lovely tonight, Anna."

"Amazing what money can do, isn't it?" she quipped, to hide from both of them what admiration in his voice could do to her heart.

"Money can do many things, Anna, but it cannot invent beauty like yours in a woman."

His tone was not consciously caressing, but there was a timbre to his voice that always drew a reaction from her, and coupled with a comment like this, it made her mouth soften tremulously. She couldn't think of anything to say.

"Come and see if you like these," he commanded softly, and opened another jeweller's box to reveal a breathtaking spangle of diamonds and sapphires to match those in her hair. She chose a large square-cut sapphire ring and diamond teardrop earrings, and waved her hands airily.

"I could get used to this!" she joked.

He was watching her with a smile that turned her insides to mush. "Good," he said.

Fifteen

It was a party at a very exclusive private address, with a long line of limos waiting in the sweep drive to disgorge celebrities, and several photographers snapping continually. Anna realized just how exclusive it was, though, only as they moved through the rooms, sparkling with glowing chandeliers, brilliant conversation and an array of jewels on nearly every inch of bare skin. She recognized numerous faces—from film, from television, and even one or two from *Parliamentary Question Time*.

"Gazi, how fabulous of you to come!" a glamorous redhead exclaimed exuberantly. She was covered head to toe with glittering gold and had an accent Anna couldn't quite place. "And this is Anna! Hellooo!" she crooned, grabbing Anna's hands and kissing her on both cheeks.

"Hello," Anna returned, unable to place her.

"Gazi says that you paint wonderful murals of Moorish palaces that he can't tell from the real thing,'' the woman said, her eyes searching the crowd for a waiter and summoning him over to offer a tray of champagne. ''I hope you will paint something for me. You must come to see me, Anna, and I will show you my small dining room and you will tell me if you can do something Greek with it.''

As Anna expressed her enthusiastic willingness, a photographer ambled over. ''Can I get one of all three of you?'' he called, and the redhead struck a pose, smiling a practised smile. Anna tried to do the same, wishing she had asked Lisbet for a few pointers.

''Of course, we want the publicity,'' the hostess murmured to Anna. ''The editor has given us a two-page photo spread in the weekend magazine.''

''Thank you, Princess,'' the photographer said, moving away again.

''My God, that was, that was Princess...Princess...'' Anna muttered in a low voice, groping for the name of one of the uncrowned heads of Europe, as they moved on a few minutes later. Gazi smiled down at her.

''She is the patroness of the charity,'' he said.

''Charity?'' Anna repeated, and then threw a glance around the glittering assembly. ''Is this a *charity* function?''

Her sense of humour was sparked, and she flicked a look up into his face, trying to suppress a smile, an effort that only added to the charm of her expression. As she met the appreciative glow in his own eyes she bit her lip and her head went back, and a crack of delighted laughter burst from her throat, causing a few heads near them to turn.

''Sheikh al Hamzeh, my dear chap! What a very great pleasure!'' a white-haired man cried in the crusty tones of the Establishment, and a moment later they had been absorbed into the group and Anna was talking to a famous television host.

The evening that followed was one she thought she would always remember. Gazi was blandly informing everyone who asked—and everyone did—that they had met when he bought a painted screen from her to put in his Barakat home.

So Anna was asked for her business card by several people who said they were in the middle of redecorating or about to redecorate and would love to have her do something, and also by the television host, who seemed to have a more personal interest in mind. That boosted her sexual confidence amazingly, because Gazi gave the man a look that would have quick-frozen strawberries in June.

Then she reminded herself that he was here to manipulate people into believing he cared. She must be careful not to fall for the act herself.

But the whole evening was made delicious by his constant attendance, the possessive brush of his hand over her back, the look of sometimes lazy, sometimes urgent desire in his eyes. She knew it was only partly true, but then it was only partly false. And it was headier than the champagne.

They stayed till after midnight. Then, as they left the party, she discovered just how much Sheikh Gazi al Hamzeh was a master of media manipulation.

"The first editions have now gone to bed," he explained quietly as they moved to the door. "They now would like something new for the later editions. Will you play along with me, Anna?"

"All right," she said nervously. "What are we going to do?"

"We are going to have a spat and make up," he murmured.

The temperature had dropped while they were inside, and when they emerged on the pavement the waiting photographers were huddled under the awning, looking miserable and stamping their feet against the cold. Most of them only eyed the couple. They had pictures of them going in, and there was nothing to be gained by another identical shot of them coming out.

Gazi paused to tip the doorman. "Don't be stupid!" he murmured over his shoulder to her in low-voiced masculine irritation, as if continuing an argument begun inside.

The lights showed a driving wet snow coming down at an angle, and although the doorman had clearly been busy with the broom on the red carpet that covered the pavement under the awning, snow was settling again.

"Why is it stupid?" Anna muttered furiously. Her blood was singing with mingled nerves and excitement. He looked so handsome and powerful in his navy cashmere coat, his white silk scarf over the black bow tie, mock anger flashing in his eyes. "It's not stupid!" She turned away from him towards the curb.

"Anna!" he commanded, striding after her, and reaching a hand to clasp her arm. Anna whirled and snatched her arm away.

"I don't appreciate being called stupid!"

The gusting wind suddenly cooperated. It whipped the split skirt of her dress out behind her, revealing all the length of her slim legs, thighs bare above her lace-top stay-ups, and incidentally freezing her where she stood. The photographers, who had slowly been waking up, now snapped to attention.

As she whirled, Anna accidentally put her foot straight

onto a little mound of cold slush. She slipped, half gasped, half screamed, and instinctively clutched at Gazi. A second later she felt her feet go entirely out from under her as electric warmth embraced her. Gazi was scooping her up in his arms.

"Excellent, Anna!" he murmured in her ear, and she felt the heat of him rush through her chilled blood.

He had his arm under her bare knees. As he lifted her, the skirt fell away, revealing her legs right up to the hip. Her shoes dangled from her toes. The photographers were scrambling now, calling encouragement and approval, as Anna, freezing, futilely groped for the panels of her skirt.

"Don't cover your legs! You will soon be warm," Gazi whispered in her ear in a firm command that was suddenly charged with an erotic nuance, and set her heart racing. "Look at me, Anna, and relent!"

Her breath catching in her throat, she lifted one arm to his shoulder and glanced uncertainly into his face. He paused for a few moments, smiling down at her with sexy promise, as if his imagination, too, had suddenly moved into high gear. Cameras clicked and flashed all around them, and then Gazi stepped to the limousine that was just purring up the drive, and after a moment she was inside.

Instantly she was locked in his arms, being ruthlessly kissed. His hand slid up her stockinged thigh with a touch like cold fire, because his flesh was chilled but still heated her blood.

Haunting music played, the windows were all covered, and recessed light glowed softly, enclosing them in their own little world. Anna was half sprawled on the luxurious leather under him, her legs angled, her dress up around her hips, revealing everything as Gazi lifted his mouth, straightened and gazed at her. But as she made a move to sit, he pushed her back with one hand, while the other unerringly found its way to the lace at the top of her stockings, traced its way over the bare skin above, and then, with ruthless precision, to a spot behind the lace of her bikini panties.

Anna gasped. She found she could make no move, no protest, to prevent what he intended. Sensation shot through her, as much from the look in his eyes as from his touch, as he carefully stroked and stroked the potent little cluster of hungry nerves.

They responded obediently to his dictates, as if instantly recognizing their master. A breathless little grunt escaped her, and her hips moved hungrily. She saw the corner of his mouth go up, and one strong arm was on her thigh then, lifting her leg over his head as he sat, and resting it on his other side—spreading her wide for his eyes, his hands…his mouth.

She understood his intent as he bent forward. His hand stopped its delicate stroking and instead his fingers slipped under the lace of her briefs and pulled it to one side, and then, just as he had promised, his mouth was against her, his tongue hot, teasing, hungry.

Her hands clenched in his hair. She could do nothing, say nothing. She was completely at his mercy, melted into submission by the shafts of pure, keening pleasure that his mouth created in her.

"Gazi!" she cried, hitting the peak with a suddenness that made her heart thump crazily. Honeyed sweetness poured through her as her back arched and her muscles clenched.

"Another," he urged her in soft command, and she felt how expertly his fingers toyed with her and his tongue rasped her to pleasure again. She felt completely open, completely helpless, as if the pleasure he gave her put her in his power. "Again," he said, and like an animal going through a hoop, her body had to obey.

After an endless time in a world of pleasure, she found him relenting. He restored her clothing, and drew her body up so that she sat in his embrace, her back against his chest, his face in her hair.

"What's happening?" she begged, hardly knowing where she was.

"We are almost at the airport," he murmured, and she could still shiver as his voice whispered against her ear.

"Oh!" she exclaimed. She had completely forgotten that tonight he had said they would fly back to West Barakat. She lifted a bare foot. "My shoe's gone," she said stupidly.

He felt behind him and eventually found it, and Anna marvelled that she had the muscle coordination necessary to slip it onto her foot. Then the limousine rolled to a stop and it was only moments before they were back on the private jet again, very like the first time, except that this time, Gazi was looking at her with a promise in his eyes that tonight she would not spend the hours in that bed alone.

They weren't long in the air when the hostess approached them with a small tray of Turkish delight and a low-voiced query. Gazi turned to Anna. "Would you like a nightcap or a hot drink, Anna? Or do you prefer to go straight to bed?"

She did not like being offered a choice. She wanted him to want to take her to bed as much as she wanted to go. So perversely, she said, "Oh, let's have some coffee."

She bit into a deliciously soft sugary cube and then stared absently at the shiny green inside of the half still between her fingers.

"Of course," he said, and she couldn't read his expression. "How much sugar?"

"Sweet, please."

He spoke to the hostess, who smiled, nodded, and disappeared into the galley.

Meanwhile Anna unbuckled her seat belt and settled more comfortably in the big plush armchair. With a little whisper of silk, her dress slithered away to reveal all the length of one leg, encased in the dark cobweb of expensive stocking he had bought for her.

Gazi's gaze was instinctively drawn, then moved up to her face, with a look that abruptly reminded her of what had taken place in the limousine. The heat of the memory invaded her body, burned her cheeks.

As the hostess set a little cup of thick sweet liquid in front of her, Gazi reached for a powdery cube of Turkish delight and put it in his mouth with a lazy hand. Anna felt electricity in the air, felt her eyes forced up to his face. He tilted his head and met her gaze, and Anna's heart kicked as if it wanted to kill her.

"I am glad you do not want to sleep," he said.

She yearned towards him, body and soul; she was almost weeping with love and desire. She said, half meaning it, "I don't intend to waste a moment of my allotted time, Gazi."

His eyes darkened with dramatic suddenness, and only then did she realize with what an iron hold he was controlling himself. He reached to imprison her hand, took the little cup from her fingers with his other, and set it down.

"Then let us not waste a moment," he told her

through his teeth, and a moment later he had pulled her to her feet and was leading her to the stateroom.

The bed with its snowy linens was inviting, the room luxuriously intimate, with the ever-present hum of the engines seeming to cut them off from the world.

She melted into passionate hunger as he unbuttoned her dress and drew it off her shoulders, and kissed him with little hungry bites as she in turn unbuttoned his shirt, his trousers, and stripped everything except his underwear off. Then at last, with desperate hungry kissing, they fell onto the bed and their hands began a passionate roaming over each other's body.

He stroked her silken legs, stripped the fine lace from her breasts, while her hungry hand found his sex and pressed it in demand.

Their blood raced up, too needy to wait, and when he stripped off the last of the lace that hid her from him, and tore off the cloth from his own hips, she cried little cries of encouragement and need, and spread her legs, her body ready for the hard, hungry thrust of his.

It was as much pleasure as he could bear, thrusting so suddenly into her, and he drew out and thrust again, to see the grimace of pleasure on her face. Neither of them knew how long they went on, crying out their pleasure, until desire and love and sensation exploded into a fireball of sweetness that burned new pathways all through their being.

They bathed their faces at the little spring, and then turned towards the dust cloud that told them how close their pursuers approached.

"It is not a caravan, Lion," she said sadly. "It is my father."

"It must be so, Beloved."

"They will kill us," she said. "I am sorry for one thing only," and he marvelled at her bravery, for her voice held no quiver, no doubt.

"What, then, Beloved, do you have regrets? I for myself have none," he said.

"Only one, my Lion. That we had nor time nor place to taste each other's love before we die."

"Ah, that," he said.

"Give me your small sword," she commanded. *"For my life will cost them almost as dear as yours."*

He pulled the little blade from his belt. *"Beloved, do you indeed wish it so?"*

"What, shall I die a coward's death at my lover's hands? How would we face each other in the other world, if I asked this of you?"

His heart wept to see her so stalwart.

"One day," she said. *"One day, we shall meet. Somewhere, somehow. Do not you feel it?"*

He was silent.

"It is so!" she swore. *"If we but wish it! Swear to me that it shall be so!"*

The Lion drew his sword and laid his hand upon the blade. *"As God is my witness, though we die here, I will wander a lost soul until your words are fulfilled, Beloved."*

"So be it," she said. *"And when we have found each other, then we will live all the life we lose now. For God rewards true lovers for their constancy. How can He do else?"*

Sixteen

It was early afternoon at the villa, and they were sitting over a late lunch on the terrace by the pool when the call came through.

Nadia was alive. Jaf had already been to see her. Gazi told her that much before embarking on a long conversation with his brother, while Anna sat waiting in anxious impatience for the details.

"She jumped off the bridge," he told her when at last he put the phone down. "The water level in the Thames was high that night. That saved her."

Anna bit her lip and tried to find the right things to say. He took her hand and kissed it.

"Someone in one of the moored houseboats saw her go. They rescued her. She begged them not to go to the police, told them if her husband found her he would kill her. The man was a surgeon. He admitted her to a private hospital. Since then she has been too ill to say anything.

When she recovered a little, she phoned the only number she could remember. Fortunately it was the number of our apartment in London and Jaf was there.''

He sat in silence, contemplating it, until she prompted him. "What about Ramiz?"

A shadow crossed his face. "The reason she felt hopeless enough to jump was—when Ramiz discovered she was pregnant, he promised to return here to West Barakat and ask us to begin divorce proceedings on her behalf. She never heard from him again.

"Yusuf must have suspected something, for suddenly she was a prisoner in her own home. She knew nothing of Ramiz's disappearance, but she knew that if Ramiz had spoken to me she would have heard. She thought Ramiz had proved faithless. Yusuf became more and more jealous, till she was frightened for her life and her child's. You were right, Anna. She went into labour and saw it as her only chance. She fled, and gave birth in a garage.

"Only then did she understand she had nowhere to flee to. We were not in town, and our apartment is the first place Yusuf would look for her. After months of bravery, Nadia broke. She caught a cab, left the baby in the cab without letting the driver know, walked onto the bridge and jumped.''

They were silent, trying to understand her despair.

"And I got into the cab," Anna murmured at last.

"Yes, Nadia said a woman was there as she got out. She said she looked at you, silently entrusting her baby to you.''

Anna shook her head. "I still don't have any memory of it. She must be very relieved to know that you have Safiyah safe.''

"Yes, of course. She regrets very deeply what she

tried to do, and we will bring her home here as soon as possible to be with her baby.''

"But you're still worried," Anna said. "Is it something about Ramiz?"

Gazi looked at her, weighing his words, and the look in his eyes made her sad with fear. "Yes, partly about Ramiz. It concerns more than Nadia, or Safiyah, or Ramiz. It is personal, but also much more than personal. It may involve the national security of the Barakat Emirates.''

Her breath came in on a long, audible intake.

"If I tell you, Anna, it will put a burden of secrecy on you. You can never mention it to anyone, not even your friend Lisbet. Can you accept this? Will you hear me?''

"Are you working for Prince Karim?"

"I am his Cup Companion. Of course I work for him. In this matter, for all the princes.''

"Are you a spy?"

"It is not my usual job. But we all do whatever is necessary.''

Anna gazed out over the terrace to the blue sea and wondered how it was possible for a life to change so dramatically in such a short time. How had it happened that she was sitting here in this fabulous villa, whose existence she had known nothing about two weeks ago, being invited to hear the state secrets of the Barakat Emirates?

"If you tell me all this, you're then going to ask me to do something?"

He swallowed, and her heart clenched nervously. "Yes, I will ask you something. But I want to tell you, not to persuade you to anything, but because I am tired of secrecy between us.''

Her heart began to thud. ''From the beginning I have been forced always into a position of suspecting you against my natural inclinations, Anna. I could not do or say the things I wished, because so much more than my personal happiness or even my sister's life was at stake. If I was indeed blinded to your true self, the whole country might suffer. Now I ask your permission to tell you the truth.''

Anna swallowed against the lump of fear and nerves that choked her. ''Yes,'' she said. ''Please tell me.''

''You know already that Ramiz was on an undercover assignment for the princes. What I did not tell you was that his mission was to infiltrate, if possible, a secret group trying to overthrow the monarchy here.''

Anna silently opened her mouth. She could hardly breathe.

''We think that it was not by his own design that Ramiz met Nadia again. We have suspected that his investigations led him to Yusuf. What Nadia says seems to confirm this.''

''Oh, my God! You mean Yusuf is part of the conspiracy?''

''Yusuf must not have known that Nadia was in love before her marriage. My father kept her secret. If he had known, it is impossible to believe that he would have brought Ramiz home to meet his wife, as she says he did. But Ramiz—Ramiz knew who Yusuf was. Pity Ramiz, whose mission required that he accept the invitation!''

''How dreadful!'' she breathed, and bit her lip, feeling how totally inadequate that was.

''Do you now understand, Anna, why I was forced to lie to you and abduct you and accuse you? It is not merely the princes' lives that are at risk from this conspiracy. A move to overthrow their rule would bring certain civil war to Barakat. Tribe against tribe, brother against brother. It would bring to the surface many rivalries now in abeyance. The repercussions would last beyond this generation, whatever the outcome. Our personal lives were less important than this.

"Can you accept that I thought and acted in this way, Anna?"

She nodded, her head bent, not daring to hope for what might be coming next. "To have you here, to be falling more and more under your spell with every moment that passed, to understand how faulty my own judgement might be...to have to suspect that you did this to me deliberately...to be forced to lie—I hope you did not suffer so much at my hands that you cannot also pity me, Anna."

Still she could not lift her head.

"Look at me," he commanded in a firm, quiet, lover's voice, and her heart kicked protestingly and then rushed into a wild rhythm as she looked at him.

"I love you, Anna. When you are here, this house, the house of my ancestors, is complete for me. Wherever I am, when you are there, too, I am home. Stay with me. I don't ask you to give up your art. Anna, I live more than half my time in Europe—we can work it out.

"You already love me a little, I think. You would not look at me with such eyes when I make love with you, if you did not love me a little. Is it not so?"

She bit her lip and gazed at him. "Oh, Gazi!" she whispered.

"Let me finish," he pleaded. "I see you with my sister's child and I know that you are the mother I want for my own children. I know that somehow, you got in

that taxi that night because we had to meet, you and I.
And we did meet.

"Don't make me let you go. Marry me, and I will
make your love grow. If ever a man could make a
woman love him, Anna, I know that I can make you
love me."

His urgency impelled him to his feet, and he drew her
up into his arms. They stood in the nook formed by the
ancient arch, against a trellis spread with flowers and
thick greenery, his strong arms protectively around her.
A delicate perfume drifted down as their bodies made
the flowers tremble.

"Gazi," was all she could say, but that word told him
everything.

*   *   *   *   *

In summer 2001, look for
SONS OF THE DESERT: THE SULTANS,
as Alexandra Sellers's sensuous series
continues…with surprise twists and turns.

Upcoming titles include:

THE SULTAN'S HEIR
UNDERCOVER SULTAN
SLEEPING WITH THE SULTAN

Silhouette® *Desire*®

invites you to enter the
exclusive, masculine world of the...

TEXAS
Cattleman's Club
Lone Star Jewels

**Silhouette Desire's powerful miniseries features five
wealthy Texas bachelors—all members of the state's
most prestigious club—who set out to recover the
town's jewels...and discover their true loves!**

MILLIONAIRE M.D.—January 2001
by Jennifer Greene (SD #1340)

WORLD'S MOST ELIGIBLE TEXAN—February 2001
by Sara Orwig (SD #1346)

LONE STAR KNIGHT—March 2001
by Cindy Gerard (SD #1353)

HER ARDENT SHEIKH—April 2001
by Kristi Gold (SD #1358)

TYCOON WARRIOR—May 2001
by Sheri WhiteFeather (SD #1364)

Available at your favorite retail outlet.

Silhouette®

Where love comes alive™

#1 *New York Times* bestselling author

NORA ROBERTS

brings you more of the loyal and loving, tempestuous and tantalizing Stanislaski family.

Coming in February 2001

The Stanislaski Sisters
Natasha and Rachel

Though raised in the Old World traditions of their family, fiery Natasha Stanislaski and cool, classy Rachel Stanislaski are ready for a *new* world of love....

And also available in February 2001 from Silhouette Special Edition, the newest book in the heartwarming Stanislaski saga

CONSIDERING KATE

Natasha and Spencer Kimball's daughter Kate turns her back on old dreams and returns to her hometown, where she finds the *man* of her dreams.

Available at your favorite retail outlet.

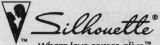

Where love comes alive™

MAITLAND MATERNITY

Where the luckiest babies are born!

In February 2001, look for

FORMULA: FATHER
by Karen Hughes

Bonnie Taylor's biological clock is ticking!

Wary of empty promises and ever finding true love, the supermodel looks to Mitchell Maitland, the clinic's fertility specialist, for help in becoming a mother. How can Mitchell convince Bonnie that behind his lab coats and test tubes, he is really the perfect man to share her life and father her children?

Each book tells a different story about the world-renowned Maitland Maternity Clinic— where romances are born, secrets are revealed... and bundles of joy are delivered.

HARLEQUIN®
Makes any time special™

Silhouette®
Where love comes alive™

January 2001
TALL, DARK & WESTERN
#1339 by Anne Marie Winston

February 2001
THE WAY TO A RANCHER'S HEART
#1345 by Peggy Moreland

March 2001
MILLIONAIRE HUSBAND
#1352 by Leanne Banks
Million-Dollar Men

April 2001
GABRIEL'S GIFT
#1357 by Cait London
Freedom Valley

May 2001
THE TEMPTATION OF
RORY MONAHAN
#1363 by Elizabeth Bevarly

June 2001
A LADY FOR LINCOLN CADE
#1369 by BJ James
Men of Belle Terre

MAN OF THE MONTH

For twenty years Silhouette has been giving
you the ultimate in romantic reads. Come join
the celebration as some of your favorite authors
help celebrate our anniversary with the most
sensual, emotional love stories ever!

Available at your favorite retail outlet.

Silhouette®
Where love comes alive™

P9-DFK-693

Also by Karen Harper

South Shores

DARK STORM
SILENT SCREAM
SHALLOW GRAVE
FALLING DARKNESS
DROWNING TIDES
CHASING SHADOWS

Cold Creek

BROKEN BONDS
FORBIDDEN GROUND
SHATTERED SECRETS

Home Valley Amish

UPON A WINTER'S NIGHT
DARK CROSSINGS (featuring "The Covered Bridge")
FINDING MERCY
RETURN TO GRACE
FALL FROM PRIDE

Novels

DOWN RIVER
DEEP DOWN
THE HIDING PLACE
BELOW THE SURFACE
INFERNO
HURRICANE
DARK ANGEL
DARK HARVEST
DARK ROAD HOME

Look for Karen Harper's next Alaska Wild novel,
UNDER THE ALASKAN ICE,
coming soon from MIRA.

Visit karenharperauthor.com for more titles.

KAREN HARPER

DEEP IN THE ALASKAN WOODS

mira

ISBN-13: 978-0-7783-0962-8

Deep in the Alaskan Woods

This edition published by arrangement with Harlequin Books S.A.

For questions and comments about the quality of this book, please contact us
at CustomerService@Harlequin.com.

Mira
22 Adelaide St. West, 40th Floor
Toronto, Ontario M5H 4E3, Canada
www.Harlequin.com

Printed in U.S.A.

Recycling programs
for this product may
not exist in your area.

For the fascinating people I met in Alaska, whose stories and amazing land I will always remember.

DEEP IN THE
ALASKAN WOODS

_1_

Alex met Lyle at the door with open arms, and Lyle hugged her so hard she could barely breathe. Her black Scottish terrier, Spenser, stayed clear of them but did his usual deep-throated guardian growl. Scotties were wary of new people, but Lyle had been in her life for months. The fact that Spenser had likely been abused before she'd rescued him made him a bit nervous around people. At least he didn't bark as if her fiancé were some sort of intruder.

"Taking care of that expensive engagement ring while I've been gone?" he asked, and kissed her again as he stepped in, pushing her with him. He had a plastic sack in his free hand, but it didn't stop him from shoving her door closed and clicking the lock. "Stay back, Spenser," he said to the dog.

Before she could say a word, he went on. "Can't believe it's this hot and muggy in good old, scenic Naperville, Illinois. Wish I was back in Scotland's late-July weather—except you're here, of course."

He had just returned from attending the British Open at an exotic-sounding town called Carnoustie in Angus,

Scotland, where he'd stayed several extra days with three mutual golf fanatics. At least Dr. Lyle Grayson, the veterinarian she worked for and was engaged to, had a passion for her, too, despite how calm and cool he seemed with those aristocratic good looks, chiseled nose and gray eyes.

"I'm jet-lagged bad, but wanted to see you, bring you these," he said as they sat close on the couch in her town house living room. Half of the space as well as part of the narrow galley kitchen was taken up with the natural homemade beauty products she sold online and to acquaintances. She'd explained to Lyle that she liked small, cozy spots, then had to assure him she wasn't criticizing the spacious home they would soon share. He hugged her with one arm as he put the sack on her lap, intentionally brushing the bare thighs beneath denim shorts she wore. Spenser sat erect at her feet, head cocked, watching with his one dark eye.

She opened the separately wrapped gifts from the sack. A white coffee mug with an image of a red unicorn, Scotland's national animal. She'd researched where he was going with his buddies. She loved to learn about new places and different cultures. She longed to go to Scotland—it was partly why she'd adopted a Scottie from the animal shelter—but Lyle was planning a honeymoon at a Caribbean island resort he'd seen advertised on TV where they'd have their own little spa pool outside their bedroom with the ocean beyond.

She unwrapped the next package. "Oh, and a Carnoustie Links golf ball mounted on a little trophy."

She didn't play golf but wished she did so she could see more of her fiancé on their days off from the vet clinic he co-owned with two other veterinarians. She and the three other vet techs there were second rung on the ladder with the vet assistants and receptionist one step lower. But what a catch Lyle was! At thirty-five, he was only six years older than she and one inch taller. She was five foot nine, and though she loved high heels, she never wore them anymore.

The last gift was a wool scarf, a lovely tartan pattern, though it seemed so alien with the heat and humidity outside. "Oh, the bars of color are striking against the white background. Thank you, Lyle."

"It's called Dress Stewart."

"The royal clan. I can see why you picked it out. I've been reading up a bit on Scotland, you see, and even watched an old Mary Queen of Scots movie on TV. So tragic she was beheaded."

"Forget all that. What I see is my beautiful girl." He tilted her toward him for another masterful kiss. She hoped her parents, who lived in England where her father worked for an international company, could be here to meet Lyle before the wedding. They hadn't set a date yet, thinking the holidays would be a great time since the clinic would be less busy and her parents could come over.

"Can I get you a drink?" she asked when he ended the kiss. He still had a good grip on her arms as if she would spring up and dart out the door. She had always loved how protective he was, but lately she'd begun to think he might actually be a bit possessive.

"No. I'm beat. I'll even take a rain check on the kind of welcome I'd like—at my house," he added, frowning, "where I won't fall over boxes of face creams and lip balms."

She was surprised at the relief she felt that he wasn't staying tonight.

He kissed her again, got up with a groan and said, "I'll call you tomorrow, and you can come over on Sunday. I take it you'll be here, cooking up your brews and pastes after work," he added, stifling a yawn.

"Yes. I need to catch up with online orders and answer questions on my blog. Despite the heat, I'll be walking Spenser in the morning, of course, and—"

"What in the hell is this?" he demanded, and snatched the eight-by-ten photo from the end table. He frowned at it. "This is a recent addition, and it seems to have a place of honor."

"I decided at the last minute to go to my high school reunion. Rah, rah, Naperville North! Those are members of the graduating class who attended. I'm there," she said, pointing, "in the back row, see?"

"Of course I see. Was that guy you used to go steady with there?"

"Mike? Yes, with his wife."

"That's him next to you, isn't it? But no wife here. He's brought his Airedale into the clinic, but I didn't let on I knew who he was. I hate that he was your first love."

"Lyle, his wife was there, but it's only the graduates in the photo."

"You got caught up with him, of course. I hope he has a happy marriage, though he probably knows by now he was an idiot to pass you up for the long haul. Any other guys there you knew well?"

"Lyle, so what? I was wearing my big, emerald-cut—expensive, as you say—ring and told people I was getting married soon. I wanted to get out. I was tired of looking at just these walls and the caged animals at the clinic while you were on a fun trip to Scotland!"

"Did he or the other guys call you since?"

"Did you listen to me? Oh, by the way," she plunged on, her voice sassy now, "I also went out to lunch with my best girlfriend from high school the next day. And guess what? There were men in the restaurant, and who knows if some of them looked at me?"

He seized her upper arms and pulled her against him. "It's just—just that you're mine now and need to act like it."

"I do. And maybe—at least once we're married—if you go to some great place like Scotland for a week, you'll take me instead of going with 'the boys.' But you don't hear me asking about any bonny lassies you might have stood next to or said 'hi' to."

"That isn't the point!" he shouted, and gave her a hard shake while Spenser started barking. "Maybe I will just stay the night!"

She fought to remain calm, keep her voice in control. "I don't think so and I'd rather you not stay. You need your rest, since you are obviously distraught and unreasonable. Please leave, Lyle. Now. I hope once you're rested—get back to yourself, that is…"

Her voice trailed off as she managed to loosen his grip on her—one hand, then the other. Lyle looked stony-faced. His eyes narrowed. In the slanted light he looked different, cruel, almost demonic. With a sudden move, almost a wrestling flip and hold, he pushed her back on the couch and lay almost on top of her.

Spenser went wild with sharp barks, but Lyle ignored him. Lyle, the gentle, caring veterinarian she had seen help animals, the suitor who had wined and dined and wooed her. He thrust a knee between her legs, then another. He had her left arm pinned, but she instinctively hit at his throat and jaw with her free elbow.

His head snapped back in surprise. She shoved him off the couch and scrambled up. Grabbing her cell phone, she ran for the front door and got it open, Spenser at her heels.

To her relief, Lyle didn't chase her, but came out past her slowly, glaring at her, shaking his head and fingering what must be a sore throat. They stood glaring at each other on the edge of the parking lot in the late blast of sun. She was sweating as she scooped up Spenser in her arms.

"I'll see you tomorrow," he told her, pointing a finger almost in her face to punctuate his words. "We need some new rules or else."

"I prefer the 'or else,' and I'll determine what that is," she said, amazed how steady her voice sounded, how sure she was of what she was doing. It all fit together too well now, and it scared her and made her sick. How could she have been so stupid and ignored so many subtle signs? She'd fallen for a controller, a potential abuser, and she knew what she had to do. It would be the same tomorrow, even if he had some rest, even if she had time to think it over. How could a man who was so good with animals and people turn so mean? Surely not just jet lag. What had she missed?

"Lyle, I think we should break it off."

"Look, pretty baby, I'm your boss. You need me."

"Take your ring back," she insisted, squeezing Spenser closer to take it off, so heavy and hard in her hand. She started to cry. Darn, she didn't want to cry. Didn't want to lose him, didn't want to admit she'd been stupid to have loved him, but he'd seemed so caring, so eager, so protective and well-off and stable, an achiever who adored her.

She pressed the ring into his hand. At least it was still broad daylight in a public condo parking lot or she wasn't sure what he would have done. Suddenly, even here, she was afraid of him.

"You'll regret this," he said with narrowed eyes and deadly calm. "You and that damn little dog, too."

He walked away, got in his car and backed out of his parking place. He squealed the brakes, then roared away.

Alex rushed back inside, locked the door. Fastened the safety bolt, since Lyle had a key. She leaned back against the door, then slid to sit on the tiled floor, holding Spenser, sobbing.

That threat, the last thing he'd said about "you and that damn little dog, too," haunted her. She'd watched a rerun of *The Wizard of Oz* on TV last week and that's more or less what the Wicked Witch had said to Dorothy.

"Alexandra Collister, you have been an idiot," she whispered to herself as Spenser whined in sympathy, thinking she was talking to him.

How…how had it happened that Lyle had turned so bad? How had she gotten this far with him, been swept away by his initial charm, his spoiling her and wanting her? And he was her boss, so there went her job, too. She'd have to find work elsewhere, though he'd probably never give her a recommendation. Her career might be over, but she knew she was right to get him out of her life.

She sat there, not sure for how long, cuddling Spenser and agonizing until it got dark outside. Oh, why hadn't she listened to Spenser? The one-eyed little guy had more smarts about Lyle than she did.

When the dog had fallen asleep, she finally put him down on the couch to close the vertical blinds to her little back patio lined with containers in which she grew many of the plants for her Natural Beauty products. But when she reached the window, she gasped.

Despite the darkness, with the streetlight coming over the privacy fence and gate only she and Lyle had a key to, she could see that her lavender plants, even her four tea rosebushes, had been violently yanked from their pots and containers, spewing their soil all over the patio. And her tall sunflowers had been beheaded.

Leaning against her Double Delight rosebush, which lay uprooted on its side, was a crudely written sign that read in big letters: You Are Mine or the End!

2

As she hurried to her car just as daylight was breaking on Friday, Alex was grateful she had the early shift at the Gentle Care Vet Clinic. She had hopes that Lyle was so exhausted he wouldn't come in. Hopefully he was sleeping the sleep of the dead, because she'd definitely decided that he was dead to her.

Surely that's what the threat on the sign meant. He was insisting she commit—and submit—totally to him or their relationship was over. But in case he was still nasty and pushy when she resigned from her job, and he meant that as a physical threat, she kept the sign so she could give it to the police. But she dreaded confrontations and hoped it didn't come to that. She just wanted out of here—out of his life.

She gripped a small spray can of mace in her hand, hoping it wasn't clogged after years of disuse. She should have tested it, but what could she spray? She heard her car doors lock as she started the engine. Her little sports car—a birthday gift from Lyle—started and purred away with no one lurking, no one following. Should she return this darling car as she had her ring?

She could just imagine these tires slashed and the deep blue finish spray painted with You Are Mine or the End!

At least going into the clinic by seven a.m. would give her a chance to ask for her last paycheck and leave the letter of resignation she'd written last night. She wasn't sure whether Lyle could be reasonable enough to give her a good recommendation to find another job, or if that was another dead end and she'd actually need to move to a different suburb and just tell her interviewer the truth, at least part of it. She'd say her previous place of employment was uncomfortable because she'd broken off an engagement.

This proved that dating one's boss could cause all kinds of complications. But she'd promised herself one thing: if Lyle harassed her or hurt her again—she had big, purple bruises on her left upper thigh and both arms—she would file for a restraining order, however upset he became at his precious reputation being sullied.

She was grateful she'd already planned to leave Spenser with her neighbor Charlene, who kept the dog during the long days Alex worked and made sure he got his walks and food. She'd hugged him when she'd dropped him off two doors down. Poor little guy, abused by his original owner so badly he'd lost an eye. Strange, but thinking of that was even more painful to her now than ever.

At each stoplight, Alex glanced at the cars behind and beside her. During her early lunch break, she planned to run home to meet the guy from the hardware store who was going to change the locks on her front door and back gate. Late last night she'd left a message at his number, stressing that the job and the timing were very important. Her mind had wandered, tormenting

her, and she'd hardly slept at all…locking her doors…
locking her heart away…locking her life to stay safe.

"Good morning," she said cheerily to the office
manager, the perky Joan, even though Alex felt—and
looked—anything but the way she sounded.

"Hey! Your fave doc's back in town, I guess," Joan
said with a big smile and a lift of her eyebrows. "Seen
the illustrious Dr. Grayson yet?"

"Briefly. He was really jet-lagged. He said he wasn't
coming in today. You haven't heard anything different,
have you?"

"Anything new with you?"

Alex shook her head and forced as smile. She considered Joan a workplace friend, though that was probably over now since Joan's loyalty had to be to Lyle and
the other vets.

"Do you think I could get my check before my break
instead of at the end of the day?" Alex asked. Her stomach was churning. She should have had more than coffee for breakfast. "I've got some bills coming due,"
she added.

"Hey, what you want is what you get around here."
She flipped her long blond hair back and hummed "Here
Comes the Bride." "I can get it for you in a little bit.
So, are you still going to work here after the big day?"

"Got to keep busy, right?" Alex countered.

She'd decided not to tell anyone what had happened,
and she wasn't sure Lyle would when he came in. If
she did leave the area, would Lyle follow her? Make
life miserable? Where would she go? Maybe her father could get her a job in England, but could she take
Spenser? She could try to become someone's virtual

assistant and work from home, balance that with her Natural Beauty business. But she knew it cost her parents dearly to live abroad, however good Dad's salary was, and she couldn't afford that or sponge off them.

She soon got caught up in the rush of caring for her feline and canine patients. Vet techs were charged with prepping the animals for surgery, carefully calibrating their meds and anesthetics and restraining them before and after treatments or surgery. You never knew what someone's pet would do when it was in pain or came to after anesthesia wore off, so the work was intense and could be dangerous. Post-op she'd been bitten on the back of her head by a German shepherd once and the pain had been bad—about as bad as her head felt right now.

Thankfully, Lyle did not come in as the morning wore on. More coffee and two doughnuts kept her going. At least she never seemed to gain weight from what she ate. Maybe another good thing from a hectic schedule and dog walking. Lyle had teased it was from strenuous sex. Oh, why did she have to think of that now? Even the way he touched her should have tipped her off to his tendency to dominate and control.

At her late-morning break, which she'd combined with her lunchtime, she tore out to her car to rush home to oversee the changing of her locks. But her car would not start when it had always purred to life so easily. It just made a grinding sound and would not turn over. She got out and looked around the parking lot. Nothing unusual. No one but pet owners going or coming with animals in their arms or on leashes.

Her stomach cramped. She got back in the car and called her auto service and requested they haul her car to the nearest garage. She left her car keys with Joan, then called an Uber to get home.

She made it just as the locksmith was pulling in. As far as she could tell, Lyle or his car were nowhere around, but she couldn't help the feeling she was being watched. Watched, wanted but hated.

"You got a problem with break-ins or something like that?" Jack, the locksmith, asked as he finished up the lock to her front door after changing the one on the tall back gate. She'd hastily swept and piled up the remnants of her plants this morning. "Remember, you got a slide bolt that will help if you're inside."

"Yes, thanks. Just thought this was a good idea, too."

He was tall, strapping and blond, very friendly and chatty. Nervous, she stood watching him work. She kept her purse tight under her arm. It had what would be her last two-week paycheck in it, the mace—and photos of her and Lyle she planned to destroy.

She stepped away as Jack worked and she called the auto service again to check on the status of her car, hoping it was something random, not that it had been tampered with by someone who knew exactly where it would be parked.

"Don't know how it happened, ma'am," the garage mechanic told her on the phone. "A couple of leads from the spark plugs had been pulled out. They're right under the hood, but I guess you didn't know how to look for them. An easy fix this time."

This time, she thought. But the mess she was in was hardly an easy fix.

As she paid Jack and he handed her the new keys, Lyle wheeled up in his black Lexus. Her insides twisted.

She stayed close to Jack. Lyle got out, slammed his car door and strode toward them.

"You're supposed to be at work!" he shouted.

"It was a challenge to keep this appointment during my early lunch break since someone disabled my car. I called Joan to tell her I wouldn't be back—today, I mean."

"And this is?" he asked, glaring at Jack.

She was so angry and distraught that she almost gave him a flip answer. Meanwhile, Jack took a step toward Lyle and asked, "You okay with this guy, Ms. Collister?"

"Lyle, please leave," she said with a nod. "What I said last night stands. And I'm tendering my resignation at the clinic. It's on your desk, though I went in today so they weren't one tech short for surgery. I hope you are rested up and more reasonable now."

"Reasonable? You owe me a hell of a lot more than a car and a thirty-thousand-dollar engagement ring!"

Jack put in, "You need to call for help, ma'am?"

"Just butt out of this," Lyle insisted, though he stood his ground away from them when she was sure he would have assaulted her if she were alone. Actually, he had done that last night, throwing her down on her couch and ramming her legs apart, which, thank heavens, hadn't gone further.

"Thank you, Jack," she said, her voice shaking. "And in case you need to know later, perhaps to have the name of this man, he is Dr. Lyle Grayson, a veterinarian here in town." Praying Lyle—this man she thought she knew—did not have a gun or knife, she punched in 9-1-1 herself but did not send it. "Lyle, please leave and stay away from me, or I will get an officer here and a court restraining order. Jack, I'm sorry you were caught up in this."

"Caught up in this?" Lyle shouted as Charlene came out with Spenser in her arms and set him down so he darted straight for Alex, yipping. "You're the one who caught me. Tricked me. You obviously don't give a damn, and I intend to see you pay me back for everything I've done and given you!"

"Like this public embarrassment?" she shot back as she scooped up her barking dog before Lyle could get to him. "Like tampering with *my* car and ruining my property last night? I'm phoning the police now and a lawyer next if you don't leave immediately and leave me alone for good. I apologize to the possible two future witnesses who had to hear all this," she added, nodding toward Jack and Charlene.

"Yeah, witnesses, both of us," Jack put in.

Alex could have cried. She was embarrassed but so grateful for the kindness of this stranger. She didn't believe for one minute that any of this was going to make Lyle back off, though. She had seen him now for what he was. Fairy-tale princes and a happily-ever-after didn't exist anymore—and maybe never had.

She called her parents that night and explained, assuring them that Lyle had stamped off and she hadn't heard from him again. They sounded devastated and concerned.

"You leave Spenser with that friend of yours, hop on a plane and come to us," her father ordered. "I'll reimburse you for the ticket, and we'll have a good time so you can forget that bastard."

"Thank you so much, but what I need is time and a

new job, but not far away, at least not that far. Besides, it would be just like him to know where I'd run to, come there and ruin things for all of us."

"You get that restraining order," her mother said. "I was reading *People* magazine over here and one of those ingenue actress types got one—it's called a TRO, a temporary restraining order, and if the offending party breaks it they can pay a fine or even get jail time."

"I told him I'd do that, and he hardly blinked. I've got my car back now, and this town house is locked up as tight as Fort Knox."

"With our precious girl inside," her mother put in, and Alex heard her sniffle, then blow her nose.

Alex was glad she was using the phone right now rather than FaceTime because she couldn't bear to look at their worried faces, nor did she want them to see her tears. Her choked-up voice was a dead giveaway, anyhow.

"I'll call you back when I decide what I'm going to do. I do want to get away for a while, but not somewhere Lyle would know about. I'll let you know as soon as I figure it all out."

And when would that be? she wondered as they said goodbye, not before they once more tried to persuade her to come "over the pond."

"Over the pond," she whispered to herself as she flipped open a scrapbook with pictures from when she'd first visited them there. The three of them smiling in front of Windsor Castle with the Coldstream Guards marching behind them. That's what she needed—a thick-walled castle and guards.

A photo fell from the album, a much older picture. It was her with her twin cousins, Megan and Suzanne, when they were all about ten. It was taken in Alaska where the twins' grandmother they did not share had lived in a rustic lodge. Falls Lake Lodge, the sign read. Ah, to be lost right now, on the distant side of a wilderness lake, protected by those towering pines, and lodged in that sprawling inn, safely far away.

But she was almost estranged from her cousins now. After she'd learned about her family's tragedy, which her mother and father had kept from her for years, she couldn't bear to be with her cousins anymore. She had never explained to them why she had pretty much cut off communication.

Leaving Spenser sleeping on the sofa, she went into the bathroom. She leaned her hands on the sink and stared into the mirror as she had so often after she'd first learned of the tragedy. Just to think, she was an identical twin, just like her two cousins.

She met her own eyes in the mirror and saw the ghost again—herself. Or was it Allison? How she wished she could confer with her sister. Maybe then she wouldn't suddenly be so afraid. How the loss of her twin she never knew still haunted her.

Years ago, she'd read up about the "vanishing twin syndrome." Her mother had named both of them when they were in the womb. Then at her next ultrasound, they discovered Allie had just vanished without a miscarriage. Some of the speculative medical literature Alex had poured over sent her into counseling for survivor's guilt, since it was thought the stronger survivor had just absorbed the lost fetus. Had she killed Allie? Was she with her, in her? Was she really two people?

She sometimes imagined what Allie would be like, even talked to her. When she looked in a mirror like this, was her identical twin staring back, blond and blue-eyed? All that was the reason she had cut off her cousins, because Suze and Meg's close relationship hurt too much.

But the two sisters had tried to keep in touch. And now—now, Alex had an idea where she could go.

3

Although Alex still felt panicked, she was panicked now with a purpose. What if her cousins wanted nothing to do with her, since she'd more or less cut ties? They'd asked her out to visit long ago, and she'd turned them down. The only contact she'd kept up was to send a Christmas card. Should she just blurt out the mess she was in, or only ask if she could visit, then make her plea once she arrived?

She'd look for the lodge's website. If worse came to worst, she could just make a reservation there for a few days and try to mend—or build—bridges, before finding somewhere to stay longer term. With her parents in the UK, Suze and Meg were the closest, though distant, family she had.

The good news was that Alaska was far away, and she had never shared anything about the twins with Lyle. He didn't know about her lost twin, either. The bad news was she'd need to drive there to take Spenser, some possessions and her products to sell, so she'd have to get a sturdy vehicle a lot larger than her little sports car.

But first things first.

Alex sobbed when she found the website for the Falls Lake Lodge online with its stunning pictures of rustic accommodations. The exterior and interior wooden walls of the lodge were just as she remembered, though the furnishings were updated and improved. Still over the big fireplace in the common room was that moose head with a massive rack of antlers staring down on the seating and tables. The three of them used to joke that the moose was watching them wherever they walked in that large common room.

Oh, and a picture of a typical bedroom looked so cozy with a patchwork quilt for a bedspread and one on the wall like a piece of art. Next to it hung a lovely painting of distant, snowcapped mountains with a waterfall feeding a lake beneath—just like Falls Lake itself. She wondered if Suze had painted that. Even as a child, she was talented. The art on the Christmas card she received from them each year was always a photo of an original signed by her. Alex also studied the big bedroom window with its view of rain forest trees. How she wished she could spirit herself and Spenser away to the lodge right now.

But what if they didn't allow guests to bring pets?

Through her tears, she studied again the photo of the smiling Meg and Suze near the "Click here for reservations" button. Other than different hairstyles, they greatly resembled each other. They were both in their early thirties, so would they even go by those childhood names anymore? They'd signed their Christmas card with their full first names. Megan's last name wasn't even Collister anymore but Metzler. She had married young and lost her husband when the bush plane he was piloting went down not far from Falls Lake. Alex had sent a condolence card and letter when she learned about it months late. Meg had a son, Charles, called Chip, who must be around five or six now.

Several years ago, after inheriting their maternal grandmother's lodge, the twins had decided to run it together, like a B and B, though they didn't want to change the name. Maybe she could help them at the lodge, even if it was to clean rooms or serve food. Thank heavens it was late July, so the big winter snows they'd sent pictures of in some of their holiday greetings would not set in for a while.

She noticed, at the very bottom of the website, a message: *Our thanks to Quinn Mantell for his help in bringing the outside world to Falls Lake. Be sure to watch* Tracker Q-Man *on the Wilds TV Cable Network, filmed in our amazing area of Alaska.*

And next to that was a picture of a smiling, handsome, dark-haired man with a trimmed beard in black jeans and plaid flannel shirt—dress Stewart pattern, no less—framed by a fir tree with a waterfall and the mountains behind him. Funny, but looking at Quinn Mantell, she could almost smell sharp pine and fresh, crisp air.

Hands trembling, she called the phone number for reservations.

"Falls Lake Lodge," came a clear female voice. "We are forty miles north of Anchorage so we can offer city life and the wonderful wilderness. The town of Falls Lake recently put in cell phone towers, so we have the amenities of the modern world in the middle of the scenic, eternal wilds. How can I help you?"

Alex panicked again. Was that a recording? If not,

she couldn't even place the voice. Megan's? Suzanne's? Someone who worked for them?

Alex knew she didn't sound like herself. She was nasal, shaky, as she said, "Hello. This is Alexandra Collister in Illinois and—"

A gasp. A shout. "Suze, it's Cousin Alex! Suze, come here! How the heck are you, girl? Are you all right? Any big news?"

Alex couldn't help it, but she burst into tears and barely managed to get out, "It is so, *so* good to hear your voice. Yes, some big news, kind of bad news, but..."

"You can tell us, hon! Blood is thicker than water, remember! Here, Suze, say hi to our long-lost Alex," Meg said, and evidently thrust the phone at her sister.

"This is Suze. Are you okay? Long time no hear and see! We can't get away, but you want to come for a visit? What's happening?"

The sisters' voices were so similar she couldn't tell them apart. Would Allie's voice have sounded like her own? Alex managed to summon her self-control and found her courage to tell them the truth and ask for their advice. They listened with very few questions for at least ten minutes while she stumbled through an explanation.

Finally, when she paused, Meg—she thought it was Meg—said, "You just come here to us where that idiot won't find you. You want to hide out, that's fine, but in God's country here, you can build a new life. We have. Hey, listen. Here's a good sign. The woman who oversaw our combo gift and antique shop just left, and if you want to run that for us, that will cover your room and board. You could sell those beauty products there, too. Thanks to a well-connected neighbor who got this area two cell towers, you could still sell online. Can't promise this climate will let you grow every herb you'd need, but—"

As if they were a phone tag team, Suze cut in, "But they do greenhouse growing here year round so that may work for more tender plants."

The two of them even finished each other's thoughts! It made Alex realize how much she'd missed having close girlfriends. She'd spent too much time at her job, on creating and selling her products—and on Lyle.

"You should see the cabbages, big as bushel baskets!" Suze went on. "You just get here soon as you can. We'll save a room and can't wait to see you. Call or text us to keep us posted. You driving a truck? Best to have one if you stay for a while, and we hope you will."

"No truck yet, but I need more than my little car to bring some things. So you won't mind if I bring my Scottie dog?"

"We have two dogs, so the more, the merrier. You'll save us on vet bills."

"I'm not a vet, but I know a lot about the basics."

"You and your Scottie will have to learn the woods can be dangerous," Meg warned. "But I think you'll find it a lot safer here than there with that wolf you're smart to get rid of—for good."

As her tears flowed, Alex thanked them again. Surely she was making good choices, even if hasty ones. As soon as she could manage—tomorrow—she was secretly, suddenly, Alaska bound.

Alex forced herself to make even more hard, quick decisions. Grateful Lyle had a big surgery schedule today, she withdrew her meager savings and closed her checking account the moment her bank opened on Saturday morning. She drove to another suburb and traded in her sports car for a used truck with a covered-back truck bed. She had never driven even a small truck before, but it seemed easy enough. At her local DMV, she had her license plate legally switched to her new vehicle.

At the last minute, she remembered to change her address and stopped in at the post office just before it closed at noon.

She parked the truck nearly a block away from her town house, hoping Lyle did not take a break from his surgery schedule to check on her in person. Evidently, since he hadn't called, Lyle was blessedly giving her the isolated, silent treatment, either hoping she'd crawl back to him or because he was planning something. Maybe her earlier threats to call the police and of a restraining order had made him back off, but she sensed that would not last long.

She gave Charlene all the food and supplies that would not store and four hundred dollars. Two hundred of that was to clear out her apartment and put her furniture and the rest of her boxed possessions in a nearby self-storage facility—No Worry Storage, ha! She paid the facility for six months and did not give them a forwarding address.

The other two hundred dollars were for Charlene's help, though the kindly woman argued about that. Alex explained that she could not tell her where she was going but would let her know when she was safely out of town and when she finally arrived at her destination, which would take about a week.

Alex hated not saying goodbye to other friends, but it would just lead to questions that might actually endanger them and her later. She had no idea if she could come back to live here again, or if she would want to. How had she ever let a man ruin her life? Here she was, ready to go to a place so foreign, so vast, so unknown.

But what she did know was that she had to get away from Lyle. It had been like some horror movie to see him morph into a monster, one she should have seen beneath the charm and gifts and protective veneer.

Last, she called her parents and told them what she had done and where she was going.

"I'm glad you'll be with family, even if it's not us," her mother admitted. "But it's so far, honey! You keep in touch and drive carefully. And we still want you to come over here, maybe in the autumn."

"I'm going to have to put down roots there, Mom, at least temporary ones. I'm going to make the best of it."

Her father's voice came in. "Of course you will, because you're the best."

"And," her mother put in, so they must have been sharing the phone, "I don't want this sad, scary situation with Lyle to turn you off men. You know what I mean. Do not let that earlier loss and then this one keep you from being you, lovely inside and out."

"I appreciate that, and I *know* you two aren't a bit biased," she tried to kid them. She had to keep this a little light or she was going to self-destruct with fear and sorrow. And her mother hadn't mentioned the loss of Allie, even indirectly, for years until now.

She promised again she'd be careful and told them she'd call briefly each night she was on the road and leave them a message. And yes, she would drive only in the daylight and use her AAA membership for car repair service if she broke down.

She did break down when she said goodbye to them. Suddenly, despite the hovering, nervous Spenser, she felt so very, very alone. Wasn't one nickname for Alaska "the Great Alone"? Or was it "the Last Frontier," because that would fit the mess she'd made of her life here, too—and the promise of going there to start over.

She checked her Natural Beauty website to see if any new orders had come in, because she would have to mail them from the stock she was taking to Alaska, so mailing rates would go up except for the west coast. But she gasped at what she saw.

Her contact page and order form had been repeatedly spammed by an email address she recognized, at least thirty, maybe forty times. Shaking, she opened one. *I want to order my fiancée back NOW! Be here Sunday morning!*

She opened one more: the same, awful, threatening message. She printed this one out so she'd have evidence of harassment if something happened to her laptop. At least, if he was threatening her that she had to come to him, maybe he wasn't coming here anymore. But what if he got a hacker to harm her website further or spammed her products with bad reviews, ruining her business that she cared so much for?

Then she saw he'd been on the products page, too. *Just like this stuff,* one review read, *you're bought and paid for.* And he had given a one-star rating to her lilac and sunflower body cream, which she loved and he knew it. At least she saw he hadn't done that with any other products yet. He'd never really appreciated how serious she was about her creations. He might even have ordered her to stop making them once they were married. Why hadn't she seen that danger, too?

She deleted what she could, wishing she could delete the past two years of her life—delete him and how she'd fallen for him, how she'd thought she loved him.

She hoped Lyle had finished taking his fury out on her website. She would have to find a way to keep him off it, but she wasn't sure how. At least he could not track her actual location, only her virtual one.

But her stomach was so upset to be attacked that way, too, that she went to the bathroom again, sitting on the toilet, holding her sides, rocking a bit, then still staying there after she flushed. Spenser pushed open the door and sat with his head cocked as if waiting for an explanation. She got up and washed her hands and petted him.

"My dear little dog, we are off on a great adventure tomorrow," she said. As she had twice before today, she braced her hands on the sink to steady herself and looked into the mirror.

Her shoulder-length hair needed washing. How long would it be before she had the money or the place to get these blond highlights streaked again? Before she found the perfect shade of blue mascara to highlight her eyes or went to an exercise class or out to a fancy restaurant? Falls Lake was not even in Anchorage, which was a big city but out in the wilderness. She supposed just like Naperville was distant from Chicago, but what a difference in terrain!

Was she crazy? A coward to flee?

No, this had to be done, and it took courage. Power and bravery, which she supposed Lyle would not have expected or respected from her. She had hardly seen it in herself.

Alex nodded decisively at the mirror, and her dearest, lifelong ally, her twin sister, Allie, nodded back.

4

As Alex drove northwest, the miles, the highways, cities and towns, even entire states blurred by: the southeastern curve of Wisconsin, the edge of Iowa and huge stretches of the Dakotas. Boy, she appreciated that this truck had cruise control. Now if she could just keep control of this trip, of the remaking of her life.

As alone as she felt, she sensed she was safer than if she'd stayed home. Lyle was probably on the warpath now, realizing not only that she had disobeyed his orders to come to his house on Sunday, but that she was gone. With stunning clarity she realized that she now feared him. At least she'd warned her parents that he might call them or even show up there. Or maybe he'd assume she'd just changed neighborhoods. And that was exactly what she was doing—big-time.

Spenser slept during the day between her stops to walk, feed and relieve him and herself. He had curled up in his open-topped carton, which was hemmed in by boxes of lip balms, skin cleansers and fragrant body creams on the passenger side floor. The truck smelled like a summer garden. And Spenser was safer that way, she hoped, than if he'd been in his doggy bed, which was stashed in the back. The little guy managed to snooze despite the fact she kept the radio on and sang along with it to stay awake. Sometimes she talked to him and sometimes talked to her long-lost sister. Allie was there, watchful, each time Alex glanced in the rear-view mirror.

At night, she slept well despite strange beds. It was at least better than sharing a bed with Lyle! During the day, she got by on fast food, granola bars, fruit and bad coffee from gas stations. She made sure Spenser had his favorite dog food before they set out each day. One night, because of exhaustion and a rainstorm that affected visibility, she pulled off, slumped down on the seat and settled sleeping in her truck in a Walmart parking lot. Her parents would have had a fit.

And when she was taking a shower at an indie called the Low Rate Motel, even over the pounding of the water and the barrier of the curtain, she heard a man's voice in the bedroom. Her mind jumped to that old movie *Psycho*, which she'd been stupid enough to watch over the summer on Netflix. Janet Leigh being slashed in the shower at the Bates Motel!

Her heartbeat pounding in her ears, she poked her head out and emerged dripping wet. Oh, music, too. Had someone turned on the TV? Would she have to scream or fight, stark naked? She had nothing to use for a weapon here in the bathroom. If she could get to her phone, she'd call 9-1-1. Had someone silenced Spenser? Why hadn't he barked? No way Lyle could have traced her, found her!

Holding her breath, with a towel wrapped around her wet body, she poked her head out into the bedroom. Spenser was lying on the bed where she'd left him, calm, sleepy. He looked up at her like, *What's your problem?*

The outside door was closed, the chain lock still on. Then she saw the TV remote was lying on the floor. He must have stepped on it or punched it somehow, and a news program had come on. A commercial ran now, one for a getaway to the very Caribbean resort Lyle had decided would be their honeymoon spot.

She began to sob so hard she could barely walk back into the bathroom to turn off the shower.

She dried herself, clicked the TV off and got into bed, sobbing silently and praying she'd get enough sleep and find the strength to go on the next day.

Alex called her parents and her cousins briefly each night, and Charlene once to thank her for all the help and wish her well. Lyle had been to see her, but she had met him at the door with a friend who was a cop and pleaded ignorance of where his former fiancée had gone. Alex could hear Charlene's four-year-old daughter's voice in the background crying that Spenser-doggy wasn't coming to visit anymore.

And then came the drag of a drive through wide Montana, which went on eternally and, wouldn't you know, that northwestern state was having an early August heat wave.

Then ahead loomed one of Montana's six border crossings into British Columbia. Thank heavens she had a current passport from visiting her parents in London. She was still going to have to drive a good slice of western Canada, then back into the US, past Juneau, to Anchorage and then even farther north. She'd be crossing another border, all right, one between her past and present—and the future.

Her cousins had told her she could stay in Canada for up to six months with just proof of US citizenship and a valid ID. She knew from working at the clinic, however, that Spenser would need proof of a current rabies vaccination. She also had that since, she'd figured, if she ever took him to England, it could be necessary. It had to be signed by a US veterinarian, so that was the last remnant she had of Lyle, for he had written his name big and bold on the paper.

She crossed into Canada late on the fifth day of her journey. She started to sing an old Johnny Horton folk song, "North to Alaska." Spenser howled along with her. It was just the two of them for several more hundred miles—then what lay beyond?

The mountains of Alaska seemed to hem her in, but she felt protected by them, too. So different from Illinois scenery and skylines.

"Hey, Spenser, this isn't Kansas or the US Midwest anymore!" she said, before she remembered that Lyle, too, had borrowed from *The Wizard of Oz* when he'd threatened her and her little dog. But surely that part of her life was over. She was safe and free. And she had the strangest feeling that—if she'd stayed home—Lyle could have been crazy enough to make sure her life was over one way or the other.

She tried to shake that off as she turned onto Route 1, the Glenn Highway, which would skirt big, busy Anchorage to the south. Just think: she could have flown into Anchorage in one day instead of driving for almost a week, but it had to be done this way.

As she turned north again, the spruce and birch forests thickened along the road. Lakes glittered through the trees, some big, some small, and she passed numerous white-water streams, a few with people salmon fishing. Everywhere she looked seemed like a stunning postcard come to life.

She saw a sign pointing toward Wasilla and remembered that was the hometown of past vice-presidential candidate Sarah Palin. As she turned off the highway onto a two-lane road to drive the last forty or so miles to Falls Lake, she had to laugh. Two houses she passed had cutouts of Palin in their doorways, and she saw one of those posters stuck on a truck window that made it look as if Palin were in the back seat of the vehicle, smiling and waving.

Strange, but after driving mostly on highways, this narrower two-lane road seemed endless. Surely everything would work out.

She saw a moose on the side of the road just about the time she saw a bumper sticker that read Eat More Moose! She supposed she'd arrive about suppertime at the lodge. Suze had said on the phone last night that they were having a salmon bake for guests, and they hoped she got there in time for that—a real Alaskan welcome. She'd also said it stayed light this time of year until almost ten thirty, so there would be no trouble with her following the signs to the lodge, beyond the little town of Falls Lake. If she went past the survival and tracking camp sign, Suze had said, she'd gone too far. Well, it did feel like she'd gone too far in more ways than one.

"Survival and tracking?" Alex had asked on the phone. "That sounds ominous. Not like—like stalking?"

"Well, kind of. More like tracking someone who's

lost," Suze had said. "Wait till you meet the guy that runs it. I don't suppose you watch the Wilds cable TV channel?"

"No. But, oh, you mean that Q-Man guy that you thanked on your website."

"Let's just say Alaskans are unique, and him most of all. He's kind of a local hero, so we watch his show here. You can learn a lot. Anyway, you've got two good teachers here, too. We'll be looking for you with open arms. Drive careful, now, this last leg. Can't wait to see you! If you arrive during the salmon bake, walk out in back, and we'll be there."

What Alex saw when she pulled into the parking lot of the Falls Lake Lodge both comforted and worried her. At least a dozen pickup trucks were there, so she'd soon be meeting lots of people. Her stomach knotted, but Meg and Suze had said to just come on out behind the lodge to find them.

She took time to comb her hair and dab on some lipstick. Yep, there was Allie in the rearview mirror, giving her a nod and whispering, "Go for it—our new life."

Alex put Spenser on his leash. Brushing off her jeans, she got out and lifted him down, then locked the truck, giving it a good pat for getting them safety here these many miles. As soon as she found the twins she'd duck back inside the lodge, use the restroom and call her parents to leave a message since they'd be asleep now.

Spenser raised one leg for the first of many salutes to the trees outside the lodge, and they went in the front door. No one was at the check-in desk. A few people were inside, but they were looking outside through the back windows, maybe to see when the salmon was done.

Spenser looked all around but didn't make a sound and stayed tight to her.

As someone went out through the back door, Alex could hear the buzz of conversation and a strumming guitar outside. The scent of delicious smoke wafted in as she picked up Spenser, opened the back door and went out.

About ten yards back behind the small crowd was a log cabin that must be the gift shop she would oversee. It was charming, with a large front window that displayed items that were too far away to make out right now. The wooden sign said Gifts and More.

Most people—maybe twenty some, a mix of men and women—were standing around the grilling site, talking and laughing. Some held beer bottles, some glasses and some cups. A few of them looked at her, nodded or smiled, so she mouthed "hi" and smiled back.

She noted a man with what looked like an expensive movie camera slung under one arm, a bottle of beer in his other hand. He was short but rugged-looking, and at least he wasn't shooting the scene. Maybe her cousins had hired someone for publicity.

At that man's shoulder was a petite, striking blonde who seemed out of place and yet her appearance screamed, *Look at me!* She should have been onstage— maybe in front of that camera—with her heavy makeup and long, blond corkscrew hair that must have taken hours to style. Unlike the other casually dressed people, she wore a leather jacket belted around her shapely body with knee-high boots to match. She seemed to be almost hanging on the guy.

It made Alex realize she'd have to keep an eye on that camera. No way she wanted to be in anyone's online pics or even on local TV. Of course, it was a million-to-one chance Lyle could ever locate her that way, but weirder things had happened.

She saw, too, that the young couple was now hovering with an older man who didn't quite fit the scene, either. Though he wore jeans and a casual plaid shirt, something about him seemed formal. He was a silver-haired guy around sixty, she guessed, and wore glasses that seemed to become a bit darker when he moved from the shade to sun. Those designer glasses and some large gold jewelry—rings and a big watch—also made him seem out of place here.

Actually, that man might be studying her, too, but she wasn't sure because of his dark glasses.

The barbecue pit wasn't what she had expected, either. About twelve large salmon, splayed, skin side out, were spitted on sharp, sturdy sticks that encircled a silvery ember-and-wood fire. A man with his black hair pulled back in a ponytail was basting the fish. Beyond were two long tables covered with green and white checkered oilcloth loaded with covered dishes, stacks of plates and glasses of what looked like iced tea—no, maybe iced coffee.

She spotted one of her cousins among the guests. Tears blinded her at first, and she blinked them back. Was that Suze or Meg? She was going to have to learn to tell them apart by their hair. Oh, there was Chip, pulling on his mother's light blue shirt and asking her something, so that must be Meg.

Meg saw her, too, and said something to Suze, who was placing casserole dishes on the table. They both rushed her with Chip not far behind. The boy had a round face, sandy hair and freckles. When he smiled, she saw his adult front teeth were coming in.

"Oh, thank God, you're here safe!" Meg cried, and hugged her first with Spenser pressed between them, still on his best behavior not to growl or bark. Maybe he sensed they were among friends and family, that—for now—they had come home.

Suze got in the group hug, then they peppered her with questions. Others stopped and turned to look. Rather than stare, they applauded, and several came closer for introductions, not shaking hands but giving her high fives, so she figured that was the custom here. A few of them who had obviously already had a few beers gave her what they called "the moose salute." Thumbs in ears, palms forward, fingers stiff to look like antlers. Chip kept doing it, too, laughing so hard he doubled over. The woman with the cameraman just rolled her eyes as if this was all so dumb, but Alex didn't feel that way.

So much to learn. So many new people, new ways.

As the rush of welcoming strangers blurred by, only a few stood out right away.

"This is Sam Spruce, jack-of-all-trades, a partner in the tracking camp down the road," Meg said of the man who had been overseeing the salmon bake. "And this is his brother, Josh, who helps at the lodge and the tracking camp."

"Wherever, whatever," Josh said with a little shrug.

The brothers resembled each other except that Josh had a tattoo of a whale on the left side of his neck, so no trouble telling those two apart.

Sam gestured to a tall man standing nearby and told her, "This is my boss and partner. Suze said you work with herbs, Alex. This guy can fix gourmet food out of herbs in the wilds—knows more wild plants and which ones to survive on than I do."

Suze put in, "Alex, this is our distant neighbor—not distant in person, just down the road a ways—Quinn Mantell, alias Q-Man."

Their eyes met and held. Oh, he was the dark-haired, tall man from their website, but he'd shaved his beard. He was the first guest who didn't high-five her but took her hand. His was big, warm and calloused. She had just the hand cream for him, but men hardly ever used it because the scent could be considered feminine. This man smelled of pine and fresh air and—well, masculinity. And they had said he knew herbs, at least in the wild. She felt her cheeks flush as she gently pulled her hand back. She had to say something and not just stare.

"I saw your picture and the thanks to you on the lodge website," she told him. "If you managed to bring the internet here, you are the local patron saint."

"Oh, I'm no saint," he said, and smiled so that his green eyes nearly crinkled shut as he reached over to scratch Spenser between his ears. "What's your buddy's name here? I had a Scottie when I was growing up."

Quinn frowned as though that were a bad memory, but he was the first person who had mentioned or touched Spenser. No yelps, no growls.

"Salmon's almost done!" Sam announced to everyone. "Come on, Josh—need some help." Though Josh didn't look too happy about it, they went back to basting each large piece of fish and touching the skin of it, as if that were the thermometer.

Spenser's nose twitched at the smell of the fish. She didn't dare put him down right now.

Introductions went on. It turned out the cameraman

was just that, a guy named Chris Ryker from New York who was the videographer for Quinn's cable TV show. He went by his last name, they said. Luckily, she'd heard Quinn tell him to stow the camera for now. The actress-looking blonde with him was Val Chambers from Los Angeles. Maybe she worked behind the scenes for Quinn's show. And the older man they'd been with was a New York lawyer somehow connected with the show, by the name of Brent Bayer. He seemed content to just watch rather than come over to be introduced. Other names blurred by.

Meg said, "Listen, let's get you inside, give you a chance to wash up first. Chip decided to call you Aunt Alex, and he'll take you and Spenser to your room. After we eat, we'll help unpack the truck. You did drive a truck, didn't you?" she asked in a softer voice.

"With all I needed for this new life, you bet. Thanks, Chip."

Quinn was still standing there, watching, listening. "I must admit," she said, "I feel like the proverbial new kid on the block."

"You're better than a new kid," he said, his deep voice softer than before, "but there's a lot to learn. You'll find folks friendly and willing to help."

Their eyes met and held before she nodded, smiled and turned away. As she followed Chip back into the lodge and down the hall, asking him where he went to school, she didn't feel afraid anymore, just totally intrigued. Surely she could make this wilderness lodge and this small frontier-type town she'd driven quickly past as well as these new people and this vast land, at least for now, her home.

5

Quinn got up with the sun at about 6:30 a.m., thinking he'd overslept. No, he was okay. They were between groups of students here at the tracking camp. A new group arrived in a few days, ages ranging from twenty-one to sixty-five from two countries besides the US this time. Two weeks later, a smaller advanced bunch. Then more survivor training after the first big snow fell.

Today he had to pick up Geoff, his cable TV producer, at the airport. They were going to map out the next series of shows. If he could pry his video guy away from Val, he'd have Ryker sit in on the planning session, too. Ryker loved this job, loved being out in nature, and his big-city girlfriend was a real distraction. Wait until Geoff, who had hired Ryker, saw Val hanging all over him. She'd already talked Ryker into renting a B and B room for both of them in town instead of his bunking here, but they could work around that.

Quinn took a cold shower fast—one of the drawbacks of this place was no hot water unless you boiled it. He got dressed in clean jeans and a new shirt and ambled over to the mess hall where Sam would probably be making pancakes. Sam's wife, Mary, was sleeping in since she'd felt queasy enough to miss the salmon bake. Besides, she had a few days off from providing the early chow line for students.

The main four buildings, one on each corner of the three-acre grounds, included his two-bedroom log cabin; Sam and Mary's, which was the same size; the storage structure; and the larger dining and lecture hall, which could seat up to forty. Behind the lecture hall in the even thicker spruce and alder trees were two bunk-houses, a fairly large one for men and a smaller one for women because relatively fewer came to the camp.

The two homes on-site were cozy but basic, and the bunkhouses even more so with the bucket showers and Port-a-Johns outside, whereas the two cabins had flush toilets and septic tanks. It was roughing it for sure, but luxurious compared to being out on the trail or track-ing in the forests around here.

"Morning," Quinn said to Sam, who was bent over the big stove, stirring something. Quinn hit the kitchen refrigerator for orange juice, then got a cup of coffee from the urn. "You're a nice guy, you know, to fill in for Mary so she can sleep late. How's she feeling?"

"So far, so good. So, you ever gonna find a woman out here in the boondocks—which we both know is paradise on earth."

Quinn had to laugh. "Don't start on lovelorn ad-vice for me. You sound like my mother. Who would want a guy who lives mostly in the Alaskan bush—alternating with a New York hotel or my mother's New Jersey condo now and then?"

"How 'bout one of them sisters at the lodge?"

"Would you give it a rest, Sam? No sparks fly, just

friendship," he muttered, and downed the juice and then had some coffee. "Hey, where are the pancakes, my man?"

"Steel-cut oatmeal's good for you," Sam said, putting two steaming bowls of it on the table. "I threw in some raisins like Mary does. Beats granola bars, pemmican and all those plants and stuff you eat out on the trail."

Sam and Mary Spruce were Quinn's closest friends here. Sam's father had been a trapper in the area for years. Trapper Jake had taught both men when they were young everything they knew about tracking and survival in the wilds, whatever the season. Like Quinn's father, Jake was gone now, but Sam and Q-Man not only carried on the special knowledge of tracking and wilderness survival, but were now sharing it through Quinn's books and cable show.

More than once, Sam had tried to teach his younger brother, Josh, some of the skills he had been taught by their father, but Josh wanted no part of it, even to escape doing odd jobs here and at the lodge. Trapper Jake had been puzzled and hurt that Josh was not interested. With the internet now available here, Josh had become an online gamer, even made money that way to supplement his salaries from the camp and the lodge.

Josh lived above the barbershop in town, though he camped out in warm weather and didn't want to stay with Sam and Mary. Maybe Josh was just a loner, not unusual in the wilds of Alaska.

"Eat up, man," Sam said. "Got to keep your strength up for the new bunch coming in. You working on a new book, too?"

"That I am."

Quinn's books on tracking skills and his occasional

assistance finding missing persons brought many to the camp to learn basic skills. Some students from as far away as Japan and Austria flew into Anchorage and paid hefty fees for lectures and on-the-field training. Some came back for the advanced classes. Quinn and Sam believed such knowledge, especially in an increasingly digital world, was as essential to the human spirit as any other heritage or history.

"So," Sam said, stirring maple syrup into his oatmeal, "you didn't take the bait about the new lady at the lodge. What did you think of her?"

"My friend, I do not need you for a dating service. She's Meg and Suze's cousin from near Chicago, come to visit and run the lodge gift shop. That's it."

"Oh, yeah, the same gift shop you told me last night you'd be glad to drop off some of our DVDs instead of my doing it this time. Not that many folks just happen to pass through Falls Lake in general, 'less they want to scuba dive the lake to look at the lost pioneer village. I swear, after all these years, I wish Mary would get over losing her grandparents there. But hey, I saw you watching the city girl, Alex. You think she's running from something?"

"Isn't everyone?"

"Never mind trying to get me off track. You're busted, man. You liked the looks of her."

"She seemed…friendly but wary. Intriguing for that reason, that's all."

Quinn was glad Sam finally cut the conversation as they downed their breakfast and more coffee, then went back to what Quinn's dad used to call "shooting the breeze." They discussed what topics might be good to suggest to their cable TV producer, Geoff Baldwin, who was bringing his wife, Ginger, with him this time since the weather was still warm. They were glad he was bringing his wife rather than sending Brent Bayer back again. His lawyer and top investor, Brent, was a control freak.

Mary came in, looking tousled, her long, reddish hair loose instead of pulled back into a ponytail. She patted Quinn on the shoulder and kissed Sam's cheek, then dished out oatmeal for herself. They were a happy pair, though he knew they wanted children, who did not seem to appear.

Quinn admired their marriage. They reminded him of his parents before the tragedy. Solid, but a bit spicy.

"So," Mary asked, her green eyes riveted on Quinn, "Sam says there was a pretty, single new guest visiting her cousins at the lodge. What did you think of her? I hear you chatted her up some. Don't know why all three of those girls are still single."

"No playing matchmaker," Quinn warned, pointing a finger at her. "Your better—I mean, your worse—half has already tried."

She just gave him a smug little smile. Maybe they'd been talking about that last night. Pillow talk. Had he been so obvious? Not to Alex Collister, he hoped.

"What, am I being tracked by both of you?" he challenged, raising his voice. "Gonna put me under surveillance to be sure I behave—or don't?"

"I know all about striking a match and causing instant flame and fire," Mary countered, ignoring his phony bluster. "It was that way between me and Sam from the first. I'll check her out myself, but Sam and I rest our case." She rolled her eyes, then went back to drinking coffee.

"Both of you have been working too hard and you're losing it, so I'm glad we have a few days off," Quinn said, rising. "When Geoff and Ginger get here, we have better—serious—things to talk about."

He washed his dishes with a scrub brush in cold water and headed for the door. He was going to stop to pick up those DVDs of the most recent *Tracker Q-Man* TV seasons and drop them off at the lodge gift shop.

"Everyone was so nice to pitch in last night to unload my truck," Alex told Suze as they stood in the Gifts and More log cabin after breakfast. Suze had just spent an hour going over the business end of things here: using the cash register, keeping inventory, storing and ordering supplies.

On his leash, Spenser followed tight to Alex's heels on the rough flagstone path as he had ever since their arrival—except when he was cavorting with Chip or trying to dig in flower beds. Scottish terriers were bred to root out rabbits and even rats. "It took no time at all," she added, "and these boxes of my herbal products they put in here are heavy."

"You'll find it's all for one and one for all in this community when there's a problem or task. Here's one of the two keys to this building for you to keep," Suze said, extending what looked like an old skeleton key. "Despite the unpopulated area, I'd lock it if you come in for a restroom break, to eat or whatever. We advertise in town, but most of our guests are our lodgers or guys who are here for the tracking and survival school."

"I figured they'd be kept really busy there—classroom and field trips, so to speak."

"Oh, guess I didn't tell you. It starts in a couple of

days, but students often come early and sometimes stay late, either here or at a couple of B and Bs in town. They have only cold water at the camp unless they boil it. Even Quinn, Sam and his wife, Mary, come in for hot showers sometimes, so we keep one room at the end of your hall for that. Their camp staff lives mostly in town, so they have gas heat and septic tanks like we do here. Listen, I have to make some phone calls, then zip into town for supplies. I'll take you with me next time, introduce you around, but I know you want to put things to rights here."

"I do. Thanks for everything. I hope to open up this afternoon or definitely tomorrow so you can mention that in town or in the lodge. I'll just make a handwritten sign for my beauty products and display them in that corner there. I'll use that old door on top of the barrel you showed me out back to make a rustic display. I'll add some flowers or plants to soften the effect. I was really thrilled to see you have a great growing season here with the cool-weather pansies and asters."

"We're not far from early hard frosts next month. Just dig up a few of the plants crowded in by the front door of the lodge—or your little Spenser will. Out there, near the tree line, is our shed, and it's loaded with planters and pots we don't use."

Suze headed out the door. Alex blinked back tears again at how kind everyone was, how helpful and generous. At home, at least since working at the vet clinic and catering to Lyle's schedule and demands, she seemed to have no close friends but only acquaintances. She should have realized she was in trouble since her best friend was her dog. Lyle had been a lover but never really a friend, because he was always her superior and let her know it. Now that she thought about it from this distance, it was as if she were his pet to be coddled but controlled—kept on a leash.

She shuddered, grateful she was safe and free, then, after assessing her own life, took a moment to assess the stock here in the store. Mosquito spray in bright metal cans. She'd overheard more than once last night that it was only the alder wood smoke keeping the "little buggers" at bay and that "real" Alaskans used more subtle, natural ways to ward off insects. Also, someone had joked that mosquitoes were the official state insect.

She saw some rustic antiques here. Over to the far side were displayed an antique-looking Antiques sign, a copper kettle and a lovely array of hand-carved duck decoys. There were examples of scrimshaw and beautiful baskets of several sizes, several made with what was labeled as porcupine quills. She'd have to keep an eye on Spenser so he didn't try to chase porcupines, if they lived nearby. Despite his small size and one eye, like his breed, he was strong-willed and could be fierce.

She fingered quilted or woven place mats on a counter that also held a display of small, charming, wood-framed paintings Suze had done of scenes in both warm weather and the dead of winter.

And now, she thought, her own prettily packaged products would be put on display. She bent to unpack her first box. Then, hopefully with help from a tech-savvy computer person, she could lock down her website against any hacking and figure out how to erase her digital footprint, or at least smudge it. That way Lyle couldn't ever find and harm it—or her.

6

Alex was on her knees, still unpacking products, when a long shadow fell across her feet. She looked up, expecting Suze was back, thinking her little watchdog should have barked, though he had his head up and his ears on alert.

A tall form filled the door she'd left open for fresh air. She blinked into the light while Spenser got up and gave a single bark of greeting, not of warning.

"Sorry to startle you," Quinn Mantell said. "I needed to drop off these DVDs of our TV show, because they sold out and—ah, some of these are new episodes." He glanced at Spenser. "Okay for a pickup? Spenser, I mean. Is it okay if I pick him up?"

"Sure. He seems to like you and he's often wary of new people—or someone he doesn't like. I appreciate your remembering his name," she said, getting to her feet but thinking how different this was from the way the little guy would have greeted Lyle.

"So, not to be nosy, but how did he lose an eye?" he asked as he scooped up the dog, wagging tail and all. Only then did she realize she hadn't unhooked his leash, so she stepped forward to do that. Again, Quinn smelled of fresh air and pine—freedom.

"He's a rescue," she explained, stepping back and putting the leash on the counter. "I'm not sure exactly what happened, but his first owner hurt him, then more or less abandoned him. I was afraid no one would want him from the shelter. It's a tough world for little animals, even domestic ones. I would have taken in more rescues or strays, but where I lived had a one-dog rule. And my living in one bedroom here means it's just Spenser and me for now."

Had she overexplained? Rattled on too much?

Their eyes met. His were like green lasers, totally focused on her before he looked down at the dog again. She watched as his big hand, the one still holding the sack, stroked Spenser's head. A big, tanned hand. She remembered the feel of his rough skin when they shook hands yesterday. She liked that he wasn't someone who had to fill the air with talk, so that what he said seemed to really matter.

"Here, let me take your DVDs." He passed the paper sack to her. "I know right where they go. So what was your Scottie's name when you were growing up?"

He hesitated a moment, almost as if he couldn't remember or had made that up, but no—he just looked sad and almost as if he couldn't speak. He probably still missed the dog. She could surely understand that.

"It wasn't very original or imaginative, but I do have a good imagination now," he added with a slight crimp of his lips. "It was Scottie. He died too early, and I—I never replaced him."

Quinn's voice snagged. Some childhood nightmare buried deep, she thought.

"So," he went on, clearing his throat when she could have kicked herself for not saying something to change the subject, "I hear you sell herbal beauty products. I like things natural and raw." He picked up one of the jars of Dandelion Body Butter she'd stacked on the counter because they were on top of the first carton.

She watched as he squinted at the small print and lifted one dark eyebrow. He read aloud, "Body butters are rich, so remember that a little bit goes a long way." Like some silly teenager, she started to blush again. She could feel it coming on, darn it.

When she thought he might tease her or even say something suggestive when he looked over at her again, he said instead, "About natural products. Take all these cans of mosquito spray," he said, gesturing and bouncing Spenser a bit as if he were a baby. "The savvy locals simply use cedar wood or smoke to keep bugs away. Mint, yarrow and sage work the same way but not as well."

She was impressed with his knowledge of that. She had a lot to learn here, about herbs and flowers she could use, about everything. And she was touched by how he handled Spenser. But she kept seeing a big, flashing Beware! sign in her head. Lyle had started out chatty, clever, though Spenser had seemed to see right through him from the first.

In the awkward silence, she blurted, "What is the one key thing you tell your students about tracking?"

"Just one thing? Pick up your feet when you walk, don't shuffle. Americans, especially, shuffle. In the wilds, it leaves a trail, and makes noise and slows you down. It's one of the things I can use to track someone, though. Drag marks and footprints can be read like—like labeling on a jar of body butter. How fast the person is moving, if they are getting tired, if they limp, lots more."

"Impressive. Okay. And in return for that, and for being so kind to Spenser, I hope you will accept a jar of Sunflower Skin Cream. For someone who is outside as much as you, it's great. It doesn't have a flowery scent, because I didn't add lilac or rose essence to this one, so it's not feminine. Just the opposite."

She kneeled again and scrabbled around in the carton at her feet, producing a jar.

He extended his hand for it—no, actually, he helped her up before he took the jar. "In exchange I'll take you for a beginner's walk in the woods sometime these next two days before my new class starts. Deal?"

"Just around here? With Spenser?"

"Over to Falls Lake but not with our friend Spenser until I point out some things about having a beloved pet in these woods—for safety's sake."

"He likes Chip. I bet he'll take him for a while. Do you know my favorite saying by Thoreau? He wrote, 'I went to the woods because I wished to live deliberately, to front only the essential facts of life and see if I could not learn what it had to teach, and not, when I came to die, discover that I had not lived.'"

She was astounded he seemed so easily, so suddenly, moved by that quote, more so than he had been earlier when she asked his childhood dog's name. His eyes filled with tears that speckled his lashes when he blinked, but he did not try to brush the tears away.

"Sorry," he said, putting Spenser in her arms but keeping the cream. "The woods—and dying. My father and my dog were mauled and killed by a bear in the woods about fifty miles from here when I was seven and had disobeyed and run on ahead, hiding from them. They were looking for me when...when it happened. I—sorry," he repeated, and wiped a big index finger under one eye.

She felt she'd been punched in the stomach. "Just a kid, you didn't know," she tried to comfort him, but her voice broke, too. She hadn't meant to trigger such a terrible memory. "I—I'm new here and maybe others knew about your tragedy. I realize I have a lot to learn."

"Hey, over fifty percent of the population wasn't born here," he said, seeming back in control already or wanting to change the subject. "They say it's a state full of renegades and thrill seekers, but it's also a place for runaways."

She just stared up at him, strangely feeling as if she were looking at another astounding natural Alaskan scene. What to say, but he held up a hand like a traffic cop. "No, that's all right. Don't apologize. You know," he added with a single sniff, "even a brief walk in the woods can restore us. I like that Thoreau quote. I'll look it up, because it rings true for me. So, I've got guests coming in from New York today and gotta go pick them up at the airport in Anchorage. He's my producer and one of two key investors, flies into town on his private jet, no less. I'll send his wife, who doesn't usually come, over here to check out your products, because she's pretty well connected there, and you never know. After all, who knew that a guy like me would end up on TV? See you then, Alex and Spenser." He lifted a hand in farewell and walked away down the stone path toward the lodge.

She had the feeling he was going to say more, to ask

her something else. But he'd mentioned a walk in the woods. At least he hadn't probed about why she was here, maybe what she was running from.

But what rattled her the most when she had decided to absolutely swear off men at least for several years was that the big stranger really got to her, and suddenly didn't seem like a stranger at all. And he'd shared a tragedy from his past, and maybe, since he'd run on ahead to hide that day his dad died, he somehow blamed himself for what had happened.

She totally understood that and felt for him. She missed a twin sister she had never known whom she may have unintentionally hurt but would love eternally.

"So anything new around here to cover or uncover?" Geoff Baldwin asked Quinn while Ginger was still in the guest bedroom. The two men sat out on the small, screened-in porch Quinn had built on the back of his cabin. It faced the rain forest that hugged his land, so thick with trees that you could not so much as glimpse the lake from here. They each had a tumbler partially filled with Scottish whiskey they kept sipping.

Quinn liked to sit out here at night, and the screens kept the mosquitoes away. He even liked sitting here in the pitch-black night to listen to the forest sounds. He could hear the loons on the lake and, from the distant tundra, the martens' squeaking shouts during mating season.

His mind skipped to Alex Collister. New topics to cover or uncover? Geoff had asked. Quinn wanted to know her better, get closer in more ways than one, but she seemed to put up an invisible barrier. And he didn't want her to bolt if he moved too fast. He had a good sense of tracking, but women were especially hard to read and she—

"Quinn?" Geoff's voice broke in. "You okay? Been working too hard again?"

"No, I'm good."

"Your ratings are, I'll tell you that. Makes it easier to attract new sponsors, maybe get a better spot than ten p.m. Eastern Standard Time one night a week. Brent tells me Ryker's doing a great job with the camera and audio, though we still need you to dub some voice-overs in the studio when you get to New York next time. Man, I wish the LA woman wasn't hanging around. Ryker told me she was coming for a weekend, and she talks him into shopping in Anchorage today before I could tell him to join us here. You let me know if he starts slipping up in other ways, though, since he really knows the ropes, I'd hate to replace him. We've got to listen to Brent's advice, too, and he thinks this Val is a ditz and a distraction."

"Ryker's work has not slipped. But yeah, she does want him to leave Podunk, as I heard her call Falls Lake. You usually don't send Brent Bayer, your lawyer, fixer and main investor, in without you. He's still a happy camper, isn't he?"

"For sure, wants to expand the show, bigger and better, always. He likes visiting here and treats the *Q-Man* franchise as if it were his baby, so I'm grateful for that. You know he likes to keep an eye on things, just like he does his other cable TV investments, though those are mostly in Hollywood."

"I worry that Val wants Ryker to try his skills in California, which would not suit him at all. He really loves the wilderness shoots, and I appreciate that."

"Well, as long as he keeps sending the studio-quality digital material. I take it she won't go out to film with you guys."

"No, I think she'd hate it out in the wilds, anyway, definitely a city girl."

Ginger joined them with her glass of wine. She was as lightly red-haired as Geoff was blond. Though both Baldwins were midfifties, she looked more like a thin model, a natural beauty like…like the woman who made Natural Beauty products. He'd actually tried some of the Sunflower Skin Cream. Smooth. He wondered if she used it on her skin. Just her hands? All over?

Ginger was saying, "This sure is a far cry from the view of skyscrapers and the Hudson River. Quinn, did I ever tell you I had a twentieth-floor, ringside seat to that so-called Miracle on the Hudson? You know, where that pilot landed on the water and saved his crew and passengers? Oh, but you were telling me one of the women who run the lodge lost her husband in a plane crash, so I won't repeat that around here again."

Geoff sighed heavily, so Quinn guessed she told almost everyone about that famous event she had witnessed firsthand, something exciting in her daily life. Hell, she should move here where there was never a dull moment. At least Ginger appreciated the scenery and could tell her Manhattan friends she'd been to raw Alaska, seen wild animals, met the primitive species of the area, including Q-Man Mantell.

Quinn reminded himself to be sure Ginger stopped by Alex's Gifts and More to check out her products. He'd take both of them over. Alex had quoted Thoreau on why he went to the woods. Quinn had to admit he had a new reason to go to the woods, to take a walk and have more time together.

Alex, with Chip and Spenser in tow, enjoyed her personal tour of the lodge by the twins that evening. There was a large, mounted TV in the common room, though not any in the bedrooms. Maybe Alaskans and visitors weren't as hung up on the news or newest shows here. Books and magazines were stashed in one corner with comfy leather chairs. Other seating arrangements were grouped to look out the back windows facing thick forest and the distant Talkeetna Mountains. She knew Falls Lake was out there, too, but you had to hike a ways to see it.

They showed her around the back service rooms, especially the kitchen where they had a cook come in to fix lunches and dinners, though the twins did some of that, too. Suze handled a hearty breakfast buffet and Meg oversaw their two maids and their handyman—Sam's brother, Josh—whom she had met. There was a small break room for the staff near a partly empty storage room where she could wedge in a worktable and electric burners to make her products. It had a window with a view of the gift shop.

Alex formally met the lodge dogs—King, a cocker spaniel, and a boxer mix named Buffy, a stray from town. She could see the boxer had an ear infection, which she'd soon clear up with a spray bottle of apple cider vinegar and water and a hot compress. Then, too, she should probably make some sort of collar cone for a few days so the dog would stop scratching it. She was so glad she could contribute in any way.

She quickly learned that Chip had small plastic toys

he secreted under furniture and behind planters when he saw his mother coming, so Meg was evidently strict on keeping the place picked up and neat. Alone in the common room that night, Alex peeked under a sofa where she'd seen him stash something. Just a Luke Skywalker flier and some other Star Wars space vehicles, quite beat up. Oh, and a World War II–era plastic bomber that had seen better days, too. She wondered if these had been gifts from his father, but she knew better than to ask, at least right now.

Out in the common room, four guests were sitting at tables playing poker and talking about what it would be like to check in at Quinn's camp tomorrow. Three other men had turned on the huge TV screen, and there was Quinn, almost life-size, pointing out different types of animal tracks and how to read where the animals were headed and how much they weighed.

She was surprised to see Josh go by this late with a mop and bucket. He just shook his head at the men glued to the TV. He looked a lot like Sam, but smaller—and then there was that tattoo. He didn't greet anyone, but was probably intent on his work. She wondered if he got paid by the hour or had a set salary. Well, she had a lot to learn around here, let alone in Alaska in general.

She looked back at Quinn on the large screen. She had to admit the man was, well, telegenic. He often looked straight into the camera, and his voice was deep and clear. And the scenery was stunning, if she could make herself look away from him.

Stop it! she told herself. *The last thing in the universe you need right now is to get attracted to some man. One horrific mistake in judgment does not have to lead to another.*

"So, you ready to turn in?" Suze asked. "Beddy-bye awaits. He kind of makes you think of that, doesn't he?" She sighed and nodded at the TV. "You should watch his episode on making an emergency camp and a warm bed and getting a good night's sleep."

They both smiled, and Alex playfully punched Suze's arm as they said good night and went their own ways. Suze had the first bedroom down the hall in the opposite direction from Alex, whereas Meg had the first one on this side of the common room, a room adjoining Chip's. Suze had said Meg and Ryan Metzler had owned a house in town, which Meg could not afford to keep after he died. So in a couple of weeks, Chip would be riding a school bus rather than just walking to his new first grade class in town.

Alex liked the spacious blue and buff bedroom they had given her with its view of the surrounding forest— every window in the lodge must have that. The room even had a cushioned window seat for reading or just looking out. She could see the tips of the Talkeetnas beyond. If she lifted her window, she was sure she could hear the waterfall that fed the lake beyond the trees.

Nearly a century ago, the waterfall had been blocked by several tumbled boulders that made the water level lower and finally disappear for forty-some years. Then a rockslide had opened the path for mountain snowmelt to feed the lake again. She recalled hearing that the years it was a small, dry lake bed, a pioneer town had sprung up there and had later been buried by tons of water.

Lives and property were lost, ended, obliterated, buried. Later, the new town of Falls Lake sprang up a few miles away and had been there for nearly fifty years. But what a shock that loss of life must have been.

Again, it hit her that there was so much new to learn around here. The wild land, the strong, unique people, different animals, the little town she'd barely glimpsed as she drove in. Though she had to be very cautious, she wanted especially to learn about one person—if he could be trusted.

7

It seemed strange to be going on a walk without Spenser in tow—stranger yet to be alone with Quinn. She had decided to take a long lunch break, told her cousins why, and they had been all for it. Alex wasn't sure she herself was all for it, but she couldn't resist.

She wanted badly to ask Quinn why he loved the wilds so much when his father and dog had been attacked and killed there. But she didn't ask that question. She could not bear for him to tear up again.

"Okay," he said as they reached the edge of the lodge's property, "I'd love for us to just have a side-by-side stroll together on this lovely day in this lovely place when I'm with a lovely companion, but you need to learn some things about staying safe around here."

They stopped walking. Looked at each other. He'd just complimented her, hadn't he? But despite this little awkward pause, more was coming.

"You need to learn some degree of wilderness savvy," he told her, sounding in lecture mode now. "Frankly, I'd advise not walking Spenser off these tended grounds into the forest or out on the open tundra, not even over by the lake. I don't want to sound alarmist, but he'd be a tasty morsel for bears, though this area is not heavy with them right now. And we both know Scottish terriers can be recklessly brave. Some people set traps for fur-bearing animals where they should not, and I've seen dogs get caught in them. If you ever came upon a bear, Spenser would start barking, and that would be like a come-get-me advertisement."

"Thanks for the warning. He's much smaller than my cousins' dogs."

"Bears can't see well but they have an excellent sense of smell. You pray you're downwind, not upwind, of them. If one ever charges, as much as it's instinct to run, don't, because that signals that you're game for sure, same with big cats."

"But what do you do if you don't have a gun?"

"Guns don't even stop them fast enough sometimes. You stand your ground and lift your arms to make yourself look bigger than you are," he said, demonstrating. He was over six feet, and that made him tower over her. "It's hard to stand your ground, but you have to learn to do that, Alexis."

"Not to change the subject but, actually, my name is Alexandra."

"Alexandra," he said, his voice softening. "My mother's a nut for British history. Like Queen Alexandra. But just remember what I said. You seem like a woman who can stand her ground. But I'm sure since I blurted out to you my family tragedy, you understand why I wanted you to know all this right away."

"Yes. I'm not sure I stood my ground, though, coming here. I think I ran."

He narrowed his eyes, waiting for her to say more, but she couldn't right now.

"Sometimes," he said in the awkward silence, "you have to run from human predators. But right now, try to follow in my footsteps, okay? If you're willing, we'll take other walks side by side, but I need to give you the newbie lesson right now."

"I'm game."

"Don't say it like that, Queen Alexandra. That's the term for prey around here. Come on, then. Even if you can't match the length of my strides, stick close behind."

"And," she said, "I promise not to shuffle. I will pick up my feet."

He nodded and grinned at that reminder of his earlier advice. They set off on a path, but he cut off it almost immediately. She was glad he'd said to wear long pants, thick socks and good hiking shoes, though she'd had to borrow those from Meg until she could get her own. Despite the warmth of the day, he'd insisted on a long-sleeved shirt over her T-shirt, too.

So, here she was, following and obeying a very attractive man, who told her what to wear and what to do, and she'd only been here two full days. Would she ever learn? And yet this was different. He was so different from Lyle—wasn't he?

Quinn pointed things out to Alex as they headed through the thick trees, then across a stretch of tundra toward Falls Lake. He could tell she was bright and perceptive. Sam had told him once that he and Mary had an instant attraction and that "If it don't hit you right away you want her in more ways than one, it may not stick."

Not exactly Freudian or even logical, but Quinn was

feeling that way about this woman he barely knew. He was glad he'd talked Ginger and Geoff into stopping by Gifts and More tomorrow en route to the airport. After the two of them had talked TV topics all morning, he was grateful Geoff had agreed to accompany Ginger into town to look for gifts to take home, so that freed him up now. In two days, his new class would assemble at the camp.

"So," Alex said, "is there any way to hide who you really are? Not you, I mean, but the human scent on us? Otherwise, we're leaving an odor trail for bears or other predators, aren't we?"

He stopped and turned to her so fast she bumped into him. He'd been going much slower than he ordinarily would have, but she was still slightly out of breath, her lips parted, an intent little frown furrowing her forehead above her sky-blue eyes.

"Good time for lesson number two," he said. "There are ways to mask human scent. So, from the wilderness plant guy to the sweet-smelling flower gal, here's the deal on that."

He took her hand to draw her over to a spot with a big fallen log. He sat, gently pulling her down beside him.

"We're sitting on a cedar trunk and that's another cedar tree over us. Now, see those cedar berries on the ground, the brownish-bluish ones? Those crushed as well as needles from spruce trees can be rubbed on your skin—or traps, or whatever—to conceal human scent. Chewing cedar berries stops bad breath, too, but that is not a hint."

She nodded and smiled, then bit her lower lip as if keeping herself from saying something. He had a huge urge to kiss her, but was it too soon? Not for him, but why had a beautiful woman like this come—maybe fled—to backwoods Alaska? And how long would she really stay?

"What do you think of the global warming debate here in Alaska?" she asked him in a slight lull in their conversation.

She was good at jumping to new subjects when silent, awkward moments stretched between them.

"It's mostly a problem north of here with melting icebergs," he told her, "but the tundra around here is being affected, too. The permafrost is melting, and farther north, some native tribes may have to be relocated. It's kind of nice our short summer season of May through September is getting a bit longer, though. Hey," he added, reaching out to grab her arm and pull her back from a tall, flowering plant she was reaching for. "Hands off. That's devil's club."

"What? Really? It looks pretty with its big leaves and so tall, it stands out. Devil's club?"

"It's deceptive, good and bad. Some pioneers and tribes used it for medicinal tea and salve, but spines are hiding under the leaves—see? They break off and dig into the skin of animals or hikers, then fester and infect. Not what they seem."

"Another good lesson from Q-Man," she said. "Thank you."

She looked up into his eyes. He had to steady himself to not reach for her. He felt her magnetic pull. But she'd built up some sort of invisible barrier he was either going to have to tear down or jump over. "By the way," he added, "I've seen animals of all sorts hurt by devil's club, so another good reason to keep Spenser out of the woods."

She nodded, stood and stepped back from him as if she were suddenly afraid. Not of him, he hoped.

"Let's go look at this end of Falls Lake," he said, "because it goes on for nearly a mile toward that closest mountain. And even if you've heard the lake's basic story, I'll bet I can tell you more. It's a hard story to hear, but people need to know the past to prepare for the future."

She looked at him again, then away. He'd thought she might say something, even confess something. But she just nodded and said, "All right. Let's go."

Alex felt deeply moved, not only by the stunning view but by the company. Quinn Martell was knowledgeable and helpful. Yet it scared her he was also charismatic and…and tempting. Except for that, in this wild, awesome, vast place, she felt safe with Quinn if not from Quinn.

"You know," Alex told him as they stood on the shingle shore and looked out over teal-blue Falls Lake together, "it's so beautiful here but ominous, too. I mean, with the trees seeming to lean in with their long shadows, then the dark silhouette of the mountain creeping closer and the muted sound of the falls feeding the lake. And it's strange to see a shore that isn't sand but boulders and these little stones. They don't look like what I think of as shingles. But the water is crystal clear."

"Cold, too, even in our summer. And actually it's a bit silty under the surface."

"Still, I should make some products with mountain water from the falls, some special Alaskan cream or salve."

"Aha. You can take the girl out of her brewing room

but can't take the brewing room out of the girl—or something like that."

"I'll bet you always live your love of the wilds," she countered.

"Yeah, that's true, even when I'm in New York City for publicity or to meet with my producer, who is here now. Which reminds me, when I drive them to the airport tomorrow evening, I'll bring them to see your Gifts and More shop. Ginger's as good as a professional shopper, comes with one suitcase or more empty, goes home with them full."

"Her husband's your producer?"

"Right. He handles finances and program control, hires the on-site videographer, liaises with our lawyer and sponsors, oversees the assembling of the half-hour shows. Geoff and Ginger Baldwin are New Yorkers through and through, so this is like being on Mars for them. By the way, have you asked Meg and Suzanne what's with the title of their shop? What's the 'More'?" he asked, turning to her, though his squinting into the sun did nothing to dim his steady green gaze.

"Just the experience of being in and shopping for lovely, unique local things in a lovely place," she told him, wondering if he was teasing again—asking if the "More" was her, like that old book about airline stewardesses, *Coffee, Tea or Me*. "And maybe the 'More' is the items we sell about your program," she said, and he grinned and nodded.

They sat on a tree trunk that had whitened like other driftwood nearby. They were silent for a moment, just taking it all in. She was so strangely content and yet so stirred up inside for being in this precious place with him.

"So what was the extra information you mentioned

about the lake?" she asked. "Its past tragedy, you mean?
I looked at one of the brochures in the shop about Falls
Lake and the little pioneer town being buried under tons
of water once, then the town it covered being submerged."

He took a breath and expelled it hard before looking intently at her again. "Buried beneath the water
here is a small pioneer prospectors' settlement. You
met Sam. His wife, Mary, had an upset stomach so she
didn't come to the salmon bake. Anyhow, her grandparents were in the little village here when the falls let
loose. Mary had been reared by her grandmother and
loved her a lot—supposedly resembles her. With others, including Mary's grandfather, the old woman died
in the sort of tidal wave. Anyway, some say the lake is
haunted at night by at least one soul who died under it."

She turned more toward him, drawing one leg up on
the tree trunk. "Really? So have you ever heard or seen
proof—suggestions—that is true?"

"Promise me you won't try to get me locked up, Sam
or Mary, either? Sam's brother, Josh, has heard it, too.
Yeah, crying, even wailing at night in the darkness,
can't tell whether it's a man or a woman."

"Do they hear it at the lodge?"

"Apparently not—maybe too tightly locked up at
night. Anyhow, the lawyer in New York who's our
main investor is pushing for the ghost stuff in future
shows. Anything to up the audience demographics is
okay with him."

"Terrible about that tidal wave. I didn't know that,
but then there's so much I don't know about my new
home."

"But it is true," he went on, shaking his head as his
voice became quieter, "that the falls do seem louder at

night, as if they'll let loose again. Anyhow, my producer and I were recently discussing whether or not to include the tragedy of Falls Lake in a segment, and I said no. I don't want an influx of people tramping through the area, looking for 'ghosts' and bothering people like my team."

"It would be like tracking the past, and an unusual, dramatic and tragic one at that."

"True. Did my advisers hire you to bring that up? Anyhow, that tragedy already brings in occasional scuba divers or historians now and then to examine the water-covered ruins, so you may see them at the lodge as well as my students. I have a good friend, a search and rescue diver, who's a professor at Michigan State where I went to college. He wants to come check it out sometime soon."

He promised to take her on a hike clear around to see the falls themselves sometime, and they headed back. Again, she felt so safe with him—that is, from anything but her growing attraction to him. But she'd learned her lesson, and she would not let those feelings show or give them a chance to grow. Not now. She just couldn't. Why, less than two weeks ago she'd been—stupidly—engaged to another man, one she didn't really know until it was almost too late.

But Quinn had given her a real gift today, and she'd thank him for that. He'd shared advice that would keep her and Spenser safe. She loved the forest, the tundra and this lake, partly because there was no way Lyle could ever, ever find her here. Besides, his mere presence would pollute this pristine, precious place.

8

"Not only darling packaging, but the products have lovely descriptions, too," Ginger Baldwin pronounced as she looked over the offerings in Alex's new display the next day. "These are useful as well as sweet but not overwhelmingly scented."

Encased in tight, black leather pants with a short matching jacket and boots, Ginger proceeded to sniff at the samplers. Alex wished she had not brought Chip's dog out here with Spenser, because Buffy kept trying to dig at her infected area. Alex had sprayed it with water and vinegar again, and the dog couldn't get to the ear because she'd made her a protective cone from a trimmed-up kitchen funnel.

"Not Alaskan products per se," Ginger went on, "but they'll still make great gifts. I like to give unique things to my female friends. Metro as they are, would you believe they all love to watch Quinn?"

"Yes, I can believe that," Alex told her with a little smile. "He is rather unique."

"And unassumingly macho. Despite the fact the show targets men, I hear a lot of women watch it, probably thinking of tracking Q-Man himself."

As they shared a quiet laugh, Alex felt a little guilty. She suspected Quinn was interested in her as a woman and not just a friend of his friends. But the last thing she needed, until she could heal and get some perspective and trust another man, was falling for Q-Man Mantell. She kept telling herself every chance she got, but it didn't seem to be often enough.

"I've only seen a little bit of one tracking episode," she admitted to Ginger. "But I'll watch more, especially since they are filmed around here, and I need to get to know the area."

"I have a feeling you'll be seeing more of the real, 'off-TV' Quinn," Ginger added with a roll of her eyes at the men who were looking at the wooden duck carvings across the shop.

"I hear he gets rather busy the week a class is in town. A few of the ones staying here until they report in tomorrow have been in the shop, mostly buying gifts for wives or girlfriends back home, a few shopping for things for their kids or even themselves."

Still whispering, Ginger said, "I'd just as soon Geoff left me home, but the weather was fine this time and so is the shopping, partly thanks to you. Listen, I'd like to take quite a few of these lilac and rose lip balms and, oh, the daisy vanilla one, too. And some of this sunflower salve and the lavender oatmeal soap. So where are you planning to concoct these here?"

"Probably in the storage room at the rear of the lodge, unless I can get a room added out the back here."

"So you're here for a while. Well, don't freeze to death. Now, I know a lot of movers and shakers in the fashion world of Manhattan, and they will love these. There may be an opportunity for you to sell them there, and I'd love to oversee that—no commission necessary, just something new and interesting to do. You see, ever since I had the horror and honor of watching Captain Sully Sullenberger save that planeload of people that went into the Hudson River ten years ago, I was inspired to help, too, though I'd never come up to that kind of a feat."

"I'm grateful. Actually, I've been harassed on my website and had to shut it down for a while. But I'll see it's resurrected soon when I find some computer-savvy person here."

"Here? Around Falls Lake?" Ginger asked so loudly Alex jumped. "Now there's a challenge. Until Quinn helped to bring in those cell towers, this place was back in the last century, buried like that little village under the lake. As much as I can't stand the airhead hanger-on who has attached herself to our videographer, Ryker, I have to agree with her that this place is pretty backwoods."

"I noticed her when I first arrived. She does tend to stand out."

"And she'd love to drag Ryker out of here, turn him into some sort of great Hollywood filmmaker. I told her, 'Dream on and move on,' but she's stubborn. Now back to your website situation, not to play fairy godmother, but give me your email address, and I'll have a tech contact you. He's in Manhattan but that doesn't matter. You do not need someone screwing up your life online or in real life, and I trust this man."

"Better take her advice, whatever it is," Geoff told Alex as he came over to the checkout counter with a carved and painted Merganser duck decoy in his hands. "I do, then Q-Man here takes my advice, right?" he asked Quinn.

"Absolutely, at least concerning business deals and scripts."

Alex felt he watched her as she punched in the multiple purchases his friends had made. They all said goodbye, and she watched the three of them trek back toward Quinn's car so he could drive them to the airport. Suddenly, she felt lonely and wished she could go with them. Ginger had been a bit overpowering but very kind. And she wasn't sure when she'd see Quinn again since his new class of students reported in tomorrow.

Two more of the very men who would be moving from the lodge to the camp tomorrow meandered into the shop.

"So, that was Q-Man himself, right?" the austere-looking man with the crew cut asked. He had a pronounced German accent. "We got a bet on that, and we'd like to buy what he bought."

She thought about making up a big list of items, but she told them, "Actually, I suggest buying some of his DVDs to take home with you. He brought those over himself yesterday."

"Do you spray something in here with vinegar to make colors shine?" he asked, looking around.

Alex heard Spenser sneeze. She turned to see him wrinkle his nose as Buffy made another attempt to rake her ear with a back paw. It was then that she, so used to the scents in this small shop, realized how kind Ginger, Geoff and Quinn had been not to mention that the place must reek of vinegar and dogs. And for Ginger to say she'd take on representing the products with her friends. Whether they were from Manhattan, Germany or Falls Lake, this place made people kind, and Alex so appreciated that. Lyle had never seemed so far away.

* * *

On his way back from the airport, Quinn parked his truck at the lodge and trekked back to the gift shop again. Damn, but he was interested in the "More" the sign promised. He didn't want Alex to bolt, but next week was going to be really busy, and surely it wouldn't be too forward to ask her to go into town for dinner when he'd only known her a couple of days. And there were a few hours of daylight left.

If that didn't fly, he'd try to stay at the lodge for dinner, but then he'd probably have cousins and dogs galore hanging on as well as Chip. He liked Chip, wanted a son of his own someday, but he'd need a wife first and what woman except the amazing Mary Spruce would want to live in a log cabin in a tracking and survival camp out in the wilds? He and Sam had kept themselves busy boiling bathwater for Ginger during her short stay. He was surprised Ginger had agreed to stay at the camp instead of insisting on the lodge or a place in town, but she'd given in to Geoff's desire to "rough it." No doubt that would be another story she could tell her friends besides seeing the "Miracle on the Hudson."

Well, if he ever did take the plunge to get married, he'd get a house in town, real high living in a place with a population of about 420, but it did have two good places to eat. And he wanted to take Alexandra Collister to his favorite.

He saw she was just closing up. She had her little watchdog, Spenser, in one arm, but the lodge dog Buffy—the conehead—was nowhere in sight. She may be nervous and shy, but she seemed so right for this place.

It was nuts, but for the first time in years, even when

he buried himself in work, he wanted a wife and family. He'd seen how devastated his mother had been by their family tragedy, how it had taken her years and a new love to climb out of the pit. He wondered if something tragic like that had happened to Alex.

"Quinn!" she called when she saw him. "Did they make their flight? Is everything all right?"

"They have their own plane, so it waits for them. But I was just wondering if it's too late to ask you to go into town to dinner. There's a good roadhouse-type place there." He reached out, wanting to touch her but petting Spenser instead. At least the dog loved him.

"Oh. You mean tonight. I—I told Meg and Suze I'd eat with them and give them a demo of my products. You know, girls' night."

He almost wondered if that was an excuse, like "I have to wash my hair."

"It's my last night of real freedom for a week," he said. "Days are busy, too."

"I—I know. I met several of your current students, two men from Berlin. They talked about the schedule you set for them with lectures, demos, mini field trips and all."

He put one hand on the door she had just locked, partly blocking her in against it.

"Queen Alexandra, I'm a very direct person, so I'll just say this. I think we could be good friends, maybe more than that. But you seem skittish or elusive or maybe you just don't want to spend time with me. How should I read this?"

She heaved a huge sigh and looked away, then back. "Quinn, I came here to escape someone I made a huge, stupid mistake with."

"I'm not him."

"I know. You certainly are not. It's just—I messed up, really endangered myself. I need time to get myself together. I'm not good at handling emotions right now."

"I understand. And if you don't want to talk about it, we won't. I can imagine it's a lot to come to a very different, faraway place with baggage—you know what I mean. I've been running from blaming myself for something terrible for years, but life goes on. My mother eventually remarried, and she's very happy."

She looked up at him right in his eyes instead of shifting her gaze away. That hadn't come out just right, so he hoped she got what he meant. Suzanne had mentioned that Alex hadn't been married so she couldn't be running from that. If she wasn't going to tell him, he'd ask Suzanne or Meg.

"Quinn, thank you so much for asking me, and for being a friend to me and to Suze and Meg. Chip, too—he looks up to you. If—if I could just take a rain check…"

"When you're ready—if you're ready—let me know. See you sometime."

He headed for his car, not going through the lodge but around the side to the parking lot. He didn't look back. He was hoping she'd come after him or at least call his name to make him turn around.

But she didn't. So, damn it, he didn't.

9

"You did what?" Suze asked, pretending to fall back as if she were stunned. "Meg, this crazy woman turned Quinn down for a date. Oh, sorry, hon," she added, giving Alex a quick hug, "because I understand with all you've just been through—but dinner with Quinn instead of us sounds like a no-brainer!"

Meg was hovering now, too. The sun was down, and the common room mostly deserted since their guests had turned in early to prepare for their 7:00 a.m. start time at the tracking and survival camp. Chip had gone to bed, taking his two dogs, who slept in his room. He was happy to have Buffy out of her torture collar, as he called it. That meant Spenser was their only canine companion up this late, but he was snoozing by the empty hearth where he could still keep an eye on Alex.

"Sure, we understand," Meg said, flopping into her seat at the dinner table where Suze had laid out a meal for the three of them. Large salads with salmon soup. "It's just that Suze had a crush on him for years before she started dating that lawyer in town. And Q-Man seems hesitant to form emotional ties other than with

Sam and Mary Spruce. He's been close to Sam for a long time. Sam's dad was like a second father to Quinn, taught him tracking. What was his name, Suze?"

"Tracker Jake—died way before we came here. He only passed his skills on to Sam and Quinn, evidently because Josh was too stubborn and refused to master tracking."

"Josh doesn't say much, as you may have noticed, Alex. He ekes out a living working here and for Sam and Quinn at the camp, but we heard he's been making some money in online gaming contests of some sort. Who was it," she asked Suze, "who told us he'd like to open up a gaming lounge in Anchorage? Sam or Mary?"

"Not my thing," Suze said with a shrug. "Don't remember."

Alex wanted to hear more about Quinn, so she brought the conversation back around to him. "Quinn said something tragic happened in his past, during his childhood." She was fishing for more information on Quinn's early tragedy, but she didn't want to blurt it out if he hadn't told anyone around here.

"Did he tell you that, too?" Suze asked. "Already? We only found out about his childhood trauma when his mother visited here a couple of years ago. She read about a bear attack in the Yukon while she was here and then told us about her and Quinn's loss. His father was mauled and killed by a bear—and Quinn found him. You think he would have become a hater and hunter of bears, instead of just a wildlife expert and tracker."

Alex put her soupspoon back in the bowl. "When he warned me about bears and keeping Spenser out of the woods, he mentioned he'd lost his father and his own dog, a Scottie, to a bear attack, but said it was not in this area. And I certainly got the message it wasn't a great topic to pursue."

"His father was a real outdoorsman, I hear," Meg added. "They were from Lansing, Michigan, but the dad loved Alaska, and they came for several summers before his dad died. I didn't know about Quinn's pet dog. No wonder he took to Spenser."

"But," Suze said to Meg as if the twins were finishing each other's thoughts, "the miracle is Quinn took to Alex so fast. Well, I didn't mean that quite like it came out."

Alex said, "Did Quinn's mother say that he at least partly blamed himself for tragedy, because he was hiding from his dad and that drew him in the direction where the bear attacked?"

"Oh, no!" Meg said as tears matted her eyelashes. "We didn't know that. It's like—well, Chip has never gotten over his father's loss, even though he had nothing to do with the plane crash. He'll say things like, 'Mom, if it wasn't my birthday, Dad wouldn't have tried to fly home a day early in that bad weather.' 'Mom, maybe he was thinking about my new bike and wasn't paying attention to his flying, just for that one second he hit the mountain.'"

The three of them grasped hands in the middle of the table and said nothing for a moment.

"So sorry, sis," Suze said to Meg, "that so many things bring his loss back."

Meg nodded, then whispered, "Let's change the subject. This was supposed to be girls' night, not a sobfest."

Alex said, "I'm thankful I'm here. That you took me in and gave me your support and trust."

They all wiped their eyes, blew noses and went back

to eating cold soup. How Alex wished there were four of them here, that she had Allie with her in body and not just in spirit. And would she ever have the moment—the courage—to share with them the huge loss in her life? Not losing Lyle and her life back in Illinois, but losing her own twin sister.

Late the next afternoon, Alex not only minded the store but cleaned it, washing windows, sweeping the floor, dusting products. Poor Spenser sneezed more than once, and she did, too. The light wind was so fresh outside that she kept the door ajar while her little watchdog yawned and slept in the sun.

Very few customers came in today now that the lodge guests had moved to a bunkhouse down the road for their first day of tracker school. She wondered how the initial greetings and orientation were managed. Did Quinn do all the lecturing and demos or did Sam Spruce help, too? She'd had so little time to meet Sam.

Spenser gave a quick, double bark-bark so she knew someone was coming.

"Hey, hi!" a female voice called to her. Alex stood and turned around from where she'd been wiping off one of the lower storage shelves.

It was the videographer's girlfriend, she of the frizzy hair and false eyelashes, Alex could see this close up. Spenser looked up, tilted his head, barked twice more in greeting, then when she came in, went back to sleep as if this visitor was not half as interesting as Alex thought she was.

"Hello. Sorry, I didn't hear you coming," she told the woman. "I'm just setting up the shop, making it my own since I arrived. I have some beauty products you might like—not that you need them, but I make them myself, so they're unique."

"Worth a lookie-look," she said with a world-weary sigh as she sauntered in. "I am absolutely bored with the gift shops in this little berg of a town."

She was not wearing her belted leather jacket this time but a hot-pink hoodie with the hood thrown back and the tightest jeans Alex had ever seen, especially around here where it seemed people went for comfort first. On Ginger a similar outfit had seemed natural, but this one—and the woman in it—looked even more out of place. With all that white-blond, curly hair, maybe she couldn't have pulled the hood up, anyway.

"Welcome. I'm Alex," she told her.

"Val Chambers, a California girl through and through. Oh, that's a cute watchdog. I thought he was fake at first, you know, like a chi-chi doorstop—and some of those bark when you enter."

She sighed again, ignored Spenser, who was sleeping, then frowned as she picked up various products and squinted to read the names and labels. Despite her large breasts, she was petite.

"I'm here because of a man—aren't we all?" she said with a sigh. "Actually, my goal in life is to get the heck out of this *Mayberry RFD* place—with my man. Why are you here?"

Alex blinked at that. Yes, she was here because of a man, but not the way this woman meant, and no way was she going to confide in her. Spenser had been right to try to ignore her. He seemed to have a sixth sense about whom to trust.

"The women who own and run this lodge are rela-

tives," Alex said, "and I was glad to escape my hometown for a while."

"Apparently, the winters around this place are deadly
boring, so hope you're planning on being here short
term. Might as well be encased in ice, I hear. Mary
Spruce says it's lovely, affording time to rest and to
spend with people, but I don't pay much attention to
her. It's pretty obvious she wishes I'd disappear. Quinn,
too—probably the whole lot of them. They're being really selfish keeping an extremely talented man back,
not to mention the salaries are pitiful around here, as
I'm sure you know..." With a shake of her curly head
she went back to surveying Alex's products.

At least Ms. Val Chambers bought several lip balms
and a skin cream, though she shook her head and sighed
at most of the merchandise as if it were way beneath
her. Not a great way to make friends, Alex thought, so
if this camera guy, Ryker, liked her, he must have a one-
track mind for what she offered. No, that wasn't fair, she
scolded herself as the woman finally left. Alex leaned
in the doorway to see her walk around the lodge without going in. In a few minutes she drove away in what
looked to be a luxury car, so out of place around here.

Sitting on the tall wooden stool behind the counter in
the sudden quiet, Alex started to nod off. At least that
woman was right that it was another world here. So far
from home...but where was home now? Strangely, she
was starting to feel at home here...

She was running away to come here, running far
across the country. Lyle was after her, reaching for her,
shouting, "You are mine or the end! A plane will crash
into the mountain, or a bear will eat you. I will find
you! You cannot hide! The end!"

She heard someone give a little scream. Her head bobbed and jerked her awake. Oh, just a bad dream. So far she'd been successfully avoiding those.

She glanced over at Spenser, but the spot where he'd been sleeping held only sun on the cedar board floor. She got up and came around the counter to see if he was eating from his bowl she'd hidden in the corner. His leash was there, nicely curled up as she had left it. If he needed to go outside to use a tree or wanted to take a walk, the clever little guy had always brought it to her, as if to say, *Let's get going!*

As her heart began to pound, she shook herself fully awake. "Spenser? Where are you?"

Surely he wouldn't have gone outside on his own. She went to the door, which stood barely ajar, and opened it wide to glance outside.

"Spenser? Here, boy. Here, Spenser!"

She stepped outside. Maybe he'd gone outside, back to the lodge to find Chip. He loved Chip, even the other two dogs, and that made her think how he'd enjoy belonging to a family.

She grabbed her purse, locked the door and darted toward the lodge. But what if he was out here somewhere, came back to the shop and found it deserted?

She cupped her hands around her mouth. "Spenser! Here, Spenser!"

Nothing. No one. Bird sounds. The wind in the trees.

She tore into the lodge. Suze was wiping some oil on fireplace mantel with a white cotton rag.

"Suze, have you seen Spenser? Or Chip?"

"Chip's in his room. Meg's making him read out loud because he starts first grade soon, and he's nervous. Wait—you mean Spenser isn't with you?"

"I fell asleep just for a minute or two—and when I looked up, he was gone. I had a customer—Val, that girlfriend of Ryker's—but she left, and Spenser would have barked if she came back."

"I'm pretty sure the lodge door's been closed, but go ahead and call for him inside here, and I'll go check with Chip."

Alex ran through the back rooms, the kitchens, the halls. She checked his little bed in her room, however futile that was because her door had been closed and locked. She glanced at herself in the mirror over the dresser as she rushed by. It was as if Allie were distressed, too, rushing to help look. *Oh, dear Lord, please don't let me have brought my Spenser all the way here just for something awful to have happened to him.*

She ran back out and saw Suze rushing toward her. "Chip hasn't seen him, and he and Meg want to help look. They're leaving the other two dogs in his room. Let's go along the edge of the forest and call for him."

Alex felt sick to her stomach as the four of them walked the perimeter of the property, calling into the forest that now seemed so dense and dark, despite the fact that night was still three or four hours away.

"Wish we would've taught Buffy or King to be trackers," Chip said, taking Alex's hand. "'Cause he might've gone after snowshoes or something."

"Snowshoes?"

"You know, the kind of rabbit. They've been around here lately."

Alex felt as if someone had hit her hard in the stomach. Scottish terriers were originally bred to root out and chase rabbits, even rats. But wouldn't he have barked to wake her if he'd gone after one? And Quinn had said to keep him out of the forest. Bears, wildcats, even just stumbling into that horrible needlelike bush called devil's club could be deadly.

But Chip had given her an idea when he'd said that Buffy and King were not trackers, because she knew someone who was. Yes, he was no doubt busy lecturing or demonstrating tracking to his new host of students, but she was desperate. Would Quinn be willing to help after she'd turned him down for a date? But none of that mattered now, at least not to her.

She had to find Spenser, get him back.

"I know Quinn's probably busy with his new group," she told the three of them. "Darkness will set in soon, too, but I need to ask him for help. If he's tied up, maybe he knows someone who could help me. I have to try, or I'd never forgive myself. If Spenser comes back, call me on my cell. I could call Quinn, but I need to ask in person."

Meg and Suze exchanged silent but very loud glances.

"Sure, but don't you go into the forest alone looking for Spenser," Meg insisted. "And if you get too far out toward the lake, cell towers or not, your phone won't work. Let us know what you're going to do, because if he can't help you, we'll—we'll do something. But it might have to be tomorrow to get a search party together, and that's usually just done for people…"

Sucking in a sob, Alex hugged them both and ruffled Chip's hair. She was out of breath by the time she got to her room to grab a jacket, her purse and Meg's hiking boots before she ran out the front door to her truck.

10

Alex didn't care if Lake Road was one lane and twisty, she drove fast. She wished her quest to get Quinn's help could have happened after she'd been here for a while. She didn't know the area and neither did Spenser. Talk about babes in the woods!

The modest wooden sign to the Q-Man Tracker and Survival School told her where to turn in. Several trucks were parked in an unpaved open space. A sign shaped like an arrow read Enter and Pick Up Your Feet. Ordinarily, she might have smiled.

"Hello there," a female voice called to her as she went past a screen of birch trees, then through a gate toward the first building she saw. "I'm Mary Spruce. Are you a friend of one of the new students? They're pretty busy right now."

"I'm a—a friend of Quinn's. I need his help. Sorry to burst in like this, but I'm Alexandra Collister from next door—the lodge."

"Oh, sure. I heard you had joined our neighbors. I'm Mary Spruce. I'm glad to meet you, but Quinn—"

"My dog is missing. Maybe wandered off in the forest, and I need Quinn's help—advice. Something."

She fought from bursting into tears. Mary took her elbow and sat her down on a bench outside a log cabin. The woman was pretty with dark red hair. Her denim floor-length skirt and jacket were complemented by her necklace with some sort of large, dangling claws.

"Please," Alex said, "time is important. I know he's busy, but if you could tell him—"

"I'll tell him. After a first day of work, they're having a welcome gathering in the dining hall. I was just getting more paper plates," she said, popping up. "You just come with me, right?"

"Right. Thank you so much."

They hurried across a grassy space that looked to Alex like a series of alleys each ending in a square soil-filled box where it seemed like one would toss horseshoes at a target or grow seeds in a slightly raised bed.

"Be careful not to step in any of these," Mary told her, pointing at the squares of sand or soil. "Examples of tracks."

Mary took her into a large, one-story log cabin with a rack of moose antlers over the door. Inside, she smelled food and coffee amid the sounds of mostly masculine conversations and laughter.

"You stand here, and I'll get him," Mary said, and gave Alex's arm a little squeeze as she moved gracefully away through the crowd of noisy men. Oh, there were also three women standing together, laughing, holding their plates and eating. Yes, she'd heard women took this beginner course, so did they take the survival skills one, too? She could use those skills now.

Alex spotted Quinn across the room, talking, nodding. She had the urge to run to him through the crowd. He was looking down at someone and then squinted her way, so Mary must have reached him already. His expression did not show surprise, but his eyes still burned her from that distance as they stared at each other as if no one else were here. She knew Quinn hid his emotions, claiming to be a "direct" person. Well, she had to be direct now, do anything to find Spenser.

He came toward her like a steady, tall ship through the shifting sea of people. Nodding at some, giving a quick answer to questions here and there, he kept coming.

"Alex, what is it?" he said, putting a strong hand on her shoulder. "What's wrong? Something at the lodge?"

So Mary hadn't even gotten to him or had time to explain.

"I'm so sorry to cut in here, but I'm desperate. Spenser's missing—walked away from the shop, I guess—and it's going to be dark soon, and you said it was dangerous for him out there, but he's never just done this, and his leash was right there, and we all called and searched..."

He took her arm and steered her into the kitchen where Josh was putting plates of food out on a passthrough ledge. He darted a look at them, then went back to serving. Mary came in with Sam right behind her.

"He saw you before I got there, but I told Sam," Mary said as the two of them hovered together across the room.

"Quinn," Alex whispered, "I'm sorry about barging in after—after everything."

"Forget that and try to keep calm."

"I need your advice and help.'

"Sam," Quinn said, turning away from her and gesturing his friend closer, "please grab me a number-four backpack and another one full of water and granola bars. And some hamburger to pass for dog food—in a plastic sack, so we don't draw unwanted guests with the excellent sense of scent."

Did he mean bears?

Quinn looked down at what Alex was wearing and nodded at the jeans and boots, then turned away again. "Mary, can I borrow a warm jacket for Alex, and make sure there are at least two garbage bags and two flashlights in the rations backpack."

Sam turned away and went out with Mary right behind him. Josh just shook his head and kept putting bowls of food on the counter. No one but Alex seemed to notice him. Yet she felt he was watchful, even judgmental.

"Don't take this wrong or let me scare you," Quinn said, "but we're going for another walk in the woods. You'll have to do what I say, and hopefully we can find him before darkness sets in."

"You—you'll go with me, take me? Oh, thank you, Quinn!"

"But you're going to have to promise me that you will focus on what I say no matter what. That requires keeping emotions in check. I know it's hard, but we can't have any tears or panic no matter what. We concentrate. Take it from someone who learned the hard way that it does not one bit of good to fall apart."

Oh, yes, she'd play by his rules. Strange, but even after being so betrayed and mentally, even physically, beaten down by Lyle, she trusted this man. But then, she had to, with Spenser's survival at stake as well as her own safety deep in the woods.

Alex hoped it wasn't her imagination, but daylight already seemed to bleed away, despite the clear sky. Quinn drove her and their gear in his big, black truck to the lodge where they piled out and went in. She had to go to the bathroom, but she didn't say a word and just concentrated on what he was saying and doing. He'd strapped a backpack on her, one with Mary's borrowed jacket and supplies inside. He had a larger pack on himself.

"Quinn, you're here!" Meg cried. "If you can find his trail, can we all help?"

"What's that old saying?" he countered. "Too many cooks spoil the broth. Same in the woods. It's gonna be just me and my new student here, and don't worry if we're out after dark," he said to Meg as Suze and Chip ran up.

"Can I go, too?" Chip asked. "I can help, use some of the stuff you taught me on our walk."

"Not this time," Quinn told him, and squeezed the boy's shoulder. "Okay, please, everybody stay back. We're going to try to pick up Spenser's trail from the gift store."

"Take good care of her and Spenser!" Suze called after them.

"The very best I can," was all Alex heard from him as he started at the closed door of the shop, held her back with one hand, then crouched to study the ground.

"You and the others have been back and forth out here," he said.

"Yes. I was desperate. Sorry."

"To be expected. I've seen lots worse than this and with people missing, not a dog. I consult with search and rescue teams in the state and beyond sometimes. Stay back until I find just his trail. I know Scottie footprints."

She did as he said, trying to steady her rapid breathing. He went farther down several paths, then to openings in the forest, not even so much on the obvious path they'd taken before. He took out his flashlight, though it wasn't dark yet, however much the shadows had begun to lean long and gray. She saw him slant the beam at what must be prints, maybe to make them stand out in sharper relief.

"Okay," he called to her. "Over here. My guess is he saw a snowshoe rabbit and went after it. See these tracks? It's called a snowshoe because its back feet are huge compared to the front, great for traversing snow or any kind of mud or tundra. See, we're tracking these four separate tracks as well as Spenser's. Snowshoe hares are forest dwellers who love bushy undergrowth. They're a lot larger than cottontails. And this time of year in their summer coats, they are grayish brown with white underparts."

"If Spenser catches it, I hope it doesn't have the tularemia bacteria."

He turned to look at her. His eyebrows lifted. "Is that what that sluggish, wasting rabbit disease is called, so you have to cook rabbit meat real well done and don't handle it without gloves? Are you a scientist or vet? See, we both know things to share. Never mind. Tell me later."

She had been going to explain about her training and vet tech job, but she could only nod as she leaned down by him when he shone his flashlight beam almost sideways at the tracks again. "Scottie dog," he said, focusing the light on the paw print she recognized instantly. "And hopping faster and faster away here, the snowshoe, with Spenser chasing it." He turned and started away at a good clip. "Come on," he called back. "Stay tight to me."

Both fearful and grateful, that's exactly what she did.

* * *

As they plunged into the woods, he was all business. Why, she fumed, had Spenser left her and safety behind when this was all strange to him? But she knew the answer to that: centuries of breeding that made a terrier a terror to any sort of prey or enemy. "Little terror," she had nicknamed him at first when she brought him home from the shelter and he didn't trust her. Yet love had changed him. And now, as scared as she was that something would happen to him, the little dog's courage gave her courage, too.

After they had walked in brisk silence deeper into the forest, Quinn stopped so fast she almost bumped into him. "The snowshoe is tiring here, thinking of going to ground."

He could tell all that from what looked like a smear of tracks?

"See, it darts off toward that thicket," he added.

He veered to the right, so she did, too. In a patch of what looked like grass and weeds, Quinn grabbed a four-foot branch off the ground and lifted some of the thicket. "Yeah, Spenser dug here," he told her.

She stepped up beside Quinn and looked down at a rough hole.

"I've seen him dig like that, in my flower beds before I had them raised. Did he—did he catch the rabbit?"

"No sign of that—no fur, blood or anything. Stand still here, and I'm going to look around the sides and back of this area to see if he rooted the hare out."

"Quinn I—I have to go—I mean, like, bathroom call. Can I just go over there and—"

"Don't go far. I won't look. But you be careful. No poison ivy or oak in Alaska, but don't let anything touch your bare skin. No wiping with leaves because there's cow parsnip around here. And uncovered skin is most sensitive, believe me," he said.

"Yes, all right," she said, nodding, then turning quickly away.

She had not a clue what cow parsnip looked like and amazed herself by blushing about what he had said, however brusque and matter-of-fact he had been. She went behind a large tree trunk, partly pulled down her jeans and underwear and squatted. *I won't look*, he'd said. But when he did look at her it was so intense, even if he was talking about cow parsnip. She had so much to learn, maybe both of them did—about each other.

Yet nothing mattered but finding her second best friend right now, second best after Allie.

11

Quinn was grateful it wasn't dark yet, but the light level and temperature were falling fast. Darn little dog with that much spunk and energy, but his paw prints seemed to be flagging. He might have a thorn in or have hurt his right back paw, too, because he'd developed a little limp, though he didn't share that with Alex.

What irony: he'd eaten alone in town last night, though several people had come up to his table to talk. He'd wished she'd come to him at the camp to change her mind about the date. Would she have come at all if she hadn't been desperate for his help? He prayed they'd find her dog, but he didn't want her to need him just for that. This whole thing hurt so much because it just reopened the wound of his causing his Scottie's death—and his dad's.

"Let's go," he said when she rejoined him quickly after relieving herself. "I've found both sets of tracks again going out the other side of this rabbit warren toward the lake. Keep close."

She did. They were making their own path now, through low brush beneath trees. He kept his head

down, squinting at the ground, using his flashlight if
he needed to bring the tracks into sharper relief. They
startled a pair of moose who seemed to frown at them,
then shuffled off.

"The setting sun and leaf litter on the ground aren't
helping," he muttered. "I'm going to have to make a
guess that the snowshoe would not go out into the open
toward the lake, but try to find a hole again, some tundra ground. But I can tell Spenser is finally flagging."

He stopped and heaved a huge sigh.

"Quinn, what is it? You haven't lost their trail?"
She peered around him. "What are those big five-toed
tracks?"

"Bear," he said, his voice breaking for a moment.
"But not tracks laid down at the same time, I think."

"You think?" she said, reaching forward to grip his
arm.

"They veer off a different way, see? We'll go on
this way."

He could see the slash of distant lake through the
foliage. It *was* getting dark since the sun had dropped
below the distant mountain. And despite the mid-August
date and the fact he'd been sweating with exertion and
nerves, the air was noticeably chilly as if the quickening
breeze was breathing on them. He sensed Alex looking
to the side now that they'd seen bear tracks.

"Quinn, what if the snowshoe eluded him, or Spenser
gave up and was thirsty and headed for the lake? With
his little legs, I'm not sure he could have run a lot farther. But I'm afraid he's come far enough that he might
not know his way back. Cats are much better at directional memory, but they can get lost, too, in strange
surroundings, especially when everything looks alike."

Quinn rose to his full height, for once not staring at the ground. He reached for the binoculars he had attached to his backpack but had not touched so far. "You sound like a veterinarian again."

"Vet tech, kind of like an assistant only more." She paused for a moment, then said quietly, "He was a vet. I worked for him."

"But didn't marry him." This was the man she left behind, he thought.

"But I didn't marry him. I was going to before I wised up—before he wised me up."

He still didn't look at her but put the binoculars up to his eyes and pointed them toward Falls Lake.

"Did he rough you up?" he asked.

"I thought he was just…ardent before, a little controlling. He roughed me up mentally, emotionally, I guess, and I didn't realize it. Yes, he got—got physical, over the line, I mean, and I ran. I can't believe I'm telling you this now."

"I just want to say again I'm not like that." He waited a moment, then went back to the binoculars. "I have some good and some bad news. Bad, it's going to be dark soon but for the stars, so we'll make camp and spend the night out by the lake. The sun will be up early, and we'll get back at a decent time."

She gasped. "Without Spenser?"

"The good news—I think there will be three of us so we'll have a watchdog tonight. I see a little blur of black across the end of the lake that may be—"

"Oh, Quinn!" she cried, drawing in a big breath and pressing her hands over her mouth before reaching for his binoculars. "Not some other animal or a piece of drift log? Chip said there are beaver dams farther down the lake."

"Not inky black ones," he said as she changed the focus to fit her eyes. "Though if your Spenser takes to chasing them before we get there, he'll get himself in even more trouble."

"It's him! I think it's him!"

"Don't call to him when we get closer. Pretty sure he's got a cut or thorn in his back right paw, and we don't need him running across that shingle shore. Come on," he said, taking the binoculars back. "Let's save your little Scottie."

He was really happy for her, even for himself. There had once been a little black Scottie he couldn't save, but maybe this partly made up for it. And her obvious relief and joy helped, too.

Even Quinn blinked back tears at Alex's reunion with the tattered-looking dog. Yet, for a moment he saw again what he had tried to forget for years: the remnants of his Scottie's bloody body where he had evidently died trying to protect his father, who lay sprawled on the ground amid bloodstained leaves and grass. If only he hadn't disobeyed to run off ahead to hide, if he'd…if…

"Thank you, thank you!" she said, cuddling the dirty dog in her arms, kissing his muddy, mussed head while Spenser went crazy licking at her chin and neck. "Oh, Quinn, I can't thank you enough!"

He bit back the too-obvious—and crude—remark that "We'll find a way," and said instead, "I'm glad you came to me, trusted me. Listen, before it gets too dark for me to make a quick camp, bring him over to the water. We don't want to get him chilled, so we'll let him stay dirty for now, but, like I said, I'll bet he's got an injury to that paw he's been favoring."

He moved closer, and they both looked. A thorn and some blood.

"I'm in awe you could spot that from his tracks. That isn't devil's club in him, is it?"

"No, those are more like big, thick hairs."

"If you'll help hold him, I'll pull it out and wash it, wrap it with something."

"We can carry him or put him in your backpack," he told her as together, kneeling by the clear, cold water, they washed the bloody paw. Amazingly, the little guy let her pull the embedded thorn out with no fuss but a few whines and whimpers. She was good at it, assured and adept, but then she was obviously skilled with animals, at least domesticated ones.

With Alex carrying the dog like a baby, they moved back from the lake toward the forest but did not enter it.

"Stay put," he told her. "I'll get some firewood and a big piece of bark from a downed tree I saw for a cover. Our sleeping bags will be those plastic garbage bags, if you want to dig those out with the water and food. See, we are dining together."

"Water and granola bars never sounded better," she said, so obviously happy now.

He moved away, found what he needed and came right back. She had taken out the plastic bag of hamburger for Spenser and was feeding him with her fingers. He put down the large hunk of curved cedar bark and arranged twigs and a few small logs for a crude fire.

"Amazing," was all she said when he made sparks to catch the kindling by twirling a friction stick amid the twigs. He blew on that to feed it and soon had a fire going. They drank bottled water, and she let Spenser lap from her cupped hands. The dog almost instantly fell asleep in her arms.

Alex looked so beautiful in the flicker of the fire with the stars popping out overhead like diamonds. He drank in her closeness, relishing the fact she needed and trusted him.

"I'm grateful for Mary's jacket," she said. "Even in a rush, you thought of everything. It was kind of her to lend it."

"She's a really good person. She gets depressed at times, partly, I think, over how much trouble they've had with having children. And—I really understand this—she mourns the loss of her grandparents in that flash flood when the waterfall let loose. She was really attached to her grandmother."

"I can surely understand that." She put the exhausted dog in her backpack with only his head protruding. She and Quinn bumped the tops of their plastic bottles in a celebratory toast as they drank again, and their eyes met and held.

"Again, thank you," she whispered as they tore into their second round of granola bars. "I will certainly pay you for your time."

"You can pay me *with* some of your time—not necessarily under the stars in the Alaskan wilderness."

She nodded. Her lips curved in a little smile. Damn, but he couldn't believe this had happened so fast, so hard. He was thinking this was his idea of the perfect first date, but he wasn't crazy enough to say so. Yet how to keep her from bolting again, just as the snowshoe must have done from the dog. He loved just looking at her.

* * *

Alex was amazed at how quickly Quinn had made not only a camp but a protective shelter for her and Spenser. With tree limbs, he'd propped up a large, curved piece of cedar bark so it came down behind her back and gave her a little roof overhead while he hunkered down in his garbage bag on her open side like another protective wall against the world.

But when they were getting settled, exhausted just like Spenser, she heard it begin to sprinkle.

"Darn," he said. "Cloud coming in to hide the stars."

"I'm amazed at how clear they are—so many of them. Suburban Chicago lights don't allow for this fabulous view, only other city lights—and garish neon, the worst."

"I've seen New York City a lot, so I can imagine," he said, pulling his jacket hood up over his head.

"Quinn, don't get wet. I can scoot over, and there's room for two—or three. You got a pretty big piece of bark."

"So I did," he said, and she wondered if he had done that on purpose. Well, they were encased separately in plastic garbage bags from their armpits to bent legs, she told herself as he scooted over, adeptly missing the propped branches that held the whole thing up. Behind him the fire had sputtered out so all was darkness in their little shelter.

Carefully, she scooted toward the curve of bark behind her while Spenser snored lightly and slept on. And to think that he used to growl like crazy if Lyle came in the front door.

The rain pattered down but not hard. Garbage bag or not, Alex could feel Quinn's body heat, his breath.

Every exhausted nerve in her body leaped alive. It was as if this was all planned somehow, orchestrated by someone, but of course she knew better.

"Do you—do you sleep outside a lot?" she asked.

"Not as much as I used to. When I have an advanced class in, we do a three-day survival trek, so then I do."

"It's good you love the outdoors, the wilds—after everything."

"That's what my father would have wanted. It's partly why I feel close to Chip, having lost his dad and sometimes blaming himself. Chip wants to fly someday, and Meg has a fit over that."

"I could tell. You know, he even hides his airplane toys. She explained Chip's guilt about his dad rushing home for his birthday. I understand."

"Is your father alive?"

"He and my mother live in England right now. He's an international broker for a US company. I miss them both. Oh, sorry, that was insensitive."

"I appreciate your telling me the truth, not avoiding it. Don't coddle me. I know what it's like to feel guilty for something."

The silence hung between them. Should she tell him about the loss of Allie? How she could not help but blame herself, even after early counseling? No, that type of in-the-womb loss sounded too far out right now. Besides, he had his own problems.

"I understand but I can't talk about it right now—not yet," she finally added.

"That 'yet' makes me think we have something to look forward to. So, you think we can build a friendship—that much at least?"

"Yes. And at the very least, I'm buying you dinner

in town at your favorite place when you can get away from your latest campers."

"The restaurant's a little wild and crazy, but then so am I."

She laughed. "I don't see you that way, just rock steady. I need to get my bearings here. Learn to read the signs and follow the right trail."

"If I can help—other than today—let me know. And we're going to have to set out at the crack of dawn tomorrow, so my newbie students don't think I've deserted them and run away like Spenser."

The dog stirred from hearing his name but did not wake. Was this a dream she could wake from? And run away—is that what she had done instead of staying to fight at home? Run away from her old life, from a man so bad for her?

"Quinn!" she whispered. Hadn't she just heard a scream? "What's that sound?"

She reached out to grasp his wrist, bumping Spenser so he came awake.

It was a strange wail, a rhythmic, repetitive singing, neither male nor female but somehow both. He'd told her about the ghosts here, but she'd only half believed him and...

"I've heard it before," he told her, not budging. "It will stop."

"You don't believe in ghosts haunting this place, do you?"

"Something or someone's out there, but no one has ever been harmed."

"But—but you mean, we just stay here?"

"I could get us back, but it's a long way, especially in

the dark. I've tried to find tracks in daylight from where the sounds seem to come from. Nothing."

"I'm scared."

He didn't even ask her but picked up the backpack with Spenser in it, lifted it over to her other side, then turned her so she had her back to him and pulled her close. Now she held Spenser next to the curved bark of their wall-roof. Quinn moved closer, spooning her. It was as if she sat in his lap, but they were both on their sides.

She felt his warm breath move her hair as his free arm came up and over her, not threatening, just making her feel safe and secure in the Alaskan wilds while possible ghosts sang them a lullaby.

Crazy, so crazy. Yet she felt content, even calm.

As the chanting faded away, Spenser yawned, still asleep. Hadn't he heard the singing? Lying in the embrace of a man she had not known a few days ago, she thought the night had never seemed more safe.

12

"Hey, you two, we've got to head back," a deep voice whispered.

Alex jerked alert, panicked for a moment. Had Lyle found her? Where was she?

It all came rushing back. Spenser was in a backpack in front of her and a heavy arm was over her. Quinn. She felt him shift his weight, roll a bit away. He must have held her all night.

"It's about five thirty," he said through a big yawn as he pulled away. "Sun's almost up, and we need to head back. Take Spenser behind a tree, but be aware of devil's club or animal intruders. And keep that leash on your wandering friend."

"Aye-aye, captain," she said, trying to sound more awake than she felt.

The two of them went different ways, then met to finish up the bottled water and one granola bar apiece. Spenser had eaten all his meat, so he just lapped water from her hands again. The sun was not up, but the sky was light as Quinn deconstructed their little camp, scuffing the ashes and even taking their bark shelter down.

He set a good pace toward the road, claiming it would be quicker to walk it back to his property rather than retracing their steps from last night. But not far on, they came to a scattering of bushes, laden with huge, wild strawberries.

"I can't believe it!" she cried. "I'm starving."

"Pick and eat fast, and we'll put some in my backpack. Fast because bears know and love spots like this. We'll take some to Mary. She craves them lately."

"Yesterday we passed other bushes with ripe, red berries, but they were small and round," she said as they quickly picked the bounty.

"Those are bearberries. They're mealy, nothing like this," he said with his own mouth full. Their lips were red and sticky.

"I can see how someone could survive in the wilds, if they knew what they were doing," she said, still eating the luscious berries, and that wasn't just because she was starved. She hated to admit that she would have liked to stay here longer to grab more—and be with him.

"You won't need to take my survival class, though," Quinn called back over his shoulder as they headed on. "I'll give you private lessons. There are lots of things to eat in these woods, maybe things you could use in your beauty products, too."

"My products are not just for beauty. Many of them are medicinal, for dry skin, things like that."

"Don't I know? That's perfect. You can adapt to this area instead of the warmer climates with your lavenders and long-blooming roses. Get some ingredients from the wild, some from a greenhouse if you can find a spot to have one built. I wouldn't mind having one, too. I think we have a lot to teach each other."

The things he was saying seemed seductive, but maybe weren't meant that way. He appeared to be so open, so up front, compared to guys she'd known, especially Lyle. She still didn't know this man very well, but she wanted to. She owed him a lot, and he hadn't taken advantage of her, hadn't pushed her. The only time he'd ordered her around was to help her to find Spenser and to keep her safe in these woods. How different that was from what she was used to.

"I see the road up ahead," he told her as the sun slanted its golden rays through the treetops and brightened the sky even more. He finally stopped leading her and came back to take her sticky, red hand and walk with her. "And beyond that, maybe a new road for both of us," he added.

"A long road perhaps, one that takes time and effort to get to."

"Compared to where we've been, we're back to so-called civilization," he said, sounding almost brusque, all business now. "Let's trade backpacks since Spenser's heavier than a week's supply of berries. I see where we are, and it's at least four miles to the camp. When we get closer, my phone will work, and I'll call someone to come get us. Ready for a trek?"

"You bet!"

Josh came to get them in his truck, an old one rusting out in spots. The open truck bed was filled with extra tires and burlap sacks of something.

"An adventure, huh?" he greeted them as they climbed in. "You should have taken a camera and filmed it for your show," he said with a quick, narrow-eyed glance at Alex in the rearview mirror.

Back at the camp, Quinn jogged to his cabin to get ready for a morning lecture to his students, and she lingered outside the dining hall while Spenser hit a tree trunk for his needs again. She could hear the low buzz of voices inside where breakfast was being served. Something smelled delicious, and her stomach growled. To think she'd never really cared for breakfast, back in so-called civilization as Quinn had called it.

A window was propped open, and she could hear Mary's voice inside. He'd said not to mention to Mary that they had heard the strange voice at night not because it scared her. Rather, he'd said, it reminded her of loved ones lost. Alex could surely sympathize with that.

Then she remembered Quinn had left the backpack full of strawberries, so she'd better take them inside. He'd said Mary loved them, and she'd been so helpful.

Once again checking that Spenser was securely on his leash, she led him through the door, the backpack in her hands. She was in the area where Josh had been handing food out into the main eating area last night. He was doing that again, preoccupied so he didn't see her enter.

No one saw her. Mary was saying to the men, "So she needs to be watched. He doesn't need a big-city fly-by-night in his life."

Alex froze, holding the backpack, wishing she hadn't come in so quietly. Mary must mean Val distracting Ryker. Or were they were talking about her?

She backed up, opened the door again and called out, "Can I come in? We picked some strawberries for you on our way back."

Sam turned to her. Mary smiled and Sam nodded, but they were blocking her view of Josh. It was awkward, and she hated that. Strange vibes, curiosity but maybe hostility, too. She held out the backpack with the berries, feeling it was a peace offering. But there was no war, was there?

"Oh, Quinn knows I love berries, and these Spruce men don't so much," Mary said, and moved to take the pack and open it. "Guess you like them, too—juice on your chin. So where's Quinn?"

"He went to get ready for a lecture. As you can see, he found my dog, and I'm so grateful."

"Sure he'd find him," Mary said as Sam turned back to the big porcelain stove and Josh kept lifting plates of pancakes onto the pass-through. "Anyone taught by Trapper Jake—he was a good tracker, too—can find anything in the dark." She tipped the backpack into a large bowl, and the red avalanche of berries tumbled out.

Alex thanked them and was almost out the door when Quinn bounded in. He'd evidently washed hastily because his face looked wet. He wore fresh jeans and a red and black plaid shirt.

"So, you like the berries?" he asked Mary. "You said lately you were craving them."

"Probably going to be craving all kinds of things now," she said with a shy smile and a glance at Sam.

Sam broke into a big grin. "Gonna need an extra room on our cabin, Quinn."

"Hey, that's great!" Quinn exploded. He hugged Mary and high-fived Sam.

Maybe Josh didn't really want to be an uncle, because he just headed out the kitchen door back into the main room—or maybe he had a job to do and had celebrated with them earlier. But here Alex stood, tears in her eyes because people she hardly knew were going to have a baby. This was a moment for these friends to celebrate, so she backed out of the room and quietly opened the door and went out.

As she hurried to her truck, she saw Josh striding through the area with the sample tracks protected in raised beds. She watched, frowning, as he scuffed through two of them.

Jealous that his brother would have a child? Tired of doing the menial work around here and at the lodge? She had the strangest sense that Josh wanted to really contribute in a big way but did not know how.

She put Spenser in her truck and got in beside him before she saw Quinn had come out. He strode toward her.

"They've been trying for a long time," he said, leaning down with his arms on the top of her truck cab. "She wishes she had more family members to tell. She still misses her grandparents who died in the Falls Lake flood. She's always been so protective of this area, of Sam—even of me. Well, gotta get back inside. Busy week."

"Which I will try not to mess up again. Thank you so, so much," she said, and extended her hand up to him, which he took and held for a long minute, then stepped back.

"And hold that thought," he said.

She nodded and he gave her a quick wave as she drove away. She'd certainly hold other thoughts of their time together. He'd held her all night, and she'd never felt safer, wild animals, weird voices or her own fears be damned. She had decided, if possible, to hold on to this man—as a friend. For now, that's what they had to be.

Alex's cousins and Chip were ecstatic to see her with Spenser. Even Buffy seemed glad to see her. They sat her down to a breakfast while she told them what had happened, including that Mary Spruce was pregnant.

"Glad to hear that," Suze said as she perched across the table from her. "I think it may help her. She has moments when she seems so depressed."

"Have you ever heard the scary Falls Lake night voice here at the lodge?" Alex asked. "I—we—heard it last night."

"Guests have asked that before. Truth is, we've always wanted to, but I think we keep the place pretty closed up at night—and its sounds are supposedly out more toward the lake. What did you think about it?"

"That must be something real—or someone. Can't say I believe in hauntings, even with the tragedy of lost lives so close there. But it was really eerie."

"To be here such a short time and hear it—wow. Wait till I tell Meg. But we won't mention it to Chip. That's all he needs to hear is a spirit ghost when he thinks his father's a ghost flying planes."

Alex devoured the scrambled eggs and toast Suze fixed, while Chip and Meg washed Spenser in the tub in the back room. Ready for a shower herself, she took Spenser to their room, then decided she'd better email her parents first. A message from Ginger Baldwin came up right on top of her inbox.

She skimmed the message. More good news! Ginger had included the email address of a man she knew in New York who could switch Alex's website to a different address with perhaps a different name and links. She would have to change her private email and Facebook pages, then contact her customers separately to tell them of the new site, or they might not find it. And he would charge her nothing because Ginger was a friend and had said she was going to help sell her products.

"Whew. What luck!" she told Spenser.

She was thrilled she could do all that even though she'd never considered herself really knowledgeable on social media. Even now she scolded herself for not immediately changing her web address, but when Lyle hadn't used it during her cross-country trek, she'd let it go for now. She was worried about her Facebook page, too, because it had pictures of them together on it, and wouldn't those just hang around like—like a ghost? Maybe this contact of Ginger's could help her erase all that, too, wipe her personal footprint off the web. She hoped that Lyle would just avoid her in his no-doubt-wounded pride.

She skimmed the long list of emails that had come in. Still nothing directly from him, thank heavens. She was starting to feel even safer here in the arms of the Falls Lake forest and mountains, though not as safe as she'd felt in Quinn's embrace.

She sighed and took a fast shower. As exhausted as she was, a rush of adrenaline kept her going. She didn't want to let Meg and Suze down by not opening the shop today. She'd go out, take Spenser, but be sure he was always, always, securely leashed and that the handle end of the leash was tied to something if she opened the door for fresh air.

Someone knocked hard on her bedroom door. Tucking her shirt in her jeans, she opened it to find Suze standing there.

"Before you go out to the store, I want to show you something," she said. She looked and sounded shaken. Her face was pale. "Chip—he just found something outside we thought you should see. Just so you know."

She grabbed a jacket she threw around her shoulders. Not willing to leave Spenser alone now, even in their room, she scooped up him and his leash before following Suze out the back door.

"Tell me. What is it? What's wrong?"

"Better just look. I mean, since you had trouble with your ex-fiancé and all."

"Did he send something?" She gasped. "He—he's not here?"

"No, weirder than that. Maybe not related at all— just weird."

Suze led Alex around the back of the lodge, to the north wall, outside her big bedroom window. She could tell it was her window, front corner. She could also see the curtains she'd partially opened just now over the window seat.

Chip and Meg stood there, staring at the window. Not looking in but at something on the outside.

"Maybe it was a bear, a big one," Chip said, sounding awed, before Alex realized what they were looking at. It was hard to see from the side, but unmistakable closer up. The boy went on. "I think it's a sign Dad's spirit came back, only he got the wrong window, 'cause this room used to be mine when we visited and he was alive."

Alex gasped, but so did Meg at what he'd said. Meg put in, "Don't say things like that, honey. I told you that is not true that he comes back."

Alex saw huge cuts—no, something like claw marks—incised vertically, deep into the log wall on both sides of her window. Spenser growled just the way he used to when Lyle was near. Her head started to pound, and her heartbeat picked up.

When Meg said nothing else, Suze told the boy, "We

don't agree with that, Chip. I mean, we don't know what did this, but not your father's spirit—or ghost."

"Do you see any footprints?" Alex asked, realizing that's what Quinn would have said.

"When Chip brought us out to see this," Suze said, "well, he'd already kind of stepped all over here. I cleaned these windows outside to help Josh's work-load the other day, so my prints are here, too—a mess."

Tearing her gaze from the massive claw marks, Alex looked down. Yes, unfortunately, Chip's distinctive sneaker prints were here. Also she saw a woman's prints, smaller, narrower.

So was this even from last night when she wasn't here, or before when she was inside? Why hadn't she or Spenser heard something, or had she when she thought the wind made branches scrape along the walls and roof?

Although she was a rank amateur at this, she also saw two blurred animal prints she thought she could recognize. A large triangular-shaped central pad and five toes with claws—big claws. Surely a bear's, like that print Quinn had showed her in the forest. She thought of the little sandbox-type squares of wild-animal prints over at his camp and how Josh had angrily scuffed through them.

She studied again the huge scratch marks raked along both sides of the window as if the animal had been trying to get in. It seemed as if the animal had looked in her window and wanted to tear something or someone apart—even as a bear had done to Quinn's dad and dog.

Should she dare to ask Quinn to take a look at this?

13

Alex, Suze and Meg stood staring wordless at the bear claw marks. Chip brooded and fidgeted. Alex couldn't believe that the picture that leaped into her head was the scratching post she'd made for cats at the vet clinic.

"Do bears sharpen their claws on trees—on wood?" she asked. "And this one just happened to choose here? I don't know, maybe smelled or saw Spenser through the window, which means it wasn't done last night."

"I guess, anything's possible," Suze said in a shaky whisper.

"Even though the ground here has been disturbed," Alex told them, "I'm going in to get my cell phone to take some pictures. Quinn's busy and has been bothered enough, but maybe I can show him later."

They heard a whine that became a roar. The women looked up, but Chip took off toward the backyard clearing.

"It's a bush plane!" he shouted. "It's coming over, flying low! Remember how they found a bear near where Dad's plane crashed? That bear that came here might have been the same one! I'm gonna wave to the plane! Come on, Mom!"

"Chip, come back here!" Meg yelled, and ran after him. "I told you that you're letting your imagination go crazy. Chip!"

They both disappeared around the back corner of the lodge while Spenser barked to be put down so he could follow, but Alex held him tight.

Suze shook her head, then wiped a tear from under one eye. "Chip just won't let go of his father," she said with a sniff as she dug a smashed tissue out of her shirt pocket. "It's normal to miss him, of course, but he keeps coming up with these far-out ideas that Ryan is trying to reach him. I try to bolster Meg, but—but with my support or not, she's mourning Ryan, too, and is really shook about how Chip's handling this loss—or not handling it. She's had him talk to our pastor, who's a young guy, and he thinks it's Chip's guilt behind it all."

"I understand. I really do," Alex said, putting her arm around Suze's shoulders. "I've felt guilty for a long time about something I didn't really cause, but feel I did."

Suze turned to face her. "You mean falling for an abuser, not reading the signs until it was too late?"

"Something back farther than that. I'll—I'll tell you both together, another time. It's just—"

They looked up as the same plane looped back and made another pass over the house. They could hear Chip yelling so they both ran into the backyard where Meg was shading her eyes and the boy was jumping up and down, waving, screaming, "See—it's him!"

"Honey," Meg cried, "the pilot just saw you waving and is giving you a little fly-around."

"No way! Pastor Todd told me about the holy ghost inside people, even if they die. If that's not him, it's his holy ghost, just like those bear scratches showed! He was trying to get in to see me 'cause he thinks I might still be in that room!"

Alex saw Meg lift her hands in frustration and bite her lower lip. Suze was sniffling. Alex felt caught between them—with her own regrets and fears—wanting to help but helpless. And here, she'd pictured this deep woods lodge as a haven of rest, of freedom from her problems, of learning to be guilt free.

The plane flew off toward town. Meg took Chip inside. Suze said, "I hate to think what Chip's talk will be about in class if they are assigned 'What I Liked Best on My Summer Vacation.'"

Alex heaved a huge sigh. It did not help to know others had problems, too, especially not the people she loved. They'd just have to find a way to help Chip. But if she thought trying to change the mood would help, that was dashed when Josh came outside from the back door of the lodge.

"Hey," Suze called to him. "I thought you weren't working this morning, that they needed you at camp."

"Already served breakfast. Gotta go back but came to pick up my pay a day early. That okay?"

"Sure, but I've got to go cut the check. Be right back. Maybe you can look at something around the corner there. Alex can show you. I know you don't track like Sam and Quinn, but—"

"Never wanted to learn," he said, frowning. "Too—well, old-fashioned. Just not me. I'm still part of the tracking team. But take a look at what?" he asked, turning toward Alex.

She was still a little miffed and puzzled about him. He might claim to be part of Quinn's team, but just this morning he'd scuffed through several of the animal track boxes at the camp. She didn't want him to damage the tracks here before she could get some photos.

She was tempted to say, "Never mind, I'll just show Quinn later," but she still felt sorry for Josh. He was a hard worker, and she admired that.

"There are some animal tracks around the side of the house that look like a bear's—and some big scratch marks outside my window," she told him, bouncing Spenser. "Chip found them and got all excited, then went crazy when a bush plane flew over."

"Yeah, seen him do that before with planes. But if he's into tracks, maybe he's the next tracker, huh? I'll take a good look later at all that." He turned away and headed back into the lodge.

She called after him. "Don't clean it up in case Quinn wants to check it out."

He kept going but nodded and raised one quick hand, which, she thought, either meant *I hear you* or *Don't tell me what to do.*

Alex was surprised he wasn't going to look now. Why didn't he seem more curious? Or...could he have seen it already? But then, why didn't he say so?

She put Spenser down, checked his leash and walked back to the window. With her cell phone, she took pictures of the claw marks on the logs. Wishing she'd asked for a flashlight to put the tracks in sharper relief like Quinn had mentioned, she took flash photos of them from several angles as well as the footprints, however scrambled now.

She wouldn't bother Quinn, knowing how busy he was, but she thought he might want to see bear claw marks and tracks. Maybe she'd risk it soon.

"Come on, my wandering friend," she said to Spenser as they walked around the lodge again toward the store she'd meant to open a good half hour ago. "Everyone has problems, not just us, right?"

The little guy's single bark was a definite "Yes!"

* * *

On Friday afternoon, Alex figured she'd had a pretty good day. She had Skyped with Ginger's techie guy in New York, and he'd set up a plan to close her old website—which had thirty-three standing orders on it she planned to fill—and shut down her personal Facebook page and set up a new business page. She'd chosen to rename her new business Nature's Naturals instead of Natural Beauty.

Then the next huge step would be—as Quinn had suggested—to create new products with new labels, using the updated business name and more local plants instead of the warmer temp ones. She'd have some time because she'd brought products to fill orders until she could switch things over by next spring. She was going to take advantage of a double-mailing her contact also suggested—that is, mail her products to someplace like Seattle so they would not be mailed with an Anchorage postmark or Falls Lake return address.

Meanwhile, despite trying to cover her tracks online, she hoped to scout around in town to find a greenhouse or garden space—unless Quinn really did want to go into that endeavor with her. She needed her print shop back east to make new labels, maybe find new suppliers for jars and tubes, though she might keep her original supplier for that if she had to.

But all that excitement paled next to a phone call from Quinn. "Sorry to track you down, but I'm good at that," he said with a little laugh. "I called the lodge and talked Meg into giving me your cell number."

"Oh, that's fine. I should have given it to you. How are things going with your trainees?"

"They all think they know more than they do and are ready to take on the world—the forest, at least, which they'll venture into tomorrow. Actually, the female students are a lot savvier than the men in some ways. The three of them run a hiking business near Denver and wanted to know more about getting off the beaten path. Listen, tonight Sam and Mary hold sway, talking about the history of this area. Mary's still feeling a little queasy, but I think she'll do okay. So anyway, that's a big night off for me as I've heard their spiel before."

She almost mentioned the bear tracks and scratches, but decided to hold off. As she checked to make sure Spenser was secure since she had the door open and several mosquito smoke pots going, she said, "I'm glad she's doing okay. I'm going into town to look around tomorrow so let me know if there's anything I can get for her."

"How about going into town tonight? You promised me a meal, though I'm paying."

As if she were a sixteen-year-old facing a first date, her insides flip-flopped. "Oh. Yes, I'm glad you can get away."

"I don't want to give you any more time to change your mind," he teased. "Pick you up at six? Very casual. The place has good, local food and line dancing. See you then."

He was gone. And she was a goner for him already, she admitted only to herself. How had this happened so fast? But she had to be careful, take it slow. Keep her own counsel, not be swayed by how impressed her cousins might be that she had somehow breeched the walls of Quinn Mantell. And really, she'd found by knowing Dr. Lyle Grayson and how he changed over time that once she was inside those walls, it could be hard and dangerous to get out.

14

The little town of Falls Lake reminded Alex of the patchwork quilt on her bed. It was a random mix of low frame houses, two of which were B and Bs. She saw trailers, a few Quonset hut homes as they passed.

"Later I'll drive you by a little bungalow I've had my eye on for a while, but I want to show you something you'll like—I think."

"Oh, look at that," she said as they drove down the only main street, though other short ones cut off here and there. "The grocery store is just called Grocery Store and the bank, Bank. I see some wooden sidewalks, too. This place reminds me of an old western movie."

"Hopefully no gunslingers or shootouts at high noon." He turned down one of the side streets. "That's the school where Chip will go," he told her pointing. "Before we hit Caribou Bill's there," he added with a nod at a wooden building that sat unattached to others on the edge of town, "I want to show you a couple of greenhouses. Maybe you could rent some space there until you can build your own out of town. I checked—

they are about four hundred dollars to build one that size, not counting the lighting."

Three humpbacked fiberglass-and-wood buildings came into view, lighted from within. She could glimpse the blur of green hues inside, even some hanging plants shot through with color.

"You do know how to show a girl a good time," she said.

He laughed. "Yeah, you go with me deep into the woods twice and I suddenly start to think about growing plants domestically."

She had no comeback for that, but then this entire place, this adventure, this man, were unbelievable. She almost forgot about Spenser, but she'd left him with her cousins and Chip for a few hours.

Most of the homes and stores had their own woodpiles and a few had small fenced gardens with massive cabbage heads as well as rows of root vegetables. Several homes had spitted salmon drying, some within fences to keep dogs and wild animals away from the fish. A few of them were covered with wire or a crude roof, evidently to keep eagles, owls and other raptors away. She thought of the bear tracks and claw marks near her window again. Should she tell Quinn, ask him about them? She didn't want to ruin their evening together.

The outside lights were just coming on at Caribou Bill's when they circled back and got out. Quinn parked the truck beside others in front of a hitching post. She let him come around and open the door for her, so this really was a date. And back in "civilized" Chicago, Lyle hadn't done that for quite a while.

She startled as the outside lights came on—Caribou

Bill's in white neon, no less. "I do not miss garish signs," she told him.

"I can do without any lights at night but moon and stars."

Inside, he led her to a booth, high-fiving several guys on their way in. A mounted caribou head stared down at them surrounded by a row of trophies on display— for bowling and Frisbee contests, Quinn said. To her surprise, he sat on the same side as she did instead of across from her. Was he blocking her in to protect her or did he plan to invite someone else to join them?

"The usual, Q-Man?" one guy asked him.

"Sure." He turned to her. "What would you like to drink?"

"White wine, please."

"And white wine for the lady," he called out.

"Oh, so they do have a bit of civilization here," she said.

"By the way, the other place in town I like is called Sourdough Sandy's but we can hit that another time. They have a microbrewery there but it's overly dark inside."

"Low lighting?"

"Mostly because they're at the forest edge of town so they have bear-proof windows that darken the place."

"Oh, there could be bears around town, too?"

"Some. The deputy tries to shoo them away. Only had to shoot one. I steer clear."

"What's a bear-proof window?" she asked, thinking they could maybe have them installed at the lodge. When should she show him her photos?

Three couples were getting up to line dance. She

didn't want to throw a pall over this evening, their first date, if you didn't count two treks into the wilds.

"Bear windows have crisscrossed metal over them," he said, handing her a laminated menu from the same rack that held condiments. "The pine blueberries are huge here and the sourdough biscuits and gravy are great."

"Lots of salmon dishes, of course," she said, deciding definitely not to bring up the bear claw and footprints right now. "Wow. Owl soup? Wouldn't that be against conservation laws?"

"It's made with ham and sausage, and should be called night owl soup. It's potent." His voice lightened a bit. He looked over at her and grinned. "Stick with the salmon or sourdough—for now."

She did. With chardonnay. And she stuck with Quinn on the dance floor where Caribou Bill himself called out the Cowboy Hustle line dance steps to a country music recording. Step, step, turn, clap. Once she got it down, she smiled and saw Quinn was watching her like a hawk—or a night owl. Wasn't he tired after all he'd done today? She had to admit she was starting to wear down.

They had blueberries and ice cream for dessert and talked. It was dark when they went out. He unlocked the truck, and she climbed up. He came around and got in, closed the door and just sat there for a moment. Was he going to kiss her? Right here, now?

"I hope we can do this again—maybe not at Caribou Bill's," he told her. "You should see Anchorage. Always something or other going on. You only skirted it driving in, but it's a big city."

"I'd like that. Quinn, I have something to tell you,

show you," she said, angling toward him on her seat. "I've been hesitant because it has to do with a bear— one around the lodge, I think."

He turned toward her, too. "You saw a bear on lodge property? Could happen, but no one needs that. I did see single brown bear tracks when we were looking for Spenser, but it appeared the bear was old and just passing through."

"I—I didn't see a bear, just the evidence of one, which is strange. I took pictures of its tracks on my phone, some claw marks, too. Chip found them, but his feet and maybe Meg's and Suze's messed up the tracks a bit, so if you could take a look at them. Sorry to spring this on you. I—I didn't want to ruin our nice evening."

"Not only Spenser needs to be careful of bears, but Chip and all of you if one's been marking its territory with scratches. Okay, when I drop you off, I'll look at what's left."

She showed him the pictures on her phone. He squinted at them. The light from the phone threw his high cheekbones and straight nose in sharp contrast and made his eyes look lit from within.

"Those footprints are a smeared mess," he said, frowning. "Josh did the same thing today at the camp over a couple of my track samples when he was ticked off about my video guy, Ryker, wanting to take Val with us on one of our easy tracking treks. I like to keep Ryker happy, but she is a pain. I thought you might like to go along, too—on that short hike tomorrow at two—and I do not consider you a pain."

"I'd like that, to learn more about what you do. But you—you saw Josh mess up your track samples?"

"No, I could tell from a couple of footprints he left

behind it was him, but I haven't settled with him yet. He's a touchy personality, always has been, for some reasons I know. Let's go to the lodge. I've got a big flashlight in the truck, and we'll look around at the marks and tracks in person. Exciting way to end a first date, huh?"

"I think our first date was when you saved Spenser."

"Then we slept together on our first date," he countered with a tight grin as he started the engine.

"Quinn—don't you be telling anyone that lame joke!"

She felt herself go into full blush, so she was glad it was getting dark. What to say? Keep it light? When they were going to look at claw marks and footprints outside her bedroom in the growing dark?

"Despite wild animals or a ghostly voice or a man I hardly knew—you—I felt safe with you in the woods," she said, her voice as calm as she could manage.

"Good. Hold that thought while we check this out. And in the days to come, we'll keep checking each other out."

He reached over the console to squeeze her knee. That touch shot all the way to her stomach, thighs— and heart.

The two of them bent over the blur of tracks. He shone the light over them from different directions, then skimmed the beam over the entire area.

"A mess," he said again, head down, sometimes squatting to look closer. "Several sets of prints like you said, a woman's tracks, too, other than yours, probably Suze's or Meg's. And yes—what may or may not be a couple of bear prints. But despite the sets of human prints, I don't see where the bear approaches and/or walks away, and those big beasts do not fly."

"Speaking of that, poor Chip went into raptures about a bush plane pilot flying over—thinking it was his dad—and saying that this room used to be his when he visited, so the scratches might be a sign from his father because a bear was seen near where his plane crashed."

"Just like a tracker, the kid's always looking for signs. I get that. Chip sometimes blames himself because Ryan was rushing home to be with him on his birthday."

"So I hear," she said, putting a hand up on Quinn's shoulder. "It's so sad that he feels that way, because he is not to blame and shouldn't feel guilt."

"I hear you, Madam Psychiatrist."

"I'm not just talking about you. I not only sympathize but empathize with Chip—you, too. Quinn," she rushed on, "my twin sister, Allie, died in our mother's womb, and I took all the nutrients—the remnants of her body—from her. Obviously not my fault, but I think of her and miss her and sometimes blame myself, when I shouldn't. I've had counseling but still..."

She sucked in a big sob as he stood and pulled her to him. She pressed her face against his flannel shirt and hard chest. Still holding her cell phone with the photos, she put her arms around his waist and held on.

"I knew there was something," he said, resting his throat against her forehead. "Something I recognized, however different it was from my—from me."

They stood there for a moment in the darkness lit only by stars, a slice of new moon and his big flashlight's beam jagging off into the darkness. "I understand," he whispered. "You even understand it but can't help hurting, right?"

She nodded. "I feel like she's with me. I resented how Meg and Suze had each other, but that's so wrong and I haven't yet told them why I stopped contact with them for so long."

He held her harder against him. "I'd better look close at the scratches," he said when neither of them moved. "Then get you safe and sound inside so your cousins won't give me the evil eye as if we're teenagers coming in late."

They stepped apart more awkwardly than they had come together. He played the light over the claw marks again, back and forth.

"Consistent with bear claws—a big bear," he said. "But there's something off with the depth of foot pads and the scratches, which should be deeper in the middle here as the bear's paws raked downward."

"Do you mean these could be human-made? I haven't seen any bear claws, except on Mary's necklace."

"That's was a gift from her grandmother, who was lost in the flood that drowned the little pioneer town."

"Oh, I see. So sad. But why would a person scratch up these outside logs? Publicity for the lodge? To scare or warn someone—me? I mean, maybe if someone knew I had that room. But hardly anyone knows me here yet."

"You're sure your former fiancé could not have followed you here somehow?"

"No sign of that, and believe me, I was careful to the point of paranoia."

"Let's go inside. If you can, tomorrow, print me out a

couple pictures of the footprints and the scratch marks from your photos, okay?"

He took her arm and steered her to the back lodge entry. They used her key to go in. The common room was deserted but for Suze curled up on the couch, reading with a tiny reading lamp clipped onto the book itself. A dim light from the kitchen cast a shaft across the room.

"Oh, hi, you two. No, I'm not like a mom or chaperone waiting up to see what time you got in. Just couldn't sleep. Alex, Chip has Spenser with him, but I can get him for you. The other two dogs are in his bedroom, too—it's like a pet shop. Or," she said looking up at Quinn, "Spenser can just sleep there all night."

"That's okay," Alex told her. "I'll just get Spenser in a little bit."

"Oh, sure. Good," she said, grabbing her book and moving quickly toward her bedroom.

"Alone at last," Quinn teased her with a little grin. "Want to sit here a few minutes before I head out or walk you to your door?"

She surprised herself by taking his hand and pulling him gently down on the leather couch beside her.

"Thank you for not only a fun evening but for helping me find Spenser and trying to teach a city girl about the wilds. Yes, I'd like to go along tomorrow afternoon with your class. If Val and those three other women are there, I won't feel out of place. I won't expect any special treatment even if I'm there at the boss's invitation."

"Sounds good. We'll set out promptly at two, and I think you get the idea about how to dress for the wilds. Those wilds, I mean. The other kind in our future relationship—very different dress code."

He smiled before she could unravel his words, and tipped her closer for a kiss. As insane as she kept telling herself this all was—too fast, too much—she kissed him back, and their mouths melded. His free hand pulled her gently closer and then, somehow, it was over, though their gazes held in the dim light.

"You know," he said, his voice raspy as his gaze stayed riveted to hers, "the room I rent here to take a hot shower on rare occasions is two doors from your room."

She almost asked him how he knew which room was hers, but then she remembered—the room with the claw marks outside. And she realized almost anyone could figure out which room was hers by looking in the window when she left the curtain open and seeing dog toys and some of her products inside. Josh surely knew.

She just nodded. He kissed her again, slanting his mouth over hers, pushing her a little, taking but giving a little more. With her eyes partly closed, she was spiraling up, not down, swirling, blinking in disbelief at how safe yet stunning this felt, watching their reflections in the black glass of the window where she could almost see her little store beyond...

She jolted alert with a gasp and pulled away.

"What?" he said, gripping her arms to steady her.

"Something out there—someone. Ran across, I think, past the food pit. At least, I think so."

"A deer? Maybe a moose? Moose migrate through in the fall and look tall with their racks of horns. If it was a bear, it would have been a lumbering gait, even if it went fast."

"I—I don't know. Maybe a funny shadow with the moon out."

"The wind's picking up. Maybe something blew across the yard."

He loosed her, turned and squinted out, but didn't stand or go close to the glass.

"I don't see anything, Queen Alexandra," he said, his voice both teasing and comforting. "Let's get your watch-dog and get you to your room for the night." With another glance out the window he stood and tugged her to her feet. "I'll wait here until you come back from Chip's room with Spenser. I'll bet Meg's in with him. After Ryan died, she slept in Chip's room to help him through night-mares while she, no doubt, had ones of her own. And with his outburst about his dad sending him signs today..."

He was right. Meg answered Alex's tap-tap on the door and brought Spenser out. She had been crying: her eyes were swollen and red. They hugged over the dog, and Alex went back into the common room where Quinn waited.

The sleepy dog perked right up and let Quinn scratch behind his ears while he walked them to their room. How silly, she thought, but she had the overwhelming urge to jokingly say, *Would you like to come in?*

Would she be joking? And what would he say? And do?

"See you tomorrow," was what he said.

She nodded. He bent to kiss her, a brief peck.

"More to come, Alex."

"Aye-aye, captain."

He patted her bottom and headed down the hall, his steps almost jaunty. She could tell by Spenser's squirming that he'd like to go with him. It scared her how much she would, too.

15

When Alex joined her cousins for an early breakfast the next day, she saw Suze had her nose buried in the book she'd been reading the night before and it seemed Meg wasn't talking, either. Chip was not in sight, but that was not unusual. Even Spenser had gone back to bed after his short walk outside—as if he were another tired six-year-old, which he very well might be.

Suze looked up from her book, her spoon loaded with shredded wheat and cut strawberries halfway to her mouth. "Oh, didn't hear you," she said. "Join us. We're both so tired lately we haven't been talking much."

She put her book aside as Alex sat across from them and read the title of it upside down. *"Into the Wild,"* she said. "I've heard of that."

"It was a movie, too," Meg put in. "Maybe you saw it. Not much time to read anymore with Chip growing up. Maybe when he goes to school in a couple of weeks."

"If I recall," Alex said, "the story takes place in Alaska. The true story of a guy who came here flee- ing from civilization. He lived off the land, foraging and hunting."

"Right. And he died," Suze said, handing Alex a plate of Danish, though she took the sugarless cereal instead. "It's a sad story, so I wouldn't recommend it to everyone, but it does give a good warning about how 'the wilds can win.' Turns out he made himself sick by eating what they call Eskimo potatoes. The tubers are good—they even grow around here—but the seeds can make you sick fast. He got very weak and couldn't even get out of bed."

"Yeah, I've seen pictures of those so-called potatoes in a book at the store," Alex told her. "Quinn says there are good things to eat in the wilds, but you have to know what you're doing."

"Hmm," Suze shot back with a smile. "What else does Quinn say?"

"Don't give me that look. He said I can join their beginner tracker group at two today just to observe, so I hope you won't mind if I close the store a little early."

Meg said, "I volunteer Chip to take care of Spenser. Anything to distract him from thinking his father is going to parachute in here—his ghost at least. But speaking of guilt, Suze said you had something to explain about—well, about that. About your feeling guilty for something? For wanting to come here after we hadn't heard from you for so long?"

Suze bumped her elbow. "I told her not to mention that early in the morning. But we did wonder how you kind of disappeared for years after the three of us had been so close, but we just figured you had another life to live."

Alex stopped pouring milk on her cereal and put the pitcher down. "I—yes, I do have another life to live in a way. You two were so great together, finishing each other's thoughts, having fun…all of that."

"Oh, and you were an only child," Meg said.

"Not in the beginning. You see, I'm a twin, too—that is, I was."

They both stared at her. She fought to find the right words.

"Your mother was pregnant with twins but miscarried one?" Meg asked.

"The pregnancy—for my sister—didn't even get as far as a miscarriage. I'll bet you've never heard of 'vanishing twin syndrome.' I hadn't, either, until I found something my mother had written years before that mentioned her two daughters, Alexandra and Allison, whom Mother nicknamed Alex and Allie. I was twelve when I stumbled on that, and she explained. See, she was pregnant with twins to begin with, but during a later ultrasound, they found only one fetus remaining—me."

Meg gasped. "I had a sonogram with Chip. We could even tell early it was a boy."

Suze put her hand on her sister's arm. "So what happened? How did Allie vanish?"

"It's fairly rare—a phenomenon, my mother was told at the time. They still don't exactly know. Usually in the first trimester, one twin becomes what they call less viable and is absorbed by the placenta or more often by the other twin. The lost twin is—is kind of flattened by the living twin, who is called the twin survivor..."

Alex's voice trailed off. Gripping her knee under the table with one hand, she held up her other hand to stop the rush of condolences she saw coming.

"And being the vanishing twin's survivor, however much my parents tried to comfort me and to explain it was not my fault, I experienced full-blown survivor's guilt. You know, like when someone escapes a tragedy where a sibling or family member they were with dies, or like soldiers in battle who lose their buddies. And so, seeing how great you two were together, I just—I just avoided seeing you for years, even had some counseling in my teens. I threw myself into my work, focused on loving and helping animals—and, I guess, threw myself at the first man who showed interest. I suppose I wanted to be loved—forgiven. So, now you know, and I'm glad you do."

The three of them held hands across the table. Meg whispered, "I understand heartbreak and loss, even of such a different kind."

"Sometimes," Alex whispered, "I think she's still with me. Surely she would look like me—the way you two resemble each other. I guess I took that idea of absorbing my twin to heart. In a way, I feel she is living through me, and I want to do right by her."

The two of them looked at each other and she probably knew what they were both thinking. That she sounded a bit over the edge? That she was making a mistake to care too much for Quinn too fast after what she'd been through with Lyle?

"Well," Suze said, "this book might be called *Into the Wild*, but life itself is about going into the wilds, one way or the other. Meg had no idea she could lose the love of her life. I figured I'd find Mr. Right and live happily ever with him and our kids, but where the hell is he?"

"I can't thank you both enough for having me here, for propping me up."

"Just you be careful in the wilds today," Meg insisted, "even though it will be close to the camp, and

Quinn and his staff will be there. You know, I was never one bit afraid to fly with Ryan, and Chip loved it, too, but I never imagined my big, strong man would crash...

"Sorry to go off the deep end again," she said, and got up from the table. "Don't mind me—just takes time. Like a lifetime, I bet. I'm going to see if Chip's up."

She hurried away down the hall. Suze loosed Alex's hand, and they sat back in their chairs. "Is it better to have loved and lost than never to have loved at all?" Suze said with a sigh.

"I don't know," Alex whispered. "I have realized lately that I have not been in love, just in want. And stupid to not get out of a dangerous situation sooner. Suze, I had a dream last night that I made those scratches on the wall in frustration and anger because I screwed up my life. In a way, I'm starting over here in your lovely Alaska, into the wilds, but I plan to come out alive and happy, safe and sane."

"Right now, that's what my artwork does for me, keeps me sane. Later, let me show you some of my paintings I have stored out in the shed. Josh always hints they're in his way. But I caught him looking at some of the scenic ones of the mountains and Falls Lake, admiring them, I think."

"I'd love to see them. I was always in awe of your Christmas card art."

"It helps me to draw and paint, but I want something more. A man. A family. And family is one reason why I'm glad you are here, even if seeing Meg and me makes you miss your sister, Allie. No wonder you seemed to understand Chip's guilt—and maybe relate to Quinn's, too, right? He's tried to help Chip. I guess he could relate to him because he lost his own father and wasn't there to help—though, of course, he would probably have been killed, too."

Alex nodded. But Quinn seemed to be so stable and steady. So strong, and how she envied and wanted that. But she had to be careful she didn't want him too much.

Alex only had two customers at the shop that morning, so she got busy. Since her product sales were going surprisingly well here and she had only brought so much stock, she phoned her supplier of jars, tubes and labels to order more. He agreed to look for the new packaging design she'd email him shortly. He was impressed she had an artist friend to design her labels, since Suze had said she'd be honored to do that.

Alex arranged to have her order sent to Suze instead of herself. She also said the check she'd send him would be with Suzanne's name, not her own. She didn't like all the cloak and dagger stuff, but she didn't want to leave any trail for Lyle or a private detective to find.

Then she unpacked a shipment of bear bells that had arrived from Juneau. She read the instructions about wearing them or hanging them from a backpack to warn bears away. She noted that, contrary to beliefs that bears were just waiting to attack human intruders in their area, the animals actually wanted to avoid human contact—hence the bells to alert them to stay away. Unless there were bear cubs in the vicinity, bear bells could help prevent an attack by allowing bears to avoid people.

She looked up and jumped as a shadow fell across the floor. Jerking her head around, she saw Val Chambers, wearing a sweatshirt over a white-collared blouse. Ironic, but the sweatshirt was emblazoned with a big-headed bear and the words Go Bruins!

"Oh, hi," Alex greeted her. She gestured to her sweatshirt. "So a Bruin is a kind of bear?"

"You're obviously not a UCLA or LA fan."

"Hardly. I've never been to Los Angeles."

"Just think the opposite of here. Warm weather. Lots of great stores—no offense. Stars—not the kind overhead at night. Great restaurants. I can't stand the ones Ryker patronizes in town and the few I've seen in Anchorage aren't much better. He loves the frontier 'ambience,' though it doesn't come near some of the awesome places back home. He'd love them if he'd try them—maybe soon."

"I've been to Caribou Bill's and thought it was charming in its own way."

"It's own way—I guess," she said with a shrug. "So, Ryker says you're new around here. Don't you miss wherever you came from—civilization?" she added with a little laugh as she turned away to look at things on the shelves.

Alex was about to deny that, when she realized she did miss some things. Getting her hair cut at her favorite salon, which she had been about to do when she left and—oh, she hadn't called to break that appointment. She missed her gym, her Pilates class. This winter her workout might just be fighting her way through piles of the white stuff. She also missed not being able to pop into a nearby deli, shopping for clothes, but who needed a new suit or cocktail dress around here? Those were all things worth losing—at least for now—for sanity and safety.

"Then why do you stick around here?" Alex asked as Val sauntered farther in. Alex could see she wore tight leather pants that looked painted on and high-heeled boots. "I mean, if you don't like it, even if Ryker does?"

"You just wait," Val said, wagging her finger so hard her diamond tennis bracelet rattled. She kept a tight hold of her big purse, pressing it under her arm as if it would drop to the floor. "He'll come around. And come home with me where he can make an awesome living and not tramp through forests and snow filming a show from Podunk, for heaven's sake. I don't care if you tell Quinn or Ryker what I said, because I haven't made my feelings a secret. Ryker likes an up-front woman, and I'm it," she added, tapping her chest just above her large breasts.

Alex nodded and decided not to say the several things that came to mind. Who was she to preach about relationships?

Val picked up one of the newly unpacked bear bells and jingled it. "Sleigh bells? You know, this store could be under tons of snow in a couple of months. Anyway, Ryker said Quinn invited you for the field trip today— or is it forest trip?—so he dropped me off in front of the lodge and I hope I can go over with you later. I'd come back with Ryker, of course."

"Sure, you can go with me. I think it's great you're making an effort to learn more about the show and what Ryker does."

"Whatever. I'm not sure I'm going farther than Q-Man's base camp. Sounds like it could be in a war zone or on the moon, doesn't it—base camp? Might as well be to me. And did you hear that one of the big bosses is coming back again to watch the action today? His name is Brent Bayer, and I actually like him, though he's kind of pushy. It's funny that his name's Bayer, you know—

like the aspirin, which I could use some of right now. I don't think you met him at the salmon bake, but believe me, he sees and knows everything. Anyway, he's going to take a thumb drive of Ryker's recent footage back on his plane with him. Can you believe the two big sponsors for the show both have their own planes?"

"Which bodes well for the future of the show. They may be putting in money, but it's obviously making money."

"Not as much as the big Hollywood type deals. Geoff and Brent are already lining up sponsors for next season. This year is bad enough but next season—ugh!"

Alex was tempted to say that she hoped Val hadn't given such an important backer the idea she hated the show—or that she was trying to lure Ryker away. She suddenly saw Val as lonely here—someone like a kid outside a candy store with her nose pressed to the window. She seemed to admire this Brent Bayer, yet disliked his passion for the show that was keeping Ryker here. Alex had to admit that though she disapproved of Val's dislike of the show and this area, at least she wanted Ryker to succeed—that is, on her terms, in her chosen place.

"You sure know a lot more of what's going on around here than I do," Alex said.

With a sharp nod, Val chattered on. "I'm not that enamored of Brent Bayer, though, really. Ryker has said he's something like Geoff Baldwin's fixer. Sounds like something mafia-related or even high-stakes politics these days, doesn't it? I told Ryker to just say Bayer's a man of all trades and be nice to him."

"Good idea and glad to have the company on the drive over," Alex lied, grateful their time together in the car would not be long. "I'll meet you in the lodge common room at one-thirty. I have a few things to do first."

"Awesome. You know, I think I'll take some of these cute bear bells. Bruins is an old name for brown bears, you know, so my LA and college friends might think these are a hoot. As much time as Ryker is in the woods, maybe I can put a couple on his camera. Damn, but that thing cost him twenty-eight thousand dollars, when he could have some Hollywood producer footing all those expenses. And he spends too much on memorabilia around here, scrimshaw carvings and even animal teeth like from walruses and bears! He recently bought an antique bear rug with claws and a skull with its ugly teeth intact—ugh! Can you take a credit card clear out here in the boondocks?"

"Unless a bear roars in and eats my machine that even takes chip cards out here in the boondocks," Alex said, past caring whether her voice betrayed her wishing Val would leave. She bet a few others felt that way, too.

She tried not to say more or so much as bat an eye as Val zipped open her leather Gucci bag and plopped it on the counter.

Did this woman want to bag Ryker because he was so different from her, from the men she must know back home? Or was the guy *that* good in bed compared to the LA lotharios she must know? But then, once again, who was she to judge another woman's head and heart when she'd made such a mess of her own?

16

Quinn could tell Alex was excited, but then he was, too. He was also nervous because Brent Bayer was going out with them today and not just visiting the camp to observe lectures. As usual, Quinn felt unsettled by the fact that he could not see Brent's eyes outside because of his light-darkened glasses. That reminded him that the man saw things from two different perspectives—trying to look good for public relations, and from his own financial, bottom-line perspective. At least the guy wore a backpack today, which made him look a bit more prepared for the day.

Quinn appreciated the support from this important investor, but was Brent thinking their Q-Man was mixing business with pleasure by spending time with Alex and having her around the show? Or was he thinking that about Ryker and Val? After all, right now Brent singled out Val to talk to. Well, maybe she'd made a beeline for him since he was from a big city and she hated it here.

"All right, everybody," Quinn announced to halt the buzz of expectant chatter in the dining hall where they had all gathered. "We're going deep in the woods today after your prep work around here. No more sample footprints in little soil boxes. As our cameraman, Ryker, here would say, 'We are going live!'"

Quinn noted that Alex had edged a bit closer to him around the side of the room. She was dressed for the afternoon trek and activities, but Val looked like a fashion plate and sore thumb at the same time. And, at something Brent had evidently told her, she'd flounced off in a huff straight to Ryker again.

Quinn went on. "Mary, Sam and I have laid out backyard-size plots in the forest for each of you to explore and evaluate. The area is heavily treed, so, although you will be in close proximity to each other—and always to Sam and me—stick to your own cordoned-off area so we know where you are. If you absolutely need help, call out your name and one of us will be there pronto."

"No bear bells needed?" someone at the back asked.

"I think the power of bear bells is a myth. If you encounter a bear, it's better to just shout loudly—and carry bear pepper spray, but we won't go armed with that today. You also stand your ground, lift your arms or backpack over your head to appear bigger than you are. Do not run, because that triggers a chase-prey response in them, and they can run about thirty miles per hour. Although we find bear tracks in this area, most of the bears are a bit farther to the east at this time where there is more open land and sunlight to ripen strawberries—though we have some nearby."

"And," one of the Germans called out, "that's why Mary scolded me for not putting the trash can lid on tight—bears looking for food."

"Exactly. They like a free lunch as much as we do," Quinn said. As ever, when lecturing about bears, his gut tightened. He never shared with his students what had happened to his father, but it was always in his head and heart.

"Of course," he went on, "you'll study and report on any unusual flora and fauna you see, identify and evaluate any animal tracks—some we have intentionally set up for you. But today your real focus needs to be on how people, intruders in the wild, reveal themselves in your area. Yeah, Steve. Question?" he asked a guy from Canada who was an eager beaver—which reminded him they had even placed some beaver tracks and old fishing lures in the three areas near the stream that cut through the property.

"Is it okay to take notes of what we observe, or do you want us to just use recall and not write the stuff down for discussions?"

"You need to train yourself to observe and later recall without notes. The truth is, for now whatever works for you is what you should do. But stopping to fish out paper and write distracts your awareness and senses you must use in the wilds. If Ryker had this assignment, he'd have his camera ready, though not the one he uses for the show."

Several people turned to look at Ryker. He didn't even realize Quinn had just referred to him, because he was in deep—and apparently heated—whispered conversation with that woman again. Damn, he wished Val weren't such a distraction, but he didn't want to bar her from the action and upset Ryker. And besides, this was a rare appearance for her, and he'd invited Alex.

"So," Quinn went on, "in other words, to each his

own, but pay close attention to your surroundings. Anybody ever read the Sherlock Holmes books? Clues, clues, clues, then, ah…instructions—I mean, deductions."

It occurred to him that having Alex here today was distracting him in a good way, while Val was just a pain. He'd admitted to himself and to Sam and Mary—Josh had overheard, too—that he wanted Alex to be safe in her new environs. He tried not to frown, recalling the photos she'd given him a few minutes ago of the footprints and scratch marks outside her bedroom window.

"So Ryker is filming us for the show today?" Jason, a guy from North Dakota, called out.

"He is, but try to ignore him so it doesn't look like you're playing to the camera. There may be individual interview time later, but today, stick to your task. Tonight after dinner we'll discuss everything you observed and learned."

He went on to explain how they had intentionally left things like candy bar wrappers, snags of cloth, pieces of tissues and cigarette butts behind to be collected and studied.

"In our discussions," he said, "I don't want to hear 'I found a cigarette butt by the trail.' I want to hear if it was filtered, if it had lipstick on it and, if so, what color? Did the smoker grind it out on the ground? Angrily? Carelessly? Do the human tracks look like a woman's? Is she in a hurry? Are her footsteps lagging? Does she limp? What direction did she go?"

"Like info for possible search and rescue?" one of the Denver ladies asked.

"Absolutely," Quinn said, turning toward her. "I've worked as an adviser on several SAR teams. By the way, Alaskan SAR teams often have a veterinarian tech consultant on board, especially in case the search dogs or sled dogs are injured."

He realized that the vet tech reference was a non sequitur, but no one seemed to notice—except Alex. He darted a glance at her, which he'd been trying not to do again. Her eyes had widened at that. She smiled, then bit her lower lip. He fought not to smile back, not to keep staring at her.

"Well, time to get going," he announced. "It will be a busy and intense afternoon."

Alex knew Val didn't like any of this, but she was surprised when she opted to stay behind. Alex could tell Ryker was both annoyed and embarrassed. Hadn't that woman ever learned you'd catch more flies with honey than with vinegar? If she wanted Ryker, she had to meet him at least partway. And she hardly looked one bit ready for a hike, clutching that big fashion purse like that.

Alex saw Ryker arguing with Val again, pointing a finger in her face, then turning away and heading out, his camera on one shoulder and a backpack on the other. Even snazzy-looking Brent Bayer had a backpack. Mary and Sam went out with everyone; Alex thought she was looking good today, and Sam had a real spring in his step. Josh, with a knife in a sheath on his belt, was going the wrong way back toward the camp with a huge plastic roll of what looked like yellow police tape, so he'd evidently been cordoning off the individual search areas. She'd seen him grip the roll by its plastic handle, then pull the stuff out with his other hand. He certainly was a jack-of-all-trades around here and at the lodge, always in the background somehow.

She followed Quinn but gave him some space, as did Brent Bayer.

"So you're not a paying guest?" he asked her with a smile that flaunted teeth so perfect they had to be artificial. He wore glasses that went lighter or darker depending on the sunlight.

"Just a friend along to observe."

"Actually, Ginger mentioned you. Glad you're supportive of the show. The sky's the limit with it if everyone pulls together. It's doing well, and we don't want anyone to rock the boat. Speaking of which, I'd like to go out in a boat on the lake sometime," he said, gesturing in its direction. "You know, take a look at that lethal waterfall that buried the little town years ago. Mary Spruce was telling me about that, and we should work it into a segment on the show, though she doesn't agree."

"Then I'd go with her feelings. Losing ones you love is so hard and never really goes away, and that should be honored."

"But history is fascinating, and people have a right to know."

She could see her reflection in his dark glasses when he turned to look at her again. He went on, "Mary is very protective of this area and the people. But she and Sam, as secondary characters, are very popular with the show's audience, even though they don't appear as much as Quinn. But the haunted elements—I hear there are ghosts afoot at night—might appeal to a bigger audience, too."

She hesitated to tell him about the night cries she and Quinn had heard. Maybe Quinn had told him, but he didn't need to know the two of them had been out all night in the woods.

They all stopped as Quinn started directing everyone to their areas. Sam and Mary gestured to people who hesitated, pointing them in the right directions. Individuals started to spread out from this point into wedges of areas like the spokes of a wheel.

Brent Bayer turned to her again and said, "Be sure and watch the segments of the programs that show the advanced survival classes. These beginner students always seem like bumblers at first, but our demographics show most of our audience relates more to them. See you later. I'm just going to drop back and observe, too."

Mary suddenly appeared on the trail where Alex followed Quinn. She saw Ryker dart off, evidently ready to film in different areas.

"That man," she told Alex, rolling her eyes toward the now-distant Brent. "A lawyer, yes, but Ryker and Quinn call him a fixer, too."

"So I heard. But here to fix what?"

Mary shrugged and shook her head. Alex almost asked her if she really did agree on including some of the local lore of the tragic loss of life under the lake, but this wasn't the place or time. Alex noted Mary didn't wear her bear claw necklace, but the deep forest was hardly the place for it.

"Wish he could fix how I feel. I'm gonna throw up my lunch," Mary said. "Don't know why they call this morning sickness. It's all-day sickness, if you ask me. Baby making and baby growing, a joy but tough, too. But, don't mean to complain about something I've wanted real bad for so long. See you later," she added and turned away to disappear down a side path.

Keeping about a twenty-foot distance from Quinn, Alex watched him work. He was good with people, helpful but firm. He asked more questions, refusing to give them the answers. Sam did the same. Ryker reappeared, came and went, occasionally darting down a side path, filming something or someone. When Quinn sometimes looked back at her, her heart thudded and not from exertion. He nodded and went back to business.

She tried to observe as he had said, but she ended up studying people rather than things on the ground. How different they were. Even among the three women from Denver, there was a leader, a tentative person and someone who really didn't want to be here.

Later Sam came up to her. He looked ahead and saw Quinn was in intense conversation with a student, so maybe he'd actually wanted to talk to him. "You seen Mary lately?" he asked. "I'm scared if she throws up out here she'll be too tired to keep going. Josh is back at the lodge, but I haven't seen her and don't want to head all the way back to look. Got to help keep an eye on our students."

"I saw her about fifteen minutes ago on the main path—back a ways," she told him. "She did say she didn't feel very good before we separated. I know where she cut off. Probably went to help someone in their area. Tell Quinn I'm just going back on this main path to where she cut off to call for her."

He frowned. "Such good news about a baby, but not if it—it makes her sick and weak. Okay, I'll tell Quinn you're coming right back with or without Mary."

Alex was glad to help. She had the feeling that Sam, even Mary, were wary of her and she'd like to be in their good graces. Next to Val, she should look pretty good to them, since she'd never cause Quinn any problems about doing his job and living here, though she'd pulled him away from the program to look for Spenser that one night.

Alex backtracked to the spot where she'd seen Mary cut off. Maybe she even headed toward the compound. Alex intended only to call for her, but she wondered if there would be a trail to follow.

She took only ten strides in the direction Mary had gone, cupped her hands around her mouth and called, "Mary. Mary! Are you all right?"

She thought she heard a murmur, but then the wind was in the trees, and she'd heard a stream that fed the lake was back this way. They had said the stream was near the only rocky outcrop in the vicinity. Quinn had warned the students to watch their footing near there, since several of the roped-off areas were in that direction.

"Mary! It's Alex! Sam's looking for you!"

Yes, she did hear a murmur, or maybe even a woman's voice. What if Mary had gotten sick or was too weak and needed help? But then, could that sound have been the wind in the trees or the stream itself?

She would just peer around what appeared to be a natural bend in the narrow path ahead. The ground had turned from soil to stone here and was on the rise. If she saw nothing, she'd head back to Quinn or find Sam again. This was the general direction back toward base camp so perhaps Mary had headed there and then felt even more ill. Certainly, knowing this area as she likely did, Mary Spruce would never lose her way.

Alex peered carefully around what she recognized as

a massive cedar tree, like the ones Quinn had pointed out to her before. Her feet crushed the brown-blue berries and needles. She spotted that dratted devil's club plant and edged around it, too. Like Mary, it seemed she had found a shortcut back to the camp. She could see the outcrop of rocky footing rising a bit more in this direction.

At least if Quinn got upset she'd gone off on her own, she'd tell him she could actually see the top of the stockade fence and part of the dining hall roof from here, so she was almost back to his property. She parted two low-hanging cedar boughs and carefully shuffled to the brow of rock about fifteen feet above the crooked stream.

She looked down and gasped. Though partly screened by foliage below, a woman—it must be Mary—was lying beside the stream, maybe throwing up into it.

Or maybe Mary was unconscious. Alex could only see her feet from here, one arm flung out and two sprawled legs not moving. What if she was going to miscarry? It was her first trimester—what if she was carrying twins? What if…

She had to get to Mary, help her. Alex called her name, then looked for a way to get down to her. People must use that path below lined with bushes. As she started carefully down, she held on to their limbs. Some of them batted at her in the breeze, but she kept carefully going, around a turn, down again. There seemed to be natural footholds here, and she could picture Quinn's campers going up or down this way. It seemed like miles but it wasn't far at all.

On the rocky ledge by the stream, Alex rushed the few feet to Mary and bent over her. The stream gurgled, as if it were retching, too. Dear God, smears of crimson. Blood?

Alex gave a little cry as if she'd been punched in the stomach. It wasn't Mary! The legs—the clothes...

The woman lay sprawled at the edge of the water with her neck at an odd angle, which made her head and hair dangle down the bank of the stream so she hadn't seen this was not a redhead at first.

This was not Mary, but Val!

Unseeing, the woman stared down at the rushing water. Her kinky blond hair was mud- and blood-streaked. Claw marks had mostly shredded her shirt. Oh, she'd made a crude necklace of the bear bells she bought earlier today, and they hung on a string, tipped toward her bloody chin. Her throat and shoulders were deeply scratched like the wall outside Alex's room at the lodge.

So Val had decided to come out, after all, at least partway. Had she fallen or a bear dragged her and mauled her? Had she fought back? Had she screamed for help?

Alex knew better than to touch her again.

"Val? Val!"

But it was no use. Dead. Definitely dead.

17

Alex scrambled up the way she'd come down and ran for Quinn, for Sam, Mary—anyone. How could Quinn have been so very wrong about it being safe from bears here?

Gasping for breath on the upper level, she flung herself past the massive cedar tree and rushed toward the main path. She saw Ryker at the edge of the first cordoned-off area, filming.

No, don't tell him yet…he would rush there…see Val like that. And they'd just had an argument, so that was his last memory of her.

Mary…where had she disappeared to? Back at the camp where Josh had gone?

She heard Quinn's voice before she saw him. He was talking to one of the Denver women, the one Alex thought didn't want to be here. She knew not to panic everyone, not scream out the nightmare she had seen. Poor Val, city girl, not wanting to even come out this far into the forest. Why had she? And alone when she'd clearly said she wasn't leaving the lodge?

Alex stopped at the edge of this cordoned-off area

and gestured madly to Quinn. He raised his head, said something to the woman and strode toward Alex, pulling her farther away.

For one moment, she was not sure how to say it.

"Quinn, Val came out of the compound. I think she fell—was pushed, I don't know. Something got her. I think she's dead, by the stream at the bottom of that little cliff."

"Take me!" He held her arm tight, almost dragging her down the path.

They walked, then ran. "It was the direction I saw Mary go," Alex told him. "Sam was looking for her—for Mary—and I saw where she went. I said I'd get her.

"That way!" she cried, pointing. "I climbed down on a narrow path beyond this big cedar by the stream."

He moved ahead of her, carefully descending on the narrow, crooked path, and she followed. She wished this was a nightmare like she'd had again last night. It had felt real, too, that she was the one who had made blurred footprints; she was the one with long fingernails, clawing at the lodge to get in, to find herself, to find Allie.

He stopped when they reached the scene and threw out an arm to hold her back. Val's sprawled body still lay on the edge of the stream. He bent to feel her neck for a pulse. He had blood on his hand when he stood.

"Yes, she's dead. Stay back," he told her. He looked stony-faced, though his eyes shimmered with unshed tears, and a deep frown furrowed his brow. He bent quickly to wash the blood off in the stream. "There are probably no footprints on this rock, but we might find some sign later. She could have slipped from above, so we'll look up there, too, when the investigators come."

"The police, clear from Anchorage?"

"State troopers and maybe the Alaska Bureau of Investigation. I swear, no bears have been around here lately," he muttered as he bent closer to Val, "but then the stream could lure one."

How stoic and brave Quinn was, she thought, for, as a child, he'd found his father and dog this way— bloody, dead.

His voice broke. "But I swear, a bear no more did that than put those claw marks outside your bedroom. She could have decided to come out to join us and, un-used to the area, fell. Or someone was with her when she slipped—or she was pushed. I see her big purse is down by the stream a ways, so she wasn't killed for it."

"Yes—yes, that's hers, but things could have been taken out."

"We won't touch it, or her again. Alex," he said, grip-ping both her arms, "I'll stay with her. You carefully climb up again. Go get Sam and tell him we need more of that flagging tape we use to cordon off this scene. Only tell him, maybe Mary if you see her, not Ryker yet. If you see Brent, tell him since he's a lawyer. Do you have your cell phone on you, because I didn't bring mine."

"Yes. Yes, it's in my backpack."

"Let me use it to call the state troopers if it con-nects from down here." He helped her fish it out of her backpack and tried it, telling her, "Good! The call area reaches here. We don't have counties in Alaska and no police per se—just state troopers."

Alex climbed up to the forest floor, then ran back toward the main path to tell others about Val. She was shocked to see Val had come out into the forest and Quinn had said a bear attack hadn't happened here. If she hadn't just fallen, that meant some human animal had killed her.

* * *

Only Quinn kept chaos away, even though he yelled at her not to climb down to the stream again. Sam came, shouting down to confer with Quinn, then went away to tell the students there had been a fatal accident, that it did not concern one of their fellow students nor the staff. They were to return to the camp dining hall because the state troopers were coming from Anchorage to investigate the scene.

Josh appeared from somewhere and, like Sam before, frowned down at Quinn guarding the body. Josh called down to him that he'd helped move the curious crowd toward the camp and that Mary had gone back to her house and was resting.

"And Brent Bayer's handling Ryker," Josh added, cupping his hands around his mouth again. "The guy's flipping out. Wants to see her now. Going nuts to think somebody killed her. He doesn't think she'd come out here on her own to even have a chance to fall. So," Josh said, turning to her and lowering his voice, "you got any ideas who might have pushed her, if that's what happened?" Talk about Ryker losing control—Josh looked and sounded panicked, like a time bomb waiting to go off.

"Of course not," Alex said, holding up both hands as if she could calm him. "I'm so sorry this happened. I was looking for Mary and found Val instead. I'm sure they'll let Ryker see her, say goodbye, when they come."

"He was shaking hard—and crying."

"Poor Val, like a fish out of water here. But if someone like Ryker—however angry he is—is crying in public…" Her voice broke and she blinked back tears again. Val had meant something to him, even though their lives seemed so different—likes, dislikes, ideas, plans for the future. Or else he regretted their argument today.

Shortly after Josh hurried away, Brent appeared. He nodded to her, patted her on the back. "I'm here if you or Quinn need me during questioning when the troopers arrive," he said, then called that offer down to Quinn before he turned back to her. "Quinn's savvy to stay with the body so no one and nothing tampers with it—with her. A tragedy. I've seen too damn many of them." He shouted to Quinn again. "You want me to come down?"

"Why don't you go back to the camp with Sam to wait for the troopers?"

"Will do." He looked back to Alex, his eyes narrowed as if to assess her mood. "I hope this doesn't change things too much around here," he said, frowning. "Our wilderness ambience is about to be invaded, and we don't need that, though I suppose, for some, it will make the area and show more intriguing."

He turned and jogged away. A big-city lawyer indeed, Alex thought, cold-blooded in a way. The poor woman had been a pain to some, yes, but a deeply unhappy woman. Sad. So sad.

She pitied Ryker, too. She recalled that, more than once today, she'd seen him go off into the forest to visit different sites and students. Would the troopers take photos for evidence? Would Ryker want to when he came to his senses? Was his shock sincere or had Val come out to continue her argument with Ryker and then...

And something else Brent had said hit her hard: if this was a murder—and not an accidental fall or a bear attack—even though they were miles from a TV station or newspaper, this place could soon be swarming with reporters. Brent had intimated that, too. Reporters with questions and cameras of their own. Quinn had asked Ryker not to film Alex or any other nonstudents to keep her location secret in case someone she used to know saw the program.

But she was the one who had found the body. If someone was arrested for murder, she'd be one of the witnesses in court. Damn, her safe and secret spot might soon be public knowledge.

It took nearly two hours before Troopers Reed Hanson and Jim Kurtz arrived with a rescue squad vehicle. Still standing at the brow of the rocky outcrop above Quinn and the body, Alex heard the distant, shrill sirens cut out as the official vehicles came closer and parked at the camp. When she told Quinn they were here, he climbed up to join her. Sam brought both troopers to the scene, and two medics followed carrying a gurney and a tarp. Quinn introduced her and names were exchanged all around.

Trooper Hanson was stocky with red hair that barely showed under his flat-brimmed, blue hat; Trooper Kurtz was tall with narrow, sharp eyes but a kind face. Kurtz seemed to be the spokesman for the two.

To Alex's surprise, Quinn knew the troopers. Kurtz told him, "Good work on that SAR team effort to find the lost kid last fall. Sorry for the tragedy here. We need to go down to the scene, but glad you've been guarding it. You discovered the body?" he asked Quinn.

"No, Alex did. She lives and works at the lodge down the road. She was here as an observer today, was looking for Mary Spruce, who works with us, and stumbled on the body. Since then, we've learned Mary isn't feeling well and is back at our camp."

Trooper Kurtz turned to her. "How about you and Quinn come down to the scene with us, Ms. Collister? We'll start with learning what you saw and did, then take photos. When the scene's secure, the medics will remove the body to the morgue for an autopsy."

"Yes," Alex said. "Anything I can do. I didn't know her well, but I did give her a ride here from the lodge today. Her—her friend Ryker would like to see her before these men take her away."

"Okay, all that in due time. Hopefully he can tell us next-of-kin information. We want him to know we are deeply sorry for his loss."

Alex dared to wonder if there was any way that Ryker could have already seen Val's body. They had been arguing, and not for the first time. Had Val really stayed behind, or had she dared to come out to harass Ryker? No, Alex told herself, she had to let these troopers—and poor Quinn, who didn't need this terrible publicity—settle all that. She had enough to worry about with her name and picture perhaps going public. Surely she and Quinn could make a plea with these troopers for her privacy, or was this all now just a matter of public record?

"Let's go," Trooper Kurtz said. "Quinn, lead the way."

Off they went down the path Alex had already traveled twice today.

Quinn could not believe this terrible turn of events— this tragedy. And he'd bet everything that a bear had not killed Valerie Chambers, even if she had changed her mind about coming out of the compound. Sadly, it had been long ago seared in his brain what claw marks from a bear mauling looked like. And he was just as sure the marks outside Alex's bedroom were ones not attached to a bear.

Not only did Val's gruesome death make him sick to his stomach, but he hated that Alex had found the body. He thought the inevitable autopsy would show broken bones from a fall, but maybe not. Someone could have killed her by the stream or carried her body there. But she'd seemed so hesitant about being in the woods—and alone?

It scared him that Sam had seemed so nervous about protecting Mary, but surely he didn't think she could be involved. He well knew both Sam and Mary fervently wished Val was gone.

But he was still convinced a bear had nothing to do with Val's death. So what or who did?

18

Alex trembled as she approached the murder site again, even though the troopers and two EMTs carrying the gurney and tarp were with her. She completely understood why Quinn had refused to leave Val's body. The murderer could have returned or someone might tamper with evidence.

Surely Val could have made the same descent down the crooked path they took now, but had she been killed here? Or thrown from above—or even hiked in from the compound, since the stream flowed from near there to Falls Lake?

The two EMTs stayed back as the troopers split up, each going around a different way to converge at the body. They bent over it—her. Quinn put an arm around Alex's shoulders. Muted daylight flickered as the tree branches shifted and the stream seemed to scold.

Trooper Hanson said, "Looks like a bear attack to me, but an autopsy will be the last word. You say that wasn't the cause of death, Quinn, I believe you."

They came back the long way around again. Quinn removed his arm from her.

"Ms. Collister," Trooper Kurtz said, taking out a small notebook, "I'm sure you're pretty shaky, but let me take a few notes of what you recall seeing when you first found her. You were looking for someone else?"

She explained about Sam looking for Mary, who was pregnant and feeling ill. "So I had just seen where Mary went—I thought so, anyway. Of course, she could have cut off, back to camp toward their house where she is now and not come clear out here at all."

"Please just stick to what happened," the trooper said.

"Oh, right. I thought I heard a voice, but I guess it could have been the stream—like a murmur."

She realized she had just given an opinion again, but this all seemed so unreal. "So I hurried closer to this outcrop and came farther and looked down to the stream. I could only see her legs and feet, or I would have seen that—that she was blond and not reddish-haired, but her head was back and drooped down and foliage partly obscured my view."

She knew she was nervous. Was she babbling?

"I guess I called out Mary's name again," she went on, "then knew I had to go down to the stream on that path we just took. I ran to her—and saw it was Val—and those horrible bear claw scratches, at least that's what I thought they were." She darted a look at Quinn. She wanted to throw herself in his arms, to have him hold her. "I didn't see her bag then, but Quinn did—later. Of course, a bear wouldn't take it."

She continued. "I—I was horrified, but thought about the scratch marks outside my room at the lodge, too. Oh, sorry, I know you're not asking about that."

"Marks like that?" Trooper Kurtz asked. He stopped writing and looked at Quinn.

He nodded and said, "Back at camp, I have photos Alex took, and printed for me at my request. I saw that scene, too, but it was at night, and the tracks were too scuffed to ID or follow—and here, with the stream and the stone..."

"Right. Ms. Collister, we'll talk to you more about the victim back at Quinn's camp where we will question everyone else, so you're dismissed right now. Quinn, you've never been on the payroll but volunteered on our searches, and that makes you semiofficial, so hang around a bit, okay? We'll have you examine the area with us a little more, then we'll let the victim's fiancé see her before we take the body and—"

"They weren't engaged," Quinn said. "They were together, but not engaged."

"I see," Trooper Hanson said, as if he really saw a possible problem there. Wait until he learned, Alex thought, that Ryker and Val had just argued. But for that matter, wait until he heard that not many people here liked Val or wanted her around at all. Her stomach cramped. She would hate for Mary or Sam—even Josh—to be suspected.

"Before I help you case the area," Quinn said, "let me get Alex back to the camp to wait in my office until we're done here, or she'll be besieged by the students, and she doesn't need that right now. I'm the one who should explain to them. I'll be right back," he added without giving them a chance to say no. He took her wrist and pulled her gently away.

"I'm so sorry," she told him as they climbed the now-familiar path. "For Val, for Ryker, for you and your plans today."

"And I'm sorry you found her like that. Sam should have gone looking for Mary himself, not sent you."

"I offered, because I haven't been sure I was much more welcome by them than Val was here."

"Of course you are."

They saw Brent Bayer, and Quinn gestured to him. "Brent, would you walk Alex to my office where she can rest until we're done here? Brent's been staying in my guest room," he told her. "I suggested the lodge, but he wanted to be close. The troopers need me, and I should get back to them, but Alex came first."

"Sure, I'll walk her there," Brent said. "Do you need a lawyer while you or the staff answer their questions? I've seen officers manage to misquote a suspect—not that I'm calling you or your staff suspects."

Alex stiffened and nearly gasped. Quinn a suspect? No, she knew where he'd been the whole time they'd been out here in the woods. She could vouch for that. But as for Mary, but especially Sam, Josh, even Ryker, who knew? And what about this man Quinn was entrusting her to? He was, no doubt, here to take care of any problems. Had he seen Val as someone who might lure away Quinn's videographer? He surely wanted Ryker to stay in his job, dedicated, not distracted.

And worse, did Val's horrid, bloody scratches, which resembled those outside Alex's bedroom, mean someone saw her as enough of a distraction, too—not for a cameraman but for the star of the show?

Quinn hurried back to help the troopers check around the body for any tracks besides his, Alex's—and now the two officers'.

"You know," he told them, standing up straight at last

after crouching to study Val's sprawled corpse again, "she said she wouldn't leave the compound, but she obviously did. Rather than coming on the paths, maybe she followed the stream from behind the camp property to here, but the obvious deduction is that she fell from the outcrop. Still—those bear claw marks. I'll bet she got scratched up after or when she was dying, because her hands don't look bloody or messed up—no defensive wounds," he said, frowning. He didn't say so right now, but he hoped no one had forced her out of the compound. She and Ryker had been arguing.

"We'll probably need to have you testify in court, my man," Trooper Kurtz told him. "So someone wanted it to look like a bear attack, so they…what? Used an unattached bear's paw to scratch her up?"

"Though bears have been in these woods, there are no tracks around here lately. I saw a few almost a week ago—a single, old bear, not near here and not since."

"But," Hanson said, "it would make sense a bear might be here to drink from the stream."

"Of course," Quinn countered, "but they seem to prefer the lake."

Trooper Kurtz cut in. "We'd like to see those photos of the scratch marks near where Ms. Collister lives."

"Actually, outside her bedroom window. You can see the real thing if you want, or you can see the photos."

"We'll be busy here for now, questioning everyone, starting with Valerie Chambers's boyfriend, but yeah, soon. We'll be here late, check things out. Guys, thanks for your patience," he called to the men with the gurney. "Once you get her up to the compound, I'm gonna let Mr. Ryker have a couple of minutes with her before you take her, but make sure he doesn't touch the body.

We'll wait here, too. And we'll bag that purse of hers for forensics."

Before he turned away, Quinn told them, "I'll send him in if he's come back out from camp—or send for him. This won't do my class this week any good. Or my camp, or the Falls Lake area."

"Yeah, sorry," Trooper Hanson called after him. "This weird phantom bear attack gets out, you'll get some TV reporters from Anchorage, maybe beyond, behind every bush."

To Quinn's surprise, he ran almost immediately into Brent on the path and told him, "I've heard Geoff calls you his fixer. Wish you could fix this. You got Alex back to camp?"

"Safe and sound."

"Don't I wish."

Alex was drained and exhausted, but she couldn't sleep. She sat in Quinn's desk chair for a while, then paced around his office. It was a small area in comparison to the big building that held the dining hall, but his house was compact and neat inside. And it somehow reeked of masculinity.

The only touch of domesticity in this room was a leather sofa that definitely looked slept on. It was probably long enough to accommodate his height, sunken a bit to the shape of a body, with a bed pillow at one end. A quilt was tossed on the back of it.

His desk, however, was perfectly organized and looked all business. A laptop was open and a yellow legal pad lay there with notes. Perhaps he wrote his tracking books here.

The house had two bedrooms, probably as small as

this room. There was a bathroom, a galley kitchen with two stools to eat at a breakfast bar and a small living room with another fireplace. She'd barely glimpsed a little screened porch outside.

She walked over again to the fireplace mantel and studied the covers of the paperback books he'd written, then the photos he had lined up there. One was of an attractive woman somewhere in her sixties who must be his mother. *Love you, always*, the neat writing in the bottom corner read, but the photo wasn't signed. No other pictures of adoring women, though she felt she might almost qualify for the role. Next to that, the picture of the man who was—had surely been—his father, since Quinn resembled him. No photo of Quinn as a boy with his little Scottie dog.

Also a photo of Sam and Quinn, both maybe in their late teens or early twenties, and a tall man between them, pointing down a path at something. *Trapper Jake* was printed below.

On the opposite wall of shelves were rows of more books and a few great photos of the area. If she ever wanted to give Quinn a gift to thank him for his kindness, she'd give him one of Suze's paintings. Yes, she'd do that soon.

And a large photo between two pictures of Falls Lake with the mountains beyond was of a stream that looked like the site of the—the murder. Did that place mean something to him, something happy, which would surely be ruined now?

She jumped when Quinn came in, knocking quietly on his own door.

"I should have told you to use the bathroom and or the kitchen," he told her.

"I did use the first, not the second. I—I don't think I could eat."

"Me neither." He came straight for her and pulled her into his embrace. She linked her arms around his waist and pressed her cheek against his chest. They stood there, just breathing, just being together for a moment.

"Poor Val," he said. "And what happened to her makes me even more upset about those claw marks outside your window. When your cousins hear about this, maybe they can switch your room."

"All of them have windows, though."

"Yeah, well, even if you want fresh air, keep yours closed. And I think we should tell the troopers that your name and face need to be kept as private as possible, even though Falls Lake is a long ways from Chicago."

"Thank you. Even the local news isn't local anymore. If there's some terrible event clear across the country, the media reports it like it's right next door."

"I'm sorry you found her, sweetheart, sorry I asked you along today."

Sweetheart? She cherished that but hardly believed it. Yet it scared her that she wanted to believe it had slipped out because he meant it.

"Stay put here for a few minutes," he said, his breath moving her hair, "then I'll follow you home."

"Quinn, you don't have to do that."

"I'll come right back. It's going to be a long, crazy night here. The German guys already told me they think we should all go out and fine-comb the woods for clues tomorrow—like they were supposed to report on today. So, I've got to stop them because a forensic team is due early tomorrow. I've also got to call Geoff back. Brent phoned him, and he's been trying to get me.

"At least I've managed one good thing," he went on, still holding her tight. "The officers have agreed that the camp and adjoining area where you found Val will be off-limits to any press or curious onlookers that show up. They're going to put up a roadblock with a trooper car and cordon off the road. They're sending two extra troopers from Anchorage to guard the area until they release it after their forensics team and Kurtz and Hanson are finished there. So that should save us from the invasion for a few days. I don't need this bunch of students giving interviews for something they know nothing about."

"I wish we could cordon off the lodge, but Meg and Suze need guests before the winter hits. Quinn," she said, looking up at him as he finally set her back with his hands still on her waist, "let's face it. Val wasn't well liked. She even argued with Ryker just before we all went out. The other day, I overheard Mary and Sam say they wanted to get rid of her."

"Glad you didn't say that to the troopers, because they surely didn't mean it that way. They'll talk to them. That reminds me, I heard Brent Bayer say he'd like to get Val off Ryker's back, and I'll bet if we checked with people she knows in LA that she wasn't Ms. Charm there, either. But let's let this play out legally. Come on, I'll walk you to your car and follow you home, because I need to come back here fast to oversee things."

As they started to leave, he stopped her at his office door. He lifted her chin and kissed her, gently, then firmly, then nearly crushed her in his arms as his lips took hers and she gave back with a passion she didn't know was there. His lips slanted, giving and taking.

One hand cupped her bottom, almost lifting her, pinning her against him, and she loved it.

They were both breathless. "You're amazing," he rasped out. "Needed that. Need you."

They jumped when Sam knocked on the door that stood ajar and called in, "Medics leaving with the body, Quinn."

Feeling flushed and a bit faint—so maybe it was good Quinn was going to follow her home—Alex went outside with him and the staff as the EMTs carried Val's body away on the gurney, encased in a bright blue tarp, which they slid into the back of their vehicle. They placed her Gucci bag in the back, too, wrapped in plastic. It probably had the sales receipt from the gift shop for the bear bells she'd quickly made into a necklace. Had they jingled when she died?

Troopers Hanson and Kurtz stood at attention as if they would salute, but they did not.

Next to her truck, Alex saw the state trooper car they had come in. It was a blue and gold SUV with the words Guardians of the 49th on it. She jolted to see what was on the central shield of blue: the big, golden face of a bear staring right at her.

19

"What happened over there?" Suze asked the moment Alex got out of her truck in the lodge's small parking lot. Right behind her, Quinn killed his engine and stepped out, too. Suze looked at him, then back to Alex and called to them. "Chip saw troopers and the rescue squad go by. He was carrying on that a plane might have crashed. It was all Meg could do to calm him down. I was just going to drive over."

As they came closer, Alex told her, "Val Chambers, Ryker's girlfriend, who was here today for a while, the one I took over to the camp—she's dead." She looked at Quinn, unsure what more to say.

He told the wide-eyed woman, "She's marked up with bear claws, but my bet is she was killed by a human predator."

Suze gasped and covered her mouth with one hand for a moment, then gripped Alex's arm with the other. "You mean—claw marks like on the lodge wall? But then—then," she stammered, looking from one to the other, "was that a warning—to Alex? The troopers are on the case? Word will spread."

"And probably," Quinn said, "bring in hoards of the curious and the media to the camp, which will be off-limits. It may mean more business for the lodge, but not good for Alex. She could be a target for reporters since she found the body."

"Oh, no. You—you did?" Suze cried.

Alex nodded. She couldn't stand to recount it all now, not even to Suze, so how would she ever get through an interview, especially if a reporter learned about—even photographed—the marks outside her bedroom?

"I can't believe she's dead," Suze said, gripping her hands so hard together that her fingers went white. "I mean, I met her at the salmon bake the day you got here, Alex. But then just a couple of days ago, she came to the lodge—I think she went to the gift shop that day, too."

"Yes, she did," Alex said, reaching out to steady Suze.

"She looked around so much inside and out that I thought she and Ryker were going to maybe move here, though she made it really clear she didn't even like our little town."

"That's Val—was Val," Alex said.

"Does that poor girl have a family to bury her?"

Quinn said, "Ryker told the officers she has a sister she's close to who lives in Mission Viejo, California. She's not married, either, so same last name. Listen, Suzanne, since you may well be housing a horde of reporters soon, here's what I've been thinking. The two troopers and their reinforcements will be cordoning off my entire property, parking spaces, the compound, the backyard and into the woods where the crime occurred. And yes, Alex could be a target for any media who show up. They will, from Anchorage at least. She doesn't need her face nor her name online or on the air or the printed page, but it may become public record."

Alex's stomach flip-flopped. Surely he wasn't going to suggest what she was thinking—what she hoped. She bit her lower lip so hard it hurt.

"My New York City guest at the compound," Quinn went on, "is leaving later tomorrow. He even has a cab clear from Anchorage coming to get him. If he tries to stay longer, I'll have him move here to the lodge."

"We could use the business right now," Suze admitted. "But I still hope we don't get inundated with the press, however much the right kind of publicity would be nice."

"Are you two following why I'm going to propose a plan?" he asked, frowning. "For now Alex needs to come live where the reporters can't get to her, where the area is cordoned off and, at least for a while, we have state trooper protection. Since Brent Bayer is here one more night, I can sleep in my office tonight, and Alex can have my room. When Bayer leaves tomorrow, Alex—Spenser, too, of course—can move into that guest room because the whole area will be off-limits to outsiders of any kind."

"But I'd need to come back and forth to oversee the store," Alex put in as her heart beat harder. "It might get busy with all the new guests at the lodge, especially if there were people here to buy things, especially if people learn that the dead woman was my last shopper and bought a bunch of bear bells, no less. Quinn, I heard what you said the bells being no good, but I saw she had strung them and wore them around her neck."

"Yeah. I saw that, too, but didn't know the source.

If Mary is feeling up to it, we can ask her to cover the store for a few days until things calm down."

"But I can't ask her to do that, learn all that," Alex said.

Suze shook her head. "We used to pay Mary to cover at the store now and then when Meg and I were too busy. She knows the ropes."

"Why didn't you tell me that before?" Alex asked. "It would have given me a link to her since I don't think she likes me very much."

"It isn't you," Quinn said. "She's wary of outsiders and protective of me. She likes what Sam and I are doing and, of course, feels protective toward the heritage of Falls Lake."

"We thought you would worry you were taking Mary's job," Suze said. "When she started to get an upset stomach, about the time you called us about coming here, we were filling in for her all the time, anyway. Sam was grateful you were here."

"Oh," Alex said as jumbled thoughts bombarded her. What else hadn't they told her? Maybe Mary did not want her here because she still wanted the job, money to help get ready for the baby. And what would Mary, Sam and Josh say about her moving into the compound even if it was Quinn's idea, especially if Mary was protective of Quinn?

Above all, as kind as it was of Quinn, as desperate as she felt about being identified publicly, was she really ready to sleep tonight in Quinn's bedroom and then move into his guest room right across the hall?

"I—it's a desperate and unusual situation, you know what I mean," she told them. "I guess, well, I mean, it does make sense, just for a little while, I hope."

Alex's heart was beating so hard she could feel it with her hands against her breastbone. Probably nothing would come of publicity over this death in backwoods Alaska. It would be a long shot if Lyle or anyone would learn of this horrid event and trace her here. And to be close, day and night, to a man she was so attracted to was not a good idea.

No, she'd be insane to move in with Quinn, that's for sure, because she was coming to care for him so fast. A romantic relationship with him—with anyone now—would be the height of stupidity and recklessness.

"Thank you, Quinn," she said. "I'll get Spenser and my things together fast so we can get back."

Quinn followed Alex's truck back toward camp. His heart was pounding. This was the smart thing to do, but he knew he had to have the utmost self-control. Meg had given him that slant-eyed *Really?* look of hers when she was told the whole situation. Chip had been upset he couldn't go, too, and kept repeating that he was glad "another" plane had not crashed.

And that darn little Spenser—Quinn was almost as nervous about having him around as he was Alex— was all protective growls and barks getting back in her truck, as if he knew what his owner had been through or thought they were off for a long trek again. Especially, in his house, Spenser would remind him of his own lost dog—and other losses. And Alex would be one hell of a temptation. He'd steered pretty clear of women because it just made life easier and less complicated—but now...

He swore under his breath as he followed her into the parking lot at the camp. Trooper Hanson had un- spooled more yellow police tape when a van with a satellite dish and bright logo on its side drove in ahead of them. Quinn could tell it was from an Anchorage TV station. They must have been monitoring police calls or had an informant to be here this fast.

Glad to let Hanson talk to them, he grabbed Alex's single big bag while she lifted out a plastic laundry basket with shoes in it, what looked like a cosmetic bag and some of Spenser's stuff. He hustled her toward the gate, ignoring the voice yelling, "Hey, Q-Man! Can we ask you a few questions about events here today before we get kicked off the grounds? We can talk in the road!"

Though on a leash, Spenser growled, then barked as if he were a huge mastiff watchdog. Scotties always thought they were bigger than they were, but it made them brave as well as foolhardy.

As if he had not heard the reporter he recognized, he led Alex and Spenser inside and closed the gate behind them, then led them to his house in the corner of the compound. He almost never locked it but he had now, so he fumbled for his key.

For the first time, his familiar, cozy place seemed tiny, dark and plain. He went to his bedroom door, thankful he'd left the room neat enough. He'd even made the double bed and had the quilt pulled up on it. They set the things down on the braided rug partly covering the pine floor.

"Small, I know," he told her as she stepped in past him.

"Safe and private is what matters."

"Right. I—everyone here—will do our best to make you two feel at home. I've got to go over to the dining hall now to calm the students, and I should look out front to see if Trooper Hanson got that TV van off the property. I know this sounds strange, Queen Alexandra, but welcome to the Q-Man Tracking and Survival Camp."

Tracking—they needed to track a killer. Survival—poor Val had not managed that. She hoped Quinn would agree that one of the troopers should go over to the lodge to look at the clawed-up wall rather than just consult the photographs on her phone or in the printouts she'd made. Because although she meant to study those photos again, and though she'd been deeply shaken to see Val's bloody scratches, she had to admit that the claw marks looked absolutely the same.

It was a challenge to be in yet another strange room, hard for Spenser, too. And downright strange, though Quinn hardly seemed a stranger anymore. From the moment she had heard he'd carried around guilt from childhood, she'd sensed a kindred spirit. His clothes in the closet, where she hung her few things next to them, the blue curtains that covered the two windows, the extra forest-green towels in a stack on a bathroom shelf—yes, the quilt and covers on the bed—all exuded that sharp pine, windswept, outdoors scent that was definitely Quinn Mantell. It all seemed so alien and new, yet so warmly familiar.

She sat in the only chair in the room and petted Spenser in her lap as she continued to look around. The wooden walls were not sanded or stained but raw and natural. The colors in the braided throw rug next to the bed echoed the quilt colors. When she'd slid her emptied suitcase under the bed, she'd seen he had stored there snow skis as well as webbed snowshoes and several long poles. And a rifle, though he'd said he never carried a gun when he tracked.

Should she go out and find something to eat in the kitchen, or should she wait until they fed everyone tonight and go to the dining hall for that? For the first time since Quinn's talk to the group early that afternoon, she felt weak and hungry. She had only grabbed Spenser's food in her hasty exit from the lodge.

Meg had hugged her and whispered, "You be careful—in more ways than one."

Deciding to venture to the kitchen, she put Spenser on his leash again and went to the door. She opened it to find Mary standing there, close, her hand raised in a fist to knock.

"Oh, I didn't hear you coming!" Alex said.

"When I get big with this baby, maybe I will walk more noisily, maybe not go out much at all. Quinn explained to Sam and me why you are here. Don't mind Josh if he's upset. Josh is always upset. Come with me, let's get some food. I crave sour stuff these days, though my appetite is not what it used to be, with all that's going on. I just hope this third generation from the water doesn't experience such bad days," she said, patting her still-flat stomach.

Alex mulled that over as she followed Mary, wondering if she was counting generations from her grandparents who were killed when the waterfall let loose the deadly flood at Falls Lake. She wanted to study Mary, try to understand and befriend her.

"It's good, considering your new condition, that you didn't have to see the worst of things today," Alex told her as they headed into the kitchen and Mary took two apples from the polished wooden counter. She took a sharp knife from the drawer and deftly cut each in half.

"That is," Alex went on, "I'm glad you didn't go all the way down that path to see Val's body but headed for the compound."

"Even if I didn't see her dead, I see her in my head, though not in my heart," she said, pouring two glasses of milk from the small fridge and grabbing some raisin cookies from a plastic jar. "My family's deaths are in my heart every time I see Falls Lake, knowing they are lost beneath."

The woman seemed obsessed with the grief of losing her grandparents and their sunken village. But then Alex could understand grieving for lost souls.

20

"We all share food here. Mostly I do the grocery shopping," Mary told Alex. Did she feel judged for taking food from Quinn's kitchen? Spenser sat alert on the floor with his head cocked and his one eye watching. Did he, too, sense the tension in the air between Alex and this woman?

They sat side by side on stools at the small, raised eating bar. Mary chopped her apple half in small pieces with her knife, but Alex ate her halved apple and cookies as they were. Alex noticed she was not wearing the bear claw necklace she'd seen once before. Her pulse began to pound. Someone had scratched Val horribly with bear claws that Quinn insisted did not come from a live bear.

She studied Mary's hands and wrists. No bruises or scratches. No blood on her clothing if those were the garments she'd had on earlier today. She dare not glance down at her shoes right now.

And Mary had been on her way back to the compound before Val was killed. Maybe Mary had convinced her to come out into the forest a little way with her or promised she'd walk Val out to see Ryker.

She saw Mary was slanting her a sideways look in the sudden silence between them.

"I meant to ask you about your bear claw necklace." Alex said. "It was so unique I wanted to see it again."

"Broke. I have to restring it. It's very dear to me. My mother's taking it away to restring it is what saved her from the flood." She minced the apple ever finer, then scooped up the nearly crushed pieces with her fingers. When she noticed Alex watching, she shrugged.

"My jaw hurts a bit if I chew something big. Besides, I like to think I am cutting it up for my baby—ha. Like he eats it direct instead of through my blood."

"Do you think you will have a boy?"

"I don't know, but he—or she—does not like me joking about him. My stomach is starting to feel funny again. I will go home and lie down. Tell Sam if you see him."

"Yes, I will," Alex promised before she realized that the last time she played messenger for Sam and Mary she had stumbled on Val's body. "Here," she said as Mary stood, "let me just walk to your door with you."

Mary shrugged, which meant either, *Thanks but you don't have to do that* or *I wish you wouldn't.* But since Alex was going to be staying for a little while at the compound, she wanted to know what and where all the buildings were. She intended to volunteer to help with Quinn's team here, and she had to know the lay of the land in more ways than one.

They walked outside toward an even smaller house in the back corner of the property. The meeting area with the food hall was the only large building here.

"We will add on a room soon," Mary said.

"That will be great. Before the snow, I would think."

Alex decided she would not go in with her, even if asked. As they approached the house, she noticed a massive rack of caribou antlers over the front door.

"Those antlers are amazing!" Alex whispered.

"They're special to Sam because Trapper Jake, who taught him and Quinn so much, had them over his fireplace at his cabin in the woods. It's no longer there—the cabin. But many places we no longer have are still in our hearts. Like the cabin where I spent so many happy times with my grandmother after my own mother died."

"I can surely understand that. You were blessed to know her. I—I lost someone I keep close to my heart too."

Mary heaved a sigh that either meant she was tired of talking or was just plain tired. Alex touched the woman's elbow when she seemed to waver. She did not pull back, but a frown crunched her face as she went on.

"I wish for no one's death. But Val was bad for Ryker, bad for our work here. I just hope Ryker stays, doesn't get discouraged or—or arrested."

"But he seemed to care for her, despite her temperament at times."

She nodded. "More fool he, but we all make mistakes we regret."

So did Mary mean that Ryker himself might have killed Val? Or worse, maybe Mary had wanted Val gone to protect Ryker. If so, did Mary now see her, another outsider, as a threat? Was she in danger, distracting the man who was the face and brains behind the classes and TV program—Sam and Mary's income and future?

No, she was letting her imagination run wild, but

what about those claw marks outside her bedroom? Was it a warning or a threat?

"I'm going to lie down now," she told Alex, shrugging off her touch.

She was relieved Mary did not ask her in. She watched the woman disappear and hurried back toward Quinn's house, glancing more than once over her shoulder and into the trees.

Alex was tempted to join Quinn and his students in the dining hall, but with Spenser curled up beside her, she fell asleep, fully dressed and exhausted, on his bed, dreaming of swimming in Falls Lake, looking for drowned people with bloody scratches on them, people she didn't know, people she was afraid of, people…

Oh, but someone was swimming with her, coming right behind. Thank heavens it wasn't Mary, but Allie with her hair streaming out behind in the water, or was that the wind? Alex reached back for her sister's hand, trying to pull her closer, closer, and save her…but then she disappeared into the floating houses and bodies…

She jolted awake as Spenser gave a single, little yip. Someone had knocked on the bedroom door. Oh, right, she was in Quinn's room, on his bed.

"Quinn?" she called out, swinging her legs over the side and getting up. "You can come in."

He opened the door halfway and poked his head around it. "Looks good. I'd like to get some sleep, too. It's finally dark and may be a long night. Troopers Kurtz and Hanson are still here. They've talked to everyone to explain basically what happened, and I promised our students it will be business as usual tomorrow."

Alex lifted Spenser down, who ran to Quinn to be

picked up. At least she could totally trust Quinn—
Spenser said so.

She shoved her feet in her low-cut boots and raked
her hair back with her fingers. She hadn't noticed before, but there was not a good mirror in here, only a
small one on the pine dresser. Well, she was hardly staying at the Sheraton or planning to go out on the town.

"If you need the bathroom, I hope you've seen it's
right across the hall," he said. "I brought you a plate of
sloppy joes and some salad and cake from the dining
hall. Josh fixed it for you. I'll wait in the kitchen until
you're ready. I'll fill you in on what's happening," he
said, and moved away.

What's happening, she thought to herself, is that, despite the horror and chaos, she was falling for Quinn
Mantell. Spenser was, too, and that little guy was the
best barometer she knew for trusting people. It scared
her that she could tell Quinn had something important
to tell her, but he was waiting.

She hurried into the bathroom. A toilet and washba-
sin, a shower and tub, too, but obviously, she thought
as she washed her hands, no hot water. At least water
ran and the toilet flushed. That's right, Suze had said
something about how they boiled water for washing
over here. So Quinn took cold showers? Maybe that
was a good thing, if he was feeling even a little bit toward her as she did him.

She joined him in the now-familiar small kitchen and
sat at the breakfast bar again. Spenser was on Quinn's
lap eating a piece of cheese as if that were the most natural thing in the world. She saw no sign of Mary's knife
or the apple and cookie crumb mess she'd left. And yes,
there was a tray of food waiting for her, covered with

tin foil. Oh, Quinn had the same, so he meant to dine with her. Dine—that was a good one around here. And yet this place seemed "so him" that she liked it, was intrigued by it all.

"The troopers are staying at the lodge tonight," he said, "but they're still on-site and plan to join us here soon before they leave. They've permitted Brent Bayer to tag along for now, since he's convinced them he's my lawyer. But I told Brent he doesn't have to stay, so he's still leaving tomorrow.

"The two extra troopers are going to take shifts and bunk in the dining hall tonight," he went on. "They'll be in charge here tomorrow when Kurtz and Hanson go back to Anchorage to report in on their investigation so far and Brent leaves. But, I'm afraid, more media are expected.

"I poured us some ginger ale instead of beer, which is the drink of choice tonight over in the dining hall," he added, gesturing to the glasses next to the trays as if she hadn't noticed the big tumblers with ice cubes. He handed her her glass, clinked it with his, and each took a swallow, staring briefly at each other over the rims.

"But let me bring you up to speed on the rest before we eat," he said. "I can rewarm this stuff in the microwave if it gets cold. See, I have some of the modern world in here—including you, right now."

He gave her a taut smile. Still holding his steady gaze, she nodded as he went on. "I'm glad you weren't in the dining hall this evening because a lot of people asked what Val's body looked like, and they would have driven you nuts with questions. Your keeping a low profile is best right now—but for the troopers, who may have more questions, of course. Trooper Kurtz told me they are rushing the autopsy results in Anchorage, though some of the toxicology tests take time."

"Do they believe you it wasn't a bear?"

"I'm not sure, but I have some cred with them. Alex, just like what was found outside your window, I'd know. Hate to bring this up before we eat, but I know what a bear mauling looks like. The back of Val's neck, maybe her entire neck, would be bitten through with lots of blood from the carotid artery. Those throat and chest scratches are deep enough to make her bleed but not to bleed out. I'll bet if we'd turned her over, we would have seen a blow or blood on the back of her head or maybe neck."

"Which maybe means whoever killed her—if he or she were from this area—might know, too, that her body should have looked different if it was a bear. By that, I mean, her killer might not be local."

"Good point. I thought at first it had to be someone from around here, and that's tearing me up. I know—and I think the troopers have figured it out, too—that Val was not liked around here, by my staff, by me. I tried to tell them who knows who she offended or even attracted in town."

"Ryker might not know about a bear biting the neck in a fatal attack, if someone needed to stage that. He kept going in and out from your students' area, darting off here and there to film. Did the troopers ask for his film footage—whatever you'd call it?"

"It's all video these days. No, not until he'd gone back to the lodge with his camera, but he let them see what he had—or says he did. The final editing goes on in New York, but I've seen him delete sections on his own. Our lawyer visitor challenged the troopers on taking the show's video, as if he were representing me and my staff, which wasn't the case and had not been decided. I know he's trying to help—he called Geoff to explain what happened—but I don't think anyone here needs a lawyer. Frankly, I'm glad he's leaving tomorrow and told him not to change his mind about that.

"Here, let me warm up this food, and we'll eat before we're questioned again," he said, suddenly looking very upset when he'd seemed stoic before.

He removed the tin foil from the trays. "I'll just put these sandwiches in," he said, sliding them with a fork onto a plastic plate, then moving them to the microwave. "I'll bet you're hungry, so sorry I held up a while. Dig in."

He came back quickly. She ate a few bites of the fruit salad with apples and oranges among other things.

"Oh, no," she told him, "I forgot to tell Sam that Mary didn't feel good again and went back to their house to lie down. I walked her to her door."

Like a kid—she'd seen Chip do this—he took a big bite of his cake before touching his salad as the microwave buzzer went off. "Sam went to check on her when she didn't come back," he said. "He said she was sleeping, which is good because she's had worse insomnia lately, wanders around the house, even sits outside until he wakes up and makes her go back to bed. Probably nervous about the baby after all this time they were hoping for a family."

He got up to open the microwave and bring their sandwiches back.

"Mary and I sat right here earlier and had apples, cookies and milk," she told him. "She did not want to talk about her bear claw necklace when I mentioned it. She said she broke it, and it had to be restrung."

Quinn stopped his sandwich halfway to his mouth. "Meaning what? What are you thinking?"

"Quinn, I've never been pregnant, but I know women can sleep more when they are, and you just said her insomnia's worse. I know people didn't like Val—I think even Ryker didn't at times—but Mary wanted Val gone. She was in the vicinity and—"

"And so were Josh, Sam, Ryker—even you. Even Brent Bayer. Mary's a haunted woman, I'll admit that. But Sam loves her, she's loyal to our project and she would not kill anyone. Alex, don't suggest any of this circumstantial stuff to the troopers, but let them work this—this homicide, okay?"

"Yes, of course. I'll only answer questions if they are put to me. Nothing leading. I'm sure they'll talk to her, too."

"First thing tomorrow, to her and Sam. They've already grilled Ryker."

"Any hint of what he said?"

"I've advised the troopers before on a couple of search and rescues, working with a friend of mine who is full-time SAR, but I'm sure as hell not advising the authorities on this beyond saying—sadly so, because it would solve all this if it was an animal—that a bear did not kill and maul Valerie Chambers. Now, let's try to eat. We're going to need our strength for what's yet to come."

"Nothing else dire, I hope," she said, and took a bite of the sloppy joe.

"Not between you and me at least," he told her with his mouth half-full and a drop of red tomato sauce on his chin. Like an idiot, she reached out with her paper napkin to wipe it off.

Their eyes met and held again. She had the strangest and best feeling he was going to put his sandwich down to reach for her.

"Just did that since your mother's miles away," she told him, and took another bite.

The tenuous moment didn't pass but hung between them. Despite living at the edge of a forest frontier, despite a murder investigation going full swing—despite her own sanity to keep in control here—she felt suddenly safe from everything but her feelings for this man.

21

Alex had been hoping that Quinn could stay with her when she was questioned again by the state troopers. But sitting in the privacy of Quinn's office, it was just her and Trooper Kurtz. He tossed his brimmed hat on the desk, so at least she could see his face and eyes better.

"I'm especially interested in Valerie Chambers's comments and actions when you spent time with her the day she died." He glanced down at his notebook. "That would be both when she visited the lodge gift shop and in your car on the way to the tracking and survival camp."

She wanted to be careful what she said. People could testify that she disappeared for a while—in the area of the murder—when she went to find Mary for Sam. No doubt law enforcement didn't rule anyone out until they had to.

Kurtz had rolled Quinn's chair out from behind the desk and had her pinned in where she sat on the couch. She gripped her hands together, then loosened her fingers as she did not want to seem overly nervous.

Before she could begin, he added, "I realize you have been through other tough times—trauma—than this, Alex. Quinn made the point that your privacy should be protected since you have escaped a dangerous domestic situation. We will do what we can to protect your identity, but I can't promise you that information won't leak out through the media. The last time we had a bear mauling death, it made big news, even in the lower forty-eight news cycles."

"I appreciate anything you can do. And yes, the fear of discovery—by someone from my previous situation—does worry me. But as for Val, she did seem to flaunt her love of the good life, city life, California life, so I wondered from the start why she wanted Chris Ryker, who evidently loved working in the wilds. She had dreams of taking him to LA, of his working in Hollywood movies. She didn't read him very well."

"And from other interviews, I take it almost everyone, especially Chris Ryker, knew she was not a fan of Alaska."

Her eyes widened. Was that a hint that Ryker was under suspicion? Maybe Val had pushed him too far, tried to bribe or pressure him to leave and he had lost control. But if he had bear claws in his backpack—and Val had mentioned he collected such items—had he ditched them now? Could he, for some reason, have scratched the wood outside her window?

Alex cleared her throat and went on. "As to what she spoke about in that store visit, it was her love for Los Angeles, the lifestyle there. She bought some bear bells, the ones she had strung around her neck when I found her, and talked about the fact they were cute and reminded her of the USC Bruins. You saw that bear sweatshirt she had on. How ironic, bear bells and a bear outfit, and then a bear—or, as Quinn says, someone wanting to make it look like a bear—killed her."

"By the way, my partner, Hanson, got a search warrant so we could take a look at Ryker's room in town where the victim was staying with him. Did she reference anything about items she or he had there?"

Alex frowned, concentrating, remembering. So much had happened. "She did say she was annoyed at how he collected local memorabilia, but I'm pretty sure those bear bells were not for him."

"Memorabilia, such as?" he said, his pen poised again. "It will help us to know what we're walking into."

"She did say," Alex told him, speaking slowly, "that his camera cost twenty-eight thousand dollars."

Kurtz's eyebrows lifted before he frowned as he wrote her words down. "So Ryker must have confided in her. Maybe confided too much, because he told me he wasn't leaving 'this gig,' as he put it, to go to California."

She almost blurted out that she'd heard Val and Ryker argue just before everyone went out to the forest. But she might as well have because it was as if the trooper had read her mind.

"Did you hear Chris Ryker and Valerie Chambers have a disagreement that afternoon, just before everyone went outside? Several others reported they did, and Ryker admitted that."

"I heard them from a distance. Although they were not talking quietly, I don't know what it was about."

"Quinn and Brent Bayer are telling me she was fed up here and he wouldn't leave—no breaking news there, only corroboration." He reached back for his hat on the desk. "Both Mary and Sam Spruce brought that argument up right away—even stressed it—so I was surprised you didn't."

"Of course, if Ryker planned to harm her, I doubt if he would have had a public falling-out with her right before," she said, but she was thinking that Mary and Sam seemed set on emphasizing Ryker as a suspect, even though they'd wanted to defend him earlier as part of their team. She realized she had just given an opinion again, but he nodded.

"Many murders are crimes of passion, not reasoning," Kurtz said. "Such is life—and death. Thank you for the information on this and your perspective, and I may need to question some witnesses here again, including you."

"How did it go?" Quinn asked when they were alone again in his office.

"All right. It seems they may be thinking Ryker, though."

"I guess they always look at the partner first, the husband, the boyfriend, fiancé—lover."

She nodded, and they were silent for a moment. He wondered if she was thinking of her former fiancé.

Their gazes met again before he looked away. He wanted to hold her, but he didn't want to press, to take advantage of this tragedy. "Want to sit out on the porch for a few minutes before bed? Or if you're beat, you can have the bathroom first and lights out. Brent's on his phone to New York in the guest bedroom and says he's going to sleep after that. I swear, he's asked as many questions as the troopers."

"Did you get what you need out of your bedroom before I take it over tonight?"

"I grabbed a few things before you even agreed to stay there."

"You were sure I would?"

"It was the best thing for you to do, and you're a smart woman."

"Thank you for that. Sometimes I wonder. I'll go get Spenser and bring him along."

Alex put Spenser on his leash and went to the porch entrance. Quinn had arranged two of the several lawn chairs tight together for them. Since Spenser could not get out, she just dropped his leash, but he still stayed at their feet.

When they sat, Quinn took her hand. The night, noisy with the rustling of leaves and owl sounds, reached in. Spenser, thinking he was their guardian, began to patrol the edge of the ceiling-to-floor screens, dragging his leash.

"Sorry you're caught up in this. What a mess," he said. "Poor, unpopular Val, fish out of water—then no water to even breathe."

"Yes. As for me, I'm used to being in a mess. I was in a mess before I even knew it."

"With your fiancé?"

She nodded. Even in the dark, she could feel him watching her intently. "I must have thought I was living a dream, and it turned out to be a nightmare."

He squeezed her hand. "We have that in common. If you know tough times, you recognize when things are better, even good."

"I agree. I'm—at least before today—determined to get there."

"What we don't have in common, we could make up for. Enjoy each other, do things together, support each other, maybe do more than just get intrigued by and like each other. Want to give it a try—more of a try than we've been able to so far—and now with this chaos?"

"Yes. Yes, I do."

"That's all I needed to know. I second that."

He turned even more toward her and pulled her closer. He tilted his head so that their lips met, slanted, melded. As tired and distressed as she was, she felt that kiss clear down into her belly and beyond. It was so different from how she felt and responded to Lyle, so... trusting and warm. Well, hot, too. She felt she could give and take here, not just give, give, give...

The kiss seemed as endless as the forest and night beyond. He tugged her to her feet, and they kept kissing, caressing. Thinking they were going somewhere, Spenser came over and rubbed against their ankles. They ignored him. He went around them until they realized he'd tied their ankles together with his loose leash.

"Your little friend," Quinn whispered, "is giving us a message. It's his version of a lovers' knot. Listen, sweetheart, I don't mean to give you the wrong idea," he whispered in her ear as they held tight together. "We both need our sleep tonight. But I hope that—"

He stopped speaking and froze. She gripped him closer. A sudden sound, a distant voice, shrill, nasal... It seemed androgynous, neither male nor female, and that sent shivers through her.

Quinn stepped out of the leash, set her back and stood between her and the screen.

"Not an owl?" she asked, whispering.

"No way."

"It sounds kind of like what we heard out by the lake."

"I've never heard it this close, not around here."

In the dark, they stood, staring out into the windy night. Suddenly, he pushed her back a bit more, then gripped her wrist hard. Spenser growled.

A dark form passed between them and the nearest cedar tree next to the stockade fence. Someone moving smoothly through the darkness inside the compound, and then that cry again, this time followed by the familiar voice that became slowly distant. To Alex's amazement, Spenser seemed too cowed to bark, but continued to growl.

"I'm going out," he whispered.

"No. Not alone, and—"

"Do you believe in earthly spirits and ghosts?"

"No, but—Quinn, maybe that was Mary. Sam said she has insomnia, walks in her sleep, and I swear, she's haunted by the losses of her people."

"Sam says he only finds her out on their porch. It's someone else."

"Can you call Sam?"

"Turns his phone off at night."

"Then let's go wake him—see if she's there. People sleepwalking can do lots of things they don't remember. Quinn, she's pregnant and could hurt herself."

"Okay, lock Spenser in the bedroom. To Sam's house, then I may go beyond."

She wanted to say, *I'll go with you if you go into the woods*, but the words wouldn't come out.

22

Quinn's big flashlight stabbed a shaft of light before their feet as they ran toward Sam and Mary's house. Alex was exhausted, and yet fear for Mary jump-started her adrenaline rush.

Although it was after midnight, they saw the Spruces' house was lit from within. Standing on the front porch, Sam was shouting Mary's name over and over.

"Quinn," Sam yelled when he saw them. "She's not here this time! She must have wandered away."

"She may have gone past my place. We saw something or someone through the porch screens. We also heard that crying voice. What if she's the Falls Lake ghost."

"No! No way! She wants to find it, see if it's her grandmother's spirit, and I can't talk her out of that. Maybe it has to do with her passion to get pregnant and have a child—but never mind all that now. We got to bring her back if she's sleepwalking again, going to the lake. I'll get a flashlight, too! I wish Josh was here to help."

He darted inside and came back out with a flashlight

that threw a beam even bigger than Quinn's. The three of them jogged the way they'd seen the dark form go past Quinn's porch.

"You think she might go out the back door of the compound?" Sam asked.

"I made sure the padlock was not only on it but shut. But I had to give the two troopers down in the dining hall the combination. If we can't find her right away, we'll get their help."

"And have them think she's a little crazy? I mean, if they learn she walks in her sleep and doesn't remember it, what else they gonna think she did and doesn't remember it?"

Alex stumbled as they darted around the dining hall, but Quinn's grip on her arm held her up and pulled her on. The lights were off inside, so maybe the troopers were asleep. She actually wished that Kurtz and Hanson had stayed here, too, because they could use their help now, but they were over at the lodge. Unfortunately, their staying a night there meant they'd be fair game to any reporters who showed up.

"Damn!" Sam muttered when they saw that not only the lock but the gate were open. "You think she remembers the combination in her sleep? I swear I didn't think she went out. Let's find her quick. If not, I'll come back for the troopers."

"Listen!" Alex said. "I do hear that voice. We can track her by that."

"You stay here," Quinn insisted. "Go straight back to the house and lock yourself in with Spenser. You don't need to be out here at night, not after everything today. If Brent is still up and asks where I am, tell him I'm with Sam."

"No, I want to help. I want to help find her."

Sam's face looked like a fright mask in the reflected flashlight beams, but she saw him nod at her.

Sam said to Quinn, "Alex wants to help. I say she comes along."

Quinn swore under his breath as the three of them plunged out into the dark.

Quinn was impressed by Alex's stamina and determination. Was that part of what had drawn him to her? Or was it her stubbornness, however vulnerable she seemed at times?

The voice was sporadic now but not as distant. Despite the darkness, they picked up their pace. He let Sam lead the way with Alex next while he brought up the rear. She knew to follow, not to talk, to keep up. Damn, but she even seemed to remember where the patch of devil's club was and skirted around it, while Sam got some of it on his pant legs.

They were almost to the lake, to the spot he always brought the beginner tracker classes on their last day for a picnic and a walk down to see the beaver dams and waterfall. He could hear the roar of that tall, silver spume that had opened its fierce mouth once to drown the little pioneer village. If Mary was obsessed with that, she probably needed psychiatric help, not for walking in her sleep but to get over eternally mourning her drowned ancestors, especially now when she needed to look after herself during a pregnancy.

They emerged from the forest through the opening he had always referred to as "the twisted path," the same one he and Alex had used to find Spenser just three days ago, though it seemed like three years. It was cloudy, so light from the moon and stars were no help, yet at the expanse of water, they turned off their lights to be able to see better, farther. A dark night at the end of a dark day—

"Wish she dressed in white instead of the dark denim she wears," Alex said as the three of them strained their eyes to search the stony shore. "What does she wear to bed?"

"Sometimes she just falls asleep in her clothes, like tonight. If she was wearing white, which she is not, she would look like a ghost," Sam muttered. "Now I will not allow that, and she will never sneak out again."

"But, my friend," Quinn said, "what if she thinks she can communicate with her family's, mourn for them this way?"

"With the baby now," Sam said, his voice angry, "she can't!"

"There!" Alex said, pointing. "Something dark moved down there."

Sam's beam illumined a moose drinking from the edge of the lake.

"Sorry," Alex whispered.

"It is good," Sam told her. "You are helping. She needs a friend."

Quinn saw Alex nod and a tear track on her cheek gilded bright in Sam's light. He figured she was thinking about the loss of her sister. "Let's walk the shore," Quinn said, "at least a ways. I wish she'd make some noise again."

But they jolted when they heard the cry, louder, even more sharp and distressed. Quinn put his arm around Alex and tugged her to him. "Just where we heard it the other night," he whispered. "Let's go that way, Sam."

"I cannot believe that can be her, out here alone, en-dangering herself," Sam said, his voice betraying he was close to tears.

Quinn countered, "You have to accept she might have done this other times. You sleep like a rock, she doesn't and—"

"Quiet!" Alex insisted. "Are we going over there or not?"

This girl had guts, Quinn thought. Despite the high odds against her staying in Falls Lake, even in this dark, the light in his head went on at last: he had found the woman he wanted to be with forever.

Their feet crunched stones on the shingle shore as, still with their lights out, they jogged toward where they had heard the voice. Alex thought it might be a woman but maybe not. A man could make that atonal, nasal sort of sound.

But all was quiet now.

They stopped, standing, waiting. No sounds but the brisk lapping of water nearly at their feet and the occa-sional call of a night bird, the rustle of leaves and the distant, almost hissing sound of the distant Falls Lake waterfall.

"Should we go farther?" Sam asked. "Should we head back? If she's gone this far before, she always comes back."

"I don't know," Quinn said. "I don't want to split up with Alex and me staying and you heading back or vice versa, but I guess we'd better."

"Is that the moose again?" Alex asked, pointing. "I think I see it this time back where we came from."

They all turned around again. "It's her," Sam whispered. "A single walker in a long skirt."

"We need to catch up," Alex insisted, "but not panic her, in case she really is sleepwalking—in a trance or something."

They moved off the shore so they would not make noise. When they stepped up onto the rough turf before the thickest trees began again, Quinn took her hand as the dark figure turned away toward the trees. Alex was instantly out of breath at the pace Sam set.

Quinn had to let her hand go as they plunged back into the dark forest, using their flashlights now.

"If we get close to her," Sam said, "we'll have to go dark, so we don't scare her."

Alex soon had a stitch in her side. It made her remember how Mary kept complaining about the pain in her stomach. Maybe she should have that looked at by a doctor as well as seeing a psychiatrist—but were there any around here?

They nearly caught up with someone on the path ahead. They could hear the sporadic voice again but not footsteps as if the voice had no body, no feet, no human form. Near the back gate of the compound, they saw a figure, standing there, not moving, just sobbing. Yes. Yes, it was Mary for sure.

"Don't startle her," Quinn whispered, but too late because Sam called out.

"Mary! Mary, we're here!"

And then the bad dream plunged into nightmare. It was not their lights, nor the wan ones from the compound door, which stood ajar, but a bright blast of beams from all around jumping at them. Strong lights, strobe lights, blinding lights.

Sam reached for Mary and hugged her to him, trying to shield her as she screamed out over and over what sounded like "Grandma!"

Quinn thrust Alex behind him, and she hid behind his back.

Reporters! At least four with cameras as big as Ryker's. Voices shouting questions in a blur of sound. Mary sobbed. Quinn shouted at them, "Back off! Stand back and turn those cameras off!"

"Just a few questions! We had to come around the back way to the tracking compound because the front has police tape!" a man's voice came from behind the bright lights.

"You are Quinn Mantell, Q-Man, right?" another voice demanded.

"We admire your show. I'm Rex Myers from *Real Ghosts*, another cable show, not in competition with yours. We're streaming live, too. If we can ask a few questions about whether the ghost could have killed that visitor, we'll clear out. Maybe just a short interview with you and the woman who found the body, Alex Collister. And if any of you can comment on the Falls Lake murder, we'd appreciate it."

Sheltered from the lights behind Quinn's back, Alex got a glimpse of Mary. Her face was frozen in fear. And catching the light, glistening, was the bear claw necklace she'd told Alex earlier today was broken and she had to restring. Then the lights blinded her eyes, made her blink. She had looked right at them, into them.

"Go!" Quinn ordered Sam. "Take her and go!"

With a raised hand to block the light, Sam moved ahead with Mary, and Quinn pulled Alex with him off the crooked path to get around the group. The lights were so bright she could not tell how many there were for sure. Someone—maybe more than one—ran along behind still shouting questions. One voice yelled the name of an Anchorage TV station.

A woman's voice now close behind them called out. "I'm Lydia Scarlet from the magazine *Secrets*. Can either of you give me a brief statement, then we can leave you alone?"

Alex covered her face with her hand and was horrified to hear another woman's voice call her by name.

Dear God, if these people had learned who and where she was, they would broadcast it, live-stream it, print it.

Quinn had a good grip on her arm as he steered her toward the back compound gate. Just as they neared it, the two troopers darted out.

"Media!" Quinn shouted to them. "Came around through the woods."

"Is the crime scene back here somewhere?" the *Real Ghosts* reporter shouted. "Trooper, could we talk to you about these haunted woods and the murder?"

They kept going, and the troopers held back the onslaught. It seemed so dark, yet safe inside the compound lit only by the window light in the dining hall.

They went farther in, Sam still holding Mary to him while she blinked at it all—and, indeed, seemed to wake up. "Why are we all here in the dark?" she asked.

Quinn also held Alex tight to his side, then turned her to face him for a big hug. The four of them listened to the sounds of the troopers disbursing the little crowd on the other side of the tall board fence: "Freedom of speech...the public's right to know..." came the protests countered by a jumble of orders from the troopers.

"Got to get her to bed," Sam said. He'd draped his jacket over Mary's shoulders, which hid the necklace—

if Alex had not imagined it. "Then tomorrow a doctor," he promised.

"For the baby?" Mary asked as they turned away. "My stomach doesn't even hurt right now, but who were those loud people?"

So much, Alex thought, for Mary taking over the store at the lodge, at least right now. And so much for her own low profile through this tragedy. Those invaders knew her name. They might now have her face. And they would certainly put Falls Lake on the media map.

23

Whether she closed her eyes or opened them, pulsating puddles of magenta and chartreuse remained from the attack of bright lights. So had she seen Mary's bear claw necklace, or imagined it? She tried to blink the spots away as Brent Bayer hurried toward them inside the compound.

"I wish I could padlock the back entry," Quinn was saying, "but the troopers were still outside. At least it sounds like the protests have stopped."

"What's all that noise?" Brent demanded, catching up to them and blocking their path. "What in hell is going on out there?"

Quinn said, "It was an attack of reporters who went around the compound in the dark and ambushed us."

"Why were you two out, anyway? Not the time or place for a romantic lovers' stroll, is it?"

They walked around the man. Alex still couldn't see well but she could sense that Quinn was about to explode. He no longer sounded stunned but furious. She wondered if he was thinking that Brent might have set this up, but there was no way he could have known they would go outside then. Quinn had told her earlier that Brent was pushing to include segments on the Falls Lake 'ghost' and lost village.

Brent came right behind them into the house and the living room. "I've been talking to Geoff for an hour, making other calls, trying to explain. Tell me what's happening, so I can call him back and fill him in on the latest."

"And will you call anyone else?" Quinn challenged. "I'm just hoping you don't want publicity for the show so much you'll go out there to give interviews. There's an Anchorage TV station reporter, so maybe they spread the word to their affiliates. Brent, there are even idiots out there from the *Real Ghosts* cable show and some tabloid called *Secrets*. Or maybe the media in LA got here this fast, if Val's death was announced there. But I think word spread just a little too fast, and I hope not by someone here."

"You better not mean me. I'm a lawyer, damn it, not a publicist! But that was his wife Sam hustled past me, right? She kept flitting here and there earlier today, and I never got a chance to meet her or pin her down."

"She walks in her sleep and went out into the woods. We went after her," Quinn said.

"In the dead of night? You're all crazy! And I heard she's pregnant. With Val's death and all, she could really get hurt out there."

"So could we all. The troopers heard the ruckus and came out. If we hadn't located Mary right away, I would have asked them to help find her."

Finally, Alex's eyes were clearing. What if this lawyer, who'd been on the phone with Geoff—and could they trust Geoff completely?—had earlier phoned contacts in the media to get publicity for filming the *Q-Man* series? As Quinn had suggested, it was amazing how quickly those people must have flown into Anchorage and driven here, found this compound and gone out around it to the back door if someone hadn't tipped them off and given them directions.

When Brent stomped off to call Geoff again, Alex whispered, "You may be right not to trust him. Maybe he's like a—a Trojan horse."

He put his arm around her shoulders and heaved a huge sigh. "You and your animals. But yeah, my thoughts exactly. I'm trusting no one but Sam and you right now. Glad you're on my side, because I'm starting to wonder who else is."

"What about Geoff?"

"He's on my side, at least the show's side. He's got too much invested here, as does Brent, so I shouldn't have lost it with him."

"Also, sorry to say this, but are you sure Josh is on board? I think he's bitter toward Sam, maybe you, too."

"It's bad enough to think Mary harmed Val, but I can't stand to suspect the others, either. I saw Mary had her bear claw necklace on again. The timing's terrible, but I'm going to ask her to let me have it so forensics can eliminate that its claws were the ones that scratched Val. She may refuse to part with it, but—like I said—I can't stand for her to think I suspect her. Alex, I'm scared my tried and true team might disintegrate. I think the troopers are looking at Ryker, got a fast search warrant for his place in town."

"I knew they'd asked for one. I'll try to wait until tomorrow for more agonizing and theorizing since we do need some sleep."

He tugged her down onto the couch that faced the

empty fireplace. "I need you, Alex, your sharp brain—the rest of you, too."

She could tell he forced the smile he gave her. She leaned her head on his shoulder. She was absolutely drained, could have gone to sleep right here and now.

They were silent for a few minutes, then he whispered, "When we get rid of Brent tomorrow, despite having to cover for Sam with the class, I'll find some time for us to be together—just us. Better get to bed now and try to sleep for a couple hours. I've scheduled a hike for the class tomorrow after breakfast, and I'll have to do it without Sam and Mary, since he'll be taking her to a doctor, probably in Anchorage."

"I can help serve breakfast, then go with you, not that I'd know what I'm doing in that big kitchen or on the hike. I'll just tell any of the students who are curious that I can't say anything about finding Val."

"Your pitching in would help Josh and me. He'll be here first thing in the morning, then go out with us on the hike. We'll steer clear of the murder site, head the opposite way. But whether I'm near or not, whatever happens on the hike, you be careful."

Alex jolted awake when someone knocked on her—that is, Quinn's—bedroom door. She heard Spenser jump from his bed on the floor and run to the door with a single bark. The strange surroundings swam in shades of gray.

The bedside digital clock read five a.m. She'd slept about four hours and felt as if her limbs were lead.

"You up?" Quinn called through the door.

"I am now."

"Bathroom's all yours. Brent's out in front waiting for his Uber ride to Anchorage."

The horrors of an endless yesterday flooded back. Val dead, Mary a mess and a murderer on the loose. The media had swarmed in and could still be nearby. And she was in Quinn's compound, in his house, his room, his bed.

"If you want me to take Spenser out," he called through the door, "hand me his leash."

She got up, turned on the bedside light. Yes, his leash was where she'd left it. She snapped it on Spenser's collar, then opened the door for him to go out. No way did she want Quinn to see her like this so she didn't even poke her head around.

"I'll walk him, bring him back to you at the dining hall."

Once she was sure Quinn was not in the hall, she padded into the bathroom. The window was cracked for fresh air, but the place smelled of men's aftershave. Was that Brent's or Quinn's? She had a great pine-scented, light green lotion with aloe and avocado she'd planned to give Quinn. Luckily, that was one of the few products she'd brought to the compound. That reminded her she had online orders to fill. She hoped her supplier sent her order to Suze soon.

She tried not to glance in the mirror, but she did. And remembered then. She'd been dreaming about looking for Allie in the forest so the killer would not get her. But she found her dead, lying all cut up by a stream, and when she glimpsed her own face in the water, she saw that she was her sister's killer.

But then she'd heard Allie crying from the darkness of the woods. "I'm a ghost. I'm with you. I love you but will haunt you…"

"No!" Alex cried, and braced herself, stiff-armed on

the basin, shaking her head, seeing Allie again in the mirror. "I didn't kill you, I didn't hurt you. I love you."

Reality crashed back in. That was her own tearful face and disheveled hair in the mirror. And yet, in good times and bad, she still felt she was living with and for her twin sister. Yes, even here in the dark of morning near the depths of Falls Lake.

Alex did not expect Josh to be in anything resembling a good mood, but she had to admit he was a good worker. He nodded and even said, "Thanks," when she rushed to the kitchen at the dining hall and volunteered to help. Perhaps Quinn had already told him what had happened because he didn't seem surprised she was here.

"I'm flipping pancakes," he told her the obvious as he scooped some up to add to short stacks in a covered warming pan. "No sausage patties today. Hard to make those without Mary's help. Put a banana on each tray, then go out and pour more coffee when they run out of it. Mary did all that."

"Yes, okay."

"Juice, butter and syrup are already on the tables, but when they come up to the window here, use that spatula to give them three-four pancakes on a plate."

"Will do."

"It was good you went out after Mary, too," he said, still turning pancakes. "She's been through a lot, takes things hard."

"I understand. I was glad to help and I want to support her."

"Good to have another woman around here. For a while."

That surprised her. It was almost a virtual hug from

this brusque man, but he'd also indicated she would not be here long.

She went to work. Time blurred as she darted back and forth from the counter to the serving window. The two troopers on-site—their faces and personalities seemed to blend into one, unlike with Kurtz and Henson's—showed up in line for food, then disappeared with their trays to eat outside or watch for more unwanted visitors or just to avoid answering questions. She did the same with the students, telling them she couldn't say anything about yesterday because of the ongoing investigation.

"You should eat some yourself," Josh said when the line disappeared.

"I will. Have you seen Quinn?"

"He ate first. Had your dog with him, gave him some water and hamburger meat. Said you're going out with us this morning. Then he went to call 'Boss Geoff' in New York."

She ate, sitting on a stool at the counter next to Josh, then they cleaned up together. The kitchen clock said it was 7:45.

Quinn showed up, carrying Spenser, though he was still on his leash. "Brent's headed for the airport," he said, leaning in the now-empty serving window. Spenser barked a greeting to her but seemed content where he was.

Quinn went on. "If we only needed a watchdog for the trek today, this guy would be it, but everyone is following clues I've set up, and Spenser tends to prefer rabbit hunting. Will he be okay, staying in my bedroom today? Then, poor guy, he'll have to switch places again when you take the guest room."

"I think he's getting used to surprises," she said, wondering if Quinn was saying all that for Josh's benefit—or hers. So far, in the midst of mayhem and murder, Quinn had been the perfect host, but their mutual attraction was a problem—another sort of danger, wasn't it?

"He'll be fine there," she continued. "It's important Sam and Mary get to a doctor, so Sam should just head out with her as soon as he gets an appointment."

"Actually, Sam plans to head into Anchorage right away, phone for an appointment there, go to a walk-in clinic or ER facility if he has to. I told him to say it's an emergency. She didn't want to let me borrow her necklace while she was gone, but I convinced her it was to clear her of any later suspicion. Sam sided with me, so she agreed. I'll let the troopers or the forensic team take it for analysis, but it's in my office right now."

Josh put in, "With her and Sam, the baby now, too, three lives are at stake, if she's going off the deep end. Sure hope she doesn't kind of blank out when she's tired or stressed, then not recall what happened."

"Sam has never said so, and I haven't seen it," Quinn said. "Nor are Sam and I worried about the necklace being examined. Mary would never hurt anyone."

"Yeah, well, I'll be back soon," Josh said, heading for the door. "Gonna hit the john in the men's bunkhouse before we head out."

In the awkward silence when he left, Alex said, "I'll take Spenser to your house before everyone comes back for the hike."

Quinn handed a contented Spenser to her, and their hands touched.

"I appreciate your help with him, Quinn."

"It's taken me too many years to get another dog.

Talk about following clues on a trail, I should have wised up a long time ago about what I really needed, which way to go in my life, not ignoring and even running away from certain things."

She wasn't sure she followed all that but she nodded. When their eyes met and held, she felt the impact of this man. As always.

"We're both running on fumes after yesterday," he said. "Tonight, maybe more bed time."

Before she could respond, Trooper Kurtz's boots sounded across the wooden floor. She wondered if they'd had a restful night at the lodge or if it was full of media already—or were the reporters just living out of their cars?

He greeted them, then said, "Some of the lodge guests—reporters—say there was a problem last night with a woman named Mary sleepwalking out in the woods. Then they say you two appeared but wouldn't answer their questions."

Alex remembered that she'd meant to call Meg and Suze, explain more to them. She should even call her parents, but she didn't want to alarm them again.

Kurtz went on. "It would have served them right if they'd stumbled on a bear or fallen down that stony ridge toward the stream. But Mary Spruce and her husband are not at their house to give her side of that."

Alex sensed that Quinn didn't know what to say, so she told Kurtz, "She does occasionally sleepwalk. The fact that she's pregnant made Sam decide they should seek medical attention so it doesn't happen again. They've probably headed for Anchorage already to find a doctor."

"I see," Kurtz said, frowning. "Don't want her out in

the forest now. It's too dangerous. That murder was in broad daylight with a lot of people nearby, but at night... Well, I regret to inform you, Quinn, that we're taking your cameraman into Anchorage for questioning over the death of Valerie Chambers. We searched his hotel room as soon as we got the subpoena. As far as we can tell, he had some bear claws he's been collecting—and they are missing—so forensics and the medical examiner's office will not be able to check if they're a match to the scratches on the victim. He tells us he doesn't know where they are," he added, frowning. "And they weren't on or near the body."

"Bear claws look the same even close up but have distinctive striations and shapes, like teeth, so if you find them, you'll get a match—and hopefully not to Ryker's possessions," Quinn said. "Speaking of which, I have Mary Spruce's antique bear claw necklace. She agreed to have it looked at—in good faith since we all know she frequently wears it. I have it in my office and can have you sign for it—very valuable, to her at least."

"Yeah, her coming forward with that's a good sign. By the way, we were impressed right away you said a bear did not kill the victim."

"I didn't tell you this before, but a bear killed my father and my pet dog when I was young. I saw the result then, have been studying maulings off and on since."

"Oh, sorry," Kurtz said, removing his hat.

"I was nearby when it happened. I found the bodies shortly after. My father was still barely alive. As a kid, I didn't know what to do. Stayed with them, sobbing, screaming. Finally, people came looking for us. I only survived because I had run off a ways and wasn't there when it happened."

"That's really tough. Very belated condolences," Kurtz said. "And I hope you can find someone else to film your TV show at least today while we have Ryker. He's waiting with Hanson in the cage of our vehicle, cooperating. I've seen your show, liked it, especially since we'd worked with you before. And may again," he said, clearing his throat, obviously moved and embarrassed. "You never know."

You never do know, Alex thought as she stood there with Spenser in her arms. She was amazed Quinn had blurted out all those details, that emotion he must have been holding in after seeing Val's corpse.

Kurtz said, "We'll be back, maybe when the autopsy's issued. And to bring Ryker back, unless something comes up there. Ms. Collister," he said, turning toward her, "we understand from talking to your cousins at the lodge that you will be here at this compound out of the reach of the reporters for a while."

"Yes, that's right. Unless they storm the area again."

"Not sure how long this will be a safe haven for you, as we may have to take down the tape and recall the troopers in the near future, as soon as forensics clears and releases the scene. They're on their way—should be here soon."

"I understand," she said.

And she understood that, as secure from outsiders as she had felt here, the entire outside area was no longer safe. Even more frightening, she did not even feel safe from herself, the way, in the midst of danger and terror, she was falling in love with Quinn.

24

The students were getting restless in the dining hall, waiting for the hike to start. Alex was worried about Quinn's not coming back yet, but she kept telling herself he must be answering Trooper Kurtz's questions about the bear claw necklace Mary was handing over.

Josh was on edge, too. "He's never late," he muttered. "Wish Sam was here. And Mary would know what to do."

"I'm going to run back to his house to see if he's okay. How about you mingle, ask them questions about what signs they're going to be looking for?"

"Yeah. Okay. Not my job, though."

She left her backpack in the kitchen and hurried out. To her relief, when she ran around the corner of Quinn's house, she saw that he was talking to Trooper Kurtz outside the front door. The trooper had a roll of plastic police tape in his hands. So perhaps he'd been closing off other areas for the forensic team, which was due soon.

"Sorry to interrupt," she told them. "Just wanted to tell Quinn everyone's ready."

His forehead crunched in a frown, Quinn told her,

"Mary's necklace is missing from where I put it less than an hour ago."

Alex stopped a few feet from them and sucked in a sharp breath. "Well, maybe she—they—had second thoughts. Had you told them where you would put it?"

He nodded. "I should have locked it in the safe, but I knew I'd be giving it to Trooper Kurtz almost immediately. I had called them on Sam's phone to explain why I'd like to have the necklace for a few days, then went over to their house to get it, brought it back—went to the dining hall, came back to give it to the trooper for safekeeping... Gone!"

"You'd said earlier you might give it to the forensic team," she said.

"They weren't here yet and Trooper Kurtz was. And now Sam and Mary have left for Anchorage."

Alex nodded and reached out to touch his arm. He had folded them over his chest as if he was trying to hold himself up. He looked even more distraught than he had last night. Mary was dear to him, Sam like a brother.

Surely he hadn't feared Mary's old claws would match the horrible marks on Val that he made it look like someone took the necklace. Or could Sam have done that?

Trooper Kurtz put in, "The forensic team should be here soon. Instead of heading back to Anchorage with Trooper Henson, I'll stay to meet them, brief them. I'll have them check your desk area and that drawer for fingerprints or DNA, not just the scene of the murder. I suppose I could even have them eliminate your prints,

but we'd have to have Sam, Mary and others here—"
he said, glancing at Alex "—give their prints."

"I'd appreciate that—if everyone cooperates," Quinn
said.

"I'll brief Hanson right now, get my stuff out of the
cruiser and let him get going with Mr. Ryker."

Quinn had to unlock the door for her to go inside
to check on Spenser. She saw several strands of crime
scene tape had been put over the closed office door.
It reminded her of a spider's web, and this was. She
hugged and petted Spenser, then rushed back out. Quinn
locked the door behind them, and they headed toward
the dining hall.

"I do have an idea," she told him. "Not about the
murder investigation or the missing necklace, but—"

"If Sam and Mary didn't take that necklace, she'll
really go off the deep end. My fault. I should have put it
in the safe. Nothing's going right—except you're here."

He grabbed her hand, and they kept walking. "Sorry
I interrupted your idea," he said. "Tell me."

"One of your German students had a really nice
video camera at breakfast. I overheard him tell one
of the Denver ladies that he was going to record some
events to show friends at home. I'm sure his work
wouldn't be as good as Ryker's, but it would get you
footage from the hike today and you could explain to
your viewers that the living conditions are primitive
and so is today's coverage of the hike or something
like that and—"

"You're a genius," he told her, and gave her a quick
kiss on the cheek. "Now if only we can solve the more
important stuff."

He held the door open for her as they went in to

join the students and Josh, who was actually mingling, though he didn't look too happy about it.

"Hey, everyone!" Quinn called out. "We've got to let the state troopers and forensics team follow clues to find who murdered Val Chambers. But today, we're sticking to our schedule, following clues in the forest as if we were looking for someone—someone lost or maybe someone who doesn't want to be found. Josh, you sure we've got enough belly fuel for the morning?"

"Gourmet stuff, Q-Man! Granola bars and good old water, but it looks enough like vodka so we can pretend."

Pretty chipper for Josh, Alex thought, then scolded herself. Maybe he just pretended to be angry sometimes. It was like still waters ran deep, like those in the lake. When she had looked below the surface of that mountain water, she could not see very far in.

Quinn walked straight to the German men, then, after they exchanged some words, one of them nodded and dashed out, probably for his camera. In this tough situation, at least she'd made a good suggestion. She hoped that Ryker would be back soon, completely cleared of suspicion. But then, if Ryker wasn't the guilty person, who was?

Quinn took the group on a zigzagging, nearly invisible path she'd never been on before, but she soon saw why. He'd laid out subtle signs and clues for them to follow to mimic the situation of tracking someone who was lost or did not want to be found. Of course, he'd laid down footprints but he'd left other clues, too. A tiny snag of cloth. A discarded bandage. A nearly hidden shred of gum wrapper. A piece of a used tissue, which he said should be bagged for DNA. And in a tight cluster of cedars, pieces of bark off the tree trunks, where someone had pushed through a narrow space.

"All right, now listen up," Quinn said. "This is universal common sense, but most people don't want to think about it. When human beings use the forest for a toilet— we'll stick to urination—men just spray anywhere and their footprints don't move much. Women crouch and shift their feet around a bit for balance and will leave more puddle than spray—and forgive me, ladies—but it's been proved that women tend to shift their feet way around sometimes, nervous someone might see them. In other words they turn around to look behind them, even if they are pretty sure they are not being observed. Human nature. Enough said—but useful info. Useful to observe the differences in the sexes in more ways than one."

Several of the men grinned or nodded. Two of the Denver ladies whispered to each other.

As they moved on, he kept his new cameraman—it turned out his name was Herman, which rhymed with German, so that would be easy to remember—close to him and sometimes suggested angles and shots. Herman seemed all business, yet delighted at the extra attention.

Alex stuck to the back third of the group, while Josh brought up the rear. She tried to keep an eye on everyone, including Josh. Was he worried about Sam and Mary? Did he resent Sam and Quinn being given tracker knowledge from Trapper Jake when he was not? But why should he when he had not been interested in learning all that, in the patience it took. At least he seemed sincerely concerned about Mary.

She raced through jagged memories of yesterday from the time Val was killed. Wasn't Josh walking around with tape to cordon off different sites for the students? He was headed back to the lodge when she saw him last, and that's where Val supposedly awaited. But why would Val head out with Josh, and what could be his motive? Did Josh feel she was not good for Ryker? Wouldn't Josh care less about that? She couldn't fathom him wanting to help the team by getting rid of Val. No, if she had to guess, it would be Ryker, however cooperative he was being with the troopers.

And where would Josh get bear claws if they weren't Mary's? And if they were, who took them today and why?

"All right," Quinn was saying, pointing at something snagged on tree bark, head high. "Gather around. Look down, look all around and don't let your own footprints mar possible clues. What is this, and what happened here?"

Staying put where they were, people leaned forward, squinting while Herman shot the scene and whatever evidence Quinn was pointing out. Oh, she saw it—strands of hair snagged in cedar bark—long, glossy strands, maybe Mary's.

People called out their ideas, but it took a while for them to put other nearby clues together: the footprints denoting a stumble, a bit of what must be fake blood on the tree trunk farther down.

"Let's say you were tracking a lost person," Quinn told them. "This is evidence, much like search and rescue teams look for. If you were tracing a lost child, the snag of hair and bloody knee or whatever would be lower. So is the person you are tracking injured? Check tracks farther on to decide. Anybody see the cigarette butt I left here? Those can be good and bad. They can cause a fire, but then can also let you follow a smoker and use the butt for DNA, just like with the blood. Obviously, what we're doing today is a general tracker experience to get you thinking about venturing in or living in the wilds. But who knows where this week's work could lead you? We've had students go on to do forestry jobs, become park rangers and even work search and rescue."

Questions abounded about putting the clues together, about how the conclusions depended on who and what they were tracking. People pressed closer, so Alex kept to the edge of the group as did Josh.

"Did Quinn tell you that Mary's claw necklace is missing?" she asked him.

"Yeah. Bet she came back for it or sent Sam. It was her grandmother's. I swear, that's who she thinks is the Falls Lake ghost, or who she herself goes out to mourn or contact. Wouldn't want my wife out at night looking for dead people."

"Do you have a wife in mind?"

"Naw. Not yet. Maybe never. Ryker shouldn't have trusted that woman, maybe didn't at the end. She played fast and loose uptown when he was at work here."

"Really? You might want to tell the troopers that. I forgot you live uptown. So what did you see or hear about her?"

He frowned. "Enough said. Not good to speak ill of the dead, even a woman like her."

He moved off into the group and started passing out granola bars when the students finally were ready to move on. It was a strange place for a snack stop, she thought, but then lots of things were strange here, including Josh. It snagged in her head that he had told her that he was glad to have a woman—her—around, but just for a while.

25

When they got back to the compound, Trooper Kurtz pointed Quinn toward the murder site, so Alex assumed the forensic team was here. In a way, they had been practicing forest forensics out here today. The idea of search and rescue Quinn had just lectured about in the woods could even include tracking a criminal.

The two men began to whisper to each other while she waited for Quinn. He nodded, then shrugged, shaking hands with the trooper as students streamed past into the dining hall. Then Quinn headed straight for her.

"The forensic team is going to work straight through, even if it gets dark," he explained. "So we're not to worry if we see lights anywhere out there tonight. They're from Alaska BCI, the Bureau of Criminal Investigation in Anchorage, and they have a tight schedule. The troopers are still keeping the media out. But once the forensic team is gone, the troopers will have to open up the area."

"Too bad," she said. "I kind of liked the peace and quiet—no shouted questions. Quinn, I know you're really upset about the necklace but can't you phone Sam and Mary and just ask them if they took it back?"

"I think they would have let me know. And I don't believe he would have let Mary out of his sight right then so she'd have time to sneak in and take it. The door was locked, but my staff—all but Ryker—have a key. Besides, Sam and Mary have enough on their minds without him telling her it's missing and her freaking out even more. Let's go back with the students. As for Val's death, I'm still hoping something turns up in the autopsy report."

As the two of them hurried toward the dining hall, he added, "After everyone takes a rest break, I'm going to talk about forest therapy and forest bathing."

"Really? I read your topics of study and activities online and I saw nothing about either of those."

"After dinner just take a seat in the dining hall, Queen Alexandra. Forest therapy is of current interest, something I've had questions on before. As for bathing, we'll worry about that later."

With Spenser asleep in her lap, Alex sat listening raptly, as did most of the others, as Quinn talked from the heart about how much the wilderness meant to him, how in a way it was a family heritage of love. Not just preserving nature, but allowing it to be therapy for the body, mind and soul. Nothing was new age about it, he stressed, only common sense.

She thought again of Thoreau's quote that he went to the woods because he wished to live deliberately, to front only the essential facts of life—and didn't that include love? To her amazement, Quinn quoted part of that, speaking for himself but citing the author. Had he read her thoughts? It terrified her that they could be that in touch with each other—without touching.

As he recited the quote, his voice was quiet, almost raspy at the end, and she saw him blink back tears. No doubt, he was thinking of his father, too, who loved the woods, who was attacked there...*when it came time to die*...

Poor Val had died in the forest, too, evidently by a human hand, someone she might have known, someone who could even strike again.

When Quinn finished and stood silent before them, some students began to clap. Herman stepped even closer with his camera, maybe zooming in on Quinn's face. Slowly, a few, then the rest of the class, stood to give their leader and teacher—their Q-Man—a standing ovation. Alex cried, not only at the power of that Thoreau quote, but because she had reminded him of it.

And tears burned her eyes, because she could fully admit something to herself: though she'd been in this special place such a short time, it was long enough to bond with a place, the people...and one special man.

"So, about forest therapy—being outside among the trees can renew and relax you," Quinn was saying with a gesture for them to sit down. "It's not hocus-pocus. It's rooted in the Japanese belief in *Shinrin-yoku*, which more or less means 'forest bathing.' Just like here, you can take other classes with trained guides to understand it more. The forest bathing idea suggests you should immerse yourself in the sights, sounds and smells of the woods, to relax, to get in touch with your deepest self."

She saw Herman still had his camera running. She heard a gentle whir from it as he walked behind her, then tilted it this way. Oh, no! Maybe she'd been so relaxed, so at home here, that she'd forgotten to keep out of his shot. Mostly, he'd had the lens trained on Quinn. She'd have to remind him to review it to ensure she wasn't in the final cuts.

"So, maybe it's time," Quinn was saying as she hurried toward the back of the room to at least now get out of camera range, "for everyone to hit the showers—another kind of forest bathing—after our trek today. Tomorrow covers wild animal tracking, nine a.m. sharp, hopefully with no wild animals in sight. After that final lesson and another dose of forest therapy for everyone, we'll be saying goodbye. Hard to believe the week is almost over. Thanks for your patience with the tragedy that occurred here this week. I'm not sure if I'll have any news from the police and forensics before they leave, but I'm sure the media will be reporting soon, anyway. See you tomorrow morning!"

Alex stood in the rear, rocking a contented Spenser like a baby, as people talked and filed out. Her little dog had been so glad to see her and had behaved very well this evening, fussed over by most of the students before he fell asleep. So many wanted to know how he'd lost an eye, and she'd told them she didn't know but that his first owner had abused him. One person had said, "There's so much we don't know, right? Like even here—life and death, the past, present, especially the future."

Quinn spent another half hour answering individual questions until the students were gone. Several times, she could tell, he looked to be sure she was still there, waiting for him.

It was nearly dark outside when they headed toward his house. She noted the back door to the compound was not only still unlocked but ajar. Even though the forensic team were in the sunken area when Val had been found, their lights caught in the trees above and made a faint halo in the dark night.

"Trooper Kurtz is going to stay out there with them," Quinn told her, seeing where she was looking. "And one of the new troopers is out in front, one by that back compound door. Let's see if we can relax a bit, wait to learn what they can tell us—if they tell us anything. By the way, Josh is staying in the compound tonight, bedding down at Sam and Mary's."

"Quinn, he said he saw and knew that Val played fast and loose in town, apparently when Ryker wasn't around. So that could mean she knew other guys who could have been upset with her for flirting or worse, or her sharp put-downs and—"

"Yeah. But I just don't think Ryker would snap to the point that he would hurt her. He could have gotten rid of her by just insisting she leave, that it was over. He's not an idiot, though he's acted like it, keeping her around so long."

He unlocked his front door. She knew he regretted having to do that in his little Eden that had now been invaded by a serpent. He'd said no one locked anything around here, but now things were different.

And with the two of them alone in his house, but for Spenser—well, that was different, too.

Quinn boiled a huge kettle of water for Alex to use for a sponge bath, while he waited to get into the bathroom for his usual quick, cold shower. When he really wanted a hot shower, he drove over to the lodge, but that must be crawling with those media hawks now.

He realized this house was not anything that would attract most women, probably not even Alex for very long as adaptive and receptive as she'd seemed about this lifestyle so far. He wondered if that bungalow in town that had caught his eye was still on the market. In its neighborhood, it was almost a palace.

But Alex had mentioned once that she'd fallen for her fiancé's lifestyle and lovely home, so had she changed enough to live like he did here? Granted, she could go with him every other month to New York City for a few days, but wouldn't that trip make all this look even worse by comparison? Of course Brent had put his two cents in on that, suggesting she'd be homesick for city life. Val she was not, but that still worried him.

He and Alex had only known each other just over half a month, so was he an idiot to want her that fast, to fall that hard? They'd had nothing but problems together, but here she was in his home and he was scared that he needed her and wanted her so bad—because he had no idea if she'd stay. And unlike some quick-hit and quick-release guys he knew, he didn't intend to share himself with a train-passing-in-the-night kind of woman.

They met in the kitchen where she had opened a can of minestrone soup and was heating it on the stove. They'd been so busy serving everyone a dinner they hadn't taken time to eat. She'd also pulled some things out of the fridge and cupboards: bread, peanut butter and jelly. It was hardly what he'd love to wine and dine her with whether in Anchorage, New York or the ends of the earth if she'd just let him.

"Thanks, sweetheart, but I could have fixed stuff for you," he told her.

"You're hungry, and I am, too."

"That's the truth," he said, steeling himself from putting his arms around her or kissing the nape of her neck as she bent over. He *was* hungry, not just for food, but the timing could not be worse. A murder nearly on his property, his team temporarily disbanded, maybe under suspicion, and he was desperate to try to woo and win a woman in the wilds? Nuts. Stupid. And suddenly of the utmost importance in his life.

They ate side by side, talking about the day, about what they might learn tonight before the forensic team left. He'd just added some store-bought cookies and ice cream to their meal when he heard a knock on the front door.

He went to unlock it. Trooper Kurtz stood there with three men. "They have permission to take both of your prints in your office," Kurtz told Quinn as Alex came to stand behind him. "I know the drawer where the necklace was and the office layout, so I'll go with them, show them."

"I understand. All right," Quinn said.

"And they'll need your prints and Ms. Collister's, anyone else's who might have had access."

"As you know, Mary and Sam are in Anchorage. I can call Sam early tomorrow, have them stop by for prints or at least tell you where to find them. Another guest who stayed here last night should be landing at JFK Airport in New York soon, but Josh, who works on-site, is in Mary and Sam's house tonight. I don't know how he'll feel about getting printed."

"He works for you, he was on-site for the murder—he'll have to play ball," Kurtz said.

They sat down in the kitchen again to eat their cookies and melting ice cream. In fifteen minutes the forensic people were back. Quinn knew fingerprints weren't taken with smeared ink anymore, but he wasn't sure how the current system worked. He soon saw they needed to just press one of their fingers on a silicon reader for a scan, which then displayed all sorts of digital information.

"The back door that leads from the compound to the forest is padlocked," Kurtz told them as they prepared to head for Sam's house to take Josh's prints. "The other two troopers will stay here tonight and take down all barrier tape in the morning before they head back, but I'm going to ride to Anchorage with these BCI guys."

"Oh, sure," Quinn said, actually wishing he wouldn't go, as he'd become a sort of security blanket here. Now, it was all on him, including taking care of Alex, and he planned to do just that.

26

They were just settling down on the couch before a small hearth fire Quinn had lit when his cell phone rang. Spenser's ears perked up from where he was lying at the end of the couch with his head on Alex's leg. Sitting so close to Quinn, Alex could hear the voice and conversation. It was Trooper Kurtz. So soon?

"Sorry to bother you again," she overheard Kurtz say. "We're still en route to Anchorage. Two important pieces of information just came in. But first let me say your employee Josh Spruce was not at his brother's house, or at least the lights were out and he didn't answer a lot of knocking."

"He told me and his brother he would be there all night."

"Maybe he changed his mind and went into town to his place. Tell him he'll have to come in to BCI in Anchorage, too, just like his brother and sister-in-law."

"Yeah, all right, but I need Josh here tomorrow."

"Hopefully we won't take much of his time. But now for the big news. I just got a call from the coroner's lab that the autopsy on Valerie Chambers is complete. Lab results will take longer to determine traces of drugs or alcohol. But you were absolutely right on what was *not* cause of death. Not a bear attack, but an initial blow to the back of the head. Those claw marks were added, not postmortem, but when she was unconscious or dying because they were so exact she could not have been moving or struggling against them."

"Which probably means her attacker also went down by the stream, maybe not only to inflict those scratches, but to make sure she was dead."

"The word *probably* means that idea is not something I can comment on right now. Additional skull injuries may have also occurred when she hit the ground. Cause of death: blunt force trauma resulting in fatal brain hemorrhage, not the fall."

"Terrible. But thanks for sharing that," Quinn told him.

The way he looked at her made Alex realize he might know she could hear everything. Her facial reaction must be obvious.

"And one more thing," Kurtz was saying. "The owners of the lodge showed me the scratch marks outside Ms. Collister's room there. As far as I can tell by just looking and diagramming them, they're almost identical to the claw marks on the deceased's throat and chest."

Quinn darted a look at her. She was aware her eyes had gone wide, but when she tried to look calmer, she only frowned. Quinn reached out with his free hand to grasp hers.

"I'll be in touch," the trooper said. "Here's the address to send your people to get fingerprints—it will be quick, as you know, but they need to make an effort to get here soon."

He read off an Anchorage address, then the phone went dead.

"You heard it all," Quinn said.

She nodded. "But what does it mean, the scratches on the wall matched those on poor Val? A warning to me to leave? Like, Val didn't, so look what happened to her? I wonder if they took Ryker's camera into custody."

"Yes, before they took him in. Ryker said they planned to check it for prints, DNA, blood. He actually didn't seem worried about that. Damn, I swear it isn't Ryker any more than it's Sam, Mary or Josh."

He laid his phone down on the table and put an arm around her, tugging her close to his side. "I should have thought of that the minute Trooper Kurtz mentioned an indentation pattern. You're...more objective in all this. And bright."

"Not really. I feel I've tumbled down a rabbit hole of new people, new places, new feelings...and, sadly, a new tragedy beyond my own messed-up life. I feel very involved with Falls Lake—with you and what concerns you."

He moved closer. "All this aside, I'd love for you to be more involved with me, and I understand if you're hesitant—leery with your past and my own messed-up present."

He reached up to cup her cheek and chin with his free hand. They looked deep into each other's eyes. She could actually see the reflection of the fireplace flames in his before he shifted even closer and his lips skimmed, then took, hers in a devouring kiss. Spenser merely shifted his position, when he would have gone berserk back home. But was this home now?

She put her free hand on the nape of Quinn's neck,

caressing his warm skin and the short hairs there. He slanted his mouth sideways to come even closer, deeper. Somehow, the kiss spiraled upward, onward.

His free hand stroked her throat, the back of his fingers sliding up and down along her skin. Could he feel her pulse pounding there? He slid his fingers lower, past her collarbone to the valley between her breasts. Every nerve leaped alive as he gently cupped a breast, kept his hand there before going lower along her rib cage to grip her waist.

She almost cried when he stopped kissing her, but, his lips close to hers, he whispered, "Our first time—of many, I hope—will be in a safe bed in a safe place we will share. I want you here, right now, in the other room, out by the lake, in our plastic sleeping bags, I don't care, but ultimately I want you to be safe and be sure. I've waited a long time for someone who would be right for me and my life, but I couldn't stand to have you only to lose you."

"Lose me like Val?" she asked. "I mean, because of those scratch marks on the lodge?"

"No! Not like that. Lose you just because you'd go back home."

Breathing so close to him, nose to nose, she told him what she'd been thinking since she arrived here. "I'm starting to wonder if—if this could be home."

He nodded, then his lips took hers again. He rained kisses down her throat, while she tipped her head back and his big, warm hand dipped up under her T-shirt and touched her bare skin.

Somehow, she pulled him closer, pinned him to her, and he slid them down flat on the sofa. Spenser protested with a single bark at having his place taken, but they both ignored him as he jumped to the floor.

It amazed her how this big man kept his weight off her, even though he had pinned her down. He worried about how she felt, he was careful how he did things, gently at first, so different from Lyle.

His tongue darted along her throat as she held him to her, trying to pull him closer. She was senseless with desire—the desire to belong to him now and always.

But as he tugged her T-shirt up, Spenser went wild barking. Oh, no, like he did with Lyle! He liked and trusted Quinn, though...

But the little Scottie was not barking at them. Quinn lifted his head. She heard knocking on the door.

"He's not scolding us, after all," Quinn said.

His weight was instantly gone from her and the couch. Looking a bit unsteady, he went to the window and, standing to the side, moved the curtain to peek out.

"Nothing. No one," he said as Spenser kept growling and ran into the bedroom, barking again.

Quinn killed the lights so he could look out another window. Feeling dazed, still dizzy, she got up and went to stand behind him.

"Oh, man," he muttered. "It's Josh with some big boxes, looking like some damn delivery man."

He tugged his shirt down as he went to the front door and unlocked it.

"What's all that?" Quinn asked. "I heard you weren't at Sam's."

"Went to the lodge. Suzanne says this stuff came in the mail and is important for Alex. She figured she might want to look through it, see if the stuff she ordered is all there. I said I'd bring it back with me."

"Thanks, Josh. That was really kind of you," Alex told him. "It's new jars and tube and labels for my products. The other boxes are ingredients I need. I'll see you get some aftershave or hand lotion for your help."

"Can you see me putting on hand lotion, Quinn?" Josh asked, shifting from one foot to the other. "Anyhow, Suzanne said she'll come see you tomorrow. But some of these are heavy, so she didn't need to be lugging them around."

"I'll help," Quinn said, and pushed the door wider open. The men stacked the four cartons in the living room.

"Had to have a hot shower, after everything," Josh explained. "I didn't want to go clear to my place in town. The lodge is crawling with reporters. And I saw they took the trooper tape down here."

Alex noticed Quinn sighed in unison with her. "Maybe I should hire a security guard for a while," he muttered.

"Oh, one more thing before I finally turn in," Josh told them. "Meg's boy, Chip, gave some kinda off-the-cuff interview to one of those Anchorage reporters. The kid said his dead dad is the Falls Lake ghost, flies a plane over the area sometimes, and the paper may run with it. Meg's trying to talk the guy out of it. She's pretty shook, so Suzanne said she might not want to leave her tomorrow, but she'd let you know."

Alex leaned against the wall, fighting back tears of frustration and exhaustion for Meg, Suze and herself—even for poor Val. Quinn was explaining to Josh that he needed to give his fingerprints to the Anchorage BCI. "Just so they can eliminate all the staff's prints to focus on who else could have taken Mary's necklace."

"Sure, soon as I get a chance," Josh said. "How about when this bunch of students leaves day after tomorrow, and I drive some of them to the airport for a few extra bucks like last time? But gotta tell you both something. I hate to say it, to even think it. I see you got a fire going tonight. I thought to do the same right when I got back to Sam's, so moved some logs off their woodpile to take inside. Behind the pile—on the outside of their bedroom wall, I saw a kind of scratchy carving of something."

Words spilled from the usually terse man like a wild waterfall.

"I mean, it looks pretty much like what got scratched outside your room at the lodge, Alex. I can't stand to believe it, but if Mary's off the deep end, she might get off murder charges, anyway, with an insanity plea—like, just be committed to a hospital. But I'm scared Mary might be behind it all, scratches on walls, even scratches on Val, 'cause that woman mocked everything, even the idea of a ghost, even the people drowned in Falls Lake."

"No, not Mary!" Quinn insisted. "That would kill Sam."

His voice trembled. Alex shook her head. Surely that could not be. But Mary had acted so strange in the woods.

27

Early the next morning, someone knocked on the front door of Quinn's house again. They were having coffee before heading over to help feed the students. Spenser gave a single "yip" as if he knew who it was. Alex supposed it was Josh again, then remembered he was fixing breakfast for the guests and sandwiches to go in backpacks for lunch.

When Quinn went to the door, she listened intently, though she didn't want to seem nosy.

She felt herself blush even now to think how Quinn had walked her to her bedroom door last night, kissed her thoroughly, then turned away so "I won't be tempted to do more, not right now."

"Hold that thought," she had called to him as he sometimes said, then he'd practically sprinted for his room down the short hall.

He'd stopped at his bedroom door, grinned and called back, "I'm gonna hold more than that, when we finally get serious private time together—get rid of the students and get rid of some lunatic murderer on the loose. I'll want to propose some things—important things. Then it's up to you."

Up to you. How different from her past, when the man made all the big decisions.

That memory fled when Quinn brought Suze into the kitchen. Alex hurried to hug her. "Oh, Suze! Is everything okay? I hear it's been crazy over there. Sorry to desert you two right now."

"And I'm sorry to just crash in without calling. We had to close the shop for a while, but don't worry. The full house will make up for it—eleven reporters on expense accounts. I see in the hall that Josh got you the supplies, so you can start 'cooking up' your products again."

"When things quiet down. This is the last day this group of students will be here, so I'm going out with them to the waterfall today."

Heading out of the kitchen, Quinn cut in, "I'll leave you two alone and get ready to go over to the dining hall."

"So," Suze said, stepping back after he left the room, "you two are doing…okay?"

"Yes. Fine. He—we're trying to stay sane and under control."

"Aha." She tilted her head and squinted.

"Really. Concentrating on solving Val's murder and holding things together here with his students. Don't tell your guests, but Val died of a blow to the head, not a bear attack."

Suze exhaled hard and shook her head. "One thing I wanted to warn you about is that the media mavens may descend on you and Quinn now."

"We're hoping to be on the hike before any of them

realize the police tape is gone. And the doors to the compound will be closed and locked—front and back, because they tried a rear assault."

"Yeah, so Josh said last night. He just told reporters who asked him anything that he was the lodge handyman, and knew zilch, as he put it. As a matter of fact, he kind of hid from them, ate in the kitchen, which is fine. But when one of them somehow learned his last name was the same as Sam and Mary's, they looked for him again but he was gone."

"I guess it's good that he's a man of few words, though he talks more now."

"As resentful of Sam—of Quinn, too—as Josh has always seemed, he's acting protective right now, so maybe that's one good thing to come out of this mess. That and the fact you and Quinn seem to have found each other."

"One thing I've learned through my stupid mistakes with Lyle is not to get involved fast, though I guess—in a way—I have."

"Well, I wish you luck."

Quinn popped his head back in when he was ready to leave. "See you at the dining hall, Alex, and see you later, Suzanne! Josh is doling out cereal, fruit and Danish rolls. We're really missing Mary's touch in the kitchen."

Alex heard his phone sound, the melody of an old John Denver song about a night in a forest.

"Alex?" Suze's voice cut in. "Are you okay?"

"Holding up. And wishing I were there to help you steady Meg."

Quinn appeared in the kitchen doorway yet again. "You won't believe this. That was Geoff. I'm invited to be on that late-morning network television program *Gab Fest* this Thursday to discuss wilderness training and a bit about tracking. Apparently there's a big audience interested in the subject. If Geoff hadn't already accepted for me, I would have tried to postpone it, but it's great publicity."

"They'll love you!" Alex said.

"I'd like to think I'm instantly lovable." He winked at her. "That show booking means we're flying pretty high. Even Ginger's excited about it. I'll leave tomorrow and do the show the next day, be gone two days. Next it'll be *60 Minutes*, then the world—ha."

It was good to see Quinn animated and joking. But it seemed a terrible time to be away. Hopefully the media would have cleared out when he got back, even if other reporters straggled in, because she would not keep staying at the compound. She almost wished he'd offered to take her with him to New York.

Funny, but she thought of the old, embroidered sampler her grandmother had hanging in her house the short years she knew her. It was of a heart surrounding the Bible words *Whither thou goest, I will go*. Grandma always said it was what she and Grandpa had promised each other when they were married. Her mother had that sampler now, though it was probably in storage since they'd traveled pretty light to England. And that memory made her empathize with Mary more, for she had lost her grandmother in a tragedy, one that seemed to hover in the air just above the water of Falls Lake.

But now, as she said goodbye to Suze at the door, she thought of her lost twin, Allison, again. *Whither thou goest, I will go*. Yes, that fit the way Allie seemed to be always with her, part of her. Like Mary—maybe like all women—there were just some things, some loved ones, you could never quite let go.

Quinn set a fast pace through the forest toward the lake and waterfall. Alex walked in the middle of the single-file group and Josh brought up the rear. Back in the compound, the students had signed a thank-you card for Mary and Sam. Alex felt better herself since she'd let Suze take Spenser back to the lodge for the day. She'd hated the idea of leaving him alone in a deserted camp, and she'd meet Suze in the lodge parking lot tonight to get him back.

Quinn encouraged people to point out anything they found interesting. He especially commented on things students mentioned that they never would have noticed before this week. They stopped briefly while he showed them moose tracks, and they followed them, noting where the animal had stopped to eat and rest and then where it had met up with three other animals. Alex could see several of the students beam with pride at the fact that they could follow those tracks.

They emerged at the stony lakeshore from yet another forest opening where Alex had not been. The lake looked crystalline today, but she made an observation. "I've noticed, however clear the surface looks, just below, the water is a little murky."

"The falls grind through rock to make a sort of silt water," Quinn told everyone. "It never seems to settle but keeps being stirred up."

Like events around here lately, Alex thought, but didn't say so.

They hiked around the far side of the lake where she had not been, past the water that covered the old pioneer village. The cedar trees were thicker here, making a skirt around the mountain that loomed above and beyond.

"Rather not see a bear today. Moose tracks and beavers will do for sure," she heard Herman say as he lifted his camera's lens to pan to the top of the mountain.

Their feet crunched stones along the lake. The muted whisper of the falls grew louder. Soon they had to shout to be heard unless speaking to a close person.

"What do you see ahead?" Quinn called back to them.

"A bunch of humps in the water," Joyce, one of the women from Denver, shouted.

"Those are beaver houses near a dam they've made!" Josh told them, coming up to join their little crowd. "Beavers are night animals."

"Nocturnal," Alex heard someone say. "He means nocturnal."

Josh frowned and hunched his shoulders, but they all plunged on. Beaver territory was easy to spot, not only with their dams and lodges of woven sticks and mud half in the water but by trees along the bank partially chewed through.

Quinn stopped them near the beaver dam where the animals had made a second little lake. The falls were so close now that he had to nearly shout. "Sorry Sam and Mary aren't here to give you better details," he told the cluster of people while Herman continued to film, "but here are a few points they would share if they were."

He climbed a three-foot-high rock to be better heard. Numerous boulders of all sizes were nearby, probably the same ones that had tumbled down with the falls that drowned the villages decades ago.

Quinn raised his voice to tell them, "Beavers were

almost hunted to extinction when beaver hats and muffs were fashionable, but they are a prolific breed and not endangered today."

Endangered—the word snagged in Alex's mind. Val had obviously been in danger. Was she in danger, too, since those bear marks had appeared outside her room at the lodge? And had Val's killer scratched up the wall outside the woodpile to threaten Mary? Or had she, in her nighttime delirium, done all of that? They were going to have to ask Sam if they knew their house had been defaced, to tell Trooper Kurtz, too. But would that cast suspicion on Mary or help exonerate her?

Her mind snapped back to Quinn's explanation. "Believe it or not, both sexes of adult beavers have a little enzyme sac inside them that produces something called castoreum. That is used by both perfumers and cigarette makers because of its smoky smell and taste. But the product I think is really far out that uses castoreum is schnapps from Sweden."

Quinn led them even closer to the falls where the mist from it reached them. "Be careful," he shouted. "Remember what we first taught you—pick up your feet. It's slippery here."

He sat on a damp rock, so the others did, too, gazing up at the powerful spill of water. He motioned Alex over beside him, and put a piece of plastic he pulled from his backpack for her to sit on. Together they looked up. However many times Quinn must have been here, seen this, he looked awed, too.

The tower of churning white water entranced her. The white pillar of spume and foam was outlined by the dark cliff above and behind the water. She could hardly imagine it dammed up by boulders for decades, building a higher lake above, then letting loose to drown the small settlement and make a new lake where one had been before.

Herman was filming the falls up and down. Everyone looked transfixed. She wondered if this beauty and power would calm Josh. She turned her head both ways but didn't see him. Surely he had not been so embarrassed by not using the word *nocturnal* that he'd headed back. Or maybe he'd just gone behind a tree for private business, because all this pounding and churning made her wish for a bathroom. She'd have to make do out here, as would everyone else who wasn't a camel!

But right then Quinn put a big hand on her knee and squeezed it. Blinking in the mist, she smiled at him.

He leaned close to say in her ear, "The other end of the lake would be a great place for a proposal or a wedding. Not here, because no one would be able to hear the vows."

She smiled and nodded. Her eyes misted, and not just because of the fine spray from the waterfall.

"Was that a yes already," he asked with a grin, "or just a nod you heard me?"

Not sure what to say, surprised at what he'd said, she took his hand in hers and held on tight as if they were on a tossing ship in a rocky sea.

Several people were digging into the sandwiches Josh had made. A few students had slipped away, no doubt for the same reason Alex needed to.

"Did you see Josh leave?" she asked Quinn.

"He probably took a bathroom break. You know, I can't tell if he misses Sam or is glad he—and Mary—are gone."

"He's hard to read. His moods change really fast. I'm sure he wouldn't just head back."

"No way. I'll go see if I can spot him, but not until the bathroom-breakers from Denver get back."

"Actually, I'm going behind those bushes or a large rock for a sec, too."

He put her backpack under the plastic on their rock and stayed put.

She found the perfect spot behind a boulder. But as she tugged her shirt out of her pants, a shadow flitted past her. She looked behind her, all around. Nothing. Then a tiny shower of pebbles skittered down the rock face.

She moved back from the rock and looked up. The top was not high. She could see a side where it could be climbed that was completely hidden from everyone. What if an animal was up there and could spring? No one would hear a scream for help with the noise of the falls.

Remembering to pick up her feet, she shaded her eyes with her hand and looked up, just in time to see Josh, on the boulder above, heave something into the churning foam at the foot of the falls. He didn't see her, was looking away.

Had he thrown a rock to see how far it would go? Something to vent his anger, thinking he'd looked stupid earlier?

In the shadow of the boulder, she shifted closer to see what he had thrown. It floated on the white-water waves a moment before it was sucked under.

Her med tech training kicked in as she watched it. She'd seen large digital pads above a larger palm pad from the underside, surrounded by fur and topped by claws—ursine. He had heaved away a cut-off bear paw.

28

With everyone around, Alex knew better than to try to tell Quinn what she'd seen. She hoped Josh hadn't seen or sensed her presence. Trying to smile, to talk, to join in the camaraderie of this group, which would be leaving tomorrow, she hiked back, keeping an eye on Josh.

He seemed normal, a bit moody, but he spoke if spoken to. Yet she wondered what he was thinking. Had he gotten rid of damning evidence that would tie him to defacing wooden buildings—and Val's body? Even if she told Quinn, if they brought troopers to that exact spot, they'd never recover that evidence to match those claw marks.

Back at the dining hall, everyone seemed to speak loudly with confidence. They were no doubt relieved the week's beginner course was over. Now they had bragging rights, now they could say they knew Q-Man.

"I don't know about all of you!" Quinn finally quieted them. "But I'm beat. I want to thank Herman for stepping in with his camera to help out. And I apologize again that your week was interrupted by a terrible crime and loss of life. I'm sure you will see more details in papers and online than I could tell you even now. I hope the hosts of the TV show *Gab Fest* don't bring up the murder when I'm a guest this coming Thursday. If you're home by then, I hope you'll watch."

Oohs and aahs about the show. Someone called out, "Autograph, please!" Josh frowned—so had he not known?

Quinn went on. "Look for some clips from our classes on the show, though Herman's work hasn't been processed yet. And I want to thank Josh Spruce for going above and beyond the call of his usual duties, and, of course, for Alex's help these last few days, filling in for Mary. Alex's personal beauty and health products are on sale online and at the lodge gift shop down the road, and you can ask her about that."

People clapped for her, Josh and then big-time for Quinn.

Eventually, as everyone trailed off to pack or sleep, Quinn asked Josh, "Are you staying at Sam's or heading home tonight?"

"Home. Still, I'll guard the front gate till you guys go get Alex's dog at the lodge. She said earlier she had to get him from Suzanne."

Josh and Quinn huddled, talking about details for getting everyone breakfast and then to the Anchorage airport tomorrow. Alex tried to calm herself. How kind and helpful Josh had been just now. But she had to tell Quinn what she'd seen, what it could mean. At least Josh hadn't seen her watching, but he was going to know soon if she told Quinn or the troopers.

Josh closed up the dining hall, while Quinn and Alex headed straight for his truck. "Like picking up our kid at the babysitter's," he teased.

"I'll phone her to bring him out to the parking lot. That's what we decided."

She called Suze first. "On our way from the camp right now," she told her. It was such a short distance. She'd tell Quinn what she saw as soon as she got him alone tonight.

But when they returned to Quinn's house with Spenser, Quinn started getting phone calls from Geoff about coming to New York. His flights had been made for him, and the boarding pass was coming in on his phone. Geoff called him back with directions and guest information about *Gab Fest*.

Nervous and anxious, Alex took a very fast, chilly shower, then groomed Spenser. If she lived here, a hot water tank would be a necessity. She changed her clothes into fresh jeans and a sweatshirt. She longed to get ready for bed, but those clothing options could be provocative.

"How about I build us a little fire?" Quinn asked as he patted Spenser on the rug, then sat down beside her on the couch.

She nodded, glad he didn't tease, didn't say more about another sort of building fire last night. How she hated to ruin the mood, but she had to say it.

"Quinn, wait a sec. I have to tell you something." She snagged his elbow to pull him back on the couch. "When I went to—to the forest bathroom today, I saw Josh throw something weird from a boulder into the white water around the foot of the falls, and I saw what it was before it sank."

"And it was…?" he asked when she hesitated.

"A cut-off bear paw—with claws intact. I'm positive."

He looked like she'd slapped him. "Damn!"

"I know. I could only think one thing."

"That he was getting rid of evidence?"

She nodded. "Maybe it had blood and DNA on it—Val's. He's hard to know, but I can't think of a motive for his killing her, can you? Maybe he just cares for all of you and was trying to keep the team intact by getting rid of Val."

"I'll tell you who he does care for, though it's nothing undercover or illicit—only, on his part, maybe regretful."

"Like what?" she asked, and put a hand on his shoulder as he put his head in his hands and stared at the floor.

"He especially cares for Mary, though you say it was a bear claw and not her necklace?"

"I'm not following."

"He's the one who—well, who found Mary first, introduced her to Sam years ago. Josh and Mary weren't an item but friends. Still, I think Sam and Mary's strong love and marriage hurt Josh deeply, because he cared for her more than he knew at first. He's never seemed that interested in other women, even when he's had his chances."

"That's so sad," she said as he sat up again and quit frowning at the floor. "He cares for both of them, but is constantly reminded that she and Sam were meant to be together, reminded of what he lost and what could have been. At least he's protective of them and not hostile. That really says something good about him."

"Let's remember that bear claws are sometimes sold around here," he said, taking her hand and holding it on her knee. "It's not uncommon in Anchorage, for example, to see bear paws or bear rugs, things like that, though they would probably have purchased them, not killed the animals themselves to get them."

"Okay, so maybe Josh was just afraid of being asked if he had any bear claws, and that's all. No motive connected with the murder, unless he thought Val was going to pull Ryker away and hurt the show."

"It would hurt the show, but we'd hire someone else and forge ahead. I really wish you wouldn't have seen him toss that paw, because the troopers could be all over him, and I'd vouch for him."

She reached out to grasp Quinn's wrist. "I'm sorry. I don't want to tell Trooper Kurtz or for Josh to know I suspected him."

He heaved a huge sigh and sat up even straighter, propping his elbows on his knees. She put her hand on his back, muscular, tense. She stroked him there, hoping to help, to comfort. Quick as a big cat, he turned to her and swept them both down on the couch with her facing him, and pressed her gently against the back of it.

Since he was taller, she seldom faced him eye to eye. His heavy breathing heated her cheeks and lips. "Sweetheart, I can't stand it if it was Ryker, but Mary—even Josh—would be worse than that. Our little team has been so good before, but now you're with me for a little while at least, which is even better. One of those phone calls was Trooper Kurtz saying he's bringing Ryker back tomorrow, not under arrest but still a person of interest because his bear claws are missing, too. He claims he doesn't know where they went."

"No wonder he's still a person of interest. Maybe Val took it, tossed it. Can you imagine her even touching something like that? And did what with it? Used it to claw my outside wall and Mary and Sam's, too?"

"I know, I know. But I couldn't bear for it to be Josh and that would really crush Sam. But I think it's Ryker, that he finally cracked trying to deal with Val, and did it with a lot of people nearby in the woods so it didn't point right at him. I believe Trooper Kurtz suspects him, too. But whoever it is, he'll be lying low, careful not to do anything else to look suspicious, including heaving a bear claw off a rock where someone could have seen him."

"Did see him," she said, and heaved a sigh. "But you've convinced me about Josh."

Quinn raised a hand to cup her chin. "I just don't want it to be my friends, my team," he whispered. "It's been tough lately, and maybe worse to come. But at least you're here, at least you care."

"I do and…" was all she got out before his lips took hers. It quickly became an out of body experience, as feelings, longing and fear swept her in dizzy circles.

She almost cried in disappointment when, his body close to hers, he tilted back a bit, holding her away, steadying her and himself.

"Sweetheart, as much as I want you, I don't want to push. I can only guess what you've been through before—with him—so this needs to be your choice. I want to carry you to bed, love you. I want you and need you, but I can wait until you're ready."

They stared into each other's eyes. He frowned in concentration, in barely leashed control. His hands on her were shaking.

Her voice came out breathless, not quite her own. "It

has been fast, but I trust you. Want you, too. I'm not afraid, not with you—not of you. Quinn, I—"

So much for building a fire here. He got off the couch, picked her up and headed for his bedroom, only stopping to be sure the front door was locked and bolted.

Spenser stayed put for once, daring another yawn as she glanced back at him before Quinn closed his bedroom door behind them.

And then, everything just exploded in her head and heart. No qualms, no hesitation. This man was her present, maybe her future—cold water showers or not, Alaskan frontier or not, big winter snows or not—and she only wanted to fan the flames that might as well have been a deep woods wildfire.

Crazy kisses, discarded clothes, hands and mouths. He was both tender and tense, and she was in over her head. Swimming together, skinny-dippy in his bed in the waves of sheets, the white-water swirl of need and love.

"I want you, love you," he whispered in her ear. "So fast I know, it happened so fast for me."

"Me, too. Yes, I love you, need you."

"And I want you to stay," he said, breathing fast. "We can get a house in town. More room, hot water—very hot..."

He was kissing her again. Delicious drowning, trying to stay afloat but going under. She held to him, kissed him back. Did he mean he wanted to marry her? Now, that was scary but so was all of this...

It was as if this was her first time, her first love. She felt cherished, and in charge, too, equal with Quinn in desire and trust. If this man lived in a forest cave, she would love him. Huge waves swamped her again, lifting and swirling.

Somehow, the old world ended and a new one had begun.

They lay together cuddled in the chaos of sheets. They barely moved until Alex got up to let Spenser into the room when he whined and scratched on the door.

"I told him to do that so I could get a good look at you," Quinn said when she darted back into bed naked. It might be August but it was August in Alaska and, as hot as she'd felt, the room was cold. Yes, hot water and a heating system needed. And Quinn.

Spenser did not ask to be lifted up, but, as if he were wise to all that what was going on, settled on the quilt that had slipped off the bed. Quinn lifted the covers back onto her and she settled in against him again.

He sighed. "Let's see, where were we when we had some semblance of sanity? What you told me about Josh makes him a person of interest, too, as is Mary. But I know them. Again, I just can't believe it was either of them. But we can't have you holding back evidence. Why don't you let me tell Trooper Kurtz instead of you in case Josh asks who saw him throw the paw?"

They fell silent again. He tugged her even closer, her back against his chest almost as they had lain in the forest by the lake, but this was so different. Had it been love at first sight? It was fast, fascinating, but frightening, too.

"Quinn, there's more I want to tell you, to explain, especially since you've been brave enough to share your childhood tragedy with me. I told you about my lost twin sister before, but I need to explain more."

Her voice caught. He gave her a little hug and kissed her shoulder. "Tell me," he whispered.

"I think one thing that draws you and me together is that we have both suffered from regret and guilt that's not our fault. You partly blame yourself for darting away as a kid and leading your dad and dog to look for you where a bear attacked them. I blame myself for surviving and taking all the space in our mother's womb and sustenance when my twin disappeared. Like you, I felt guilty, though it wasn't my fault. With Mary's problems—Chip's, too—I realize my lost twin still haunts me, but not in a scary way—in...an inspirational *I'm with you, I love you always* way. Does that make any sense?"

"It does. I sometimes think that about my dad, that he's with me. He would be cheering me on as much as he loved the wilderness—even wildlife, including bears. He would have loved what I'm doing with my life, my career, sharing it with friends who are almost like family. So, I agree that you and I have more in common than we think."

He reached down to pat her hip. "I'll ask later more formally," he went on, "but I hope you will consider staying here in Falls Lake so we can make a life together. But I don't want you to feel rushed or pushed. If you'll consider it, I'll bring a ring back from New York and ask you properly and formally and, of course, get adoption papers for Spenser."

She had to laugh at that. Her little rescue dog gave a single bark when he heard his name. Whatever befell them, whatever they decided, she'd been rescued by a man she trusted and adored.

29

Before dawn the next morning, after final goodbyes and good-lucks, the tracking students piled into rental cars, one airport limo and a truck. The line of headlights stabbed the darkness, then the bloodred taillights disappeared down the narrow road. Ryker had driven two of the students Josh had planned to take, since Josh was going to stay here as caretaker of the camp while Quinn was in New York.

Ryker seemed both glum and nervous, which Alex and Quinn understood, though he had not been charged. But they had to admit he was a "person of interest" to both of them, too.

"At least they beat what may be the onslaught of reporters," Quinn said, and took her hand as they followed Josh back into the compound through the gate. Using a flashlight, Josh carefully locked it behind them.

"Thanks, Josh!" Quinn called back as he and Alex headed for his house.

"Nice you still trust me at all!" Josh shouted.

"What's that about?" Alex asked. "Did you ask him about throwing the bear paw away?"

"Yeah. I'll explain. I told him I'm still deciding whether or not to tell the troopers what he did. I've been putting it off but I'd better let Kurtz know, so he doesn't think we're hiding something. Josh took it pretty well, and I gave him the idea I'm the one who saw him, so he's not ticked at you. But what do you say to my plan once it gets light? We go out the back door and have Josh lock it behind us before the next assault of reporters. We'll take the back trail to the lodge where you can hole up while I'm in New York."

"Geoff should send his private plane for you."

"I've been on it—a first-class six-seater—but not this time. Ah, the rich if not the famous. I can make good connections, and he'll pick me up—his driver will, anyway. Brent has a private plane, too, but smaller."

"How about you carry Spenser in your backpack, and I'll take my clothes and things back in mine? Suze thought most of her visitors would clear out today since they're getting nowhere here and—hopefully—the tragedy is now in the troopers' hands. And I do feel better after Sam phoned."

"Me, too. Hopefully some anti-anxiety meds will help Mary. I guess they have to be careful with what they prescribe and dosages, since she's pregnant."

"And I'm sure you noticed there have been no cries from strange voices in the night since she's been gone."

"Maybe the so-called Falls Lake ghost will go away now. If so, we'll really think it was her."

He only shook his head, then called out, "Hey, Josh!" when the big man lumbered from the darkness toward the dining hall to clean up. "We're going to grab some breakfast at my house, then hike over to the lodge through the woods to be sure no one spots us. You'll lock up, after we go out the back way?"

"Yeah, good idea to still lay low. But what you gonna do if those TV hosts ask you about the murder during your interview?"

"Tell them ahead of time I'm only there to talk about the tracking and wilderness experience. Then just say I can't comment if they try to bring that up."

"Wish it was that easy," Josh muttered. "I'll be over at the lodge later—drive my truck, if Alex would rather just hide in the back to get over there."

"No, thanks," Alex said. "I'd like a nice, quiet hike this morning before Quinn heads out for the big city."

"Fine," Josh added as he turned away. "Let me know if I can help. Sure like to get our team back together soon!"

"I mean it about bringing back a ring from New York," Quinn told her after they had scrambled eggs, bacon and toast and fed and walked Spenser. "If you want me to keep it for a while before asking you, I will. If you want to wear it but set the date far off, that's okay. If you change your mind—not okay, but I would understand. I know this is all fast, but I've never been more sure of anything."

She lifted Spenser to settle him in Quinn's backpack as they stood in the bathroom where Spenser had run. The little guy "kissed her" by licking her chin. Quinn laughed. "You sure that dog's not French instead of Scottish?" he asked. "Looked like an attempt at a French kiss to me."

"You are both bad," she told him, and stood on her toes to lick Quinn's chin, then dart a quick kiss on his mouth. "And about the ring... I want to say yes, but we do have some things to be arranged. I've told my parents about you, but not everything. As you said, it's so fast. After I just emerged unscathed from my terrible relationship, they'll be worried."

"Tell you what. We'll make a trip to visit my mother and your parents as soon as I survive *Gab Fest* and the advanced class coming in here in a week. Let's just talk that over as we head out," he said. "I want to get you safely over to the lodge and come back so I can pack. Geoff said to wear something 'woodsy.' This is going to be one quick trip and, after, maybe we can make all our trips together."

She glanced in the mirror again as he headed out ahead of her with Spenser on his back. Allie was staring at her from the mirror. She looked a little nervous, but she nodded her okay as Alex turned away and followed him out.

They took a western path Alex had never been on or even seen before. Josh locked the gate behind them. This trail was deep enough in the forest that they could not see the road, but they could hear the occasional vehicle on it and wondered if the reporters were making another, last assault since Suze had said they'd been recalled and had checked out.

The trail wound around natural obstacles—thick brush, a few boulders that must have come not from the waterfall but from ancient glaciers. They completely skirted the rocky outcrop where Val had died. They sat beside another noisy, crooked stream. It had stepping stones in it, but they didn't cross yet. Quinn turned to her and spoke over the sound of the stream.

"I phoned Trooper Kurtz about Josh heaving that bear claw away—and that I phoned Sam and they don't have her necklace. Of course, Mary's very upset, so those anxiety meds better kick in soon. Again, I got the feeling the troopers are considering Ryker as the killer, so we'll have to be wary of him. I'll consider replacing him, though I'd hate to break up the team. Nor do I want to cut him adrift when he's been through so much."

"What did Josh say when you told him you knew he tossed the bear paw?"

"He claims it's an old one he had since high school, and can't remember where he got it. He found it recently in a drawer. After someone killed Val, spur of the moment decision to get rid of it, he said. To protect you, I implied I'd glanced up and saw him heave it."

"So he didn't seem upset at all—like he'd been caught doing something that could get him in trouble—but he still knew to get rid of it?"

"Sam and I decided to trust Josh long ago. He's protective, not harmful, when he could have been bitter over losing Mary to Sam. Unless Josh has just buried that pain so it wouldn't explode. But let's talk about us. Have a seat on this log by the stream and let me clear the air on something."

They sat and she petted Spenser's head before they settled, shoulder to shoulder. The constant current of the stream burbled around its stepping stones.

"Alex, about last night. I know I said we'd be somewhere safe before our first time making love. Lately, the compound and surrounding area is not safe, but it just seemed the right time—the necessary time."

"I feel safe with you. I did then."

He reached for her hand and held it on her knee. "If

you'll marry me, we'll get a place in town, use that compound house for a hideaway—and, of course, stay there the nights we have students. With the advanced classes, which are so different from what you saw, I go out in the wilds with them for three nights. The thing is, I didn't want to push you, to take over, because I don't want to remind you of the idiot you ran from. I don't ever want you to run from me."

"Run after you, more like, Q-Man," she said, bouncing their hands once. "And you gave me the choice last night, so I'd say we're equal partners in this."

He nodded. Spenser yawned. Quinn kissed her.

"Let's keep on keeping on, partner," he said with a touch of western drawl. The man had tears in his eyes. When they stood, she got on her tiptoes and kissed him again.

"Onward," he said after a long embrace. "Together. Just the three of us."

Stepping from stone to stone to keep their feet dry, they forded the shallow stream together. She smiled and blinked back tears, too. She had never felt so happy or so safe.

Chip spotted them the moment they approached the lodge property from the woods. He was sitting in the middle of the backyard with a pair of big binoculars.

"Hi, guys!" he called out, and ran toward them. "Mom and Aunt Suze said you were coming!"

"Looking for wild animals?" Quinn asked, and ruffled the boy's hair.

"That's what I told Mom, but I'm really looking for planes."

"Yeah? Well, I'm taking one today to New York City."

"But not bush planes," Chip said. "I like little planes. That's where you really get the sense of flying and being in control."

Alex and Quinn exchanged silent glances at that adult talk. It was as if Chip's father were here saying that, just as he'd obviously said it to his son.

Alex took Spenser out of Quinn's backpack, snapped his leash on and put him down.

"Chip," Quinn said, "how about you run Spenser inside and tell your mom and aunt we're here? Aunt Alex is going to move back into her room for a while."

"And open up the shop," she said. "Also, in a day or two, start cooking up some beauty products in your kitchen here when it isn't being used."

"Like soap?" Chip asked. "What about toothpaste?"

"I haven't ventured into that yet, but maybe it's next," she said.

Holding Spenser's leash, Chip ran inside with his binoculars bouncing.

"I've got to head back," Quinn said. "I'll come here as soon as I return from New York."

He kissed her, lingering. She hugged him. With a sigh, he let her go and headed into the forest as Suze and Meg ran out to greet her. It was almost like a homecoming, and here, she'd hardly been away.

"The place is pretty much cleared out—of reporters at least," Suze said, and hugged her. "Come on in!"

Meg caught up, and they did a three-way hug. If only, Alex thought, families could be like this. Last night and this morning, Alaska had never seemed so warm and wonderful. So why did she sometimes feel the forest had eyes, that someone was watching her?

She glanced back to be sure Quinn wasn't there but saw no one.

Maybe she was just thinking of Allie again. Maybe, once she wasn't with Quinn, where she felt so safe, she's just remembered the bad things like losing Spenser or finding Val dead. Or perhaps it was just her old fears lurking, of being controlled, the nightmare of being possessed and abused but not really loved.

She'd go in and call her parents, tell them more about Quinn, about the love and safety she'd found here.

30

Although Alex was so happy to be back with her cousins and Chip, she immediately missed Quinn. That afternoon, everyone was excited about his being on "regular" TV tomorrow. She kept busy by sweeping out the Gifts and More shop she intended to reopen.

She didn't have Spenser with her, because he was serving as a kind of comfort pet for Chip right now. The boy had especially bonded with the Scottie over his own dogs because Spenser was missing one eye, and Chip felt sorry for him—as he did for himself.

"But see how well he does without that eye?" Alex had told the boy earlier. "In life, if tough times come, and we lose something or someone, we keep on, being brave, looking for good things and helping others. I mean, just like Spenser helps you and me. He helps Quinn, too, since he lost his dad when he was young, like you did. And Spenser helps you just like you help your mom."

A quick knock on the door jolted Alex from that memory. Meg opened the door as if Alex's thoughts had summoned her.

"Guess what?" Meg blurted as she darted into the shop. "We thought we were rid of reporters, but there's one who just checked in at the lodge from the *Anchorage Daily News*. Thank heavens, he said they've killed the story idea about interviewing Chip about his father being a ghost! I'm going to have that boy see a psychiatrist in Anchorage, so I'll see what everyone learns from Mary's experience there. Anyway, this reporter's here on the story about Val's murder. He's already been over to the compound looking for Quinn, so I told the guy he's out of state right now. He also asked about who else he should interview."

"You didn't tell him I'm here?"

"Josh was nearby when the reporter checked in and piped up to say you were with Quinn in New York. He outright lied, but I went along with it. In other words, lay low out here, and I'll let you know if he leaves. He tried to interview Josh—guess he had his name, too—but Josh just kept saying, 'No comment,' that things were under investigation, and no one was supposed to talk."

"Quinn says Josh is very protective, and I agree the more I get to know him."

"The guy is full of surprises. He even carted your boxes of supplies back here in his truck since you decided to work on your products in our kitchen and storeroom. The boxes are in the work shed, so just ignore the snowmobiles stored with the other stuff. Suze has some of her paintings in crates, too. In short, it's pretty crowded in there." She waved and popped out as fast as she'd come in.

So Josh was a good guy in the disguise of a curmudgeon. She should have known that since Sam, Mary and Quinn obviously trusted him.

She finished putting some of her products back on the sales table and decided to open her cartons in the large shed, however crowded it was in there. She fumbled in the drawer for the box cutter and a flashlight. Peeking out to be sure no stranger was in the backyard or looking out the lodge windows, she went out.

Geoff and Brent took Quinn to Tavern on the Green in Central Park for a late dinner. "I figured you'd feel more at home with the outdoor, garden seating," Geoff told him. "I kind of miss it in the winter, especially when this place is full of tourists."

Quinn liked the place okay, especially outside. It was spacious even inside, but he enjoyed the fresh air and the plants all around. Yet he always had the sense of people pressing in from the tall buildings. He'd like to bring Alex here someday, though. Even if she was from near Chicago, she'd worked in a suburb, so he hoped she'd share his feelings about cities versus smaller towns and countryside, especially an area with deep forests, mountains and lakes.

"So," Brent cut into his thoughts, "would you like to go over possible interview questions for *Gab Fest* and run your responses by us?"

"I'll do best if it's kept spontaneous," Quinn said, reaching for his iced tea. "Geoff showed me the video clips the show will use so I know how to speak to it when they run it."

"You feel steady enough after everything?" Brent went on. "The hosts have promised questions about the murder are strictly off-limits. I consider myself strictly off-limits, too," he said, taking a sip of his martini. "I told Trooper Kurtz that when he called me about getting fingerprinted here and sending them digital to their BCI in Anchorage. No way I had motive or opportunity to harm that woman, and you didn't, either."

"Brent," Geoff cut in, "how about another topic besides poor Val Chambers? Meanwhile, Quinn, how serious are things between you and Alex? Brent tells me he got the idea that you two might be an item."

"Despite everything, I admit I'm serious about her, and that's about all I want to say on that right now. But, Brent," he went on, turning toward him at the table, "I don't like your earlier suggestion that we do a show on the so-called Falls Lake ghost. We don't need those woods and the lake crawling with ghost hunters, and I've had a reporter from one ghost TV show poking around already in the dead of night. And that would upset some of my team."

"I think you're off base there," Brent said, sitting forward. "I can see that haunted angle as a great way to build our audience."

Geoff said, "Let's just help Quinn stay mellow, in charge with whatever backwoods charm he can manage for this gig tomorrow. But, Quinn, I see Brent's point about growing our audience however we can. Actually, I'm the one who arranged your guest spot on *Gab Fest*, and Brent wasn't all for it. But your interview is bound to get us more viewers, women at least. By the way, I hear you had three female students in the most recent group."

"Yeah, that worked out well. I'd say we're averaging about fifteen percent women in the beginner groups but barely five percent in the advanced. So, Brent," Quinn said, "if you want to build our demographics, why have you been against going for the huge, dynamic women's audience? Times are a-changin', my friend."

And then Quinn had a revelation. Could Brent's attitude toward focusing the show on a masculine audience be the fallout of his bitter divorce? His ex might have been married to a brilliant lawyer, but she'd come out on top with a huge settlement. Clarissa Bayer had hired a legal shark and managed to take half of Brent's assets when she left him besides getting custody of their adolescent son, since she'd proved Brent was having a recent affair—a second one. And his latest lover had testified against him in the divorce hearings.

"You do realize," Brent said, gripping his drink with one hand and pointing to emphasize his words, "that the fact you're single gives a boost to our male-oriented ratings, Q-Man in the wilds and all that. Then we get the female audience with your macho star appeal, not by softening the impact of the show with more female students or women characters—a girlfriend or a wife."

"Look, I don't see this as a hunk show or I'd be out of there."

"I didn't mean that," Brent shot back. "But you don't see it as a family show, either, do you? We've hardly mentioned that Mary and Sam are married, and she's been pretty much in the background. And that's the way I see the show's trajectory. I don't care if it is the equality-for-women, #MeToo era."

"No personal life for the title character?" Quinn shot back.

"I didn't say that. Only your team are all outdoorsy people, and someone like Alexandra Collister being part of things feminizes it, and we don't need that. Besides, I got the idea that she wanted to remain private—in the shadows—because of an unfortunate previous experience of some kind."

"I can't believe you're saying all this when you managed to get me scheduled on a female-focused show like *Gab Fest* tomorrow," Quinn shot back, feeling very defensive and protective of Alex. And he did not want to discuss her frightening domestic background. "Are you still thinking about some backward world where a woman's place is in the kitchen and the bedroom?" he challenged. "Or just watching 'women's shows'?"

He turned to Geoff again. "Geoff, Ginger's a big part of your life and likes the show. Talk some sense into our adviser-investor here."

Quinn knew his voice was rising, but he couldn't help it. He was on edge, had to watch his temper lately, especially here where he felt crowded, pushed and, despite people everywhere, almost lost. How did Brent really know Alex was running from something? Worse, he had just used Alex's entire name, so had he been researching her?

"It's just food for thought right now, Quinn," Geoff insisted, leaning forward and gripping his wrist. "But let's all face it, the appeal of the show is mostly to a male audience, not ghost aficionados or women who want to go out tracking."

"And you two have been researching Alexandra Collister?" Quinn demanded, unwilling to let that go. He tried to keep his voice down as their steaks arrived. "I don't recall either of you knowing her full, legal name."

With a huge sigh, Brent leaned back in his chair, crossing his arms over his chest. "I think I heard her tell her entire name and say something about previously living in the Chicago area and having a bad relationship there, that's all. We can get back to this discussion about the show's future trajectory later. Let's enjoy our meal."

"Look, Quinn," Geoff said, back to his usual calm, controlled voice, "we care about you and your staff—and friends—and have promoted you for your personality, character, appearance and occupation, not to mention your passion for the wilds. Yes, we're selling a product in a way. Look at all the good you're doing to keep America green. You profit, we profit, as long as we don't get crazy and mess things up. It's a tragedy the murder happened, but we'll get through it. Valerie Chambers was not good for Ryker, who is evidently under suspicion for her death, and we just hope that Alex is good for you. Let's face it, your relationship with her, whatever it is, happened pretty fast."

Frowning, Quinn took another swig of his iced tea. "I'm against people being used," he told them, leaning forward to pick up his fork and stab a few fries. "If I sense that is happening with the people I chose to work with, I'm done at next contract time."

The two men glanced at each other without moving their heads—or mouths—for once.

"Agreed," Geoff said. "Our concern is for you above all."

Quinn nodded and ate some fries. He didn't tell them so, but his concern was not primarily for the show. It was for his staff, but now more than that. As soon as he was done here, he was going to unwind by taking a solo walk under the streetlights through the winding footpaths of a wooded part of Central Park called the Ramble. It was near a lake, too, and he was suddenly so homesick for Falls Lake—and to have Alex with him.

* * *

The door to the shed was not only unlocked but stood ajar, so Meg must have known she'd be going in to get her boxes soon. Alex was glad she'd brought a flashlight. Though there were two windows, they were small and the forest shadows loomed large outside. And as Meg had said, it was crowded in here with three snowmobiles, some stacked furniture, crated oil paintings, paint cans and who knew what else.

And yes, her four boxes were piled near the door, which she kept open for more light and air in the dusty, stale atmosphere. She realized she hadn't smelled anything musty since she arrived in fresh-air Alaska.

She cut into the first box and pulled out the new labels she'd had Suze design to give more of a rustic flavor to her renamed products. As soon as she became really acclimated here, she'd research what local plants she could use. And that greenhouse Quinn had mentioned…and that house he'd talked about, a cozy bungalow…

She scooted the next carton away from the wall and noticed a large roll of yellow tape hanging on the peg behind it. Maybe it was the one Josh had used to cordon off the students' observation areas the day Val died. She remembered Brent with his backpack on—which was so unlike him, however casually he dressed—pointing here and there when Josh probably knew more about the layout than a city lawyer ever would.

What scared her was that whatever was used to bash in Val's skull could have been the handle on that roll of tape. Or, of course, the handle of Ryker's camera or even the camera itself. Could it even have been a piece of wood from the forest, which anyone could have wielded, or almost anything hard someone had hidden in one of the backpacks that day?

A chill racked her. Quinn had said he'd call her, but she'd left her purse with her cell in the shop. She had to go back and get it. He'd said after midday New York time, but…but she wanted to talk to him now, just to feel better, to not feel all alone out here.

It was a crazy idea, but she almost felt she was being watched—just nerves over poor Val's demise, no doubt.

"So we meet again," came the whisper of a too-familiar voice behind her. "Why the hell did you run and this damn far away? I told you. You are mine or the end!"

31

After dinner with the show's two movers and shakers—and they'd certainly shaken him up tonight—Quinn walked through the Ramble, missing Alex, wishing he was with her on the path they'd hiked yesterday. Strolling lovers or couples necking on park benches made him miss her even more. For sure, he told himself, he'd stop doing the show when his contract was up next year if he couldn't have her in his life because of it. He'd produce and finance the show himself, or get new sponsors—something.

That is, if things between them worked out. If…if.

He stared across a stretch of water, wishing he was home, then walked east toward Fifth Avenue. Streetlights and lit-from-within window displays made the area look like day. He leaned against a store wall and punched in Alex's cell number. It rang…rang. He'd told her he'd call her about now, but maybe the distant time zone had mixed her up.

Her voice came on, asking him to leave a message. "It's me," he said. "I'll call back later. Just wanted you to know I'm heading to look in the windows or a jewelry store I just might visit tomorrow. Hope you'd be as excited with that as I am."

He called his mother and filled her in on the murder, made sure she remembered he'd be on *Gab Fest* tomorrow. Then he explained he was in love, would bring Alex to see her as soon as he could—and admitted he was hoping to buy an engagement ring.

"But you haven't known her long, my dear."

"Long enough. Are you going to lecture me, too?"

"Too? You must tell others it's not their business, unless you mean Alex herself."

"My producer and his lawyer."

"Well, no lecture from me! I knew that your father was the man for me about an hour after we met, so I'm not one to scold, at least on this. I can't wait to meet her. You can probably only imagine a mother's wish for her son to find 'the one,' and I have visions of grandchildren dancing in my head. Now tell me more about her…"

And he did.

Her pulse pounded so hard she heard it thudding in her ears. The words barely came out.

"L-Lyle. How did you find me?"

"Did you doubt I would? I've been watching you for a couple of hours, hoping you'd wander somewhere out here instead of the shop where others could see you from the lodge. I saw one of your female friends out here earlier, and she left this place open. Ah—fate that you joined me, but we need to get going now."

"I'm not going anywhere with you."

"Remember the 'or the end' part of my promise?" he asked, and lifted a gun she hadn't seen to point it at her.

She sucked in a breath. Nightmare. Not happening.

The hole in the barrel seemed huge...dark. And then she saw the gun had a large handle, which he was gripping so hard the weapon wavered.

"A few days ago, did you hit a woman on a rocky ledge looking down at a stream?" she asked, her voice not her own.

"Are you crazy? I just got here, though I saw that in the Anchorage paper. But hell, no. I'm after you, and you're going with me right now, quietly, willingly, or else. Move. Out into the forest for a little chat, maybe more or—I repeat—the end."

Maybe, she thought, someone would see her from the inn and get help. If she went missing—even if it took a while for people to learn that—surely Meg or Suze would call for help. But the one who could track her was far away.

Pieces of panicked thoughts bombarded her. Lyle had never had guns, had he? What if he didn't control that one well? She had the blackest feeling she could not just talk him out of it—this abduction, maybe a shooting. Surely she knew this area better than him and could shove him somehow, get away. And that futile thought reminded her again of how very far away Quinn was.

Then she made a very calculated decision. If she left here with Lyle, she was doomed, gone, the end indeed. She had to make a stand here, close to the lodge, her family, civilization.

She stepped back but another carton was in the way. Lyle leaped at her, seized her, clamped a big hand over her mouth when she opened it to scream. He gripped her face so hard her teeth ground against the soft inside of her mouth.

She yanked one hand free and lunged for the plastic

tape hung on the wall, hoping to use it for a weapon. But he threw her down, his hand still clamped over her mouth. He grabbed the tape. She tried to kick at him, knee him, but she knew he was strong. He'd pinned her down in better times and was enraged now, his face distorted in an expression she'd never seen.

He ripped off a jagged piece of tape to wrap around her mouth—no, he pried her mouth open and, when she tried to scream, jammed some of its stiffness in her mouth. She gagged, gasping for air. The tape blocked her airway so she started to suck in air through her nose. Did he mean to kill her right here?

Out of breath—still struggling. He ripped off more tape—and wound it around her wrists. Getting dizzy, hurting. Was this a nightmare or real?

If she could only get to her box cutter for a weapon, but it was out of reach. Despite her bound wrists, she tried to claw him. Out of air, out of sanity. She tried to protest through the plastic gag, but he ignored her. He dragged her to a sitting position, hefted her up over his shoulder and carried her out, closing the shed door behind them before he strode for the nearest forest path, the one she and Quinn had walked just yesterday, the one that led to the stream.

The remnants of her breath bounced out as his shoulder banged into her stomach. She almost threw up.

However he had found her, he was here. He must mean to kill her. This was real—the end.

It seemed he carried her forever. Maybe she was unconscious, but no, she knew where she was, who held her captive. How did he know his way here? Who had told him where she was, not only in Falls Lake but at the inn? He seemed to know the lay of the land.

And Quinn—more than half a continent away. He was supposed to call her about now. She'd just been going to get her phone. What she wouldn't give for a phone. The only good thing was that Spenser had not been with her, for Lyle would have hurt or killed him to keep him quiet.

Quinn, Quinn. She tried to send a message to him all those miles away. *I love you, need you.*

For a moment, she'd thought she heard footsteps on the path behind them, but no one was there.

Lyle carried her a good ways, crossed the stream, ignoring its stepping stones and just plunging in. He sloshed cold water as he went, even up into her face and on her back. He was furious, kicking his way across. For a moment she thought he might be taking her clear back to Quinn's property. Surely he wasn't going to take her all the way to Falls Lake and drown her, make it look like an accident or suicide. But Meg and Suze would know better.

She managed to cough the wadded plastic toward the front of her mouth, push it out with her tongue, though it would do her no good to scream now. But if someone noticed she was gone, maybe finding that chewed yellow plastic would tell them which way they'd gone—if they didn't just think it was forest litter from any passerby.

He sat her down on a rock across the stream from where she and Quinn had stopped. Was that only this morning? Did she and Quinn have only the past together?

He did not loosen her wrists. "Don't bother screaming, because no one is going to hear you this deep in the woods."

She gasped for breath. "Why don't you just go on with your life—leave me alone. Find someone else?"

"Oh, I will, but you've publicly shamed me, and you don't do that to someone you claimed—and vowed—to love and marry. You are a very sick woman."

"Look, Lyle, there's been a murder near here and the Alaska state troopers are still patrolling this area."

"I hear the authorities have done their thing and left the scene. And have a suspect in mind."

Her head snapped up. Had he been talking to someone local or had he read a newspaper? But still, how did he find her?

At least it was getting easier to breathe. Although he had put the gun in the large black leather bag he wore over one shoulder, she made the decision she was going to have to calm and coerce him, not fight him. She would have to lie, not tell him how much she detested him, but she had to know more about something he'd just said.

In as calm a voice as she could manage, she asked, "So you've heard about the murder here and the authorities' investigation and the aftermath? From whom? It was so clever of you to locate me, but how did you do it?"

"A little bird—actually, a big one," he said, and dared to laugh as if he enjoyed tormenting her, which he no doubt did. Why hadn't she seen through his controlled facade? Could you ever really know someone you were intimate with and thought you were close to?

"Now let's talk," he went on, perching on a rock higher than the one he'd put her on. "Let's just see if you're willing to cooperate with me, apologize and see the light—or it's lights out, pretty baby. Lights out."

Lights out, but not, she vowed, life out!

32

Lyle leaned back on his rocky seat for a moment, to take his black bag off his shoulder—maybe to keep his gun dry since the stream splashed over some rocks. She needed to risk everything now.

Though she was tied hands and feet, she exploded at him, banging her shoulder into his chest. Had to get that gun in the water, hit his head on a rock—anything! Desperation made her strong and wild.

He hit his head on the pebbled edge of the stream, but he writhed to right himself, got to his feet. She rolled away, but he came at her like a wrestler, looking for a hold, for a pin.

She kicked and struggled, but he dragged her into the cold, frothing water and shoved her in, facedown. She held her breath at first, but that was futile. She was going to suck water into her lungs…stop breathing. He'd untie her then, leave her here, and who knew if a bear would find her, or another killer…like poor Val…

Pictures of those she'd loved flashed through her mind in a vivid blur. Her poor parents would suffer so.

Meg, Suze, Chip. Dear Quinn. Her beloved little dog. Quinn or Chip would take Spenser…

Fear nearly drowned her, though the water had not. If only this was a nightmare, but Lyle was real and here.

He stumbled up on the bank, sopping wet, and, breathing hard, hauled her after him. She had to try to play along, not fight him like this. Apparent obedience, acquiescence, even admiration was the only way to deal with this man.

She took a deep breath and steeled herself not to scream at him. Her voice came low and shaky. "I just couldn't stand to be tied up like this. Panicked. Please, take the tape off. I won't run. I've run enough and am grateful you found me. Our early days together were wonderful. I'd like to try again."

His expression wavered between distrust and hope. Did she have a chance with this ploy? It made her sick to her very soul, but she had to keep him from using that gun.

"How clever of you to find me," she went on, still spitting water and even blowing it out her nose. She sucked in another deep, ragged breath. A pain at the back of her head burned. "I just had to get away for a while—to think things out."

"And have you?" he asked, sitting back on the big rock again and pushing her down to a kneeling position below him.

"Yes, lately I've missed home. The way things were. And you were a huge part of that. It's been hard because I was so angry with you at first for—for being so physical, dominating, but I have begun to realize I missed you, too."

She assumed he did not know about Quinn, hadn't

seen them together. Could this tactic possibly work? She needed to be untied. She needed that gun. She needed to stop this terrible man she had so stupidly fallen for.

"Okay," he said with a tight grin she was shocked to see. He was obviously going to gloat. "Connections are how I found you. But I'll tell you just two words, then no more. License plate."

That slammed her in the midriff. He'd somehow traced her license plate? Was it recorded when she crossed the Canadian border? By local law enforcement? But that would be the troopers and wouldn't Kurtz or Hanson have warned her? No, of course it wouldn't have come through them. But someone must have seen her truck, someone must have located her license plate and her, then contacted the authorities—or found him. But only her cousins and Quinn knew about Lyle, and surely none of them had betrayed her.

She wanted to scream at him, but she said, "As usual, you're way ahead of me. I regret I panicked and ran. I just couldn't stay to face you after I'd let you down and ruined what we had."

She tried to look crestfallen. It didn't take an acting job to cry. Her tears mingled with the water still on her face. She was scared and angry. She had to get away from this man or get help somehow. But her rescuer was several thousand miles away.

"I didn't even use a private detective because I didn't want to be traced, and I knew you could be," Lyle said, going into a familiar let-me-explain, boasting mode now. "Since you tried to leave me, your life has become one big mistake, Alex. You had everything with me and you threw it away."

She shook uncontrollably from being wet and chilled as well as from nerves.

"But I must admit," he said, his voice mocking, "for a stupid woman, you did a fairly good job of covering your tracks online and with your friends. If my contact who traced your license plate had not worked out, my plan B was to call the company that supplied your pretty little packaging materials to give them some song and dance so they tell me your new location, mailing address or whatever, but I didn't need to leave a trail that way. Bet you thought you didn't leave one, either, huh?" he said, his voice taunting. Yes, the dominant, pompous, clever Lyle was here, but could she use that against him?

"By the way," he went on, obviously enjoying himself, "everyone at the office thinks I'm distraught you couldn't handle the pressure of work and wedding. So, like you, I needed a little time away. I'm supposedly in the Caribbean for a week where I actually have a reservation. But here I am thousands of miles away from there, and you are going to pay for all the insults and trouble you've caused."

Her mind reeled again from the realization he must mean to kill her. If he could get away with it and get away from here, people might think Val's murderer had struck again, even if in a different way.

She had to outsmart Lyle but she felt weak and nauseous. With Quinn so far away, would it even pay to try to leave him traceable clues if they left this area, or would this maniac shoot her right here? She could only think of one way to play for time, and she hated herself for that. She had to try again.

"Actually," she said, "when someone murdered that

woman who was also visiting the area, I knew I'd had
enough of this place. Everyone hates a murderer. But it
really made me miss home even more. Lyle, I've been
so scared, so confused and lonely for my old life," she
lied. But she was not faking anything when she burst
into hysterical tears.

She dared not look up as she sobbed into her still-
tied hands. If she could just get him on the trail, get
that gun, use it to make him flee or walk him out to
the road, then to the lodge. At least Quinn had taught
her some wilderness survival skills but not against a
deranged man with a gun who must intend to kill her.

"Whatever you think of my falling apart back home,"
she choked out, looking up at him, "I should not have
run. I just wanted to get away and think things out—
then I started missing you, but I knew you'd be furious with me and not want me back, and I couldn't face
that—"

He interrupted. "So who are these women who run
the Falls Lake Lodge?"

A new fear sliced through her. She must not let him
take her back to the lodge. He'd been asking around
town for sure. As much as she needed Meg and Suze
to know what had happened, that she was at best a prisoner and, at worst, soon dead, they must not be hurt.

"Cousins I hadn't seen in years and was kind of estranged from. I told them next to nothing about you—
us. Just that I was running from a situation that had
panicked me. I wanted to mend bridges with them, just
as I—please forgive me, Lyle—wanted to do with you
but I was just so overwhelmed when you blew up at
me like that."

He snorted. He didn't believe her. He fished the gun

out of his side pack. Again, she thought he was going to kill her—right now.

"We can't stay here," he said, rising. "This water source could draw wild animals or campers and hikers, and we need to be alone. Then we'll talk and maybe more so you can prove to me you mean what you said."

Grateful to live longer, to have a chance to escape or stop this man, she thrust her feet out, straight-legged before her. "I can't go one step with you if you don't cut these bonds—the ties on my wrist, too. The woods are a dangerous place to be tied and awkward. Please, Lyle. We could go back, try again, start again. Being far away like this, I know what—who—I've been missing now."

He shrugged as if she or that request was nothing to him, but he pulled a big jackknife from his pack and cut her ankle ties, then her wrist ones. As she massaged her wrists, she prayed it wasn't too late now.

Quinn was really nervous, not about being on a national TV show tomorrow, but about maybe picking out an engagement ring tomorrow. Besides that, he was upset Alex still wasn't answering her phone, but he kept telling himself she was busy at the lodge, that she may have screwed up the timing of when he'd said he'd call.

Maybe he should wait until he asked Alex what style of ring she liked. Too many glittered here in the window, perched on dark green waves of velvet that looked like little hills.

The window glass reflected his anxious face superimposed on the rings with diamonds cut in different shapes, mostly round or rectangular cut, some with two-pointed ends. Would she prefer yellow gold or white gold for the ring itself? He did not like the really fussy ones, encrusted with tiny chips of gems crowding the bigger ones. Alex needed a classic-looking, timeless one, not supermodern. And wouldn't she want one that would kind of fit with the wedding ring? Maybe those should be bought at the same time. Hell, why did he think this would be so straightforward and simple?

Would she expect him to keep his word and come back with a ring? Or was it better to take her into Anchorage to choose one? But he thought if he had one in his hand, ready for her finger, they could get it fitted. But then, as controlled and abused as she'd been by the idiot she had fled from, maybe she'd really want a say on her rings, not just have to accept what he chose.

With pedestrians and traffic rushing by in the background, he heaved a huge sigh and stared again at his reflection in the glass. Alex had said she thought of her lost twin when she looked in mirrors, that she felt she saw her there, staring back. He had felt that same way in forests when he was growing up, that his dad was there watching, waiting…sometimes even wanting to say something, to warn him of danger.

He took out his phone to call Alex again.

"You go first, and don't try running ahead or anything funny," Lyle told her, pointing with his gun at the familiar path toward the compound.

"All right. You tell me which way to go," she said, hoping her obedient attitude might calm him. Actually, Quinn had once told his students that compasses were only of minimal help in deep, thick woods with rivers and mountains, because travelers were at the mercy of those natural barriers and random, twisting paths. Here she was at Lyle's mercy, but she had to find some way to turn that gun on him. She prayed harder for that, asking for stamina and a chance to live.

Her legs were still shaking uncontrollably, but she had managed to live through the first trial: Lyle could have shot her and left her in the stream or buried in brush. He'd snapped to nearly drown her, but she had some time left—she hoped.

She intentionally stumbled every now and then, digging the toe of her shoe as best she could into the dirt path, trying to leave directional arrows. Why, she didn't know, because Quinn was in New York, and she'd be gone one way or the other when he got back, unless Suze or Meg realized she was missing and called for help. Called the troopers, even called Quinn.

Her back blessedly to Lyle—although she felt she was a huge target if he chose to shoot her—she tore a tissue from her pocket into tiny shreds rolled them tight and dropped them piece by piece on the ground.

It seemed hours had gone by, the shadows lengthening. She was thirsty and hungry, still cold from the stream, weak and so scared.

"Lyle, can we stop for a second? Do you have water?"

"I hear there's a whole freshwater lake of it back here somewhere."

So he didn't really know this area, and she did. She'd had the best teacher, and she loved Quinn Mantell, would always love him, no matter how much time she had left. "I know where the lake is," she told him, but she turned more toward Quinn's compound in case Josh—anyone—was there.

"Stop!" he ordered when she led him toward the compound. How she wished the troopers were still around. Would Suze and Meg call them when they realized she was gone? Surely her cousins wouldn't think she'd taken a walk on her own. *Oh, please, God, let someone know I'm not just out on my own, that I need help, that I need to find a way to turn that gun on Lyle before he uses it on me.*

Quinn was relieved that at least Suzanne answered her phone. She had caller ID, because she blurted out, "Quinn? Where are you?"

"In the Big Apple, wondering how little Falls Lake is doing. Listen, I've been trying to call Alex, and she's not answering. Maybe her phone is messed up. Can you put her on yours?"

"We can't find her."

"What? What does that mean?"

"Meg and Chip are out looking for her around the backyard, the shop, the shed, even going a ways into the forest. She was in the store—left it unlocked—evidently went to the shed, but she's not there and didn't even take her purse or phone with her."

"Is Josh around?"

"He doesn't have to be here for over an hour. Haven't seen him, either."

Quinn felt a belly blow. He actually doubled over, braced himself against the park bench he'd returned to.

"Suzanne, listen. Don't call the troopers in yet in case it's nothing—in case they would go in like storm troopers. Don't put Spenser on a leash to go into the woods, looking for her, not yet. And get Meg and Chip back in the lodge. Don't let anyone mess up any foot-prints on that single forest path that leads away from your back property near the shop. I never should have left, not now. I'm coming back as fast as I can get there. Call me with anything—anything."

"But you have that big interview tomorrow. Everyone's psyched to watch."

"I'll find a way. Then, if she's not back, I'll find her. I'm calling Sam to tell him we need him back at Falls Lake. They were coming back tomorrow. With Val being killed in the woods—hell, I'm sure Alex is all right but I need to be there now."

"Sam? But he's still in Anch—" he heard her say as he punched off. How he wished these city trees and bushes and this lake could be the ones at home.

33

Quinn knew Geoff had gone back to work. He called him immediately, insisted he be brought out of what his secretary called "an important meeting with a new sponsor."

"Please. Now!" he repeated. "This could well be a matter of life and death!"

"Are you all right? Ill or an accid—"

"Now!"

An endless wait, then Geoff's voice: "Quinn, are you okay? Whatever it is, keep calm. You're not still upset about my bringing up Alex at lunch, are you, bec—"

"Geoff, you need to cancel my appearance on the TV show tomorrow. I'm serious. This could be life and death, and please don't ask for a blow-by-blow right now. Time is key, and I have to get back. I need to use your private plane. I'll pay you for the pilot, time, gas. Please just tell me where to get it, because flying commercial would take too long."

A slight hesitation. If Quinn had been with Geoff, he would have shaken the life out of him to get an answer.

"Quinn, even if you head to La Guardia now, it will take hours to get back."

"Damn it, please do this or forget everything with my show because I'll be living like a hermit in the wilds, and you'll never see me again."

"The plane's in hanger 54 at La Guardia. I'll call the pilot, Steve Mason, to meet you there. You'll have to go through a checkpoint with your bag."

"I'm leaving my bag here, leaving now for the airport. Geoff, if Steve can't be there right away, hire someone else."

"It's something about Alex, isn't it? You'll still have to land in Anchorage. Keep in touch. Take care of yourself above all."

"There is no myself without her anymore. I'll call the troopers in later if I need them, but this has to be done quietly, just me for now. I can't let them throw up barriers and make noise with search dogs to try to find her their way."

"Alex is missing? Are you sure?"

"Just listen, please. No choppers in the sky to panic her or whoever may be involved. I just hope to hell I don't find her hurt—or worse. I'll keep in touch."

But he felt so out of touch, so far away. He wanted to touch her, hold her. Unless Meg or Suzanne or Josh could help, she was on her own, at least until he could get back.

Alex knew there were not many hours of daylight left. She could not bear a night with Lyle in the woods, her and Quinn's woods. She'd always felt so safe with him here, but now her greatest fear had come true. Lyle was here, a vindictive, violent Lyle.

"Hold up!" he ordered. "I think the path that cuts off to where I left the car is near here."

So he could be easily lost or led astray? Maybe led in circles until Suze and Meg realized that she was missing and sent someone to look for her? She feared Lyle finding his rental car more than his being lost in the forest. Would he put her in the trunk? She did not have her ID to get on a plane with him. Or would he drive them back east? Had he planned all that, too, or did he mean to leave her body in the woods?

He frowned down at his compass, tilted it a bit, tapped it, then shook his head. She was almost brave enough to leap at him. But again, he held the gun, a bit loosely, but could she risk physically fighting him even though her wrists and ankles weren't tied now?

Then she realized where they were. A big patch of strawberries was growing just off the path next to a thicket of that awful devil's club plant. It had those dreadful spines that caused infection. Maybe she could get him to pick berries, then shove him into the devil's club and pretend she just stumbled. Could she wrest his gun away, run or turn it on him? She knew the path to the lake, then where to find several other rugged paths leading from there, one toward the compound, one toward the road.

"Lyle, while you're doing that, I'm starving. See those strawberries? Can I pick a few? I'll pick you some, and you can eat, too. That will be almost as good as a drink of water. Please, will you let me?"

He squinted at her during that plea. His hand tightened on the pistol. "This is not some romp in the woods picnic. You make one wrong move, you make me think you're trying to get this gun, then you will get this gun in another way!"

"Why can't this be a new beginning? I admit I made a huge mistake. I've learned my lesson. I missed you and city life—especially here in this awful backwoods town. You still love me enough to come after me, to take me home with you, don't you?"

"Without that damn dog. I love dogs, and they love me, but that little bastard hated me from the first. I saw him with that kid back there."

"I'd be happy to just leave the dog with him. We sure see enough dogs at the clinic—if you'd take me back, or if you just want a stay-at-home wife to have kids. We can get a dog of our own. I've also come to realize how much I want children—ours."

She saw him waver. God help her, she'd never want a child with him. Was she laying it on too thick? She was not a very good liar, but she had to be now. So she was trying to play to his sick fantasies of control and his need to be obeyed. Why had she not really seen him before? She'd been blinded by the mirage of a perfect life and man when none existed. She had wanted things, a lifestyle, when she'd give anything now to just have a tiny house with cold water and Quinn in it.

"All right. Pick a few. Go ahead. But I'm watching."

She edged closer to the low-lying berries and the taller devil's club. She could see the noxious spines on the woody stems. She actually pictured herself cutting Lyle's face and neck with them, but then she'd get her hands all cut, and would it give her time to get that gun?

Picking the strawberries, she gobbled a couple for strength, for their juice. But even that made her feel more sick to her stomach. It had been hours since she'd eaten breakfast, and she was dizzy, almost felt she was floating.

"Here," she said, extending four big ones to him as she walked closer. If she grabbed the stems of the devil's club far enough down, maybe she wouldn't be cut up by them. But could she quickly break them off, thrust them at him to get that gun?

In that moment, she heard a snort, a shuffling sound behind them. Lyle turned, gasped, lifted the gun straight-armed and shot at a big bull moose as he huffed down the path past them, as startled to see them as they were to see it.

"Lyle, no!" she shouted too late. "Don't hurt it!"

She leaped at him, hit at his arm still extending the gun. His next shot went awry. She grabbed for the pistol, fought for it. He slammed her back and she went down, hitting her head on something…on something… maybe on a rock in the stream or at the waterfall or somewhere…

And then, waiting to be shot, she saw Allie reaching for her, holding her. How much they looked alike, were alike. Dearest Allie was always with her even if she was shot, even if she was dying in Quinn's beloved wilderness.

In Allie's arms, she clung hard before she realized it was Lyle. She wanted to scream, to thrust him away.

"I only shot it in its back haunch," he said. "It startled me. It just kind of stumbled, snorted, then hurried on. It looks all right. We do love our animals, don't we? You only went for the gun so I wouldn't shoot again. Maybe we can work together when we get back."

A glimmer of hope he wouldn't kill her—that he believed her—shone through her panic and despair. Yet reality hit her hard again. She had hugged and clung to Lyle, dizzy, thinking it was Allie, but at least that must have convinced him to trust her some. And he evidently thought she'd only gone for his gun so he would not shoot that beautiful, wild moose again.

"It startled me, too," she said, wishing the world would stop spinning, the trees tilting. "Sorry I hit your arm. I've seen them around here before. I know you wouldn't hurt it, not with your loving veterinarian's heart," she added, feeling she'd throw up as much as from her lies as from her spinning head.

But in a way, Allie had saved her just now—that is, the image of her. Never could she have clung to this man like that if she had not thought it was her long-lost sister. But would she join Allie soon, lost forever at Falls Lake?

On the jet heading west, Quinn kept himself sane by planning out what he would do to find Alex—and stop someone if she'd been taken by force. He kept seeing Val's body, sprawled by that stream under the rock outcrop.

He could not bear to think of it. Alex knew that basic area now and could not be lost! And it still bothered him that Josh had tossed that bear paw away despite the fact he trusted him.

He breathed out hard. He had a hired chopper waiting for him at the Anchorage airport to take him immediately to the Falls Lake Lodge. At least Chip would not think it was his lost dad again, for a chopper was a far cry from one of the single-engine bush planes that set the poor kid off.

"You okay back there?" the pilot's voice came over the intercom.

"Yes, thanks, Steve!" he shouted toward the open cockpit door from where he was stretched out in the closest leather seat.

But he was hardly okay. This was torment worrying about Alex, what was happening to her now.

Then there was the other sliver of torture he couldn't let himself face. If it wasn't for the fact the Collister twins and Chip had her beloved, little Spenser, the other fear that gnawed at him chattered away again: that she'd flee Falls Lake as she had Naperville. That he and his rough lifestyle would not be enough for her.

But above all, he feared she was in danger. And he was going to track her, silently, carefully, if it was the last thing he ever did—and if that was true, so be it. For Alex, he was willing to die trying.

Lyle was still holding the gun, despite the fact that he seemed calmer, warmer, toward her. He was obviously inept in the forest, even with his compass, especially since night had fallen. He kept muttering about being certain he should turn south near here to find the road and his car. He'd produced a flashlight to read his compass, but it wasn't doing him much good to illumine the mazelike forest surroundings.

She felt as if he'd beaten her—felt beaten in general. But thank heavens he had thought her attempt to grab his gun was so he wouldn't shoot the moose. Before they'd left that spot, she'd seen a blood trail the poor animal had left. At least it hadn't been her blood.

But if she got the chance, she was planning to turn on Lyle.

She startled when he spoke again and pointed. "Talk about seeing the forest for the trees. I figure the lake is near, right through those trees. I heard in town there's some legend about it, that a bunch of people drowned, so behave."

Did he mean to drown her in the lake, make it look like an accident, just when she was starting to feel safer?

He went on. "I have a map in the car that shows the lake and if I can see how it's laid out in person, even in the dark with the stars and moon, I'll bet I can figure out which way to walk to find the road and the car. You don't know, do you?"

"Lyle, hardly. This is a huge stretch of forest, and it's so dark in here. Granted, if you can find the lake, it will be open and lighter. I'm totally impressed you've planned things out so well—compass, flashlight."

"Gun," he added.

"It's the compass and light which are key to finding our way out."

"Yeah, like that 'our,' baby. You and me together!"

He pulled her toward the lake glittering in the moonlight. She'd run out of tissues to tear and leave for a path. Walking with him and the small stones underfoot made it impossible to leave the scuffed arrows to show the direction they were heading, so she wrenched off her link bracelet and dropped it behind them. Being at this lake with him would dirty it for her, tarnish the memory she had of sleeping side by side with Quinn nearby.

Quinn, so far away. Quinn, so far from her forever now?

As Lyle nearly dragged her on, she felt sick to her stomach and sick to her soul.

34

"We're going have to drink some of this lake water," Lyle told her. "I figured we'd be to the car by now. Damn. I gave up trying to find directions on my cell phone around here hours ago."

She didn't tell him she knew a few places it would work out here.

"I heard this water's kind of silty," she told him.

"I don't care. We're not near some damn toxic manufacturing plant to pollute it, like in the States."

"We are in the States."

"Doesn't seem like one to me—more like Siberia. Russia owned this land once. And in case your cousins send someone looking for you, we won't sleep out in the open, but back in the forest a ways."

"What about bears?"

He looked not only angry but scared. "I asked around in town. This area's not supposed to have that many of them—like other places."

"Or moose herds, either, but we saw one up close and personal. And all it takes is one bear looking for those luscious strawberries."

"I have a gun. More bullets, too. I should have let you pick more strawberries. I hope my car doesn't get towed."

"Here in the Falls Lake forest on that dead end road?"

The moment she'd blurted that out, she wished she hadn't. She wanted to give him the impression she didn't know the area. And dead ends were not what she wanted to think about or bring up right now.

He dragged her by her arm back a little ways along the shore. She prayed he would not notice the bracelet she'd left behind for a clue, but she could say it just came off.

He knelt by the water and pulled her down beside him. She was thirsty, and he was no doubt right about the water being pure despite its murky appearance. She'd just close her eyes and think of the water Quinn had always made sure he and his trackers had. Maybe Suze and Meg had called for help by now, but if they told the troopers, she dreaded the idea of search helicopters flying over or even a search party that could panic Lyle. If only Quinn was not so far away.

The lake water tasted like chalky medicine. She swallowed a little more, then—when she didn't keel over—Lyle drank, too, managing to keep an eye and the gun on her. Didn't he trust her enough to put that damned thing down? And if she could grab it, did she have the courage to use it? She knew just holding it on him would not be enough because he'd risked everything to come after her, thinking he would force her to face "the end."

"I'll have to tie your hands and feet so I can grab a couple hours' rest," he said. "Let's find a vine or some kind of natural rope for the girl always making natural products," he added, and spit into the lake.

"Lyle, I'm hardly going to run off into the forest in the dark. I need you and that gun for protection. This is the wilds, you know."

He yanked her to her feet. "Quit lecturing me! You deserted me, Alex! You tried to throw everything away!" He pulled her toward the edge of the forest where lower plants grew. He aimed his flashlight beam into them. "Now, get some of those vines!"

His voice echoed. She had thought she was making progress, calming him, but—out of his element—he was definitely panicked. And, of course, he could assume people would be looking for her. If only the one she really trusted in the dark were looking for her.

She found some sort of vine running along the ground next to a taller, purple blooming plant. Oh, those were the Eskimo potatoes, which were edible but could be toxic. If she could just get him to eat some of that— but then he'd make her eat it first. And it surely wouldn't act right away. She needed some other sort of miracle.

She thought perhaps she could knee him and grab his gun while he tied her wrists, but he stood behind her to do it. Then he hugged her to him, kissed the nape of her neck, while she tried not to shudder, not to thrust him away with her hips.

"Mmm," she said, fighting the urge to scream. "I haven't forgotten you that way, touching, kissing me."

He took her back a bit more from the shore, sat her down on a fallen tree trunk and tied her feet. "We'll get to that. Stay put. I'm going just a little ways to try to see the shape of the lake to figure out which direction the road is for first daylight tomorrow. Then we're out of here. Sit right there so I can see you when I look back."

Of course, she thought as he walked a bit away and

craned his neck to look around in the wan light of a rising quarter moon, his knowledge of this area was next to nothing, but she'd never realized before he was clueless about directions. Why hadn't he tried to orient himself with the sinking sun since he'd still been muttering about his cell phone not working? But in so-called civilization, things were laid out on grids of streets and signs. He should have prepared more, but in this way and so many others it was crazy to try to compare him to Quinn.

He came back over, still with the gun in his hand. "I think I got it," he said. "I just need a little rest. Hopefully your friends won't panic you're not back yet. I'd like to use this time for you to lie down next to me and prove that you really do love me, and that I'm boss. I'm sure you'll be happy to do everything I say."

"Lyle, we're both exhausted and this ground is hard."

"You know, I shouldn't have tied your legs. I'd really like them wrapped around me."

Her insides cartwheeled, and she had an almost overwhelming urge to throw up. Lovemaking with Lyle. Never again! Not anywhere, especially not here, near where Quinn had held her, protected her, the night they'd found Spenser.

He forced her onto a grassy patch and lay down beside her and, for the first time, put the gun on the ground behind him, far out of her reach.

With one hand he held her chin so hard he forced her lips to pucker. He kissed her hard and with the other hand fondled, then squeezed, her breast.

She steadied herself and tried to force herself to kiss him back. He meant to hurt her, shame her, make her prove she meant the words she'd said. But even if she did respond, would he just kill her in the morning? Was she tricking him or was he tricking her?

"What's that?" he demanded, and lifted his head.

She listened, praying it was someone or something that would make him stop, that would let her grab that gun even if her hands were tied.

She looked up. It was a bush plane flying over from the direction of that falls toward town. She thought it was the one that Chip went into raptures over, the one he thought was piloted by his dad's spirit.

"Do you think they're looking for you?" he asked.

"Coming from that direction? No way. I've seen that plane fly over a lot, almost every day. Besides, it's not circling, is it?"

He heaved a sigh. His hands on her relaxed and withdrew.

"We'll get more of that when we get out of here tomorrow," he told her, pulling her onto her back and lying down beside her. "You owe me big-time for putting me through all this."

She let her breath out slowly, afraid to show just how relieved she felt that he'd stopped. Lyle had made a lot of mistakes, underestimating the forest, underestimating her. And these hours when he'd sleep would give Suze and Meg time to get Sam back from Anchorage to track her, to call Quinn, maybe the troopers. It was Quinn, miles and miles away, she wanted right now and always.

Quinn stared at the blur of runway lights below as the jet landed in Anchorage. He hoped the smooth landing was a good omen. It was barely morning, but light dusted the horizon. When they had taxied to a gate that took an eternity to reach, he unbuckled and shook Steve's hand after he'd popped the outside cabin door open.

"Good luck on your quest," Steve said. "By the way, Geoff said to tell you this flight is all on him."

"Then thanks to you and him," Quinn said, before hurrying down the stairs and sprinting toward the exit.

He felt the burden of finding Alex was all on him. She'd been gone for hours and now the dead of night. Thank God it was not the depths of winter when the dark was endless, but it seemed like that to him now.

In the long arm of the terminal, he looked up to read signs. He sprinted toward the hangar number he'd been given to meet his helicopter. The most important tracking quest of his life had just begun.

Suze and Meg were both waiting up for him when he landed in their parking lot and the chopper took off again. It was getting light, though the remnants of the aurora borealis still hung in the sky. He hugged them both fast.

Meg blurted, "We figured you wouldn't have your tracking or hiking stuff, so we have some of that. And we put a few things in a backpack. I hadn't thrown out Ryan's clothes, so I figured…" She gestured to a pair of pants, a sweatshirt, running shoes and a khaki pilot's jacket with a logo of air force wings on it.

"My shoes will do, but I'll take everything else. I owe you both. Is Spenser with Chip?"

"I'm telling you," Suze said, nodding, "he's like a therapy dog. Oh, in the backpack we put a change of clothes for Alex. We just can figure what happened. After, well, after Val we're scared to death."

He frowned at how she'd put that. "Again, thanks to both of you." He grabbed the things laid out and sprinted for the bathroom off the common area.

He tossed his city clothes, used the toilet, dressed in these things Meg had brought him. Ryan had not been quite as tall, so the pants grabbed in the crotch and hit his ankles wrong. It didn't matter. Nothing did but finding Alex, safe and alive.

As dawn dusted the sky and then segued to morning light, Alex didn't care that her head was partly on the grass and partly on a flat stone. She was alive. She still had a chance to get away when he untied her. Maybe she could signal someone if they came along on the road when they found Lyle's rental car.

The pistol was still on his other side, out of her reach, and she'd wake him if she reached for it, but soon, maybe…

But again, could she actually shoot him to get free? She'd overheard Troopers Kurtz and Henson talking about people blaming law enforcement for killing someone threatening their lives instead of just wounding them. They'd told Quinn that a suspect full of adrenaline, rage and sometimes drugs could still shoot or stab an officer if their bullets just hit a limb, so forget the wounded-and-down theories of dealing with hyped-up, desperate people, and Lyle would soon again be that.

So should she shoot to kill? If, that is, she got a chance? If they made it to his car. She was so used to Quinn's skills that she wasn't sure the increasingly inept and uptight Lyle could find it. Would he even let her get that far or decide to just be done with her and hide her body here in the deep woods?

He was sound asleep, snoring, but she knew he'd wake if she shifted around too much. But all she wanted was Quinn's arms around her. Only Quinn's, but for now she let the morning forest sounds and breeze caress her. Alaska—Falls Lake. Whatever happened, this was a lovely place to live and die.

35

When Quinn ran back into the common room at the lodge, he was shocked to find Suzanne dressed to go with him, holding two backpacks.

"In case she's hurt, you might need help," she told him. "You know your phone will only work a little ways in. You can send me back out with a message if you need to."

"Thanks. Don't take this wrong, but I'll move faster and be quieter alone. If I don't come back by noon, call Trooper Kurtz. But thanks for reminding me to put my phone on mute," he said, digging it out to silence it. "I know exactly where it will and won't work out there."

He was already moving toward the back door. "You two have been great. Nothing like the bold, beautiful Collister girls, all three of them."

As he opened the door, he thought he heard Spenser bark, but that might be his imagination. Yet maybe the little guy had heard his voice and thought Alex was with him. She would be—she had to be—soon!

He jogged across the backyard, past the shop to the shed. Of course her cousins—Chip, too, even Spenser—

had been back and forth here. Yet at the edge of the property, he saw a stranger's prints, a new-looking running shoe with a distinctive, crisp design on the sole, so that should be easy to follow once he got farther along the forest path. New, probably expensive running shoes. Those shoes didn't fit anyone he could think of around here. His gut twisted tighter. What if her ex had found her? The "how" didn't even matter right now, only the question of where she was.

He started down the forest path he knew by heart. If he lost her, if she was hurt, it would be the torment of losing his father all over again—worse! And no way would she have wandered off in the woods alone. She knew better. He had taught her better.

Meg and Suze had said they'd checked the shed because they knew she'd been inside, but he could not see her tracks coming out. The man must have surprised her, taken her in the shed. But again, he could only find the man's shoe treads.

The tracks were deep so he must be carrying weight. Alex? Surely alive. If she were dead, wouldn't he have left her in the shed? He would have been even more foolhardy—or possessive—than ever to kill her in the shed and carry her body out. Besides, Suzanne and Meg had said there was no sign of blood in there.

He followed the trail easily enough. The man was trying to move fast but was a little more wobbly than usual, no doubt because of carrying Alex. Since his toes were not making deeper impressions than usual, it showed no extra frontal weight, so she must be over his shoulder for better balance and speed.

Damn, what if another reporter had been hanging around, waiting for something to happen? Maybe he'd accosted Alex, and she'd refused an interview, then things got out of hand.

Quinn backtracked quickly to see if he could find where the man's footprints originated. If he had a nearby hideaway, maybe he'd take Alex there in a roundabout way. He easily located a little spy's nest not far from the rear of the lodge's backyard, so the man must have hunkered down waiting and watching. The forensic staff could get fingerprints off the litter here: an empty plastic water bottle and a torn sack from the town bakery that looked like it had held doughnuts—which the ants were crawling over now. Yeah, it could have been a new reporter who'd come back for a second try at this story and knew to watch the lodge.

But what if it wasn't?

On his way back to the path, he saw a discarded, large can of mosquito spray. Only an outsider would carry a can at all—let alone one this big—because Alaskans would know to use something different. And to litter like this—highly unlikely in this green state.

It was no local who had been hunkered down here. Again, what if— But no. No way. Alex had covered her tracks when she came here to Falls Lake.

Forcing himself to concentrate, he followed the trail again. He tried to shut out forest sounds: the wind in the branches overhead, birdcalls, his own soft footsteps. He focused on trying to hear voices, heavy footsteps, even hard breathing, anything.

But he heard nothing like that. The mystery man had a huge head start—hours—but damn it, he'd follow him somehow to the ends of the earth.

At the stream where he had stopped just yesterday morning with Alex, he found she'd been alive, at least this far, because that was what was really scaring him. Her captor had put her down, evidently to sit on a rock Quinn now examined.

Finally, something!

Tears filled his eyes. He saw her footprints, shifting a bit near where she sat. Her feet were parallel and so close together that she must have had her ankles tied. He didn't see the other set of footprints here, the outsider's, but he could have walked on the rocks or even in the stream.

And then more pieces of the puzzle. Shreds of neon yellow plastic tape, snagged along the stream, not police tape but the kind Josh used to cordon off the separate search areas for students to find clues. So that was what she must have been tied with, no doubt her hands, too. Yes, there was a knot in one piece of tape. Could her captor have let her go here?

Scanning the area, he saw a crude arrow she must have scuffed on the path. He looked up and down it until he picked up the trail again. The man had untied her feet; she was walking in front of him, surely not leading him—but then what if he had a weapon?

"We've slept long enough," Lyle muttered in her ear. His bad breath pushed against her face. "Wake up. We're out of here in case another plane goes over or they try to find you on the ground. Got to get to the rental car, before someone finds it. I'll untie your feet again. Let's go," he ordered, rising and yanking her up.

"Lyle, please untie my hands as well as my feet. I need to go behind a tree because nature calls."

"You've hardly had any liquid, but then, nature sure does call around here—shout, too," he said with a little laugh at his stupid joke. "Too bad. I think you're better with hands tied," he said as he went behind her and cut through her ankle bonds with a jackknife. "We'll be out of here pronto, because I've figured it all out."

"The way out of this maze of trees and paths?"

"You think I'm stupid?"

"Of course not," she said, but he was crazy to think there was any chance she still loved him. Had he fallen for her fake change of heart last night? Or did he just want company in the wilds because he knew he was so inept and scared in this Alaska, which was also called the Great Alone?

Alex tried not to drag her feet, though she was stealthily leaving directional arrows on the path again. Even though she still knew so little of tracking, she didn't want anyone—if someone came after her—to think she was an outsider like Lyle. Whatever happened to her, if Quinn came along this path when he returned, she wanted him to know she had listened to him to pick up her feet but also learned to leave signs—that she had valued his lessons and him.

I went to the woods because I wished to live deliberately, Thoreau had written. She had shared that with Quinn and he had quoted it to others. *And see what it had to teach, and not, when I came to die, discover that I had not lived...living is so dear.*

How she hated to admit it, but she was more convinced than ever that Lyle, if he did not shoot her, intended to tie her to a tree out here, maybe gag her and leave her. In the dense forest, in the thickets here, they might never find her, though an animal could smell her human scent—her grief and fear—and come to her.

She thought of Quinn's father and little dog attacked in a forest. She pictured her own dear parents and her little dog. She remembered long-lost Allie, and was glad that her twin sister lived on in her head and heart, and that was not a curse but a gift. And how amazing she had never told Lyle about her twin but had told her cousins and Quinn so soon. How could she have fallen for this man who held her prisoner now?

"Damn!" Lyle's voice broke into her agonizing. "I was sure this was the way back to the road."

She did not tell him that it was, that he had actually stumbled on the right path, though they had a ways to go yet through twists and turns.

"Surely it will lead there," she said. "If not, to a trail that does."

"What do you know about it?" he shouted, yanking her around to face him. "I studied a map. I bought a compass! My direction finder on my cell won't work in this damn labyrinth! I can figure most things out, but never quite you—did I? You had to hate me to leave me, embarrass me like that!" he shouted, shaking the compass as if he could convince it to give him answers.

She wanted to scream that she'd more than embarrassed herself to trust him, to so much as think she loved him. But he was getting red in the face, losing control, and she'd seen that before—and fled.

But now she couldn't. Now she was trapped in lies, in fear, in deepest regret. She felt it on her face and body like a brand that she had ever trusted and cared for this man. With Lyle, she still felt scratched to pieces, like poor Val had been. Poor dead Val.

She stared wide-eyed at Lyle, someone who had

seemed to love her once, to love animals, but now she knew he loved only Lyle.

He threw the compass to the ground and raised his gun toward her as a shaft of sunlight split through the trees and slanted across his face. He blinked and jerked his head.

She could tell he was losing control, but so was she. He dragged her on, several steps toward a slight swell of a hill with a tangle of vines and weeds below. No way she could defend herself with her hands still tied.

Suddenly she was sure he had worked himself up to act—to be rid of her, to kill her and shove her down into that wild forest growth. He must have known she was lying, that she detested him. She could only be grateful that he did not seem to know about Quinn, had not seen them together. If only Quinn were here…

She knew it was now or never. She ducked, threw herself at his knees, rolling into him and taking him down. His gun went off but she wasn't shot—yet.

36

Quinn jerked his head up. A gunshot? Distant. A hunter possibly, he tried to tell himself, but he hurried toward the sound of it.

As sunlight sifted through the thick trees, he looked down again to read the tracks. Still two sets of footsteps, Alex's and the man's in single file, she walking ahead of him because he blurred some of her prints.

Now, tiny bits of shredded paper. And more than once another deep-toed arrow to show their direction, as if he needed that. Yes, that was his girl, his beautiful, clever and bold Alex!

But the tracks were scuffed here. And dried blood! Drops, then smears of it, but perhaps from a deer, which had left tracks. No, a moose, a big one, maybe a bull with a full rack of antlers, magnificent to see. What kind of jerk would shoot at that?

So had some passing hunter seen Alex go into the storage shed at the lodge and decided to risk kidnapping her? No way, not with those fancy new shoes.

Quinn was out of breath, but he pushed himself to jog at a speed which still let him keep his head down to watch for tracks. The animal must have been shot, staggered a bit, but went on down a side path, limping. With the dried blood, that was obviously not the gunshot he'd just heard. Maybe her captor was trigger-happy and probably nervous as hell. If it was her former fiancé—Quinn's biggest fear—what kind of a vet shot a beautiful animal that would probably not attack?

At least it was not bear tracks he was staring at. The ripe berries this time of year could draw them to areas where they didn't live.

Time was ticking and Alex's captor must have some sort of escape plan, maybe including having a plane pick them up on the lake. If they left the area, she might be lost forever.

He was even more torn when he double-checked and saw footsteps heading two directions, one toward the lake, one toward the road. Why would her ex take her toward the lake unless he was waiting for a plane—or meant to drown her?

Quinn chose the direction of the lake and hurried on.

Alex slammed into Lyle, then the ground hard, but so did Lyle. Her breath whoofed out. They both scrambled for the gun. She was closest to it, picked it up in her tied hands. No time to get her finger on the trigger and aim, so she got to her knees and heaved it as far as she could. The only good thing that had happened so far: it landed in the middle of a tall, blooming bush of devil's club.

She was shaking all over, hot and cold. She would have never shot him in time before he grabbed her or got the gun—and used it himself.

"Damn you, Alex!" he shouted, and kicked her in the stomach before he scrambled to his feet.

Doubled up in pain, she could barely choke out her words. "I just…didn't want you to shoot another animal. Or me when I—I've been so relieved to see you, make things up to you. I'm sure we're on the path toward the road."

Still lying on the ground, she dry heaved. She had nothing in her to throw up. Her head pounded, and her belly throbbed. Never had she been so scared and so miserable—well, maybe when she was with Lyle those last days.

"That looks like a bunch of thorns where you threw it," he said, looking away.

"Those prickers are toxic," she gasped, wiping her mouth with the tail of her blouse. "Lyle, we must be close to the road. Leave me here and just go on. I don't know if I even have the strength to walk anymore."

"And leave you to make up some story about my kidnapping you? Get up, damn it!"

He yanked her arm nearly out of its socket. She got to her knees, her feet. She was absolutely sick of pretending to care for and obey this man, but she wanted to live. She wanted to live here in Falls Lake, now and in the future.

To her amazement, he knocked her down again, almost as if it was a football tackle. He pressed her down, lay on top of her.

"You stupid bitch, I ought to take you right now, then tie you up naked and leave you, but you may be my ticket out of here. Swear to me you'll go with me, keep your mouth shut."

He pulled her hair so hard her chin jerked up. Her

eyes watered and she began to sob. If Lyle still had the gun, she would be gone, not that he couldn't strangle her, knock her head with a stone, the way Val had died.

"Yes, I'll go with you. I—I said I would. Lyle, you have got to trust me if we're going to be together."

"Remains to be seen," he muttered, and hauled her to her feet again.

One of her shoes had come off in the scuffle. He saw it, but kicked it off the path, pulled her away from retrieving it and shoved her on.

Earlier, Quinn was confused that his quarry had evidently turned toward the lake and the road. So Alex was letting her captor wander, hoping for time, maybe for a way to escape. But on the shingle shore, he'd lose their tracks.

Sticking close to the trees, not on the water's edge, he jogged around this end of the lake. And there, closer to the water, glittering in the sun, was a thin link gold bracelet that must be hers.

A struggle had caused it to come off? No, even the delicate lobster claw link was intact. Weird but he pictured the wedding rings in the jewelry shop window again. Gold. She liked gold. And graceful, delicate things.

Like herself, his golden girl. Graceful, but not delicate. Strong and sturdy except when it came to missing her lost sister. And now, Alex might be missing, too.

He heard and saw nothing but two loons landing on the lake with their crazy call that sounded like a yodel and the distant murmur of the waterfall. The lake sometimes sent back an echo. He had to try the other path.

Jamming the bracelet in his pocket, he turned and

sprinted for the trail that led to the road, then down it, jogging again, eyes alert for any signs—signs of how Alex was holding up.

Down the path toward the road, something silver caught his eye—another treasured clue, a larger item than the slender bracelet? A metal compass glinted in a shaft of sun. Surely Alex had not left that for a clue, too. Quinn picked up the compass, holding it by a big leaf, preserving fingerprints, not leaving his own. He dropped it in his backpack and scanned the ground again. Had her captor lost or tossed it?

He knew one thing for sure: her captor was the metro man she'd thought she'd loved—Dr. Lyle Vet, whatever his last name was.

But he'd figure out how the bastard had traced her later. He pushed on, not far—then, over here, it looked as if two bodies had hit the ground and writhed a bit. Both got up again and went on. Had he attacked her sexually or had they fought? He couldn't tell.

Then yes! They were still on the trail ahead. Even running, he could see their footprints again. Alex was flagging, dragging her feet. He prayed she wasn't injured. And not wounded by the gun he'd heard go off, but he saw no blood.

He came to a place where there had been another scuffle, near a bad stand of devil's club. Her shoe was there, just one shoe. Surely the monster who held her was not undressing her. At least two sets of footsteps appeared again and went on, Alex with one shoeless foot.

So head down, hurrying, he went on, too.

This trek was turning into an out-of-body experience. It was way beyond nightmare, beyond the hope she could escape, or that Suze and Meg would send troopers to rescue her, if they could find her. No sounds of search dogs, no helicopters flying over.

Even better, she prayed someone had reached Quinn in New York, and he would tell them what to do, that he would be back as soon as he could.

One foot in front of the other. Paying the price for falling for Lyle—trying to keep from falling. Maybe she should pretend to faint, to collapse at least. It would be so easy. Maybe he would run off and leave her. He was tired, too, frustrated, panicked he'd attempted more than he could control.

She knew they must be close to the road, for this was the same path she and Quinn had taken out of the woods. It seemed so long ago.

She was full of regrets. The minute she knew that Spenser distrusted Lyle, she should have taken that for a sign, but she thought the little guy would get over it.

"Lyle, I'm too sick and weak to go on. Just leave me and go."

"Lied to me about wanting me back, didn't you?"

"Let's just say the way you have treated me on this trek has not been like someone in love who wants a rec-onciliation, like I do."

He yanked her arm to spin her around to face him. She nearly fell, tried to keep her balance.

"How about I take your clever suggestion you just stay here, and I'll go on alone?" he ranted.

He pushed her, back against a tree so hard she hit her head. Dizzy, spinning…

She watched him through slitted eyelids as he grabbed a broken tree branch from the ground and swung it at her head. Somehow, she turned away in time, and it banged against the tree trunk. The limb shattered—bark flew, rotten inner wood peppered her. Rotten to the core—he meant to kill her!

Move, crawl, run, fight! an inner voice screamed at her, maybe Allie's voice.

"The end!" he was muttering. "The end, the end!"

She scrambled to her feet and ran, but she heard him coming after her. He was between her and the road, but could she lose him in the woods she knew better than him? Wouldn't someone, Suze or Meg, Josh—anyone—come looking for her?

Her wrists still tied, she darted down a narrowing path, around a sharp turn, and there was salvation. Quinn! It was really Quinn, here now, running toward her!

"Lyle! He found me, wants to kill me!" she cried, and nearly vaulted into his arms. He was solid, really here!

"Is he behind you?" he asked, setting her back behind him and moving off the path. "I don't hear him. Does he have the gun I heard go off?"

"I threw it in the devil's club back there."

"That's my girl. Stay here." He dug a jackknife out of his pocket and pulled it open, put it in her hand. "Saw yourself free and stay put. I'll get him. He's the one in trouble now. You're safe, sweetheart—I'll be sure of that."

Quinn had hoped to spot Lyle, but maybe he'd have to chase and hog-tie him, then drag him to the road until they could get troopers here. Or could he be hiding in the thick foliage here? He must have seen or heard him and decided not to chase Alex, to run. Thank God she was safe, staying behind. She'd obviously been beaten and dragged around, but she was alive. He'd make all this up to her.

But he had to find and capture her bastard kidnapper. The guy must be clever to have once won her, fooled her. Quinn wasn't a violent person, but he could not wait to get his hands on Lyle.

Then, around a turn in the path, he saw his quarry, just standing there when Quinn had figured he'd run. The thing was, they were both prey now: Lyle was standing like a statue on the path about twenty feet ahead of him but not looking this way because he was staring down a bear Quinn could see off to the right of the path. The large black bear had reared up on its hind legs, sniffing the air and watching Lyle in return.

Quinn's pulse pounded so loud it nearly drowned his thoughts. His eyes widened. From the depths of dark memory, he saw again his father's and Scottie's bloody bodies.

The bear looked at him, too, then back to Lyle, who hadn't moved. The guy was a domestic animal vet, but at least he must know not to run. Lyle looked from the bear to Quinn, then back to the bear again. His features were frozen in fear.

Standing still, Quinn lifted his hands high to make himself look taller. Of course, his instinct—human instinct—was to run. To tear back to get Alex away, to protect her and himself.

Steady. Stay. See it out. At least she's back a ways behind you.

He stood stock-still with his hands in the air as if Lyle had got the drop on him in an old western-style shoot-out. Off to the side of the path, near the tangle of berry bushes, the bear stared, too, the three of them forming a triangle.

And then, damn it, without turning back to look, he heard Alex's slow, careful footsteps on the path. Why hadn't she stayed back?

In a quiet, steady voice, he said, "Bear at three o'clock. Don't move. Stay behind me." Then he said a bit louder, "Don't move, Lyle."

"Yeah, sure," Lyle said, his voice high-pitched with nerves. "So you can haul me in? I think my car's close."

He turned and tore away. He had a head start when the bear ran after him, but Quinn knew what the result would be.

Alex hugged Quinn from behind, holding tight. She was shaking, but he was, too.

"He didn't know not to run," Quinn muttered, fighting the tears of memory. "A vet but not with wildlife."

They heard one sharp scream, then a ragged cry, and that was all. He turned and held Alex hard.

"There may be more than one around with the last of those berries," Quinn said, his voice breaking. "Let's head back for the lake, and I'll call for help for him on my cell in case he's still alive. It's either there or the road for phone reception."

"Yes, we'd better be sure he isn't suffering after that attack, call for emergency help."

Carefully, fearful the bear might still be near, they followed the path. Lyle's body lay in a pool of blood. His arms were wrapped around his head but his shoulders were bare and clawed. Strangely, she pictured a German shepherd she'd cared for which had been hit by a car and lay on the road. No, this was Lyle, a human being, even if a sick, evil one.

Looking all around, they knelt on either side of him. Quinn felt for a pulse at the side of the base of his neck, then shook his head. "Dead," he whispered. "At least it was fast. I pray it was so for my dad and dog. Let's call for someone to retrieve the body. We'll phone out on the road rather than at the lake, then come back here to wait—protect him as he never did you."

She realized that as cruel as Lyle had been to her, she was crying. A release from fear, a final release from poor, sick Lyle.

Quinn sniffed hard and pressed his lips together. His words came out raspy and broken. "He didn't... hurt you, force you?"

"He wanted to. He would have. I lied to him to keep him from shooting me. Somehow, he didn't know about us. He said he found me through my license plate."

"But someone here must have helped him trace that plate number," he muttered as they rose and headed for the path to the road to call not for a rescue squad but a coroner's vehicle.

37

Quinn stayed at the lodge that night in her room, sitting on the bed, holding her, then lying down outside the covers so he didn't have to let her go. Twice he had to put Spenser on her other side, so they didn't press the little dog between them. Spenser seemed to be guarding her, too, as if he knew what his mistress had been through.

His *mistress*. Spenser's mistress but she would promise again to be his wife as soon as she woke up and was herself. The local doctor had checked her out: dehydration, black and blue bruises, but no concussion.

She'd fallen asleep sitting up while Trooper Kurtz had questioned her, even when the BCI team member asked her about her kidnapping ordeal. The forensic team had gone to retrieve Lyle's body and survey the scene. It was Quinn who had to tell them where to find the gun in the devil's club.

Trooper Kurtz had told Quinn, "I'd thought at first Lyle Grayson might have murdered Valerie, but obviously no connection, and we verified he was cross country then."

So no answer yet to that looming question. Ryker was

still a person of interest, and Val's murder cast a pall over many other people who had been around that day.

When Alex woke, it was still daylight—no, it was daylight again, for she had slept all night. The horror crashed back over her, but she was safe now. Lyle was dead.

Why had he been so sick to stalk her after she'd fled miles away? How did he find her? Someone must have tipped him off. Officer Kurtz didn't know how, nor did the others at the lodge she had asked before she'd absolutely collapsed from exhaustion.

She squinted at the curtains over her bedroom window and heard Spenser yawn. A new day. A good, beautiful day. Back to normal life—a better one, one with Quinn. She'd hire Josh to get those marks off the outside of her room, then suggest he remove the claw marks by Sam and Mary's woodpile, if they agreed. Or maybe, in case a person was arrested for Val's murder, those marks would be needed for evidence.

She shifted her weight and realized she was sore all over. And then she felt a body much bigger than Spenser's next to her. She opened her eyes a bit, then wider. Quinn! Quinn fully dressed, sprawled on her other side, asleep facing her. Oh, that's right. He'd been with her when she'd finally gone to bed after all that questioning and more to come. More to come...

As if he sensed that she was awake, he opened one forest-green eye, then both.

"A new day, a new start," he whispered.

She reached out to touch his cheek. At least two days of beard growth there. She knew he grew a trimmed beard in the winter. She'd seen it when she first looked at the lodge website, which seemed eons ago.

"I came back too fast to bring a ring," he said. "How about we pick one out together, do a lot of things together—if you'll say yes."

"Yes. Absolutely, positively yes."

His eyes shimmered with tears. "I don't mind sharing you with Spenser, though I suggest we change his last name from Collister to Mantell soon."

"Sounds like a plan," she said, and lifted her hand to his, palm to palm. Their fingers touched, then intertwined, holding firm and strong.

One month later

Their engagement party on the patio of the lodge reminded Alex of the gathering she'd walked in on the day she'd arrived. Again, Geoff and Ginger were here from New York as well as Brent. The two men kept talking, probably hatching, Quinn had said, trends for the *Q-Man* show. Also, Trooper Jim Kurtz and his wife, Janice, were here, though Jim looked so different in casual clothes.

It was a salmon bake again, though the fish were not fresh out of a stream but had been frozen since the season was over. Another season, a special one for her and Quinn, had just begun.

On a table separate from the food, Alex had set out little sacks with gifts from her renovated products line. The new art on the packaging Suze had created had pretty forest and wildflower labels.

Spenser was on a spiffy new leash—red, no less—and was getting used to the bungalow in town they would close a deal on next week. The absentee owner, a friend of Quinn's, had already let them come and go anytime to renovate and furnish the place. Her furniture and other possessions were being shipped from Illinois. With Suze and Meg's help they had been painting the rooms.

"Oh, this little bedroom will be good for a nursery!" Mary had said when she had dropped by. "Maybe we will raise children together."

"You know," Alex had confided in her, "you are not the only one haunted by past family losses. I lost my twin sister before we were born, and I sometimes believe she is still with me, but in a good way."

"A good way," Mary had repeated. "That's how I will remember my lost family now, too."

Mary waved and smiled at her across the mingling guests. Proudly showing a bit of a belly, she was helping Suze and Meg serve salmon sliders and a variety of side dishes. Quinn and Alex thought her weekly psychiatric counseling sessions in Anchorage were really helping her.

As for the Falls Lake ghost, Mary had admitted she had sneaked out to cry and mourn at night, hoping to honor her lost grandparents and praying for a child. Hearing that, Sam had smiled and said, "Was it a prayer to have a son?"

"It might be a girl!" Mary had protested. "One I will name after my beloved grandmother."

Sam had also confessed to them and Trooper Kurtz that he had been the one to take and hide Mary's bear claw necklace so that it could not possibly be lost when it was taken to Anchorage to be examined. He was certain, he said, Mary had not harmed Val. The necklace had been examined and given back to her when the claws did not match the marks on Val. Since it had been his wife's property, no charges had been brought against Sam.

Alex noted that Sam and Josh seemed especially close tonight. No doubt it had been hard for Josh to have Mary choose Sam instead of him when they were younger, but both brothers seemed finally reconciled to that. Everyone was glad to see Josh had brought a date from town tonight, a redheaded waitress from Caribou Bill's.

Chip was everywhere, still toting his dad's binoculars, which Meg felt comforted him. The boy looked up at all kinds of planes that flew over, so he did not fixate so much on just one. Surely her dear boy would work his way out of his problems, she'd told Alex and Quinn.

Geoff had managed to patch things up—producer to producer, he'd said—with *Gab Fest*, and Quinn was being rebooked on the show next week when he and Alex flew to see his mother and her husband, then on to London to visit her parents.

Geoff had insisted on a round of champagne, which he'd arrived with, and his voice cut through the chatter.

"All right, everyone. Raise your glasses. Here's to our future bride and groom, from all their friends and family!" He lifted his goblet high, and they all—except Chip and Spenser—did, too. "Although the *Q-Man* TV show will reach out mostly to men, we're going to have Alex and Mary on it to emphasize that women can be wilderness trackers, too."

"And anything else they put their minds and talents to," Ginger chimed in.

"Ah—exactly. That will bring up our viewer numbers with the female demographic."

Brent shook his head, but Quinn grinned as everyone lifted their glasses and offered best wishes. Alex saw Meg grab a glass out of Chip's hand he must have snatched from the table.

Spenser barked. Alex and Quinn kissed to cheers and applause. She had never been happier. After all they'd been through, surely they would have smooth sailing ahead.

Everyone went back to eating and chatting. Meg disappeared into the lodge and returned, trailing the local postal carrier, who covered a huge area around the town. Meg gestured to Quinn and Alex, and they went over.

"Certified letter for you, Quinn," the man said, handing it over along with Quinn's usual stack of mail. "You got to sign for it."

He thrust out a form on a clipboard, and Quinn signed.

"Best to you and the new missus," the man said, evidently thinking this was a wedding party.

"Help yourself to some food before you go, Larry," Quinn told him.

"Well, don't mind if I do," he said, and moved away.

Quinn stared down at the letter with its handwritten address partly obscured by the green form attached to it. He frowned.

"Not just fan mail?" Alex asked.

"I think it's from Valerie Chambers's sister. Remember, Val said she lives in Mission Viejo, California, and has the same last name. See—Mission Viejo and Melanie Chambers," he said, showing her as if she wouldn't believe it.

"My address is on my website, though most people write through email. I hate to duck out of our party," he said, "but let's step inside for a sec and read this."

They went into the common room, sat on a long couch and huddled over the letter as he opened it. "Yes,

Valerie's sister, thanking the people who knew Val—not including Ryker, she says."

"Maybe she suspects him of killing her."

He nodded and went on, "She appreciates Val's friends here who may have helped her," he summarized as she saw him skim the letter. Another piece of paper, different from the letter, fell out on Quinn's knee and Alex retrieved it.

"She thought we should have this primitive drawing Val did," he went on reading, "because maybe it means something to someone there—kind of strange, and she can't tell what it is, she says."

Alex opened it carefully and smoothed it flat on her knee. It was small and crisscrossed with creases. She bent over it, then sat straight up. "What?" Quinn asked as he moved closer to study it.

"It's a sketch of the bear claw carving outside my bedroom window—like the one outside Sam and Mary's. But why would Val's sister in California have this? Val must have sent it to her, but why? And why is it so…scrunched up?"

He turned back to the letter. "Near the bottom, she writes that she's sorry the paper's a mess, but she found it hidden beneath the lining of Val's purse, which was returned to her with her other things. Just wait," he muttered, frowning, "until I tell the troopers their forensic team missed this when they emptied her purse."

"So could Val have copied the design from this to carve it outside my window and on Sam and Mary's house? But I can't see her trekking around to do that—and then she ends up with something similar scratched on her body. I don't get it. But look, there's some really tiny writing scribbled next to some of the marks."

He took it from her and held it up to the window light. "I think it says, *Worth it!* Then *$50,000* and *LA here we come!*"

"Let me see," she said, crowding close to him. "You're right—and over on these other claw designs something else. Is that…a phone number? And there's another sentence here—I think it says 'Use only b. paw Br bought in NYC, not Ry's—then give back.' Quinn, I'm not sure, but do you know what that could mean?"

He kept squinting at it. "We have to be sure. Have you seen a magnifying glass around here?"

"I think Suze might have one in the junk drawer."

She got up and went into the kitchen, which was in some disarray as a storage and serving place for the food outside. She checked some drawers but found no magnifying glass. She'd have to ask Suze, but they needed to return to their guests. She heard Quinn come in behind her. "I can't find it, but maybe we found the murderer."

"It can't be him. Too long distance. Too far out in other ways."

As if their fears had summoned him, she spun around to see Brent standing alone in the doorway. Starting to tremble, she told him, "We're coming right back out."

"Someone overheard you received something from poor Val's sister," he said. "A bear claw drawing and what else?"

The reality of her fears hit her like a punch in the stomach. "Oh, just a thank-you for our finding and caring for her body before the troopers and squad could get here."

"I see."

"And I see, too," Quinn said. "I just managed to pick out a New York area code and phone number I recognized on Val's drawing of bear claw designs. I'll check it on my phone to be sure it's yours, Brent, but she also had a large sum of money listed alongside the words *worth it*."

"She asked me for my number in case she ever needed a lawyer for Ryker, since he was acting erratically. She was afraid he might try to dump her one way or the other. I still believe he's the one who killed her."

"Really?" Quinn said. "I can't picture her making the bear claw marks in the dark and walking the woods at night, but if she had a diagram to follow and had been promised a large sum of money—and a job for Ryker in LA, that might have been enough to make her do it."

Brent was facing Quinn, but Alex could see the older man tensing his body, as if he would run. He flexed his fists while Quinn didn't move from blocking the door. She prayed he didn't have a gun. Quietly, carefully, Alex opened the drawer again where she'd seen a rolling pin.

Quinn said, "Trooper Kurtz isn't in uniform, but let's get him in here and in on this."

"And ruin the festivities?" Brent demanded, his voice rising. "I think you both had better get back out there."

Alex felt they knew the truth now. Brent Bayer had not wanted to get his hands dirty or possibly get caught for making the bear claw threats, so he'd bribed Val to carve the claw marks, promised her money and a job in LA for Ryker. Then something had gone awry— she wanted more, she threatened to tell, something. Or she just wanted to give the bear claw back which he'd brought from New York so it couldn't be traced here.

But when he saw he'd misjudged, Brent had either not been willing to lose the series videographer, or he just wanted to be rid of Val—and scare Alex away from Quinn with marks outside her bedroom at the lodge.

Then to make it possibly seem like a ghostly curse, he'd decided to have Val do the same to the wall outside Sam and Mary's place. Maybe in Brent's mind they were expendable for the series, too, so he could isolate and control Q-Man.

Quinn said, "You were wrong, Brent, about not featuring women on the show or building an audience for them. But you wanted to draw more viewers in by exploiting the ghost angle. I think you and I need to sit down right now with Geoff and Trooper Kurtz to hash this out—"

Brent ducked and tried to lunge past him. Quinn went off balance, reached out to snag his arm, to stop him, but the man vaulted through the door and ran across the common room toward the front of the lodge. No wonder he'd driven his own rental car from the airport for once and parked it right outside.

Quinn was right behind him, with Alex leading up the rear, rolling pin in hand. Suddenly, Kurtz arrived, too. "What's going on in here?"

"Brent bribed Val to do his dirty work, then she rebelled or wanted more money, threatened to expose him," Alex said. "You killed her, didn't you?" she shouted at Brent, throwing the wooden rolling pin at him as he reached the front door with Quinn in pursuit.

The rolling pin bounced off Brent's shoulder. Quinn grabbed him, swung him around. Kurtz helped Quinn subdue the struggling man, who shocked them all by bursting into tears.

"She had it coming!" Brent exploded. "Can't trust women at all, any of them! You'll learn that, Quinn— they'll screw things up one way or the other. This messed-up world is letting women take over! Glad I tracked down

Alex's jilted fiancé. I understood the poor guy she'd deserted…made him an offer, too, but of course she ruined things again!"

"You can make any statement you want after I read you your rights," the trooper told him.

Alex realized the pieces all fit now, broken and awful as they might be. She bet Val with her big purse and Brent with his backpack had met just outside Quinn's property to exchange money—or a bear paw. Maybe she'd asked for more, maybe she'd said she'd talk—and he'd killed her and scratched her up, thinking a bear would be blamed.

She scrambled for a clothesline rope so Kurtz and Quinn could tie up Val's briber, hater and killer, the man who had betrayed Alex to Lyle so she was almost murdered, too. A powerful, bitter man who hated women because a woman—maybe more than one—had hurt him.

When she got back with the rope, Quinn pressed Brent to the floor, and they tied him, then the trooper used his cell to call for backup. "Yes, murder suspect, under arrest…" was all she heard as she and Quinn moved away. "I'm going to read him his rights now," she heard Kurtz say into the phone. Brent kept glaring at her and Quinn, standing arm in arm.

She knew then the best, maybe the only, thing she could do to help punish Brent for killing Val and siccing Lyle on her—besides testifying at his murder trial someday—was to let him see how much she loved Quinn. She recalled Quinn had said that Brent's wife had betrayed and left him. Was that the cause of all his bitterness toward women?

She wrapped her arms around Quinn's neck and stood on tiptoe to kiss him.

"Hold that kiss!" Ginger said, suddenly appearing.

Geoff trailed behind along with Sam and Mary. Gasps and questions followed when they saw, across the room, Brent tied on the floor.

Hadn't Ginger and Geoff's marriage—Sam and Mary's, too—shown Brent that there were love matches that lasted through tough times? But maybe that had made him even more bitter.

Quinn kissed Alex again and tugged her away, gesturing to the curious onlookers to go back outside, too, that he'd explain everything soon.

Suddenly her pounding pulse began to slow. She felt peace and happiness surround her as Quinn's arm encircled her and steered her outside, away from the noise and questions. Despite the chilly night, she and Quinn went out on the back patio where they had first met and held tight to each other.

"Sad someone could be so sick and hateful—at women in general," she whispered, cuddled close with her head tucked under his chin. "I'm sure the world's recent strides toward women's equality made him more desperate."

"I don't feel desperate anymore—except to marry you. I'm more than willing to let you take over my world."

"And the same to you, my love."

She lifted her face for a kiss. Overhead, stars glittered in the sky to match the diamond on her finger. Despite past dangers, deep woods and the desperation of sad, broken people, with her hand now in Quinn's, she was safe at home.

* * * * *

Author's Note

I love writing trilogies with connected heroines, so I hope you will not only enjoy this book but the two Alaska Wild novels to come, *Under the Alaskan Ice* and *Edge of the Alaskan Cliff*, which will feature Megan and Suzanne Collister.

I never had a sister—wish I did, however much I love my brothers—and the idea of having an identical twin sister really intrigued me. When I stumbled on the concept of vanishing twin syndrome online at www.wombtwin.com, I found yet another fascinating possibility of twindom.

Unlike many suspense authors, I always begin with a setting that will work for a frightening story. I look for some place that is unique, beautiful and challenging for my characters. I had originally thought to set this novel in backwoods Michigan, with which I was very familiar, but both my agent and editor suggested I take that "wilderness/deep forest" setting to a whole new level by using Alaska.

That idea suited me perfectly as my husband and I had enjoyed a trip to "the Great Alone" state, and I had written an earlier Alaskan romantic suspense novel called

Down River. Besides the vastness and natural beauty we saw on our trip, I was totally intrigued by the bold, unique people. In a way, the wilds of Alaska are "the last American frontier." I remember speaking with a young woman who was going to marry a man she had not known long and move to "the woods." "I'm glad," she said, "we will have electricity next year and running water not long after that." (!) On the other hand, Anchorage is a huge, dynamic and busy city so the state has great contrasts.

I was also intrigued by a book by Tom Brown, Jr., who teaches tracking skills. I read both *The Science and Art of Tracking* and *Field Guild to Wilderness Survival*. His information is not only fascinating but useful, even for someone who usually takes walks in city parks.

Delving into information about Alex's love of making natural beauty products was fun, too, especially *101 Easy Homemade Products for Your Skin, Health & Home* by Jan Berry.

I also owe a lot to a vet tech whom I interviewed—Emily Pickard—who is very knowledgeable and loves her career. I had no clue about a vet tech's training and specialties; I thought "a vet assistant" was just someone who helped out, but techs are so much more. Emily was generous with her time and advice.

Also, thanks to friend and writer Patricia Matthews (who writes mysteries as Olivia Matthews) for her information about the career of videographers. Her husband is a videographer for various sporting events nationwide. Without their information, I would probably have been back in the "film" universe. Ryker—glad he was innocent!—thanks the Matthewses, too.

The other piece of the background/research puzzle was learning about search and rescue, or SAR, although that knowledge will come into play more in the next Alaska Wild novel. Thanks to former SAR team member Martin Roy Hill for sharing his expertise in a class I took online. SAR rescues are not focused on missing persons but on lost persons. (Missing persons entails a criminal element—someone kidnapped or a criminal intentionally hiding. Lost implies someone who has wandered away—no crime involved—though these lines can blur in an emergency or when a child is involved.)

Thanks also to my friend Sally Pickard for arranging my vet tech interview. Also to longtime writer friend Susan Elizabeth Phillips for info on Naperville, Illinois. And, as ever, to my husband, Don, for proofreading. Always thanks to my guides through my rom/sus novel writing career, editor Emily Ohanjanians and agent Annelise Robey.

I hope you will look for books two and three in the Alaska Wild trilogy, featuring Meg and Suze, though Alex and Quinn will be around, too.

Please visit me at my website at www.KarenHarper-Author.com or my Facebook page at www.facebook.com/KarenHarperAuthor.

Karen Harper
July 2019

Setting as Character

In the more than three decades I have been published, I have learned so much about writing not only from reading but from other authors. One of the things that surprised me is that most novelists begin with a plot idea or particular main character in mind, whereas I've always begun with a setting I love or that intrigues me. In my writing, the setting is key, and then the other story elements will fall into place.

This is even true of my historical novels based on the true stories of actual women. I always start with British or American settings and eras and then find my heroine's story from there, because those two countries are the cultures and places I know best.

For my contemporary romantic suspense novels, where I place my plots in the US is of key importance to me. As a born and bred Ohioan, I have used my home state in a variety of novels, especially my Amish stories. Often, however, I'm impacted by a place I visit which grabs my imagination. If I find a place intriguing, a story usually starts forming in my head, hopefully later to be brought to life.

That was the case when we visited our nephew in

Denver and stayed at his home high on Black Mountain above Conifer, a suburb. I had no more returned to Ohio than a heroine, her predicament—and her home area—came to me for the novel *The Hiding Place*, because I liked the unique setting. Likewise, my visits to and knowledge of Appalachia led me to write the *Cold Creek* trilogy set there.

The point, however, is not just to choose a beautiful, challenging or intriguing place, but then to bring it to life with details so that it becomes another character—a key character. Setting as a character in novels interacts with the human characters and may change during the course of the book, just like a person.

The best example I can think of which everyone might be familiar with is the doomed ship *Titanic* in numerous stories and movies. The (character of the) ship begins as a safe haven for other characters on the dark, cold sea. It's a warm, glitzy, friendly, welcoming place. Of course, then—in the best style of a murder novel—the ship turns into an enemy to escape from and then a killer, a mass murderer.

Another classic setting with a great character arc that goes from lovely to scary is the "friendly" beach and ocean setting in the book and movie *Jaws*.

The Alaska setting in *Deep in the Alaskan Woods* begins with a place that is a protective haven and retreat for Alex, who is fleeing an abusive relationship in "civilization." Through Quinn, who is very tied to the setting, she comes to realize that the area, which can be dangerous, can also be a desirable friend. Quinn, too, having lost his father and dog as a child to "nature" has had a changing relationship with the wilds. When Alex is abducted, the forest could have quickly become her enemy, but she then knows and cares enough about this "character" that she can use it to fight for her freedom and her life.

I'm sure you have read novels that glued you to the page but could have taken place anywhere. I prefer to read and write ones in which the setting is very special, an essential element, because the place really is part of the novel. That doesn't mean that a writer who begins with a character in mind or a theme/plot doesn't write a great novel. Many have. Writing with the setting as the first consideration works for me, and I hope my readers enjoy those setting and stories.

Karen Harper

UNDER THE ALASKAN ICE

**is the next book in *New York Times*
bestselling author**

KAREN HARPER'S

new trilogy set in rugged Lost Lake, Alaska.

The truth always surfaces.

When a small bush plane smashes through the ice at Falls Lake Lodge, it's a chilling reminder of everything Megan Metzler has lost. Three years ago, Meg's pilot husband died in a similar crash, a tragedy Meg and her young son, Chip, have struggled to move on from. Still, Meg does everything she can to assist when Commander Bryce Saylor arrives to investigate, even as working alongside the handsome pilot stirs up painful memories—and an attraction that catches them both off guard.

Bryce knows time is of the essence as he plunges into the frigid water in search of clues. But when vital evidence is destroyed, it soon becomes clear this downed plane was no accident. With someone tracking them from the woods, Meg and Bryce must race to unravel a mystery as indomitable as the Alaskan wilderness, or they might be the next victims to crash and burn...

Under the Alaskan Ice by Karen Harper

Available October 27, 2020, from MIRA Books.

Connect with us at:
Facebook.com/BookClubbish
Twitter.com/BookClubbish
Instagram.com/BookClubbish

mira

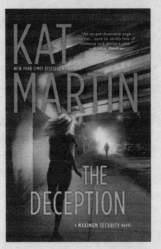